The Hustler's Touch

A NOVEL BY

Nanette M. Buchanan

Type of Work: Fiction Romance
Creation Date: 2016
First Edition: 2017
ISBN- 978-0-9793883-6-1
Cover Design: Ekthesi Advertising/Fideli Publishing
Cover Model: Natasha Jiles

I Pen Books
www.ipendesigns.net

Acknowledgements

This is my tenth novel. God is with me, and I am humbled, I owe a lot of love, hugs, and kisses to family and friends who have journeyed with me since my first book in 2007. It's simple to say, "I've got your back, or I'm there for you" and mean it. I'm fortunate to have those that have kept those words true. The complaint from Indie Authors is often the lack of support. I would say there are those who expect that their circle of friends and family will be with them on the journey, every step of the way, always.

I would be lying if I said that wasn't an expectation I had as well. But, there was a woman of knowledge, one who spoke so softly to a small audience in 2008 and offered her words of wisdom. Her presentation was offered to give direction to those of us who were apparently "newbies." She named authors, book clubs and stores I did not know of; she gave us rules, tips, and warnings; she offered her services and yes gave us CDs and notes for an experience that would never be ending. Ella Curry stood before me, before us, and I never let her go. Her words then, I follow today... "Don't be surprised if your audience doesn't include those you expected would be there. You have to build an audience. You have to work hard to be an author."

So with this being my tenth novel, I want to thank Ella Curry, CEO of EDC Creations, for always being there. Always being a phone call away and giving me my first dose of reality. There is a list of authors, publishers, promoters, and book clubs and their members that have held me up and kept me from taking a detour. Often when I was in a funk, I found them, and their words of encouragement to be a necessary part of my journey over the years.

This writing stuff ain't easy without support. So I want to thank you all. If you've given me your time, Alisa Green, your support is amazing and never-ending. Old friends and new friends I wish relationships like ours would be like a virus of love ...you catch it and spread it, not caring who catches it next. That's what love like ours is. Reading my books just because, because you love the writing, I hope, has kept me on point.

My family, my husband, we're almost there. The years have flown by and looking into the near future; I am so glad I'll be sharing this chosen journey with you. It's my passion to write, and you've helped to open the doors by welcoming each book and the process.

To my children, take the time to do what you love. You've pushed me in that direction; please allow yourself to unwrap your passion and live it through. There's nothing more rewarding than fulfilling a dream, seeing your vision clearly and stepping out on faith. I'm learning and living this through my journey as an author.

Natasha Jiles, you are beautiful. Your picture on this cover depicted the main character in this story perfectly. Thank you for allowing me to use your beauty to display my work. Though this story is pure fiction, it is one filled with romance; one that lives in the lives of many. Thank you for being a part of this written expression of love.

Forward

I decided to write a romance novel with the ripples and splendor that love often reveals. As I've said many times, the couples that survive years of love have survived the ripples.

If you have read my novels, you know that it wouldn't be my style to write the story without the twist. So yes, this is a romance, a true but a questionable love. Well, you let me know ... is it love or a hustle?

Dreams & Reality

Chapter 1

The view of the topaz water creeping upon the white sand brought the peace Seychelle longed for after quarreling with her father. She was pleased with her decision to move into the beachfront home her family owned. It was her solace, a place with no restraints. It was where she could dream; it was where her visions became clear.

Seychelle Tudjal was a native of the Seychelles Islands, East Africa. She took pride in bearing the name of the islands. She had been told she was just as beautiful. Her family lived on the south side of the Mahé Island. Seychelle shared their beachfront home located on the north side of the island with her sister Sasha. The splendor of Seychelles Island captivated her throughout her younger years. She held back her tears as the thought of leaving it all behind crossed her mind.

The Tudjals often traveled to the United States. Family travel became frequent as she and her siblings continued their higher education in America. She returned home after graduating from Florida State University with a Master's Degree in Business Administration.

Seychelle followed her brother's footsteps as requested by her father. Their father, Cole Tudjal was a businessman on the island who owned an import and export business. Tudjal Imports, one of the largest businesses on the island, was to continue through the family just as Cole had inherited it from his father. He was expecting Seychelle to honor the traditions of the family.

It wasn't odd for a woman to work on the island, have their own business there, or be involved in the trades that brought wealth to the islands. Many worked as single mothers while keeping their homes intact. Seychelle loved her current position in the business, but her dreams were to travel, leave the island and explore abroad with a clear conscious. She didn't want to disappoint her father, but she couldn't live her life wanting so much more. Her visions exceeded tradition and loyalty to her father's wishes. Seychelle reminded her father he had a son, the eldest of the three Tudjal children. It was her brother Aiden, who was born to be responsible for the legacy of Tudjal Imports. Seychelle tried to explain her vision and no longer sought her father's approval. She refused to argue the point any longer.

Aiden left the island shortly after his return from college. He too held a Master's Degree in Business from Florida A & M. It was their father's intention for his children to become educated and self-sufficient. His son would return to the island, and the business would expand and continue to flourish.

There was a celebration held in Aiden's honor after his graduation. The festivities with friends and family turned into a dispute between Aiden and a childhood friend. Ibn Stilton, unknown to any of the extended family, was asked to leave after disrespecting an elder. After Aiden escorted him to the door, he offered to shake the man's hand. Ibn punched Aiden, and the fight began. It didn't last long as they tumbled and tussled across the lawn. Aiden raised his fist in frustration and rose to his feet. He turned his back to walk away. Ibn, not much older than the twenty-one-year-old Aiden, jumped on him. They fell to the ground, once again swinging punches. Aiden hit his assailant in the temple, and all movement stopped. Ibn was rushed to the hospital after he was unresponsive lying on the ground. He had a spinal injury, which left him paralyzed. His family sought revenge. Cole spoke with the family often explaining it was an accident. He offered to assist in paying the medical expenses. They wanted Aiden to pay dearly for their son's condition.

2

Cole paced through his dimmed lit home each night for weeks. He pleaded with the people on the island to help him explain Aiden's position. This boy, Ibn, invited himself to their home and now his family wanted to take all that belonged to them. It was to be decided by the courts. Aiden was allowed to stay with his family until the case was presented. After months of testimony and deliberation, the courts determined that Aiden would not be penalized. His actions were not deliberate as he acted in defense. It wasn't long after the court's ruling that the Tudjals were harassed and threatened. There was a fire set to the fields close to their home with the promise that the business on the docks would be next. Cole and Naomi, his wife, agreed Aiden would have to leave the island. Their firstborn moved to Los Angeles with hopes he would begin his life with his own business. He apologized to the family whenever he was reminded of his father's dreams. Lately, he hadn't contacted them or sent any gifts.

Sasha, the youngest of the three became a teacher after her years in college. She unlike her siblings studied on the island. She taught in the private school system on the Mahé Island with no desire to learn the import business. Seychelle and Sasha were close, and both loved their parents and respected their traditions. The women agreed it was time for their father to face the truth. Seychelle would eventually leave the island. She would tell her parents and Sasha her plans during Sunday dinner. It was then her father began his rant.

"You do not need to leave the island or your family; this is your home." Cole stood at the head of the dining table and continued. "I forbid you to leave. Where will you go? You know nothing about the American ways or traditions."

Naomi was well aware of her husband's fears and her daughter's dreams. "Cole, please sit, finish your dinner. Let us discuss this matter as a family after we have eaten." She would miss her daughter, and she knew her husband's words were falling on deaf ears.

Seychelle lost her appetite the minute he stood on his feet. Her father's voice boomed through the house as it had when they were children. His appearance was always enough to settle a dispute in the home. Her mother was soft-spoken and could calm the temper of a gentle giant. Cole took his seat and didn't speak again until the table was cleared. Naomi invited her children and husband into the den.

The open bay window allowed the refreshing sea breeze to enter the room. Naomi loved the room's intimacy. It too had a calming effect. Sasha broke the silence as they situated themselves in the smallest room of their home.

"I don't know the last time we all sat in this room together."

"It was when Aiden was told to leave," Seychelle stated without giving the harshness of her words any thought.

"But he left on his own, didn't he?" Sasha looked at her parents and her sister. All had assured her it was what Aiden wanted. Sasha was more upset than any of the family when he departed.

"It was the right thing to do. You were too young to be concerned with the details." Cole responded no longer evading the topic. "Now, Seychelle should do what's right also."

"Right for who father, the business, the family, who? It is right for you! We will not lose anything if I don't become the next CEO of Tudjals Imports."

"We will lose to whoever buys the company from my children when I die! Is that what you want? All that I have done for our family will die with me!"

"And you sent Aiden away without a thought about the business dying or you for that matter. You had the money for lawyers; you didn't see to defend him and save the business? You gave no thought to the future of the family business then. Aiden has been allowed to move on, and I must stay?"

Cole had no response. Sasha and Naomi sat silent, shocked at the verbal exchange between father and daughter. Although the children were of age, no one dared to question their parent's decisions. Naomi knew of her daughter's wishes; none included an argument with her father.

"Father, I trust your wisdom and Aiden begged you to allow him to stay and avenge those who wanted to see him in jail or put to death. I've heard you say time and time again what should have been. It's too late. I don't want my time to past. I want to marry and be happy just as you and mother are. I want to return to the islands and live knowing I stepped out on faith and succeeded."

"Child, we don't know what the future holds. I know that a young woman, alone, in America is trouble."

"Father, how can you say that? You've never lived there and...."
Sasha's words were cut short. She was silenced by her father's look of disapproval.

"Sasha, I won't take that talk from you. This is your sister's desire and the family business. You saw to it that none of this would be your responsibility!"

"Cole! Enough of this! We won't have a family if this kind of talk continues. I won't listen to it!"

"Naomi! Naomi!" Cole stood and shouted his wife's name as she walked out of the room. "Seychelle, you have upset us both. I suppose this was not your intent?"

"No Father, it wasn't but...."

"But, no more." Cole put his finger to his lips. "Silence my child. We'll have no more talk of this. I will come to the beach tomorrow. You and I will talk about your plans. Sasha if you are leaving too, be there with your sister. We will discuss this without your mother's heart being broken again."

"Father, I never said I was leaving," Sasha said, ignoring his gestures for silence.

"Father, I think this decision breaks your heart as well. Once again, this is about your feelings and how it affects you. What about our hearts? Sasha and I are a part of this family. We all have concerns about my travel. I didn't want a private discussion or an argument. We are all adults, and my desires should not be taken as the cause of family discord. We can discuss this now or not at all."

Cole often spoke of the pride he held for his daughters and their independence. Now as Naomi looked back at them from the hall, she knew he would listen as Seychelle told him about her business plans. Cole took his seat praying his daughter wouldn't be leaving too soon.

Now watching the waves hit the shoreline, the soft breeze from the ocean touched her overheated skin. Her thoughts drifted from the argument to what she'd leave behind. The heartwarming culture she grew up loving she hoped she would find as she traveled throughout the United States. Seychelle smiled as she looked out at the formation of the rocky glaciers that became the backdrop for many of the postcards she received while away from home. She'd miss the serenity and all it offered, but as her mother often said, "The beauty of the islands lives in each of us. You will take it with you wherever you go."

There were swimmers in the water; the temperature was close to ninety degrees. A perfect day for tourist and visitors. Seychelle wouldn't deny travelers the opportunity to be a part of the paradise she called home. Her business would bring that serenity and beauty to all who chose her resorts.

Chapter 2

Aiden couldn't explain how his plans to start his own business failed. Upon his arrival in Los Angeles, he asked for support from his parents until he found a job. It was the monthly deposits they made that kept his rent paid. After eight years, they still sent money as though he were away at college. He worked two jobs for food, transportation, and other necessities. There was no money left for extras. He lied whenever he called or wrote letters to his family. He sent pictures of the office buildings where he sought work and luxury apartments that helped support the lies of his desired lifestyle.

Initially, he lost a bit of what he saved on investments not understanding the "American way," but his father would not hear of him returning home. Cole told his son that unfortunate experiences made boys into men. There were those who preferred to scam Aiden rather than do business with him. He didn't understand the lesson and how it related to manhood. He refused to admit any lost. He could no longer hold long-term jobs; the longest was a month or slightly more, and now years later he had no desire to work in corporate America. Aiden preferred to make it on his own. At the time, he was sure his obstacles were merely a temporary setback.

Seychelle contacted her brother hoping to spend time with him in Los Angeles. She called weeks in advance so he could get himself together fearing he was living as a playboy. He spent weeks preparing his apartment. His sister had no idea how he struggled and lied about his business and success. After hearing her plans, Aiden made strategies of his own. The phone rang; recognizing the number he sighed with relief as he answered.

"Hello, Sasha?"

"No, this is Seychelle. I'm using her phone. She decided to travel with me. There is a delay. Our flight missed the connection in Florida."

"Have they booked another flight for you to Los Angeles?"

"Yes, everything is good. Aiden, Sasha said she told you she'd be visiting too. It is okay right?"

"Of course." He answered looking around the partially filled apartment. "How did mother allow her to leave with you? The last time we talked, you were still arguing with Father."

"Sasha's returning at the start of the school year at the end of August. It's a vacation, a summer of travel for both of us. I will return to the island with her. If everything goes well, I will return to the States and launch my business. Do you have the package I sent you?"

"Yes, I've been reading through it. I'll wait until you arrive to talk about this business of yours."

"Aiden, you do think it will work, don't you?" Seychelle saw no flaws in her business plans. It would take time, money and chances, but she prepared for the risk. "I have saved my initial investment, and I think we can make this work."

"Yes, we'll talk. Have a good flight now. What time will you arrive? I will be at the airport to pick you up."

"The flight will be there at seven. So I'll see you then."

Aiden hung up the phone and glanced at the papers on the kitchen table. He hoped his sister was right. He wouldn't have to explain his failures or the money he owed. He would convince her that she needed him to be a part of her dream.

It was twelve o'clock. Aiden still had time to move the few pieces of furniture around and make the place look cozy. It took almost all of his savings, but the risk was better than the gambling bets he lost. The collection calls stopped with the last payment he made, but that would be short-lived.

Aiden's gambling began when he realized his reality no longer matched his vision or dreams. He wasn't one that was open to receiving advice. He began to gamble, an excuse not to get drunk and wake up with a nameless woman. Gambling quickly turned into a weekend habit. He won a few big returns, but he soon learned it would never match what he lost. He borrowed from a few who thought it was for his living expenses and then he met with those who wanted monetary returns. Alcohol became a comfort and his first friend.

Aiden met Jon Mikels, an investor while seeking a loan at First National Investments Bank. Jon became his sponsor at his monthly AA meetings. He became a confidant after a few nights of too many drinks. Aiden would openly admit, his new friend saved him.

Jon looked into Aiden's finances. He promised Aiden he could get him out of this crisis if he stopped gambling and drinking. He simply needed to listen.

Aiden talked with him about Seychelle's plans for her business. Jon looked at the business plan that Aiden glanced over. Seychelle wouldn't listen to his list of pros and cons. He explained his sister would listen to an investor and he'd set up the meeting. Jon agreed, she needed an investor, someone that knew real estate investments and other financial aspects of the business. Jon was sure if they worked together they all could be financially set. The business plan proved to be worth the investment; far better than any of Aiden's hot schemes.

Jon told him no new business was an instant success. Aiden would have to keep a job and clear up his finances. Aiden began paying who he owed as advised. He now worked as the head of Environmental Control at Los Angeles Regional Hospital. The pay was more than he expected. Although he preferred wearing a suit, the title "manager" stitched on his white shirt inspired him. The job gave him no other satisfaction. His pay would be deposited directly in the bank. Jon would remind him not to be a spendthrift as there were a few collectors still looking for their money. Aiden was slowly recovering; he hoped his sisters wouldn't see his flaws. "Jon, this is Aiden." He spoke into the phone as though someone was eavesdropping. "Both my sisters are coming. I don't think I have enough food. I'm tapped out until payday."

"My friend, you sound as if you've got them there with you. Have they arrived?"

"No, they'll be here by seven. I didn't go to the bank and now...," Aiden paused. "I'm gonna need a drink to get through this." Aiden leaned on his kitchen counter, waiting for a response. His anxiety would lead him to the first drink he had in months.

"The food is on its way. When you mentioned your sister was arriving, I did some shopping online. It will be delivered by four. I'll stop by to make sure there is nothing else you may need. You'll be okay. Listen your sisters are not visiting to judge you. This visit is the start of your purpose. You went to school and got all of that business sense to help your sister. In helping her, you will build your own. You'll see. We'll talk and then celebrate."

"Alright, thanks, man. I just feel useless, I mean if you knew my family you'd know why. I'm what my father would call useless."

"Well, you won't be seeing him so soon. You've been sober for eight months, and you've moved into a better place. You've got a job, my friend, and I'm here for you. Keep your head up."

Aiden learned quickly, during his college years in the states, not to take things Americans said literally. He found in business and relationships, if one was to survive he needed to take what was said as what they meant. Jon interrupted Aiden's temporary depression with words of encouragement. Once Aiden disconnected the call he thought about taking that drink. He sighed and retreated to the bathroom to freshen up.

Looking in the mirror, he admitted he needed to shave. It was too late to get a haircut. The familiar odor teased his senses. Just one drink, maybe two would put him at ease. He ignored the urge and took his time pampering himself. He would have to drop his habits that would lead to questions he wasn't ready to answer. After a quick shower, he faced the mirror again. The urge to fill a glass was nagging and annoying. He brushed his hair and smirked at his reflection. His sisters didn't need to know who he had become over the past few years. It would soon be time to pick up his sisters. He needed to be sober.

Chapter 3

Jon Mikels was new to the west coast when he arrived in California. Searching for a new start, he left the east coast seeking to be an associate in a newly developed investment firm. His ability to speak Spanish, and fair complexion, opened a few doors upon his arrival. He was told he'd be an asset as a bi-lingual associate. However, he soon grew weary of never being invited to the boardroom meetings or presentations. Those with less knowledge then he acquired during his college education were Presidents and CEOs with placards on their office doors as proof of their rewarded differences.

Jon realized he could do better and he did. He began to invest in small businesses. He gave business start-up seminars and workshops. Organizations soon called on him to speak to an audience who found themselves sinking in debt and their business in foreclosure. He met many who found drugs and alcohol to be a temporary relief to their permanent problems.

It was a year later when Jon stopped by Alcoholic Anonymous to give inspiration to those in attendance and a monetary donation. It wasn't what he expected, but he was financially in a satisfied state of mind and sought to give back. After visiting group meetings on a regular basis, he became a sponsor. His dreams became secondary, visions that faded, as he allowed himself to attach to those he sponsored.

It wasn't until he met Aiden that he began to dream again. He saw an opportunity to help someone who thought as he did. Aiden had been in California for eight years. As he told his story, he confessed his mistake was believing it would only take five years for him to develop his own business. It was the night of his confession, after months of attending the AA meetings, he decided he didn't have a reason to live. The leader of the meeting, Stan Becks, stood slowly; shocked, without words to penetrate the frozen air.

"What is your name sir?" Jon asked. Stan sat down slowly apparently unable or unwilling to offer assistance.

"Aiden. Aiden Tudjal." He answered and hung his head in shame.

"How long have you been here, in America?" Jon ignored the signal to be quiet from Mr. Becks. The group began to whisper amongst themselves.

"A little over seven years. I've tried working for others, you see, but that is not what I was born to do. I was raised differently. My family stands on their own. I have failed them, my father, and my lineage." Aiden sat down and held his head sobbing. "I can't go home, and I have nothing to live for here. They have lost my money, and this alcohol has drained my spirit. I am no longer the man I was or should be. Don't you see Mr. Becks none of your counselors understand this? None of them come from another country; no one understands the depth of my sorrow."

"I was not born in America, my friend. Let me talk with you alone." Jon turned to Mr. Becks for his approval to assist Aiden. Jon and Aiden left the circle. Mr. Becks was pleased that Jon would handle the awkward situation. He resumed the session as though Aiden never spoke of possibly killing himself.

The two men got situated in another room. "Have a seat. Let me get a chair for myself. Would you care for water?" Jon asked as he spotted the cooler in the corner. Aiden didn't answer, and Jon took two cups and filled them. Returning with the cups and pushing the chair across the floor, Aiden offered to help.

"It is a bit difficult, right?" Aiden questioned not expecting an answer.

"Yes, my attempt was worth the results though. I got you to realize you're not ready to die." Jon stated, aware that Aiden wasn't talking about his dilemma.

Aiden had no response. He realized the depth of what he said, and it was at that moment he knew he was vulnerable. As they adjusted their seats the tension between them eased, Aiden told of his journey and listened as Jon shared his. Jon had been through two transitions. He was born in the Dominican Republic. His family moved to New York before he was ten.

"Yes, in my father's home, we lived as though we were still living in DR. He made my brother, and I work at an early age. He worked two jobs. We owned the home my mother dreamed of after his death; but his dream of a store, the reason he saved his money, never became a reality. He wanted to return to what he loved at home, where he was born. My mother loves the United States and the B.S. they tell her of the American Dream.

My sister, Anna, married a banker and they live in Queens. They moved my mother with them. Ana quit her job and enjoys knitting and sewing. Her dream is complete. She and my mother now have their own business. They make clothing for babies and children. They're doing very well."

Aiden didn't see an immediate connection then the story continued.

"My father died before we were teens. My brother was older, and he got the auto shop. I wanted no part of the dirt and grease, so they all got together and paid for my college degrees. However, New York isn't the best place for an independent investor. I could have worked for an investment corporation, but I didn't trust the system. They robbed from my father's business for years. He paid money to everyone. I wanted my own. I sold drugs, took drugs, drank, ran through the clubs and fell flat on my face. I embarrassed my mother, my sister, and the only one to shake me was my brother. I'm here to shake you. Aiden, life doesn't need us to redirect our journey. We have to live and enjoy what God has planned for our journey to be."

"What? Man, I go to church on Sundays. I pray, Monday through Friday. I don't know what God has planned for me. My journey has been treacherous." Aiden shook his head but continued to listen trying not to be rude.

"Aiden, to live your dream, you have to see the vision. You have to plan how you will live this journey. You can't change your destination if you keep walking the same path. Aiden, you can't reach your destination killing yourself in the bottle, wasting your money away, while living in the past."

"So are you a support, or a counselor here? I haven't seen you here before. I thought you worked with the banks."

"I'm sure you know I'm an investor. You work at the bank right?"

"I don't anymore. I quit. I came here to get my own, and I failed. I would go home, but I can't. My journey is ending quickly."

"Hmm, I wouldn't say that. What choice do you have but to climb upward? You agree you have nowhere to go. I am a speaker, and I've invested in this place here. So I'm already vested in you. C'mon, let's go to my place. You'll stay with me a few days and then we'll return to your world. If you still don't see a reason to continue your journey, I'll leave you to your fate."

Aiden's brow wrinkled. His reaction didn't stir Jon enough to explain his words. The men left together and now eighteen months later, Jon felt his investment would finally benefit him.

Aiden requested that his sponsorship be called a friendship. He clearly had traditional rules from his upbringing on the islands regarding friendship. Jon agreed, if they were to be friends, they had to build a relationship of trust. The traditional rules for Seychelles Islands were no different than those in the Dominican Republic. Men were to work to uplift themselves, family and community. There would be no secrets when it came to health or finance. Many rules immediately created a partnership. Aiden promised within the next two years; he would be equally able to uphold and manage his finances. He didn't trust himself and needed Jon to help him be worthy of carrying the Tudjal name again.

Jon was sure Aiden would drift back to being the soul that sought no redemption and only wanted his life to be done. However, it had been months before Aiden mentioned a drink or defeat. Now with his sisters' visit, Aiden feared they would detect his faults and defeats. Jon wouldn't allow it.

It was their plan that they held on to and it kept Aiden's new vision the priority. Jon and Aiden would be a part of Seychelle's business. They were sure that was why she asked to visit and stay with Aiden for a few months. She finally was prepared to start the business she had envisioned. Jon advised Aiden not to push their ideas on her. If they allowed her to suggest, or when she realized an investor and a bidder would be needed to buy or build on the property for her resorts and spas, they would offer their services. Seychelle would have to admit she couldn't take on that type of business in the United States alone. Jon had all the answers she needed.

Chapter 4

"The view is beautiful." Seychelle was referring to the aerial overview of Los Angeles. The plane was circling the LAX Airport preparing to land.

"It doesn't impress me as much as the islands. Each time I flew during school break I thought of the differences. Even from the air, our land looks like nature intended the earth to be. America has done so much to the natural beauty of their land. Even the vast areas of grass and the difference in the ocean, it all looks abused. The natural beauty is gone. I suppose it is because it's so crowded." Sasha replied, looking over her sunglasses through their shared window. "I guess I will always love our islands; there are no other like them."

"And what other islands have you visited? Sasha, of course, you will always love Seychelles Islands. It's our home. I agree, but the world has so much more to offer. The differences make the beauty. You will see. My resort will give you the opportunity to travel all over the world and visit the beauty of other countries."

"None can compare I'm sure, but I love to travel, and I will not pass up the opportunity to travel free."

"Who said it would be free?" Seychelle teased.

Sasha tapped her sister's arm laughing as the stewardess passed them cautioning everyone to return their seats to an upright position. She attempted to sound enthused as she spoke into her headset.

"We will be landing soon. Please secure your trays and gather any items under your seats. Check any small children for their safety. Please do not forget any carry-ons in the overhead compartments or beneath your seats. Thank you for flying Delta Airlines."

The sisters checked their surroundings and secured their seat belts. "Look there, Sasha. Those are the next to be included." Seychelle pointed to the cruisers in the Pacific Ocean.

"Your dreams, I pray they all come true for you. I can stop working then."

"Sasha, they are no longer dreams. I'm here to bring this vision into reality. You, father and mother, can retire. It will be done."

"I'm happy for you, for us. I hope you don't mind me taking a real vacation though. I haven't been in the states since I graduated. I haven't been on a real vacation since I began teaching. I don't know if I'll be any help to you."

"You will. I need someone to visit spas, resorts, and casinos. You can do that right?"

"Girl, can I? I love your vision more and more."

They stood ready to depart the plane. "Good, I've saved for years, and it's time to begin. It's not what Father thinks. Sasha, I've planned it out. If it doesn't work, I'll return to my job. Father thinks I quit. If I told him I took a leave of absence, he would have said I didn't believe in myself. It will work, but I've got to put forth the effort, network and spend money."

"I know you didn't dare tell Father you were spending your savings."

"Didn't tell him or Aiden. Aiden would want to spend it with me. So as far as either of them knows, I'm using money from a research firm."

"A firm? I know Aiden didn't believe that." Sasha grabbed her carry-on from the overhead compartment.

"You're right, but I told him they might be potential investors, so they were willing to put up the money for my findings and written reports. Aiden doesn't need to know the finances. Be careful what you tell him. He sounds like he's been failing with his ventures. I hope not, but he always sounds lost to me."

"I understand. Aiden doesn't share much about his progress. Father said men don't brag or tell it all as women do. I wanted to ask what that meant, but Father changed the subject. Well, I'll watch him, and you concentrate on getting the business started. Maybe this is what he needs, a new beginning."

"A clean beginning Sasha. He loves to gamble and take risks. I can't rely on him until he proves himself."

Passengers began departing the plane. The sisters traveled many times to the airports in the United States. The rush of the crowds no longer scared them as it had when they began their international travels. The signs for baggage claim led them to pass eateries, a temptation they hoped they could suppress.

"We'll go eat before Aiden takes us to his place, I promise," Seychelle spoke before Sasha could suggest they give in to their stomachs call.

The island beauties turned heads as they walked swiftly through the crowd. Both were proud of their height; Sasha, taller than her sister at five foot ten inches, walked in her stilettos as though she were a model. Their bronzed skin glowed, their shapes pronounced in their form-fitted tank tops and matching skirts. Neither watched their diets, and their curvaceous frames attracted smiles of approval. Seychelle ignored many of the glances, while Sasha loved the attention.

"Where are you from?" An older woman asked as they waited at the carousel for their baggage.

Sasha smiled knowing Seychelle wouldn't answer. "Seychelles, it's in East Africa."

"Beautiful, I would imagine. I don't often travel abroad. I've always wanted to take a cruise. Your accent is so different."

"Yes, and it is beautiful. You should; you'd enjoy it."

"Sasha our bags, or at least yours is coming around," Seychelle stated walking closer to the carousel.

"Well, you will need to be more polished my sister. You are pursuing a people business my dear. You have to be approachable."

Seychelle rolled her eyes, deliberately ignoring the comment but understanding the reason for Sasha's statement. She had never been a social butterfly. She loved watching from a distance. She surrendered with ease whenever questioned about her dating. She was more than willing to explain it wasn't a priority and as a loner, Seychelle had a list of better things to do. The two maneuvered their way through the parting crowd as others moved from the carousel, an expected courtesy.

"Do you think Aiden will be on time?" Sasha asked looking at the crowd toward the exit. There were a taxi and rent-a-car signs that caught her eye. "Does he have a car?"

"I would hope so. He told us that you have to drive everywhere, things are a distance." Seychelle replied not sure of her answer.

"Well, where are we to meet him? Did he say?"

"Yes, on the opposite side of the street near the taxi stand. Flight pick-ups are done there. He said we should see the signs. I think I'm going to mention getting a rental."

Sasha gave her sister a questionable look. "It may be a better rate, but it could have been included in your airfare. We have time, and I agree. I don't want to have to wait for your brother as we visit these resorts."

Seychelle pointed to Aiden who was waving across the street. "Girl look at him, cool huh? Why is he not crossing to help with our bags? He won't change I tell you. C'mon they're stopping the traffic."

The walk sign flashed as an officer posted himself in the middle of the street and beckoned the travelers to move quickly. The small crowd crossed mumbling where their cars or connecting transportation would be parked. Aiden pushed the button on his keys releasing the lock to the trunk.

"Welcome my beauties. How was your flight? Here let me help you. I have a few things in the trunk I can move over."

"You've lost your manners, my brother. Americanized?" Sasha teased as she sat her bags at his feet.

"What did I do or not do to that sister of ours?" Aiden asked Seychelle. "There were men there to assist if you needed help."

"She's teasing, I'm sure. Besides, I wasn't giving a tip for bags we can carry. Here this small bag can fit there."

The trunk of Aiden's Honda had plenty of room. He made sure to adjust his seat, allowing Sasha to stretch her legs.

"I'll take you around town at some point. You'll learn quickly once you get familiarized with the roads and the area. There are plenty of stores for you ladies to browse and we can search the web for places I have not explored myself."

"Aiden, you must have been up and down this coast on business. Father talks about your business often. How is it going?"

"Well, not good, I can't tell Father that the business efforts have failed. I'll explain once you get settled."

"Do you go to the beach here?" Seychelle changed the topic before Sasha could insist her brother explain what had obviously become his disappointment.

"No, I have not been. I've been working on me, to be honest. I know where it is and I know you love it, so we'll go while you're here."

Seychelle looked at her sister who knew not to say anything more. The sisters listened as Aiden became their tour guide. Aiden apologized for not cooking a welcome dinner for them. Seychelle insisted they eat out rather than cook, which they would often do during their stay. Aiden nor Sasha put up an argument when their sister told them she would pay the tab.

Seychelles Island

Chapter 5

The temperature reached ninety degrees before Cole took a break and called home. His new morning ritual gave him peace of mind. Summers on the island had included drop-in visits from his girls. Now, since his daughters were away from home, he made a point to call Naomi before noon.

Cole walked out of his office in deep thought. Naomi shared her concerns about their children. She was venting, and he understood her reasons. The conversation was cut short when the noon bell alerted the dock it was time to shut down for lunch. Cole wanted to walk the beach and clear his mind. Another summer habit he shared with Seychelle and Sasha.

Naomi suggested she meet him in town later. An early dinner at their favorite spot would allow them to share the fears they held to themselves. Cole agreed, hoping their impromptu date would linger into the night. Their marriage was filled with love. The love for family was first and foremost. Now with their children away from home, it was time for the couple to embrace each other.

Naomi was a beautiful woman. Cole remembered how he'd tease her about her conservative dress and matching head wraps. She loved the colored patterns and matched them well with handmade jewelry. Cole was a native of Seychelles Island. Naomi's home was Nigeria. They met while she was on a tour of the hospital and other medical facilities on the island. As a nurse, it wasn't hard to transfer to the island and settle down with her new husband.

Cole smiled at the thought of their walks along the beach and their soft conversations. Naomi would tease him mockingly speaking faintly above a whisper. He always felt that his voice was loud and needed to be toned down. He softened his baritone voice for her. He towered over his wife at six foot three. Naomi was shorter at five foot even. She gave up her heels that decreased his towering stature and no one other than Cole spoke of the difference.

Cole walked the length of the loading dock. He waved at the workers who sat in groups eating their lunch. He was respected and seen as a fair man. He couldn't help but think about Aiden returning home and continuing the business. He couldn't see selling what took years to build. His son would be back hoping there was a place for him. Aiden was lost in America. Soon his problems on the island would be forgotten. He could come home. Cole prayed for it each night.

The air lacked the humidity it held earlier in the week. Cole returned to his office wishing his walk had put his mind at ease. He dialed the number and waited for his son's voice.

"Father good afternoon. How are you today?" Aiden answered hoping his sisters didn't prompt his call.

"I called to see if you were okay. Your sisters can work a nerve, you know." Cole laughed, pausing for Aiden to comment. "Seriously, how are you holding out? It's been, what, three weeks, a month?"

"I would say about a month. They haven't been here. They're here a few days in the week, and I guess to follow up the calls they make. They're not in the way or working my nerves."

"So have you showed them around? It sounds like they're on their own. You know Aiden I let them come there so you would keep them safe."

"They're safe. We know where they are and where they're going."

"We, we who?"

"My friend and I. Jon is an investor. I met him at the bank. We talked about my business, and now he's talking with Seychelle. He's a blessing, Father, if I had him when I came here, I would be so much further in my work."

"What, you can't help her? What about your business? Further in your work? Have you made any progress? Seychelle is not going into business with you, is she? Aiden you do not want her to lead your dream. What is this Jon to tell her about your business? Aiden has a million dollars of emptiness? This will be a reason for her to abandon the nonsense. If you, a man, could not make it, how can she? Yes, once she understands, she will return home. Aiden, if you must know, this vision of hers is more than any businessman can handle. There are no women who head the type of corporation she will need. Besides, how is it this Jon can help your sister but not you? Has he taken over all you have? Is that why you haven't told your mother or me there is no business? What does he really want? That's why I didn't want those girls traveling by themselves."

"Father, no one took anything from me. The girls are safe. No one wants anything from them, especially Jon. He's an investor, a man of good faith. He has his own wealth, and he willingly shares his knowledge."

"No woman should be traveling as though she has no respect for herself and where she's from. You are the man they should be looking up to and traveling with. How did you pass on your obligation to a stranger?"

"Father, they didn't come here for me to watch them. What they are doing is respectful, and Jon wants only to help them. He got me out of my depression when I got here. I'm taking it a step at a time. It took some time to repair my faith in me."

"So how is your business? Are you still gambling and entertaining those women. Church, your belief in God, will restore you. I told you, have faith in no other. He will provide."

"Father, I have to go. Can we discuss this later?"

"Are you sisters around you?"

"Yes." He lied.

"I don't want them knowing I'm checking on them. I'll wait for them to call. Aiden, you're the man the only man in their lives now. Protect them. Women will say they know what they want and how to get it, but without us, they will fall. Do you understand?"

23

"Yes, I have to go Father, and I'm still not properly dressed to leave."

"We will talk tomorrow at length. Aiden, they will lose themselves in America. You know that right?"

"Yes, I do. Father, have a good day."

The dial tone sounded through the receiver. Cole pushed the "end" button and put the phone on his desk. It wasn't often that he got a bad feeling about his son's honesty. It was then that he realized, Aiden needed his sisters more than they needed him and as their father, he wanted to know why.

Chapter 6

Naomi watched the clock. She didn't want to be late for her date with her husband. He agreed without hesitation or her pleading that they hadn't been out in months. Walking the beach at sunset would ease the tension between them. She respected her husband's point of view, but she couldn't help but wish Seychelle the best.

As a mother, she knew Aiden wouldn't do well in Los Angeles. Even as a child he'd play before buckling down to get any work done. Playing cost him on the island. She sensed it would take him time to settle as a man. The men were expected to work hard. Many times Cole would go to the school or the athletic events and lobby Aiden's case. His father protected him for the future of the company. Naomi would disagree, they'd argue, and Aiden would be free to do things his way again.

Seychelle called her mother when they arrived in Los Angeles. She confirmed her suspicions within her first week of their visit. Her daughter described Aiden's mood, his home, and his menial job. It wasn't until she spoke of Jon, Aiden's friend, that Naomi understood the truth. Jon was handling Aiden's business, keeping him in line with his finance. He motivated him and kept him encouraged. Seychelle overheard Jon giving Aiden a heart to heart. She told her mother she suspected he was Aiden's sponsor.

Naomi didn't quite understand what Aiden would need with a sponsor. He never was into drinking or drugs, what could be so overwhelming that he needed a sponsor? Her daughter didn't understand either, and she ended the call promising her mother she'd find out more. She and Sasha agreed it was best their parents knew, Aiden was not the same.

Naomi hadn't decided whether to discuss this with her husband or wait until Seychelle and Sasha phoned with more information. Naomi would continue to pray. It was this living she feared for her son. He was their firstborn, and it was his father's doting that bore the results. Cole was hard on his daughters because of his failure with his son. Aiden would have to explain, once again, his need for assistance. Naomi didn't trust a sponsor; she would insist he come home.

One last check, looking in the mirror, she agreed with Sasha she didn't look her age. The women in the village worked long hours, entrepreneurs of handmade products; many businesses were established for tourists and exports. The islands flourished because of these women. Naomi had the privilege of raising her children, taking care of home and the needs of her family. Her time as a nurse was "as needed". She left the full time hours once her children finished college. Cole worked long hours. It was those hours that kept Tudjal Imports as the leading import and export franchise. Many of the men on the island worked for the Tudjals.

Naomi closed her eyes in prayer thanking God and praying for all of the families on the island. She grabbed her car keys, locked her home and convinced herself that the night would be a new chapter in her marriage. It was time to reignite the sparks before the flame of their love became a small glow. She missed the warmth they had.

Chapter 7

Parking would be a problem near the shoreline. Those who chose to walk the beach would park near the restaurants. Tudjal's Imports was quite a distance from the restaurant of Naomi's choice. She circled the block hoping to find a space. She smiled as she looked into the rearview mirror. Cole stood near the curb waiting for her to park.

Her husband seemed always to be where she needed him to be. She learned it was not just by chance but in his character. Their love for each other was classical, a symphony of understanding the other's needs. They married young, against the wishes of Naomi's parents. She had returned home twice in the thirty years of their marriage. After the funeral of her parents, she saw no reason to reunite with her siblings. She was a Tudjal, a family of wealth. Her siblings, four remaining, called when in need; Cole loved her through it all. They promised their children would value family not their monetary worth.

"Naomi, you look fabulous. I may have to take you out more often." Cole teased her as he kissed her cheek. "What news brings you to suggest this date as you called it?"

"As you've said more often, you work hard, and I need to know that we still exist. We need to make time for us. Let Tudjal Imports

27

take care of itself as well as our children. We'll have dinner, wine, conversation and that walk along the beach I've been longing for."

"This may be a new beginning. You know I love it when you start stirring things up."

"Well, where would you love to eat?"

Cole took his wife's hand and led her toward their favorite eatery. They walked along Main Street taking in the air with the mixed aromas of the smaller restaurants. Many of the patrons waved and smiled. A few owners extended their hands for Cole to shake, an island tradition. The music from a few businesses played as dancers performed on the paved road, an attraction for the tourists. Creole and French conversations were whispered among the tables that sat on the sidewalk.

The couple decided to eat outside. The soft wind reminded them that the beach wasn't far. The warm water was felt as the air carried a refreshing mist. The waves splashed against rocks along the shoreline, making a perfect backdrop for romance.

"Cole isn't this nice? When was the last time we really relaxed?" His wife's questions humbled his thoughts. He had prepared for a spat while hoping she would side with him. His worry for more than a month had been his children, his girls.

"Naomi, let me say I am sorry if I've not been attentive lately. It's not easy with Sasha and Seychelle romping in the States."

There it was out. Cole brought up the very topic they needed to discuss and put to rest.

"Did we not raise them? Did we not talk to them about our expectations? We are proud parents, aren't we?"

"Yes, yes we are." He reached for her hand. "My dear, I still have my fears. I think it is because of the problems that Aiden has met. He talked of his failures; failures that would take time to repair. A man has a lifetime to recover from his mistakes. Women need to be ready for marriage and motherhood. They can't waste time on fantasy and dreams, stepping into a man's world as though they seek to run things. This is not proper."

"What is not proper Cole? The world has many women who are successful. Are you comparing them to Aiden? His failures are not theirs." She moved her hand slowly over his, not to upset him but preparing for his temper to rise.

"So we accept this notion of running a business in America? We have a business here. Sasha teaches here. Their life, their start is here."

"Cole, it need not be their start and finish here. Seychelles Island is not the world. You suggested they get their education abroad. You introduced them to life off the island. Now you condemn them. They are not us, Cole. Look at the chances, the hope, the belief they have in their dreams. We instilled that in them. We have to trust their judgment. If this is not for them, they will come home."

They sat sipping their tea in silence, each deep in thought.

"Sasha is not giving up teaching is she?" Cole had not asked his youngest her intentions. His conversation with Seychelle was enough to upset him for weeks.

Naomi smiled and patted her husband's hand. "No worry Cole. Sasha is spending the summer with her sister and brother. She will return to the children she loves when the summer months are over. Each of our children Cole has their desires. They are young, and like us, they are free to make decisions for their future."

"The sun is beginning to fall. Let's start this beautiful walk. There is nothing we can do but pray Naomi." He reached for his wife's hand as they stood together. The two walked toward the shoreline.

A bridge crossing from the diners and shops held others who seemed to be captivated by the orange hues surrounding the setting sun. They took slow steps smiling and waving as they passed others enjoying the evening air. Naomi slipped off her sandals as they approached the white sand. The clear blue water splashed against the rocks. The soft sound of the waves blended with the conversations, whispers, laughter, and soft music that became an audible setting for the couple's walk.

"Times have changed. A father has a son who learns the trade and works knowing it will soon be his concern. His life is guided, predetermined by what the father does. The daughters seek to marry and become a wife then a mother. You know, Naomi, work for a young woman was not heard of until after she had her education. She was to stay close to home, learn to cook, clean, the things a wife does. Times have changed."

"We want them to have the best Cole. That was the reason you sent them to school. They have the best education compared to many here on the island. Do you regret this?"

"Naomi, you and I know the answer. I wanted so much for them, all of them. Now they're all just wandering in another country with no intention to give them what they deserve. Aiden couldn't make it. What will Seychelle do there with no husband, no brother, and no father to watch for her?"

"Do you think she needs a man to be someone or become someone? Cole, you can't believe as the elders did during our younger years. These are times when women have their own. Have you been blind to what is going on here? Many women are working, using their talents, running their homes, and businesses."

"And this is against the law of nature. Men provide, work and keep the family going."

"And women, Cole, just what should we be doing?"

Naomi waited hoping the conversation wouldn't turn into a debate. When he didn't answer, she knew he hoped for the same. They continued to walk and decided to stop when they realized they had the same distance to walk back.

"All our food will be long digested, and a new hunger will nag at us if we continue to walk." They took a seat on one of the large boulders. Naomi smiled and leaned in to kiss her husband. The kiss sealed their understanding. It was time their children made their own choices. As parents, they could only support their dreams.

Just Visiting

Chapter 8

Seychelle sat at the kitchen table where brochures, promotional material, and her calendar were stacked and scattered. It was Monday, the day she set aside to plan the upcoming week and evaluate her findings from the week prior. She didn't want to agree with her father or brother, but it was a bit much. Researching spas and resorts was tedious; visiting as a guest, observing the clientele and enjoying the amenities took time. Seychelle was determined to prove her vision was not a fairytale. She would build the Tudjal name. Resorts, spas and travel were doing well on the islands. The chalets along the beach served well for short stay travelers. The newer resorts were all inclusive, an American tourist novelty. Seychelle wanted to be a part of the new revenue. She'd expand with locations worldwide.

For the first month of their visit, Seychelle and Sasha traveled along the Pacific coast. California had a lot to offer. Her vision included adding a difference to existing establishments. She enjoyed the conveniences she and Sasha received, but she needed to meet with those who sat in the corporate offices. Her interest was in the management, the investments, and finances. She'd buy a few of the existing properties that were said to be failing. A few modifications would attract the money from other investors. She would purchase properties and build.

Sasha suggested giving the resorts a touch of the islands. The layouts and floor plans, business outline, financial disbursements, and expectations were in the paperwork that surrounded her. She needed staff. An area she hadn't explored. She needed a mental break.

Seychelle watched Aiden's daily routine. Monday's he worked around the house. She'd use the morning to discuss her plans with him. Aiden wasn't the same outgoing soul their mother described. His apartment, his dress, and even his attitude did not indicate that he was happy or heading toward his success. Seychelle remembered their last conversation before he left the islands. It seemed his vision was not clear; he somehow had lost his drive.

The apartment was smaller than he described, although he said he had moved. There was no furniture, at least none that was suitable for the space he had acquired. It appeared as though he hurried and scrambled to move; Seychelle wondered if his move was a run from trouble. His friend Jon seemed to always be in the shadows as though he was protecting Aiden's secret. Monday was the best day to approach him. No Jon until the evening and Sasha filled her mornings exercising at the gym.

Aiden had never been one for decorating beyond the necessities. Seychelle's past visits with her brother included adding her touch to his living quarters. This apartment was different. Something was missing. Aiden's spirit, his thumbprint or ownership just wasn't there. It was as though he didn't belong there or didn't want to be there. The boxes stacked in each room indicated that he was in no hurry to get settled. The apartment seemed staged. A feeble effort, Seychelle thought, as she stood and began looking through each cabinet, closet and storage space.

"Bonjour."

"Hey, good morning," Seychelle replied unaware of her brother's entrance. "I noticed you haven't begun to unpack. Your belongings would give one the impression you're not staying." His sister continued to explore the empty spaces.

"I am. Where else would I go?" Aiden's response was as sluggish as his walk to the counter. "Do you want coffee?"

"I have juice, thanks. Aiden what's going on? You seem different. Why did you move? Your place was banging, what is this? Talk to me." Seychelle turned to face her brother.

His white t-shirt and shorts were tattered. Their father would never have approved of his wear, even in his own home. Seychelle was stunned but held her comment.

"I had a setback." He walked out of the room before she could ask another question. Aiden closed his bedroom door. His truths were slowly unveiling. He had no real plan when he arrived in the United States. He had the finances and a dream. It was as though he was living the aftermath of a nightmare.

Aiden knew it would only be a matter of time before his sisters would question his downfall. It had been so easy to disguise the disgrace he felt with his family living on the island. His depressive state painted the walls of his apartment as it had painted his spirit. He wept. He needed a drink.

That's how it started after the final scam. Aiden allowed himself to accept another con. Drinking didn't numb him as it took away what he knew was logical. Now sober, it didn't change the circumstances. He couldn't afford another loss. He'd explain it all to them in time. "Humph," he sighed. He told himself he wouldn't talk about his state of mind. They didn't need to know he prayed for a rescue and God sent them to California. He fell back on his bed hoping sleep would overcome his stress. He watched the doorknob waiting for his sister to come in without an invitation.

On the opposite side of the door, Seychelle listened for Aiden's voice. She thought against knocking on the door for an approved entrance and returned to the work on the table. She'd talk with Sasha. Maybe the talk of achieving her goal and her new venture disturbed her brother. The reality was Aiden needed help, more than their father would be willing to give.

She drank her juice slowly, savoring the chill and flavor that quenched her temporary thirst. It wasn't long before she was engrossed in her plans to visit other resorts.

Chapter 9

The four ate dinner prepared by Sasha and Seychelle.

"This is delicious. I mean the restaurants here don't serve a meal as well prepared as this." Jon raised his glass to Sasha and smiled. Seychelle brought another platter to the table. "What more?" Jon's eyes glistened as Aiden showed no interest.

"It's more of the sautéed spinach and shrimp. I know I wanted more. How is it Aiden?"

"I think the last time I had smoked catfish, I was home. Jon tells of a place near the wharf that does a good job. I told him there's nothing like the food on the island. Now he knows the difference." Aiden replied reaching for the platter.

"He had nothing to compare it to, right Jon?" You're right, now he knows. I think if he continues to eat the food like this, he'll want to live there soon."

"Not quite Sasha. There would have to be more. I'm enjoying the food, your company and if there was anything else, well you may be right."

"Ah, my sisters arrive, and you want to leave for the islands?"

"No, no I mean no harm. It's hard to pass up good cooking, beautiful women and island living. Ah, there's the third thing Sasha. Let me know when to pack my luggage. I'm leaving with you."

They laughed as the platter passed around. Seychelle suggested they cook hoping it would bring her brother back to life. He seemed nervous until Jon arrived. She wondered did Aiden invite him so he could avoid her questions. She was prepared to talk to him after dinner. Jon's presence didn't matter.

Seychelle began the conversation asking how Jon and Aiden met. Jon took a seat next to Sasha on the couch leaving the answers up to Aiden. He began slowly with the details picking up the pace. Seychelle listened intently trying to focus on his words without thinking that Jon, too, was looking to take advantage of her brother's weakened state.

It was more than a question and answer session. Sasha had questions of her own, more about Jon and his background, more than what Seychelle was interested in hearing. Sasha's input did lighten the tension in the room.

"Investments, that's my forte. I've had a few clients that decided to wing it, and failed I might add; but for the most part, I've come out on top."

"Jon is one of the Los Angeles elites." Aiden's spirit seemed lively. After a few glasses of wine, he poured Ginger ale into his glass. Sasha raised her brow without commenting.

"So how did the two of you really meet? You said you worked at the bank, and you were a customer, but you're close." Sasha's observation brought on a moment of silence.

"Aiden, you have to know that—"

"That what, Seychelle? What difference does it make? We told you how we met. I worked at the bank, and he was a customer. I wanted to know about investing."

"Isn't that against the policy of the bank? You looking to work with a customer for personal gain?" Sasha questioned looking at Jon.

"What difference does it make? I was part of a bad deal, and he gave me good advice. I'm recovering, that's all."

"Recovering from what my brother? Tell us what it is. You never mentioned this friend, Jon, not once while I spoke with you. We meet this man and, excuse me, Jon; you depend on him for everything. What is going on?"

"Tell them Aiden. Tell them the whole truth, and we all can move on."

Aiden hesitated. He stood, ready to run out of the room. He wasn't willing to tell it all. They looked at him as the jurors did, as the men and women in the group did, as he did whenever he looked into the mirror. He was well aware of his shame. The shame he felt would fall upon the Tudjal name.

"I'm an alcoholic." He mumbled. "I'm sorry. I've been clean for over eighteen months, but I'll always be an addict. Jon is an investor, my sponsor, my friend. My plans fell apart, and I did too. Jon was there to show me I could get back on my feet, start again and be somebody again. It doesn't help to say it over and over again. It's embarrassing to have to have—"

"It's okay. You're not the first to be an alcoholic in the family." Sasha stated firmly. "We have them in the family as you know."

"Yes, those Father will not deal with, or have us mention."

"Yes, his brother," Seychelle said solemnly.

"So if you want to tell them, I understand, but I rather you didn't. I'll tell them when it becomes necessary for them to know."

"What do you mean?" Sasha wanted to understand his reasoning.

"I want to give them back their money. I want them to know I recouped what I lost."

"I see, and Jon what is it that you gain from this relationship."

Jon told his story. They talked for hours, and the four agreed they could expand the Tudjal name. Now that the sisters understood their brother's plight there were no more questions.

Jon and Seychelle talked about the possibilities of owning or investing in properties for resorts. Aiden and Sasha looked at the resorts and the amenities provided. It became clear. If Seychelle's dream were to become a reality, she would need a team to work with her.

Two plans fell immediately into place. As Seychelle suspected her brother needed her as much as she needed him. It became apparent that Jon would be an asset as well. Aiden's ability to articulate business proposals, plans and develop modules coupled with Seychelle's vision and concepts gave them the groundwork for Serenity Resort & Spa. Sasha suggested Sérénité Spas. It seemed that neither Aiden nor Seychelle gave a second thought to the French translation. Seychelle played with the words with her pen and pad. She smiled as she thought of the calligraphy for a logo.

"I love it! Truly I do." Seychelle wrote the entire name in the fancy script for them to see. "We need a logo. Jon, Aiden, what do you think?"

"French, do you think that will attract more business? Jon smiled anticipating Seychelle's answer.

"Hopefully. I would think tourists would travel as they do and include our resorts as a place of interest. Sasha before you return home you must help with the décor and colors. Aiden, can I leave the logo design to you and Jon?"

"When are you returning home??" Aiden asked solemnly.

"Don't sound so glum. We have another six weeks to work this through. Sasha has to return to prepare her classroom. I, on the other hand, will return to the islands in September. I'm hoping I can stay with you Aiden. If not I'll have to find a place. I don't want to travel back and forth for business meetings. At least not while we're building."

Seychelle turned the pages of the paperwork Jon prepared for her signature. The letters seemed short but requesting to meet investors, bankers and corporate lawyers didn't need lengthy details.

No, you can stay here, of course. Where else would I have you stay? It's better to work this way, I guess. We have no office to work from so here is fine."

Jon was surprised Aiden had no objections. It took the month of June and longer sessions for Jon to explain to Aiden his sisters were no threat. They wanted the best for him.

It was early for a meeting of the minds, but they agreed on the paperwork to launch the business had to be signed and returned to the attorney's office. The four would meet with the lawyers and real estate brokers during the week.

The California sun was comforting although Jon stated he preferred a cooler temperature.

"It's a nice day, refreshing even. The islands holds a different type of heat well above what you would call hot. You'd have to travel off the coast to know warmth like that." Sasha was teasing Jon. Seychelle looked up from the papers recognizing her sister's cunning ways. She hoped Jon didn't find her tactics attractive.

"Why not? If you're extending an invitation, a promise to be my escort, and maybe teach me the island traditions, I will be there."

"Sure, I'll await your call sir."

"You doubt there will be a call, why?"

Jon's subtle hints started when they met. Sasha blushed as he compared her beauty to that of a queen, no less than a princess. Seychelle snickered knowing the game played between them was fair. Sasha smiled, and they all openly laughed.

"My father would surely take out his gun to you. That's traditional and rightfully so. Men who respect the women of the island would not accept such an invitation." She raised her eyebrow and winked.

"Well, we have six weeks for you to teach me what I need to do to see you. I don't wish to disrespect your father or the traditions of the island. I understand the reason for your return. I don't intend to interfere with your career. I respect you and your work."

Jon took her hand moving her to the living room. Aiden and Seychelle gave the couple a questionable glance.

"Now you won't find anyone else who would wait a year to see you again. I mean, that is if you don't have a man in your life. What I'm trying to say is I'd like to know you better, and I can't say that I'd wait a year."

Sasha had no response. Since their arrival and meeting Jon, she thought she was between dreams. The thought of travel, meeting people and being complimented constantly was intriguing. She hadn't imagined how it would be, but her nightly visions peaked her excitement. She dreamt of meeting someone mysterious, but a gentleman who would smother her with attention. Seychelle received most of the attention on the island. Sasha was considered the last of the Tudjals. "Pretty and spoiled," was the definition she overheard during her college years. She didn't date much, so there was no man to compete with Jon.

"More papers?" Sasha asked her sister, welcoming a chance to step away from Jon. "What did we leave out? Jon, I thought you gave us the necessary paperwork? Oh dear, let me check the list."

"He did Sasha. We need to show the notary our identification, that's all. Our signatures will be binding then. Jon, we included you as our Financial Advisor and something regarding investments. I hope you don't mind. Sasha, you are one of the people listed on the Board of Directors. I'm sure, after talking with the lawyer, the Wilkins Law Firm will represent us and will sit on the board as well."

"Sounds like a lot." Sasha shook her head in admiration. She stood over the table where her siblings sat. "Well, your dream is now a reality."

"Yes, what's next?" Seychelle asked addressing her brother and Jon.

"The bank, an account needs to be established." We can go there first. Jon watched Sasha as she busied herself helping to clear the table. He would wait for the answer. Sasha's actions assured him, she wouldn't leave without letting him know when he could visit.

The Plan

Chapter 10

They stayed on schedule visiting the west coast resorts, lodges, and hotels. The coastline, rugged by nature with plenty of fishing was the main attraction for vacationers. The breathtaking framework added to the resorts that nestled in the majestic landscape. The sisters were amazed when they were told there was skiing and other winter activities in northern California. They decided, during the last night stay at Bacara Resorts in Santa Barbara, to travel to Mexico or Las Vegas.

The oceanfront property included the natural beach for two miles. Seychelle complimented the décor and stunned the others when she said she wouldn't mind duplicating the resorts atmosphere.

"I love the coordination of their colors, don't you Sasha?"

"My, my Seychelle," Sasha whispered, "This had to be expensive don't you think?"

"Investors, my investors." Seychelle looked away from the table. The music of the jazz band caught her attention. Aiden and Jon agreed to meet them before dinner; it was close to seven.

"What do you think about Jon, I mean now that we know his true relationship with Aiden?"

"Sasha, please don't tell me you're attracted to his quick wit. He's nice but not charming if you know what I mean. He doesn't fit my definition of, what can I say—"

"Say no more, keep it to yourself; they're headed this way."

"So you like him?" Seychelle asked ignoring her sister's warning.

"Yes, Aiden did you take that nap?" Sasha feigned a smile and summoned the waiter to the table. "We'll order now. I'm rather hungry, Seychelle what about you?"

"I am. We'll take a moment, thank you." The waiter nodded and waited for the men to order their drinks.

"Water with lemon." Aiden was pleased there was no response from his sisters. "Iced Tea is fine for me." Jon looked at the ladies, as did the waiter.

"Oh, sorry, I'll take a Moscato." Seychelle placed her order without a thought.

"I'll have a Piña Colada, thank you." Before the waiter could step away, Sasha blurted out, "Listen, we can't be on edge every time we order drinks. Let's be clear; you guys are okay with us drinking right?"

"It's not a problem, Aiden you're okay right?" Jon was sure Aiden could handle the matter.

"I'm good. What are we eating?"

Sasha and Aiden began their conversation leaving Aiden and Seychelle to enjoy the band while sharing a platter of hot wings. As they waited for their entrées, they reminisced naming the bands from the islands.

"Do they still have the Friday night at the beach concerts?"

"Yes, it has become the main attraction. Father hates the traffic on Friday afternoon, but Aiden it has brought so many to Mahé Island. I want our resorts to have those type things, something different."

"So what has Father said about this venture, now that he knows you're not giving in to his wants?"

"Aiden, I can't. My dreams are not Father's. He would have Sasha and I handling invoices for Tudjal's Imports until we were island elders. We talked, and talked, and to be honest, I think he hopes this trip will prove him right."

"Right? How? He doesn't know or understand the business you're seeking. What did he think? He knows you've researched the business.

41

This trip wouldn't prove much. You're not allowing his thoughts to persuade you, are you?"

"No, not at all. I don't know what he thinks. Strange I feel that most men consider it strange that I want my own business."

"What do you mean? Did we give you that impression?"

"No, not you or Jon, but talking to the bankers today. Did you see the reaction when Jon told them I was the primary and Sasha and you were secondary? Even the lawyers, did you notice the stares? Sasha did."

"Maybe it's the proposals. There may not be many women who invest in building resorts. I'm sure plenty have invested as shareholders."

"Aiden, I want to be an owner. Build and own; maybe I'll start with investing but eventually, I want my own."

"What's up, you two? The conversation is getting serious or what? You should see your faces." Sasha was feeling her second Piña Colada, but it didn't stop her from ordering a third.

"I was telling Aiden it's rather uncomfortable to be in my position talking to the men we've met. They seem to be uneasy with doing business with me."

"Seychelle, it's not you sis," Sasha stated reaching for a wing. "It's the fact you're a woman," Sasha whispered as if she was passing on a secret.

Jon shook his head. "Listen, business, big business, it's like a network. Everyone is leery of the newcomer. You come in looking like money, depositing, money and talking money. They want to know where you came from and who you are. It's business. No one wants to move down a notch because you took their place or the place of someone they know and trust. You're new; we're new. Your ideas, your determination, you're just starting, and they know you'll work until you fall apart. That's what they're hoping."

"Listen, they trapped me because they feared me. I fell for the traps. Jon and I won't let it happen to you, but you've got to be strong to push your way up. Your presence is more than enough — they definitely notice you. They just don't take you as a threat, but you have the money. You have what most didn't have when they started. That puts you in a different category. You're a threat they'll have to watch. They'll toy with you and watch who you become attached to. Sis, there will be those who hear you and believe, they'll invest and work with you. It's the trash you have to move past as you climb the ladder. Are you scared of heights?"

"There's a way around this. Listen, let's just complete the schedule Seychelle has planned. None of us are scared of heights, right?" Jon winked at his table of friends.

Sasha smiled. "Pass me a wing."

Chapter 11

"Las Vegas and then Cancun, Mexico." Sasha placed the calendar on the table between Seychelle and Aiden. "I booked all the arrangements; we're set."

"Will Jon be joining us? Has he said what he is expecting in salary? I've been thinking about the staff that we need on a regular basis. I definitely won't be doing clerical work, nor will you have the time Sasha. We'll need someone to do the books, and arrange our travel."

"Not for some time I'm sure, right Aiden?" Sasha shook her head in disbelief. "You'll have time to get the staff. After all, you must purchase the properties and then get the staff. Is this the pitfall Father expected? I hadn't thought about staff for the office or the resorts, silly me."

"Has Jon mentioned a fee?" Seychelle waited for an answer. "He hasn't brought it up to either of you? That worries me. Aiden what does he expect in return? What do you expect?"

"I won't be working with the resorts full time. I'll keep my job — maybe change my shift. I won't be expecting a salary until we're on our feet. Jon didn't mention a thing. I'll call him and tell him we need another sit-down meeting. We shouldn't talk about the internal needs on the road." Aiden spoke giving a dose of reality to Seychelle's dream.

"Aiden's right. Until the resorts are bringing in money, we can't expect to be paid. I can be your Personal Assistant until then, maybe longer. There's not much I can't do from home, after school hours."

"I don't want this to change anyone's lifestyle." Seychelle sighed. It was a pitfall. She had it listed as one. Now it was in need of immediate attention. They were to meet the lawyers and brokers after their return. Sasha would be heading home in three weeks. Her accomplishments over the past few weeks didn't seem like much. She had visited the resorts. Those she was interested in she highlighted. Each stay was no more than three days, enough to get a feel for the atmosphere and their amenities. Each cost put another dent in her funds. Although she had minimum funding set aside for employees, it wasn't enough.

"Yes, call him. We'll need to meet after Sasha, and I arrive in Vegas."

"Jon and I should arrive a few hours after you. I'm meeting him at the airport there. His flight from New York lands about two hours after yours."

"Everything is set. Remind me of the names that need to have a written introduction to our company."

"Jon is working on some additions to the list. He's separating the list by the types of ownership."

"Yes, let's talk when he arrives. He's flying out in the morning right?" Seychelle gave a quick eye to Sasha who was pleased to answer.

"Yes, his flight leaves at eight. I booked him on an early flight. His meeting there is at ten."

"I don't know Aiden. Do you approve of her dating your friend? Father would have a lot to say. Jon is Spanish you know."

"Actually he's Dominican, and it doesn't bother me. I think they're teasing each other. Long distance romance is a trying affair if an affair at all."

"Hello, I'm here. We are not in a relationship, nor have I teased him." She felt the stare from the two of them. "Well, not enough for an affair. Certainly, nothing that needs Father's attention."

"I do agree with you; Father need not know. That would be another reason for him to interfere with my business."

"It's the beginning ladies, and our father has never been able to handle non-traditional beginnings. So if you are interested in Jon, don't keep it a secret from Father; that's if it gets serious. Seychelle, don't wait until all fails or falls through to ask for help; from Jon or me. We won't make any drastic changes in our lives or our employment, promise." Aiden had a change in attitude. He seemed more relaxed and less stressed. Sasha mentioned it to Seychelle before their visit to the resorts in Berkley, California. It helped not to worry about him or his addictions.

Sasha and Seychelle packed the night before. They avoided the morning rush as they caught a mid-morning flight. It was more like a shuttle flight certainly shorter than the flight would be going home.

Sasha took the opportunity to nap while her sister read through financial reports. She was overwhelmed by the amount of money she hadn't calculated. She wouldn't disclose her disappointment, but it was hard to suppress.

Seychelle spent many hours planning, saving, and praying she'd be ready to open her first resort. Jon spoke with a few bankers and brokers. Aiden was right. Unknowingly she would have fallen for a few of the scams as he had. She appreciated Jon and Aiden and hoped they wouldn't have ulterior motives of their own.

The plane landed, and the sisters exited the airport looking for the hotel shuttle. Just as they suspected there was no hour where there wouldn't be a crowd at the airport. They wheeled their carry-on luggage giving no thought to waiting at the baggage carousels. The debate to fly back to Los Angeles and then to Cancun ended when Aiden agreed to bring the luggage with him. There was a change in plans. He wouldn't be with them in Vegas. He would be networking with the investors in Cancun before their arrival.

"Girl, it seems without that strip, as they call it, there are miles and miles of land. Plenty of room for more, I guess, but did you see a beach?"

"Sasha, can we wait until we reach the hotel. There's our shuttle."

A transport bus adorned with gold "MGM" lettering pulled up to the curb. An over-friendly driver jumped out speaking a scripted greeting as he opened the door for the luggage and assisted the women with their first step on the bus.

"Hope you beautiful ladies had a nice flight. Things on the strip are heating up. If you like, I can give you the tourist details, or you can ride and ask questions. We're here to help you while you stay with us at MGM."

"We'll enjoy the view and ask questions when needed if you don't mind." Seychelle wasn't in the mood for his rehearsed lines during the entire ride.

"I knew you'd tell him that. Seychelle you've got to become more, what do they say…sociable? Really!" Her sister whispered exaggerating her disappointment. Sasha smiled at the driver as she extended her hand.

He nodded and stood at the door waiting for other passengers. They found they had a choice of seats. They were the only passengers boarding at the airport. The bus began to fill as they stopped along the way to the renowned hotel.

Chapter 12

There was more than enough time to check-in and explore the MGM Grand. Seychelle and Sasha walked through the casino to the escalators on the opposite end. The glamour, lights, and sounds of the machines added an anticipated excitement to the air.

"Did you think of adding a casino? It brings in money or so it seems? I've never been into the gambling thing?"

"Sasha that would be a temptation for our dear brother. Maybe in a few but not all."

"Had you thought about casinos at all?"

They walked into the bar and took a seat. "No, but I'm sure the investors and Jon have. Sasha, I have the ideas and the desire, but I never thought it was this deep. Father may be right. It's more than I ever imagined. Just the little we know has added to my ideas of what the perfect resorts would be. I want this Sasha, I've always wanted to create the dream getaway."

"Father does not know this business. Don't become your own obstacle. Let's wait and see what Jon has found out. I told him to call when he checked in. Look around, this place didn't just happen overnight. One idea, investors, and boom…"

"I didn't think of it that way. I knew we'd have investors but Sasha that puts them in deep with our profits."

"Girl, please. Look at how deep those profits will be. Look around. A resort with or without the casino would bring in a profit well over the cost. I could only guess what it brings in. Other than the businesses on the island our father doesn't know anything unless it's tradition. The traditions are slowly fading away. The world is changing. Seychelle the world is changing. Our home has always seen the women work with the men of the island helping to build for their families. You can build too, but who says it has to be on the island. Father can't think you'll be living there all of your life. I've got news for him; I may be tempted to leave the island."

"Where are you going?" The two laughed knowing the answer.

"That's Father's question," Sasha said as she mocked their father. "You have nowhere like this. Where can you live among people who know and understand God's gifts and live man's dreams?" The women laughed.

"I see him saying that all the time. That's why this has to work Sasha. I've saved more than enough and I invested in stocks that will continue to grow. I didn't think beyond that. There's so much more I don't know."

"Well, that's where Jon and Aiden fit in. Listen, I'm sure there's more than one person managing these resorts. You'll be in the same position as the other owners in a few years. It's destined to be."

The bartender refreshed their drinks. An hour later Jon met them for an early dinner. The restaurant seating began where the outsized mahogany bar ended. Centered, was a large stage awaiting promised entertainment or attempted karaoke. Jon greeted them with a smile and hug. The bartender watched the island lovelies maneuver between the tables tipping in their stilettos. They left him smiling at the thought that Jon left the bar with the eye candy he had admired for the past two hours. The bartender and other male patrons found themselves scanning the area for other beauties that appeared to be alone.

"You ladies left quite a stir back there," Jon stated as he pulled out their chairs for them to sit.

"Please, any woman would turn their heads. I doubt they were worth the time." Sasha nodded her head in agreement.

"I didn't even notice," Sasha said looking at Jon's reaction.

"Okay, you two, what's up? Let's get that straight first. Are you dating, flirting, screwing or what? It's obvious something is going on." Seychelle looked at her sister and Jon. Her expression demanded an answer.

"Nothing that grown folks don't do, huh Jon?"

Jon smiled and raised his eyebrow in Sasha's direction.

"Your sister is a beauty and as you know a flirt. No, there is nothing between us other than a friendship that I'm sure will blossom in time."

"So you see sister, no need to worry. If things get started between us, it will be a distant affair."

"I wouldn't say that my dear. I promised your sister we'd get this ball rolling before the two of you are set to return to your home. I keep my promises."

"Well, promise me—" Sasha moved her hand closer to his.

"Can we discuss the business, then you two can continue whatever you want to call it." Seychelle waved her hand to the waitress serving their table.

The trio talked through dinner. Ideas and pitfalls were a part of the discussion. It was when Seychelle mentioned locations that Jon gave her an alternative that would change their lives forever.

"So Jon, if I hear you right, we should invest before building our own?"

"Sasha, both of you looked confused, listen ladies. Investments mean money in return. Corporations don't invest, buy or build without knowing there's a return. So you buy someone out, bid on the resort that is fading out. Add your touch, services, and whatever to make it fabulous. Yes, it will cost, but you're seeking to regain the customers they may have lost and curious vacationers. Now that's not where your money stops. You invest in various sites. A golf course, a company that will bring those amenities to you. Investments will keep your money moving. You don't want to put your money into your resorts without a better return for your overhead. This will matter when you're charging those vacationers to come and stay at your resort."

There was a silence among them. Without the words, Jon knew they had questions. He pulled out statistics and prepared folders from his satchel. He gave each of them a folder. As they glanced through the paperwork, Jon ordered another drink.

"Would care for another drink ladies?"

"Yes," Seychelle replied taking a deep sigh.

"Oh yes, I'll have another, thank you." Sasha never took her eyes off the papers in front of her.

"I've given you the results of those I've researched and carefully looked into their statistics over the years. This overview should give you an idea of expenditures as well as lost profits. You can't afford to go in blind. I think these are the best for startups and you can move on from them without losing. The locations may not be what you expect but...."

"Jon, how much are you looking to get paid for your work with me, I mean us?" Seychelle shot a quick eye to her sister, hoping she wouldn't speak out. She was surprised when Sasha didn't close her folder to give his answer full attention.

Jon was caught off guard. He and Aiden hadn't mentioned their money. He hadn't considered working as a part of Seychelle's company. He would admit he intended to make his money before she lost hers. He would disappear long before she realized she had made a bad investment. As the friendship between him and Aiden changed so had his intents. Jon found Sasha attractive and his interest in her grew each time he was in her company. He wanted to spend time with her alone before making long-term decisions.

"I didn't consider that. I just wanted you to see what the possibilities are for the business. It is a sound investment this way. If you still want to build, you may find yourself in a bind. I don't know what your accounts look like, but if you were to build, you'd be paying out more than receiving."

"Okay, so we build on what is already established and invest. Who pays the staff and all that other stuff you mentioned? I thought I would be doing that as well."

"There are agencies; you pay them. These places have staff. The packets you have there, shows a line item for each payment you will make. The suggested investments are behind the brochure."

"You can't think you're giving me all of this and not working with us. As I said, I thought about a Financial Advisor, or accounting, and sales, but I had no one in mind. Aiden and I talked about it at length. I thought I would take a few leads from him since he was supposed to have a business in place."

"God's work." Sasha firmly stated.

51

"What?" Both Seychelle and Jon frowned, confused as she repeated herself.

"God's work. Jon was put in Aiden's life to save him from obvious self-destruction. You, on the other hand, are the one who is blessed with the business sense. You'll be fine, we all will."

"We? What are you saying, Sasha?"

"Well, you said you would need an assistant. I'll be that assistant, give me another year with the students. I'll give them another year. This is a big endeavor; you'll need a team you can trust. I need a future, Aiden needs a future, and Jon, tell us what you need?"

Jon took a drink from his glass. "I need you and me to have our first of many dinners."

Seychelle shook her head. She took that to mean he'd be with Sérénité Resorts & Spa. She felt tears filling her eyes. Excusing herself from the table, she left them to discuss what was next.

Seychelle slowed her hurried steps. She didn't want them to see her crying. She could release the anxiety that kept her from sleeping over the last week.

She entered the restroom and freshened up. Lingering at the sink, she smiled at herself as she heard her mother's peaceful voice. "The world is yours; others just live in it. Take control of your life, and you'll find your purpose. Follow your internal voice, and you will be blessed for years to come. You'll be fine my child; you have your education and common sense. Be patient, and you'll find there are no challenges you can't face." Her thoughts were interrupted as two women entered the restroom. Seychelle gave a slight smile and went toward the exit.

"She looks like money." The taller of the two women stated.

"Girl, the women come here to pick up the big spenders. The owners roam around, and that's who they get dolled up for."

Seychelle wanted to laugh loud enough for them to hear her response. Sasha would have done more than that. As she repeated their remarks in her head, she did laugh. She was soon to be an owner.

Chapter 13

The music was soothing. Sasha convinced Jon that Seychelle wouldn't want to tag along. She wanted to see the rest of the casino and get closer to the melodic tune that was being suppressed by the band at the restaurant.

"Do you hear it? I wonder if that's, do you hear it?"

"No. Who do you think it is?"

"It sounds like that song by Mariah Carey." Sasha rose to her feet. "Seychelle you don't mind do you? You can sit here; we'll be right back."

"No, you two go ahead. I'm sure you'll be safe with him. Right, Jon?" Seychelle teased.

"Yeah, she definitely won't be allowed to roam." He winked as he stood. "Are we meeting you here?"

"No, I'll go to the room. Don't rush." She knew they wouldn't.

Seychelle hadn't heard the tune that Sasha claimed was drawing her in. The band playing at the restaurant wasn't bad. She ordered dessert and coffee. As she flipped through the folder, she heard a voice. Assuming it was the waiter she didn't bother to look up.

"Sure you can put it there, thank you."

"You allow anyone to put it there?"

The deep voice came from what she would later describe as God's way of teasing a woman through the voice of a man. She imagined her hands touching what had to be soft baby skin. She'd admit he needed the beaches of the island to give him the perfect tan, but she'd dated men of mixed races before. It was obvious he had a faint bit of Caucasian blood, but his native ancestors would be proud of his tribal features. Seychelle was in awe, but she quickly realized she hadn't answered his question.

"I'm sorry. I thought you were the waiter." She noticed his facial expression and felt the need to apologize. "You wanted to do what? Please forgive me." She hoped he would repeat his question without her having to apologize again.

"I asked would you mind if I joined you."

"Oh, no I don't mind. Please do."

She thought to herself, *"I sound desperate. What is wrong with me? My God, he is delicious, I mean gorgeous."* She glanced around the room hoping Sasha and Jon didn't notice him approaching.

"I noticed the couple leaving; I hope I'm not intruding?"

"No, not at all. Pardon my manners." She put away the folder deliberately giving him her full attention.

She examined him further as he attempted to explain his reason for wanting to talk to her. His dark hair was slightly wavy. His heritage peaked her curiosity.

"I haven't seen you here. Did you arrive today?"

"Well, this is a large place. I doubt you know everyone that visits."

"Just about everyone, especially those with beauty. Also, you don't look like the gambling type. You're more like the reserved type. Mellow music, quiet dining, relaxing resorts, and the beach. Should I continue?"

"No, you've read me well, Mr.—?"

"Ah, if I told you my name you would then Google me and find out what I do."

He looked at her as she smiled. He watched her earlier with the other woman, whom he assumed was a friend. When Jon arrived, he hoped he wasn't there to be with the island beauty that caught his eye. It was her height that caught his attention after her initial presence teased his instincts. She had to be a model. Perhaps in town for a show.

"I don't think I would be that interested in a name."

"Good, I'm Vance, Vance Chase and you are?"

"Seychelle Tudjal."

"Nice, beautiful name for a beautiful woman. What island are you from? Your accent is different."

"Seychelles Islands in East Africa and you. You speak French?" She surprised herself. It wasn't often she would be specific about her island.

"Ah, my accent gave that away. I am from Canada, born and raised there."

"So you are a long way from home as well."

"Not as far as you but yes quite a distance. Here on vacation?"

"Yes, I'm with family. My sister and I have come to visit them in the states." She didn't know why she volunteered the information, but it added to the conversation.

"I am here often, business. I've not been to Africa. Maybe Seychelles Islands needs to be on my itinerary. So you're named after the islands. It must be beautiful."

"Thank you, and yes my father named me after the islands. He's lived there all of his life."

"Do you plan on staying there? I mean any plans for the States?"

"Not really. I don't see myself settling into one place for a while. I live there now, but I want to travel. See the world."

"So if you don't mind me asking, what do you do?"

"I'm separating from my job there. I was working in the family business. It's profitable, but I've worked there since High School. Not sure what I'll move on to." She lied and didn't think twice about it.

"Well, that's life. Traveling through it, I do that with my business."

"Salesman, or Insurance Agent?" Seychelle prepared herself for the disappointment. He would be trying to sell her something. She prayed she was wrong.

"Investor. I'm invested here. I don't sell anything; I buy and collect. It's very profitable. Just what would you say if I told you most of the hotels on the strip have my signature on their paperwork?"

"Impressive. Have you ever wanted to own?" She saw the opportunity to pick him for information.

"Too much aggravation. I invest, get my share every month, and it's without a headache. It's not a bad business. I come here and a few other spots and relax. I enjoy seeing people enjoy themselves."

Seychelle looked closer as he spoke wondering his angle. *Why did he choose to talk with me? Why am I engaging in this conversation?*

"So you come to see how your investment fairs?"

"I guess you can say that. Not that it matters, my investments are secured. I come to see if what I've invested in pleases the patrons. I don't want to bore you with all this talk. Let's talk about you. You're a lot more interesting than the business I deal with daily."

Seychelle enjoyed his conversation. They walked through the casino onto the strip. He became an instant guide, giving her the history and updates on the oldest and the latest additions to the busy boulevard.

"Do you find yourself bored with the atmosphere? I mean I would think it becomes mundane."

"Not at all. This is exciting, people releasing stress and relaxing. I'm in business, but I don't let it take over my life. I too need time to relax." He smiled and offered his hand. "You see my dear my business is relaxing. I travel and understand that it is this type of atmosphere that people will always spend their money on."

She took his hand, and they continued their walk. It was at that moment she knew they would be spending more time together. Vance laughed as she talked of her travels to the United States and her attraction to resorts. Seychelle explained without revealing her business that she and her sister were resort hopping.

"Looking for that male from another island? Most women seek to find a man for marriage at these resorts." Vance gave her a tempting look but was unable to keep a straight face. He laughed and together they shrieked like old friends.

"No, that's not true for my sister or me. My father would have our heads if we were seeking husbands during our travel."

"Why? Do you have a pre-arranged marriage waiting?"

"If he had his way I'm sure he would have done that right after our graduations. My mother would not allow that though. It is done as a cultural tradition, now it is advised, persuaded, recommended, well you know. What about you? Now that you have admitted that you relax and it's not all business."

"I've dated a few times over the years during my travels. But most women want to be settled, and I wasn't quite ready for the commitment. As I get older, I find myself thinking more about it. Who knows, I may have to go to the islands and ask Mr. Tudjal for a meeting."

Seychelle gave him a pert look and watched him as he ordered drinks for them. They explored a few of the casinos along the strip and walked back to MGM to have a final drink. She was enjoying his company and wished they could have a full day together. Vance Chase was a man worth knowing.

"So where will you and your sister hop to next?"

"Cancun, Mexico and the Seychelles, our home."

"When do you leave for Cancun?"

"In the morning. We have a mid-morning flight. We're meeting my brother there."

"I see. I've enjoyed your company. I don't know if I could or want to say goodbye."

"You don't have to. I'll be back in a month. Maybe we can meet when I return."

"Or in Cancun, I have to be there by Thursday. That gives me three days of relaxation. I'd love to spend one of them with you."

"I don't know what to say." Seychelle hesitated to make any other comment.

"Say you'll see me when I get there. How long are you staying there?"

"A week, we'll leave Sunday afternoon."

"That's perfect. Let me give you my card. You call me when you've settled in."

Seychelle looked at the card in his hand. She didn't extend hers to receive it.

"If you don't call, I'll know I am often overconfident. You don't have to say a word, don't call and I'll understand."

Travel Meeting

Chapter 14

"So, you met him in Las Vegas, and he flew down here because he wanted to spend time with you? Seychelle, doesn't that sound a bit strange? Who does that?"

"Vance Chase, I googled his name. He's an investor, a rich investor. He's from Canada, he's single, and if my spirit is right, I can learn a lot from him."

Sasha dabbed her mouth and put down her coffee cup. "It's not like you to talk to someone so openly. Does he know what your business is?"

"Our business was never a question, nor would I have told him. I told him I worked in the family business. I didn't even tell him it was Tudjal Exports. After his statement about Google, I'm sure he'll do his researching. Our business will not have a connection to me, at least not one that is easy to find. Not right now."

"Okay, so he's an investor. You want to be an owner, why not allow him to be the first investor. He'll take a chance on a woman he's interested in, won't he?"

The thought crossed Seychelle's mind during the flight to Cancun. She couldn't trust having her dream controlled by anyone but herself. Vance had teased other senses. Sleeping the night before their travel was an arousal of emotions and sensitive responses. She wanted to know more about him, the man, not the investor.

"He would I'm sure, but Sasha he's someone I could see myself with, mentally and physically."

"Whew, you sound like you went there already. Physically? Really? Okay, so you are going to call him and make that date official."

"Not yet. There's a meeting he's attending on Thursday. I think there's bidding going on. In conversation, he said that was what most of his meetings entailed. I don't know where to look for the information. Jon will have to check. Sérénité Resorts & Spa needs to put in a bid. We have to get our feet wet. Jon and Aiden need to secure a spot at the meeting."

"Seychelle, we know nothing about this bidding. What if you lose your money and can't recover it? Why take a chance and rush into this? Are you going to talk this over with them or just tell them this is what you want?"

"I want us to talk it over. I was expressing to you what I see as an opportunity. It's not until Thursday. We've got three days until Thursday. I've got three days to learn more from Vance."

They finished their breakfast and returned to their room. They chose the Moon Palace Grande for their unlimited breakfast buffet. The Boulevard or strip, as most travelers called it, was filled with resorts and entertainment. It was the perfect island for a getaway. The sisters agreed to wait for Aiden and Jon to explore the sights.

"How was your date with Jon?"

"No, no, you see it wasn't a date. We found that distant sax that was playing. Believe it or not, it was on the street. The guy had a speaker and an amp, right there on the street. Vegas reminds me of New York. When we would visit New York City, our heads would be doing a three-sixty. So much going on, every night, all night, non-stop. I loved it."

"Okaaay, get to the date." Seychelle laughed watching her sister squirm. Sasha was always outgoing and sociable. Her sister was happy for her and hoped Jon was sincere and not just looking to catch her off guard.

"We listened to a few of his songs before we decided to walk the strip. It was beautiful. I mean, not in a romantic way but just the energy in the atmosphere. Everyone was having a good time and sharing smiles and pleasantries."

"Sasha, what are you doing writing in your journal! Talk to me girl. What did you do or not do? You left me like you needed to tackle the man and now you won't tell."

"Well, I didn't tackle him if that's what you want to know. We talked." She raised her eyebrow as she thought of Jon wanting to be tackled. "He did mention what he could imagine us doing. I laughed coyly, and I'm sure my reaction teased him as much as it did me. So I decided to tell him I wanted to be sure. I don't want to regret meeting him or being in business with him. That's the real problem."

Seychelle let the words sink in. Sasha was right. Personal involvement swayed decisions when it came to business.

"It takes a strong relationship that's for sure. Did he agree?"

"No, I didn't tell him, girl! Ruin my night with that serious mess? No, we talked and walked. It seemed like forever, but Seychelle he is a good man with a good heart. He wants so much out of life. I could see us in a relationship, but we agreed that getting this business off the ground was important. We want this for you and us."

"Now I feel guilty. I was going to tackle Vance if you tackled Jon."

The women laughed hysterically. They could barely hear the knock at the door. Seychelle waved her hand in the air causing another burst of laughter. Sasha answered the suite door for her brother and Jon. They entered bewildered as they greeted the sisters who were still giggling.

"Good joke?" Aiden asked as he sat his satchel on the table. He pulled out separate copies of papers and placed them where they each could review them.

"Girl talk. What have the two of you been up to? Those packets look serious."

"Sasha, come on over here. They are Seychelle; we arrived here just in time for a bidding."

The women looked at each other and nodded their heads realizing Seychelle had been right.

"You knew about the bidding?" Aiden's question was secondary, and Seychelle didn't bother to explain.

"Not important. Did you find out how we could be included?" She looked at Jon. "Can we?"

Chapter 15

After looking at the pages filled with numbers and statistics, it became obvious that the women did not know how they would assist Jon and Aiden in deciding which property was worth their bid. The numbers were beginning to blur, and Jon's excitement as he explained the pros and cons turned into babble.

"I don't want to sound disheartened, but I'm lost." Sasha flipped another page as she sighed. "I need to understand, how do we decide? They all look worth the investments, but you said we need to be careful. What are we looking at?"

"I've circled those that would be best for us. The others are properties I've listed that will probably be up for bid over the next six months to a year. This is where we need to start."

"Aiden we can't wait six months to start. I wanted to purchase and be ready for next year. If we wait six months, then with the upgrades and repairs, it will be the fall before we kick off a grand opening."

The men had discussed Seychelle's timeline as expected. Jon explained the differences between her timeline and waiting six months.

"If we wait, purchasing the next property will have to be delayed. I was seeking to purchase or bid every six months with the proceeds. Of course, the purchases would soon slow down."

"Whoa, are you thinking there will be enough revenue in six months?"

"Jon, I have enough money to cover bids, and with investors, we'll be okay without the revenue. I don't want the investor's money to be our stronghold."

"That's sounds reasonable to me. What do you think Aiden?"

Sasha watched her brother, as he seemed to prepare his words before answering. She wondered had the men talked it over before presenting the paperwork to them. For a moment she thought the circles and other markings were planned to force Seychelle to think their way.

"We weren't thinking about the money you had, your savings Seychelle. You can't continue to travel as you've done and not need more money. Once you buy property, you've got to invest in others or be certain your revenue can bring returns. New properties may not be worth bidding on each year. You say you want to build? You'll need the investors to support you once you've started."

"I believe they'll respect our business more if we can and are willing to support ourselves. Matching their investment, or even seeking money for rehab projects shouldn't be questioned if we can prove ourselves over the first two buys. Right, Jon?"

Seychelle wasn't as naïve as they thought. She was right. They needed to be seen as buyers on the rise. Once they were noticed as such, they would need to be stable. It would take her money to prove stability and the investors backing would be secondary.

"C'mon guys, I don't want us to owe them the minute we finalize the deals. They are about making money, and so am I. That money needs to come from our revenue. They can't feed off us."

The meeting confirmed Seychelle had done the research and decided what type of business she would run. Aiden and Jon were clear. There would be no bidding without a discussion. They had no choice but to agree. Neither had the funds to change any decisions once Seychelle said they were final.

Aiden made excuses to get back to his room. Sasha and Seychelle agreed they needed to unwind after their first meeting. Jon stayed in the room hoping to answer any other questions.

"Is he okay Jon?" Seychelle questioned as Aiden closed the door.

"Seychelle! Aiden will hear you!" Sasha stated firmly.

"We need to know, and Jon is his sponsor, right Jon? Listen, I don't want to sound cruel, but this business has no room for deceit. What did Aiden promise you? Salary, partnership, what? There has to be a reason you're taking this on. What are your plans?"

"I don't know what you mean Seychelle." Sasha felt a chill run down her back. She hoped Seychelle's assumptions were wrong.

"Listen, your brother asked me to sit in with you and him to discuss the business you proposed. To be honest, I didn't think there was much to it. More like a vision that would never fully materialize. I won't lie. This market is rough and often cutthroat. Your brother made it clear that he didn't think you knew enough to handle the investors or the bankers. You would need to have someone you could trust. Yes, he did say we could make money and possibly be in a better position than with our current jobs. I'm willing to take the gamble."

"So what's his problem?"

"It's a constant battle. Alcoholism is a daily battle. Situations that bring on stress bring on the urge to drink. He's getting better, but we'll always be facing a battle."

Jon packed his satchel to leave. Sasha left Seychelle at the table in deep thought.

"Jon, were you always an investor?"

He turned from the door to answer the question. "Yes, of sorts. Mostly flipping the property or rehabbing for rental units. It's lucrative but Sasha this is the next level. I want your brother to be well with this. I don't think he is. I have to find out why."

"We are a proud people. He needs to feel needed. He needs to have some control. He's in business with his sister who has control. I don't know how long he can pretend he's okay. My father would rather it be my brother making the decisions. Aiden seeks to satisfy my father."

Seychelle heard Sasha's response and decided to speak her thoughts. "He can't satisfy anyone until he's pleased with himself."

Chapter 16

T heir first official meeting put a damper on the balance of the day. Sasha finished summary notes to be filed and sent e-mail copies to the others. She and Seychelle decided to relax on the beach the balance of the afternoon. Neither mentioned inviting Jon or Aiden.

The beauty of the beach was soothing. The breeze from the water invited them to take a quick dip before relaxing on the lounge chairs with refreshing drinks. They preferred the beach although the crowd at the pool seemed to be enjoying the bar and the live entertainment.

"I think the pool and beach is a must. Having a choice has to be a plus." Sasha stated not expecting a reply.

"Most of the resorts that are near water have that option. I don't know that people concern themselves with the beach. We do because it is a part of where we lived all our lives. The idea of having a pool and bar is more of what they want; the beach is attractive but not a must. I don't know; you may have a point."

Seychelle adjusted herself on the lounger and took a sip of her drink. She sighed and closed her eyes.

"What's wrong? Are you worried about Aiden?"

"Sasha, this business is an expensive risk. One that I want to be sure Aiden can handle. I don't want it to push him to the edge. I mean, if he can't deal with the pressures, maybe including him is a mistake. Tell me I'm wrong Sasha, please, I want to be wrong."

There was a silence between them. It happened often. Since their childhood, they had a way of communicating without speaking. Sasha knew they would have to talk about taking a chance with Aiden.

"Do you think it's more than alcohol?"

"Sasha, Aiden has to be stronger. I don't want Jon negotiating deals for me without one of us. I don't want to be there on Thursday bidding against Vance. I've thought about it. I want to pick and choose but stay away from the bidding wars and investors."

"So you'll have to trust Jon or at least give Aiden a chance." Sasha's voice faded. She knew Aiden chances were dwindling.

"He can't even stand to be at our meetings. I know what he's feeling. Being inferior to us, that's what is on his mind. Did you not see the look on his face? It was the look Father had when he said I was selfish. Imagine me wanting my own and being successful. Aiden is upset with my plan to bid, buy and build. The thought of the women in the family flourishing is what has crushed him. This my sister is why he drinks."

"He had his chance. He chose to gamble it away."

"True but our Father has taught us all the ways of the island. Aiden was what Father has hoped for, prayed for. A man-child to carry on the business or one of his own. Don't you see Sasha? I've added pressure to our brother's being. He failed Sasha, and that's what he doesn't want anyone to see."

"Seychelle, you can't think that Aiden would fail again. He has to recognize this as a second chance. Father will bless the business and him. Let Father think his son is the...."

"Is the what, Sasha? That's just it. This is not his business, and I don't know if he's comfortable with it being my dream or idea. I think he and Jon were looking to come in and convince me to sit in the background."

"Well, you said you didn't want to go to the bidding war or sit with the investors."

"Sasha, the business needs a face. Right now the face needs to be a man."

"And?" Sasha sat up as a toned bronze body approached them.

Seychelle lifted her large hat that laid on her face as they carried on their conversation. She couldn't understand her sister's questionable pause.

Vance winked as Seychelle blushed. He was as she imagined. He looked as though he had spent his morning in a tanning salon, but she knew it was from the rays of the sun. Vance tilted his hat, acknowledging Sasha's presence. Seychelle's eyes disrobed his black trunks and the matching sleeveless beach jacket. Although she admired his fashion sense, her imagination gave her a better vision.

"Good morning, join us." Seychelle pointed to the empty beach chair beside her. "This is my sister Sasha, and this is Vance Chase, the man we were just talking about."

"Boring topic I'm sure. I must say there must be a rule for the women of Seychelles Island."

"Sasha, tell him one of the rules for women living on the island."

Sasha laughed. "A woman never speaks to a man in public knowing he is not an islander. The visitor, the man, must be properly introduced by a male of the island."

"Okay, I was going to say you all must be beautiful. I will remember that when I visit your home."

"And what would be your business on the island, Mr. Chase?" Seychelle teased. "There aren't many resorts looking to be bought out."

"Yes, I googled it." They both laughed. Sasha frowned not understanding the joke. "It's an interesting place. Not at all what I thought when you said you lived there. It's beautiful. I was curious, you see, I wanted to know more about you.

"So now you know. How was your flight?" Seychelle changed the subject and hoped he would too.

"It was a flight, the norm. I was hoping you, and I could have some time to view a few of the resorts here. After you told me you enjoyed the travel, I thought you should see some of the amenities that most vacationers don't know too much about. Uh, your sister, Sasha is it? She can join us as well."

"No, I would only be the other ear. I'll find something to do."

"It's not like that. Vance, I can meet you later this evening. I promised to do some shopping with Sasha."

"Sure, give me a call when you've returned." Vance leaned over and kissed Seychelle gently on her forehead. He stood looking in no particular direction. The ladies watched, anticipating his departure.

"Nice meeting you Sasha, maybe tomorrow we'll all hang out."

"Yes, that sounds like fun." He nodded as his reply while walking away. Sasha waited before she spoke again. "So Mr. Chase seemed disappointed. He is obviously not an American."

"He may be, but he's a native of Canada. His accent is similar to ours. I believe he said his native tongue is French like ours." Seychelle watched as Vance found a seat at the bar. "I should have paid more attention to the conversation we had. I became distracted. He's soothing on the eyes, yes."

"He is that. I suppose Father will be disappointed with our choice of men."

"I only tell him what he needs to know. You can second-guess your choices and reveal them to Father if you like. That's a mistake I won't make."

"Shall we check on Aiden before checking out the island's amenities?

"Let Jon handle it; he's the mentor. Although, that will put a damper on your plans with him if you made any."

"Men, I guess we'll have to teach them along the way."

Chapter 17

Jon sat waiting as Aiden read over the sales sheets again. After explaining the abbreviations and codes, he circled the resorts that interested him. Aiden hadn't looked up from the paperwork to give any opinion.

"I don't know what this guy Vance Chase will bid on or purchase. I don't think he's just an investor. My thought is we're not on his level."

"Yes, that's understood. Has Seychelle seen these sheets?"

"Aiden, she expects us to be ready for this. You are the lead. I'm simply the consultant — at least that's what I will be telling Seychelle. Once you understand this process, I'm willing to step into being an investor as well."

"Jon, this is not the same as proposals."

"Don't make excuses. Listen, take the reins and steer. Wherever you lead us, we all will follow. I've given you the map; study it. What do you see there?"

Aiden rubbed his head. He needed a drink or thought he did. His mind drifted for a moment.

"Aiden, stop thinking about it. There's no escape, no backing out. This is an opportunity man, and your chances don't come this easy. Your sisters have given you a reason to stay sober."

The word sober echoed. The taste of alcohol teased his taste buds. It didn't matter Gin, Vodka, or Hennessey straight; he had no preference. The real alcoholic signs began after three drinks or more.

"Okay, so let's talk to them. We'll need them to see the descriptions and cost before I make a final decision. Have you been to one of these bidding events?"

"No different than the usual real estate bids or sales. Yes, I have bought and sold a few properties. I'll admit, your sister's business venture has my interest. We'll be okay, I'm sure."

"Jon, if this fails how will I survive?"

"The same as always my friend. Let's take some time to enjoy this island. Maybe unwind a bit."

Chapter 18

Vance and Seychelle enjoyed dinner and a show. Their small talk brought on silent thoughts between the couple as they watched the performance.

"Do you enjoy jazz? I guess I should have asked before purchasing the tickets."

"No, I enjoyed the show. Thank you." Seychelle's mind had wandered during dinner.

Mentally she was preparing for the next meeting with Jon and her brother. Aiden told her there was another approach to purchasing the property they needed to discuss. The sales were to begin at nine in the morning.

"Would you like another drink?" Vance asked.

Seychelle smiled hoping he didn't detect her mental distance.

"Yes, I'll have another." She thanked the waiter and attempted to give Vance her full attention.

"So what have you and your sister planned for tomorrow? I was hoping we could spend a few hours together before I leave."

"Oh my, I didn't realize you were leaving tomorrow."

"I'll be leaving on an early flight Friday morning."

Seychelle listened to his itinerary. She would soon be flying across the states and countries.

"Do you find much time for yourself or others?"

"No, not really. I have the freedom to change my schedule. And there are no 'others' as you say?"

"I didn't mean to pry. I just thought with your traveling it would damper a serious relationship. I'm sure you'd make time for family matters."

"Not that I've been in what I'd consider a serious relationship, I don't foresee a problem. Do you?"

"I wasn't speaking of you and me." Seychelle blushed.

"Of course, but women tend to feel my business includes meeting pretty ladies such as yourself. They don't want to compete."

"It takes a special man and a confident woman."

"How confident are you?"

"It depends on the qualities that describe confidence to you. Some men assume that an out-spoken woman simply doesn't know her place, or the woman who sets goals and accomplishes them is too independent. My country frowns upon the confidence of a woman. Liberated women are often outcasts when it comes to relationships."

"I see. Well, I think I'd admire those qualities. I haven't met a woman that quite fits that description. Women are a sign of strength, period. They don't really need to do much to earn my respect. All of the definitions used for women usually don't give credit to who they are."

"But you would agree you wouldn't want the self-sufficient woman as a wife, would you?"

"Trick question." Vance raised his hand for the waiter. "Would you like to walk the boulevard? There's usually a street filled with entertainment. I'm sure you'd love it."

The end of the conversation was more than obvious. Seychelle wondered was Vance that special man her father often spoke about.

"Tell me more about Canada and your business. Do you invest in other businesses?"

"Canada is beautiful, but I travel quite a bit. My office is wherever; I don't have an office set up there. As for my investment, well that depends on the return."

"Really? Don't you find the need to keep an order of things?"

"I do have an office in my home. As an investor, as you say, I travel with my office. My laptop, phone, and reminders on both keeps my business in order. It's convenient, and I send it to my home office. You never mentioned what your family business was or did you?"

"We do imports and exports. It's a third generation business. I'm looking to explore other options."

"I see. What is your interest?"

Just as she was about to answer his question, a street performer handed her a rose. She smiled and nodded her thanks but found herself a part of his performance. Vance watched his date being escorted to the center of a semi-circled audience. The gentleman, a street magician, smiled as his on-lookers applauded Vance who nodded his approval. Seychelle drifted thinking of the crowd that surrounded them as the magician accepted the voices that cheered.

The pastel scarves fell gently on her shoulders. As the magic man spun her around with a simple touch, each became budded roses. As the magician collected them, he stopped Seychelle and handed her the beautiful bouquet. The crowd hushed in amazement. Seychelle turned once again for the entire audience to see. The roars and applauds began again as Seychelle returned to Vance's extended hand.

"Beautiful flowers for a beautiful lady."

"Thank you, this is…." Seychelle's response was interrupted by the ringing of her phone. "Excuse me; I have to take this."

Seychelle answered the call as Vance watched as the magician performed his next illusion.

"Hello, Sasha is everything okay?"

"Yes, I'm sorry to interrupt your date but will we be meeting tonight or before the bidding tomorrow."

Seychelle looked at Vance standing a few feet away. His planned departure raised an urgency in her nature. She didn't know why but she needed the intimate moments, to begin with, a touch of more than his hand in hers. She was mesmerized by his voice. She had no intention of ending her evening early. He teased her senses, tickled her nerves and peaked her curiosity. He ignited a flame that hadn't been lit in years. Seychelle couldn't remember being as giddy as she felt whenever he was near.

"Seychelle, tonight or tomorrow morning?"

"Neither." They both laughed softly. "Girl, I can't stay focused. I'm falling."

"Get up girl. It's too soon. Hold on to the thought you're here for business. A business, I might add, that's he's here for as well."

"Okay, focus, you're right, too soon? I could say the same about you and Jon. The bidding starts at nine. Let's meet at seven, our suite. Sasha don't wait up for me."

Seychelle ended the call before her sister could respond. Walking up behind Vance she gently touched his hand. They allowed their fingers to adjoin.

"Shall we continue?" They continued their walk on the boulevard. "Is everything okay?"

"My sister was just reminding me of an early morning appointment she made for us."

"I see. No late night for you."

"Quite the contrary." Seychelle couldn't help but smile. She was willing to have him tuck her in.

Chapter 19

Sasha, Aiden, and Jon agreed to meet at the Grande Fiesta, the hotel where Aiden and Jon chose to stay. Sasha and Seychelle stayed at the International Resorts, where those interested in the bidding would be in the morning. There were couples walking along the shoreline as the sun began to set. Sasha sipped from her second Margarita as she waited poolside for the two men to arrive.

She thought of her father's warnings regarding American men. He wouldn't have to worry since Jon was Dominican. After talking with him regarding traditions and family values, she found the Dominican lifestyle and traditions were similar in many ways to those of her family.

Sasha never introduced any of her friends to her family. Her dates were no secret, but an introduction to the family wasn't suggested or required. She didn't see the point in the interrogation from her father or the bogus smiles from her mother. They didn't know their baby had thought about marriage twice since her senior year in high school. She came close to being a mother and spent the night in a Florida hospital during the miscarriage. The young man's family paid the bill, and Seychelle sat at her side as she wept.

Aiden stopped introducing her to his friends after that close call. He nodded his head as she laughed at Jon's joke about the two of them getting together. She understood it to mean she had her brother's approval. That approval would weigh heavy as she introduced Jon as a love interest to her father.

As the two men approached the bar, she sighed. It was all a dream. Jon had not done anything but teased about their being together or him visiting her on Seychelles Island. Her past taught her not to live in her dreams. The reality was she always pushed harder than the men she got involved with; maybe too hard.

Jon stopped talking as he spotted Sasha sitting on the stool at the bar. The length of pool separated them, but he could feel her eyes and smile as though she was touching him softly. Although he teased her and Aiden about getting to know the island beauty, he found himself mesmerized each time they were together. His past was filled with meaningless relationships. He never was the "playboy" or a "Prince Charming." He thought of mentioning his attraction to Aiden, but he couldn't find the words.

"Ah, there's Sasha. Jon, do you see her there at the bar?" Aiden began to quicken his pace. Jon reached out and grabbed his arm.

"Hey, let me say something. Aiden, man, I don't want to be rude or anything. I want to get to know your sister better. I mean seriously get to know her, your family, and of course this business."

"And?" The tone of a protective brother was not expected.

"What do you mean and? I wanted you to know because I don't know how long I can pretend I'm teasing about being with her."

Aiden gave him a hardened glance.

"C'mon man you knew it. We've been traveling with your sisters for the last two months. We've spent a lot of time together. I've kept in touch with Sasha even when I went on business trips of my own. Aiden, I want us to be close but not if it will alter our friendship or cause you any problems."

"You and I come from a different type of people. You know what I mean. She's not just my sister; she's a Seychelles Island woman. They don't sleep with just anyone or just fall for any man. They are strong women not like some of the women here. Jon, my family, is not looking for a rescuer to save our traditions or our secure our finances."

"What are you talking about?"

"Listen! My father, our father would not be pleased with me if I just let anyone date my sister simply because she's been around us for months."

"That's not my reason at all Aiden. I wish I had met her or maybe if she weren't your sister you'd understand. I want to take it further, and I don't want to disrespect you. I mean, seriously I want you to be okay with me asking her, properly I might add, to consider dating me. I didn't want you to think I was doing it behind your back."

"No in my face is so much better. Would you have been a part of the business if Sasha wasn't here? Is that a part of the deal you want to make with Seychelle and me?"

"No man, you got it all wrong. I love the idea, and I'm totally committed. That has nothing to do with Sasha. But I do want to get to know her and love her. It doesn't stop us from being friends, business associates, or whatever. I'm not asking you; I'm telling you I will be asking her to extend our friendship, beyond the distance and time we may spend apart. I want to visit your home, meet your parents, and become a part of her life. Aiden I think I'm in love."

Aiden stood looking at the ocean. He heard Jon, but there was something about his confession of love that didn't sit well with his spirit. He knew Jon as a good man. He knew he and Sasha would be good for each other. He knew his parents would accept his Dominican friend and approve of his desires to be with their daughter. Aiden's fear was he would be alone again. Jon would be closer to Seychelle and Sasha.

"You're okay Aiden." Jon patted him on his back. "I'm still with you my brother. I will never leave your side. This will bring us closer and your family will understand. I would never bring any of you any harm. Have I done you wrong?"

"No you haven't, and I thank you for that."

Bidding Wars

Chapter 20

"So when the bid is made, there is no connection with Seychelle Tudjal. It falls under the resort's name. If searched, the names of the investors and the bank will appear."

"Jon, we are the investors, the trustees, and whatever seats need be filled." Seychelle didn't understand the blind bidding tactic that Jon had explained over what seemed to have been the last hour.

"We have interested investors. They're interested in buying shares of the business. The gentlemen you met at the bank are more than interested in investing and being a part of your dream."

Seychelle smiled slowly. It took a moment to set in but as Jon passed her the contracts and other required documents for her signature she felt relief.

"This is so much more than I ever thought. So you and Aiden will set up the paperwork, and one of the investors will attend the bidding? How much do these investors want?"

"If you want them to be there they will. They're only there to carry out your business. If not, the bidding goes in as a blind bid. It is considered with the rest of the bids, and if we win the bid, the site hosting the bidding will contact the bank. I took it for granted that you wouldn't want any of us to be at the bidding. It would be easily traced that Aiden was your brother, or I the consultant to your business. It is better to have representation. If there is a need to counter bid, you have someone there. A blind bid gets no counter bid."

"I see." Sasha looked at her sister for a response. "Seychelle this is what you wanted."

"It is. Okay, Jon, who will bid tomorrow? Are you and Aiden attending the bidding? It will be too late for us to call one of these people in." Seychelle passed the papers across the table without signing them.

"He'll be here tonight if we call and give the okay."

"Well, according to the paperwork you have there, we're on our way. After we win this bid and before we leave on Sunday we should meet to get all a proposed budget for the immediate needs. Well, family, we're on our way. Do I sign before the meeting tonight?"

"Do you have questions? I would hope not." Jon held the papers waiting for Seychelle's answer.

"Jon I asked my brother to explain to me what you and he wanted in return. Some investors seek to profit from the returns. Do you understand that although this is great timing, I have nothing to pay anyone?"

Aiden and Sasha looked at Jon who was stunned by the question.

"Seychelle, we're in this together. Your brother questioned us when he brought attention to his business. I introduced him to two of the bank trustees who were known for investments that made them lucrative. We gain when you gain. Nothing more. You can break ties with us, and if you read the paperwork, we can break ties at any time. It's business. We want to make money and to do that we give you money to work with."

Seychelle took the papers and flipped through them again. "We're good, Jon. I don't want to regret this."

"You won't. Great, Aiden call the bank and ask for Mr. Whelan. Let's have a conference call with him before we all get lost in leisure." Jon flipped through the signed papers.

"Calling now. Sasha hand me that book near you."

Seychelle walked to the large window that looked out over the beach. Her first chance to buy. This moment exceeded her plans.

"Do we get to view the properties that are up for bid?"

"Yes, Aiden and I took the liberty to pick a few just in case we didn't win the bid for this one. It's located in Las Vegas. A new property, but it has so much potential."

"New? How did it fall through before it got started?" Sasha picked up the photos. "Oh my God. Seychelle look at this it's beautiful."

"Westlake Village. I knew that would catch your attention. The layout of the resort is what caught my eye. They have a man-made river that flows through the length of the property. One can start at the hotel and float to the beach. There are various stops along the way, all within the perimeter of the resort. The final funds for payment fell through. The owners were given adequate time to finish the renovations and make the payment. Last month was the deadline."

"So what's needed?" Sasha turned her back to the window. C'mon, do we want that debt?"

"What debt? Seychelle, Jon worked as a magician. The money from the investors will pay for the renovations. Your dream is materializing." Aiden stretched out his arms to her.

She needed the hug. Tears fell, and she didn't understand why. "Aiden I'm scared." She whispered as she put her head on his chest. "This is bigger than I ever imagined."

"Listen, we walk daily never looking to step into shit." Seychelle stopped crying and quickly wiped her fallen tears. She frowned waiting for Aiden to finish what she thought would be a ridiculous comment. "We don't purposely watch where we walk, but if we could avoid the troubles that would delay our steps or go another way … well Seychelle we would never arrive. What I'm saying this is not just your walk. We are walking with you, the investors are now with you, and none of us want shit on our shoes. This is the business of hit or miss, and often money is lost, or it prospers. We all want this to work."

Seychelle backed away from her brother. "Okay, let's get this business started. I think I have a way in. The person can't know what I'm doing so if you're introduced we are not in business together."

"Are you talking about Vance Chase?" Jon's question was sharp. It cut through all Seychelle wanted to say.

"I saw him with you earlier. He's a big-time investor."

"Do you know him?"

"No, not personally. I know he's someone to learn from."

"My thoughts exactly."

"There's a few that have prospered well; he is definitely one of them."

"Hmmm, Mother spoke of playing with the enemy." Sasha laughed and passed the last of the paperwork to Seychelle.

"I'm not playing with him. Just so you all know. I don't want him or anyone knowing the business. I think I'll be seeing more of Vance but I don't want him to think I want his money. I definitely don't want him in my business."

No one answered. The silence was her assurance. Vance Chase would have to search deeply to find a connection between Seychelle's love for business and the new love she began to feel for him.

Chapter 21

I f anyone asked Seychelle to give details of the first bidding she attended, she'd have to lie. She couldn't possibly tell anyone fear replaced the confidence she had a few hours prior. She held on to Vance's hand as he led her through the crowded lobby.

After a brief phone call, she agreed to attend the bidding with him. He explained his meeting had ended and he could meet her in the lobby of the MGM. It was still early. Coffee and breakfast baked goods were prepared at different food stations for the guests and those waiting for the conference room doors to open.

"We need to get the packets for the properties. Usually, they have them prepared and placed on a table out here." Vance led her through the crowd of people who were cordial waving hello and politely excusing themselves as they moved out of his way.

Seychelle was amazed at the number of people mingling and making small talk. They all seemed to know each other. Vance parted from her briefly to approach one of the men who seemed to be directing the traffic and answering questions. He returned with two packets.

"You may want to browse while I'll try to explain what's going on."

Seychelle feigned a smile. She wanted to watch and summarize the actions for herself. She promised Sasha she wouldn't blow her cover with questions. She hadn't met Mr. Whalen or his associates so they wouldn't be surprised about her attendance.

Jon explained they would be seated in the conference room while he and Aiden would remain in the V.I.P. room. She was to call them if Vance suggested they go to V.I.P. room after the bidding.

Vance pointed to the doors as they opened. Seychelle stepped in line following the crowd. She felt comfortable although she wondered how much money the room collectively represented. She was glad she was dressed properly. No one stood out, and none seemed to be impressed by another's appearance. Hello's and hugs were the greetings for the women while the men shared firm handshakes. Everyone seemed to know each other.

"These people bid against each other?"

"All the time. It's business. I keep a record of who to watch. Some will overbid another to keep them from having the property. Others will underbid to draw in an unexpected bid. It's a financial war. The key is to know who the players are, who they represent, and how much they are worth."

Seychelle was pleased when she opened the packet. It was the same information she reviewed and marked that morning. She tried not to show her excitement. She was ahead of the game. Vance looked over the papers, flipping through the pages quickly. He took out a pen from his inner pocket.

Seychelle took the time to give him the once-over. His casual dress reminded her of a school professor on the island. He wore black linen slacks with a black silk muscle shirt under a gold linen sports jacket. It was the simplicity of the clothes that spoke to her. He was sharp. She gazed around the room and noticed the other men dressed in similar fashion some with buttoned shirts, none with ties.

She began scanning the room for couples. She couldn't tell. There weren't many women, and none seemed to be interested in the men in attendance. Vance did say it was "business, " but she wondered if the women were significant bidders or potential arm pieces.

"Anything of interest?" Seychelle recognized the page Vance was reading. The property on the page were marked by Jon and Aiden. It was their second choice. She wanted his opinion.

"Okay, look at this one. It has all the amenities, great reviews, a good price and it has growth potential. However, the owner has spread himself thin. Investors have backed away from him since his purchase of, wait let me show you." He flipped the pages back to another listed property. "His firm lost this property a few months ago. I believe he's lost most of his backing."

"So as an investor he's not worth the money?"

"No you invest, and then he takes off, and the resorts struggle until a new buyer is found. He's not a rebound owner. There are a few who may lose a property or two and build on what they have and recoup what they lost. There are buyers and investors; buyers lose more than an investor. Usually, return on my money is made in the first five years. If the property is kept past the first five, I make a profit."

"So the first five years is a good time to measure if the resort will make it or not?"

"I'd say so. There are a few that struggle but pick up by the third year. You have to watch the figures, reviews, and the vacationers. A lot of them run promotional vacations to draw in timeshare buyers and consistent vacationers. It helps to keep the property vibrant. A lot of these buyers are too anxious to buy more property. Being impatient causes financial mistakes."

"Did you come to buy or to seek out new buyers?" Seychelle wanted to know his intentions.

"Not a buyer, my dear. I have seen a few properties that if bought by the right persons, I'll invest. Now if you were buying I'd invest."

Seychelle smiled but kept her focus on the pages she held. Vance leaned closer to her and whispered.

"I wouldn't care if I lost. Just the opportunity to be a part of your life is worth all that I have."

"Well, as you said there's a difference between an investor and a buyer. You see Mr. Chase to be a part of my life may require a purchase. An initial investment may lead to a conflict of interest."

"Hmmm, you just may turn me into a buyer."

"Yes, buying is a serious commitment. It may stop you from future investments."

"Other than property my dear, I am not invested in anyone."

"Vance Chase, I was wondering if you'd be here."

The woman that interrupted his teasing stood behind his seat. She nodded in Seychelle's direction as she pretended not to see that they were practically entangled.

"Excuse my manners. Cheyenne Minnows, this is Seychelle Tudjal, my friend from the Seychelles Islands."

"I see, and is she here for a visit?"

Seychelle wanted to tell her she was a buyer. She felt anger creeping down her spine. She didn't quite understand the woman's rudeness.

"Actually, she's with me for the week. I'm trying to convince her to fly back to Las Vegas before she returns to her home."

Seychelle fought back her initial attitude pleased Vance acknowledged her as more than just a friend.

"Oh dear, are you still using that line? Honey, don't let his overall appearance bait you. He's a tease. Aren't you Vance?"

Cheyenne turned her attention to a hand waving in the distance.

"Nice meeting you. I'm sure they'll be another before the night is over." She laughed, although neither Vance nor Seychelle understood the humor. "No worries, Vance and I go back a few years. I guess I wasn't one he could mold. He likes them, dark and pretty, picture perfect. Oh Vance dear, there's Russell and that urchin Paula. Well, I've got to get to my seat. Good luck sweetie, he's a good catch if you can keep his roving eyes on you." She began waving her hand as her reply. "Vance leave something on the table for us lowly folks."

She stepped away with an intentional signal from her hips. Vance shook his head hoping he didn't have to explain the embarrassing moment.

"Hmmm, an ex or a playmate? Either one, she seems annoyed you came with someone. My question is, did you ask me to join you knowing she would be looking to be with you?"

"No. As she said, we dated a few years back. I was naïve to the business and the women I would attract. I invested in three properties during that session. I received calls, gifts, and women at my room door. I've learned a lot since then. I travel alone by choice, and I don't date or romance women who have hidden agendas."

"If their agenda is hidden. You, a man, would never know. What was her agenda just now? To embarrass you or to send me a message?"

"I guess a little of both. Her intention is to get us to discuss her as opposed to continuing the conversation we were having before the interruption."

"What have you learned about women in business?"

"A lot. They work harder for what they want. They seek to be hustlers. I understand that more now than before. So I don't mix business with pleasure. They are distinct and separate."

"So why am I here? Is this not a mix?"

"You are not in business with me nor are you the competition. I would like to consider you as a friend that I'd love to know better. Have you considered what I said about Las Vegas?"

"Yes, I heard that indirect invitation. I'll let you know. I must go home to check on business there."

"Oh, you made it seem as though you worked for your family."

"I do, but I run the business with my family. Mr. Chase, I work for no one."

Vance heard the words fall from her lips. Although he had heard many women express their independence many times before, Seychelle's words were enticing. She was the type of woman who could have it all if she just asked. He knew and recognized immediately, Seychelle would never ask. He would have to give his all and show her what he felt she was worth. He leaned in and kissed her lips. As she relaxed, she softened their connection. It was clear, they both wanted more.

Chapter 22

The bidding process was easily understood. Seychelle felt a rush of excitement knowing her bids were among the mix. The property Aiden and Jon set their eyes on would be with the last round of bids. There was a fifteen-minute break before they would return to the atrium and then to their seats.

"So what do you think?" Vance asked as they walked to the lobby.

"It's exciting. I didn't think I would enjoy the process. I guess I thought about the auctions at home. They too have this bidding process for equipment. I've never been to one, though my father says it's frustrating."

"I've read a little about your island. It sounds beautiful. I can't imagine living there. Seems like a fantasy getaway."

Seychelle held her comment. If Vance were waiting for an open invitation, he wouldn't get it from her. It was too soon to determine his intentions.

"I see the sign for the bathroom, where will you be?"

Vance pointed to an area where three men stood. "I see a few friends. I'll be in this area when you return."

Seychelle followed the sign for the V.I.P. room. She hoped Vance hadn't noticed her detour. She looked for the room marker that matched the badge Aiden gave her that morning. She opened the door to what appeared to be a meeting. Jon and Aiden along with three men she didn't recognize. Sasha was standing looking out a large window.

Seychelle immediately observed Sasha's stance. "What's wrong?" Sasha turned to face her sister. The smile on Sasha's face eased Seychelle's fears.

"Westlake Village! Sister, you have a blessing coming your way!"

"They have yet to bid on the property," Seychelle responded not understanding her excitement.

"Aiden and the others decided to bid higher and not worry about the others you spoke about."

"Why? What if we don't win the bid? Without bidding on the others, we leave with nothing Sasha!" Seychelle's whispered harshly.

"Listen, talk to them. Westlake Village has four locations. If they can't sell it as one bid, they'll break them into separate properties. Talk with Aiden, as he explained it you could get all if you don't bid on the other properties."

"So when was I to know about this decision? What are they discussing now?"

"The money. That's Mr. Clayton Whelan, and I can't remember the man in the middle, but that fine one on the end is Mr. Kevin Gaines. Girl, you need to go over there and find out if he's available. Oh, the one in the middle is Mr. Claude Brooks. They're your investors. They've been working figures since they got here."

Seychelle sighed deeply. It seemed her business was slipping away. Aiden nor Sasha understood it was her dream and her money. Now there were six people who wanted to be a part of the dream, and eventually they'd be looking to own a piece of it.

"Aiden, introduce me to our new investors." She approached the conference table hoping no one would notice her fake smile. The men stood immediately, as though she held a prestigious position. Their reaction eased her anger.

Aiden gave names and years of investment experience for each of them. It seemed as though he memorized their biographies. Seychelle would later tell Sasha she was impressed. Each shook her hand tenderly as though she was glass. She took a seat at the table. Before she could express her concerns, Jon pushed a folder to her. It was then she remembered Vance.

"Seychelle, they're calling them back to the atrium."

"Aiden, Jon I trust you know what's best. Let's get this business rolling gentlemen." The men rose again, and in unison, they responded, "Indeed."

Vance was where he said he would be. The conversation ended as she approached the trio. Cheyenne was now a part of the threesome.

"Vance, look, sweetie, she didn't leave. Maybe she did understand the process after all. Dear, what did you say your name was again?"

"I didn't. It's Seychelle, but you won't care to remember it." Seychelle gave a noticeable smirk and turned to Vance.

"Vance, sweetie." She spoke deliberately mocking Cheyenne. "They're beckoning us to return to the atrium."

"Yes, Vance you get along now. Call me and let me know about that property. I believe you can beat whatever deal you think will have been made. Who knows you can have the property and the amenities on the table if you contact me sooner than later."

Cheyenne smiled as she offered her hand for more than the handshake Vance gave her. Disappointed she snatched her hand from his grasp maintaining her sinful expression.

Vance took Seychelle's hand and led her through the atrium without a word. They got to their seats with a moment to spare.

"Where did you go?"

"The line was long at the first restroom. I found another near the V.I.P. Rooms. Your friend is desperate?"

Vance laughed.

"You're laughing, I'm serious or is that the wrong word."

"Please don't substitute another." Vance shook his head. "Listen, there's nothing she would love more than to rattle you or me. She plays a lot of games."

"Hmmm, or she's been played."

"Seychelle, don't let that nonsense upset you. Are you keeping up with the program?"

"It sounds like she has upset you more than me. Following the program is not difficult at all. Did you see one worth investing in?"

"Yes, it's coming up, Westlake Village. You may be right after all. I may want to buy."

Chapter 23

S eychelle couldn't speak. Her response was trapped between the thoughts that raced through her mind. As mixed emotions heightened, the temporary paralysis held her tears. Her immediate thought was why Vance hadn't noticed her shock.

"Cheyenne brought its value to my attention. I guess I missed it browsing through the bids earlier. I can't see myself allowing a woman to buy the property knowing she'd only toy with its possibilities. She's a buyer, but she has no clue what to do with the property once she owns it. Her team of, well let's just say many of the properties that have gone up for bid have had a connection with females looking for a hobby. Purchasing this type of property is a buyers dream. I hate to say it, but this business is strictly for investors and buyers that know the value of what they bid on. Most women don't generate the funds or continue to care enough about the property. They buy and sell after they tire of it. Cheyenne is in for a fight."

Seychelle listened. It was obvious what property Cheyenne was talking about before they returned to their seats. She wondered if Cheyenne had always been a buyer. Vance didn't seem concerned that she had no reply.

"I'm glad I didn't bid earlier. I hope she tried to con a few into letting her have the property. This deal is sealed."

"Does Cheyenne usually purchase?"

"Not really. This is her way of pulling in the buyers who have an interest. Pull them in and see how deep their financial backing is. Most women have a man pushing them. It's the hustle. Seychelle, I don't want you to think I'm against any woman wanting to get into this. Most women aren't that interested, and I haven't met too many that will hustle as hard as the men in this circle."

"Hey, Vance, man what's up?" A man seated across the aisle threw his hand up. "Did Cheyenne find you?"

"Excuse me Seychelle. Let me see if he's going after it. This is a hot one."

Seychelle reached into her handbag for her phone. She texted Aiden:

> Getting Westlake Village is a must. It's hot and there's many who don't think anyone will buy it. The whispers are it will go at a low price because no one noticed it. Vance did. I'm following his lead. Aiden, we have to leave here with property. I want this brother. I need this.

The sound of the gavel brought bidders to their seats and silenced the room.

Chapter 24

"Where is Seychelle? Did she call you after the auction?" Sasha was yelling in the phone. "Aiden where are you?"

Her questions didn't allow Aiden a chance to answer, so he waited for her to pause. "She's with Vance in the conference room. He must have an interest in one of the properties. He's making his connections. Clayton and Kevin are in the same room. Jon, Claude and I are at the bar celebrating."

"Wait she's calling me. I'll call you back."

"Sasha! I own a resort. All four of the Westlake locations! Can you believe it?"

"Where's Vance? Can he hear you?"

"No, he went to talk to owners about being an interested investor. Girl, he gave Clayton and Kevin a card. They talked to him for a minute or two. Aiden told them who he was. I'm trying to calm down before he returns."

"Can you get away a minute? I mean we need a minute!"

"Sister, this is just the beginning. I don't want it to look obvious, but I can't stop smiling. Did you see that chic's reaction when they said sold? I wanted to say remember my name now!"

"Huh?"

Seychelle forgot she hadn't explained Cheyenne's role in the situation. "I'll explain, we do need a minute. I'll call you back. Sasha, this has changed so much."

She turned to see if anyone was interested in her conversation. She lowered her voice to a whisper. "Sasha, I imagined going through this process over and over. Westlake Village is it."

"For now my sister, for now. I am happy for you. Happy for us, but honestly Seychelle you will return to this bidding process once you become bored with the Village. Don't change your goals. You wanted to share the resort experience as you envisioned it. You can't stop with one resort."

"Vance is coming this way. We'll talk later."

Seychelle returned her phone to her handbag while keeping her eyes on Cheyenne as she quickened her steps behind Vance.

"Turn around; you have a shadow," Seychelle stated sarcastically.

"Vance, what happened?" Cheyenne tried to sound reserved but the lost to an unknown buyer was overwhelming. "Who is the buyer? I saw the name but who are they?"

Seychelle heard the same defeat in the answer that Vance gave reluctantly.

"New buyers or new to this arena. The Whelan Investment Group are the investors, or so I thought. I took the liberty to introduce myself. They have invested in a few properties before; nothing with as much promise as this property. It's unfortunate for both of us. They're new, but they have their own money. I gave them a card, offered to meet with them. They, in turn, gave me there's and suggested I look them up."

"Well, what did you find? A new investment group with no background I would imagine." Cheyenne gave Seychelle a snide look. Seychelle saw an opportunity to step away without a word.

"Quite the opposite. They're based in California and have been in business for more than ten years. The son Clayton Whelan inherited his father's group after his sudden death. Cheyenne, they may be serious competitors."

"So do they keep the properties or sell them at a higher price. I can't see the three of them running resorts."

"I saw a list of properties. Most on the west coast. This may be the first resort. Which means my dear you lost the so-called bet. Let me just say as I've said before; this business holds no place for a woman."

"Vance you don't believe that. Money has no gender. Therefore, this business is open for those who can pay to play. I've dealt with The Whelan Group before, there's a reason for their interest. We just got played, but I don't believe they're the buyers. Just like I don't believe you, and the Queen of the Nile will last too long."

"She's not you." Vance expected the conversation to lead to Seychelle.

"No, and you can't expect her to be. You can't believe that you can deny yourself each time we meet. Oh, and having one on your arm is nothing like having me in bed."

"I must say you're persistent. We had our run if you can call it that. Listen, I've had better."

"How would you know? As I recall you refused to give me a chance."

"I thought you were worth the time. Strictly business my dear and I'm sorry if I crossed the line. I can't trust you either way."

"I'm determined to change that. Say no more; your fantasy island babe may be upset to hear you say yes to what you know is just a matter of time."

Vance had an answer, but Seychelle's smile as she approached him and Cheyenne silenced him. The thoughts that raced through his mind as her walk seemed to be a slow walk to heaven. There was no need to continue the conversation with Cheyenne, but he did need to make a statement.

He reached for Seychelle's hand and delivered words he knew would stun Cheyenne. "Glad you're back babe. I was just telling Cheyenne our time has been limited. I need an intimate moment, some quiet time." He kissed Seychelle softly on her cheek. "Until next time Cheyenne."

The couple walked away leaving Cheyenne to watch Seychelle. She was sure they would meet again. She nodded her head; an acknowledgment that Seychelle Tudjal was in her way.

Love of Money

Chapter 25

I f either Seychelle or Sasha were to discuss their evening; each would have to explain their discretions. Vance asked Seychelle to lunch but she convinced him that time spent during dinner would be better. He agreed to meet her in the lobby of her hotel at seven. They walked on the Boulevard holding hands. There was an undefined silence between them. Each had their thoughts on what the next few days would bring.

"I leave tomorrow morning. When will I see you again?" Vance realized his question sounded desperate. "I mean will I get a chance to see you again. Wow that sounds just as bad." He wished he had a better way to express his feelings.

"It doesn't sound bad at all. I understand."

Seychelle pointed to seats in the courtyard of the Le Grande Resorts and Hotel. The décor reminded her of the eateries on the islands. The flowers and large vases decorated the perimeter, and the tables were covered with matching multicolored linen. There wasn't a crowd, but the waiters seemed busy preparing for expected customers. The couple picked a table, sat and browsed over the menus.

"Really? Don't you think that sounds desperate? Well, explain it to me."

"Vance since we met we've been, what can I say, on spontaneous dates. We've talked about business, briefly about family and nothing to confirm what type of relationship this is or could be. I've enjoyed it, really I have."

Vance responded softly. "So it's over? Listen, I don't want you to think—"

"Think what and is what over? We've never started anything. You were in Las Vegas on business. You are here on business. My sister and I are vacationing. I'm tagging along with you because you asked and I've enjoyed your company. Is there more? I don't know. Vance, I do hope so. But I don't want it to be attached to the business, not yours or mine."

"I understand." He reached across the table to hold Seychelle's hand. He was once again enchanted. Her beauty was beyond compare. He admired her choice of clothing. A Bohemian dress and a hint of matching eyeliner that teased his emotions. It was enough to put him into a trance. He told himself as he had during the day, she was breathtaking. She was flawless with a French accent that softened his being.

"Do you? I don't know if Cheyenne or the others would understand. She seems to be interested in your social life as well." She smiled hoping he would understand the humor in her statement.

"Cheyenne Minnows is a competitor. It's all a game to her, business or personal. When she loses, she becomes fierce. I've been on that side of her once or twice; that's how we met. I've invested in properties that wouldn't allow her to buy shares. She's a buyer and investor, depending on the property. Today it was Westlake Village. She thought I was her competition. So she was offering more than whatever the property was worth. I was determined not to let her have it. Foolish, just to prove a point, I know. Well, The Whelan Group will be tormented with Minnows Investors' unethical methods and relentless calls. On a personal level, she's still a tease."

Seychelle watched Vance as the waiter approached the table for their order. Vance asked her choice of wine, and the two agreed the special for the evening dinner would be fine. She was comfortable in his company. She imagined their relationship beyond business inquiries or auctions. His touch aroused her. When they kissed, she knew she wanted more. His clothing outlined his physique. Through them, she could see his body was sculptured and well defined. She remembered her thoughts after seeing him at the pool in his swimwear. She would only imagine what wasn't exposed. His linen suit and sandals reminded her of words from her father. Cole Tudjal told his daughters a real man dresses properly for all occasions even when he's relaxing. This type of man only existed in her dreams. A fantasy come true? There had to be a thorn somewhere. Cheyenne Minnows had to be it.

"Personal level? So the two of you attempted to have a relationship?" She wanted to say more as she felt the summer heat that topped what she knew was rising anxiety. She hoped he wouldn't ruin their meal admitting Cheyenne had been in his bed.

"No, nothing like that. She used me to get her an account. The complete story I won't tell. After I realized what she was doing, she attempted to come on to me. She's been teasing me about it since then. I never accepted the challenge nor did she get that account."

"I didn't see many women there. Has she been in business long?"

"I don't think so. There are a few women who are in the business. Their attendance depends on their interest in the properties listed. Cheyenne goes to most of the auctions. That's why I think she hasn't been in business long."

"I'm sure she's seeking more than properties." Seychelle smiled and tapped his hand. "What type of properties do you invest in?"

"Those that bring a return. New projects like Westlake show a promise. On the other hand, any investment is a chance these days. I understand what you said Seychelle. Our time together hasn't been what either of us would consider the start of a relationship. I'd like to begin, here and now. Would you accept my apology for being so forward? I really don't want this to be our so-called last date."

"You're flying out in the morning. I'm here until Sunday. That's where this relationship stands as of now. After Sunday, I'll be on Seychelles Islands."

"That leaves us tonight. If it's a start, I'll take that. If it leads me to visiting the islands or you visiting Las Vegas afterward, my dreams will have come true."

"Well, it's the end of the week, Mr. Chase. Are you really returning to Vegas to work?"

"I don't want to sound pushy. I'd love to be with you until your flight departs. Will I be considered a stalker? I mean, I want to do what's right for you, for us. I have this feeling about us, and I don't want it to be wrong."

Seychelle allowed his words to echo in her mind as she sipped her Moscato. Vance waved his hand to get the waiters attention.

"Check please." He sighed. "Should I be worried that you're quiet? No response could mean many things."

"No response could mean I agree. This is all going so fast. Relationships, if you can call this one, take time not distance."

"Seychelle, I agree. I don't know if I can deal with a distance relationship. You came to Cancun a few days before me, and I missed you. Seychelle it's unexplainable. Tell me I have it wrong. Tell me you don't feel what I feel and I'll stop."

"I can't; I would be lying."

Chapter 26

The soft music and wine set the atmosphere for soft talk and foreplay. Seychelle and Vance danced to the rhythm casting shadows on the drawn drapes in his suite.

"I've canceled my flight." Vance began to kiss her neck gently.

Seychelle would later blame her willingness to give in on the heat of the moment, the wine, the softness in his voice, and his mannerism. The long list of excuses would be a cover for the truth. She wanted him in his entirety. She wanted him to explore her. She needed him to take her. Her desire to scream yes was quelled with her soft, enticing moan.

Vance understood her response and took her by her hand. He led her to the bedroom. Disrobing was a choreographed dance between the two. Neither took their eyes off the other. As his pants fell to the floor, followed by his briefs, Seychelle rolled the rim of her laced front thong hesitating before exposing herself.

She stepped toward his erection allowing him to feel the lace and a desire he hadn't felt in months.

Vance took the offer and aided her in taking off the thong. Laying her on the bed, he started from her feet. He closed his eyes allowing his imagination to lead him to where their desires would be fulfilled. He kissed her legs as he massaged her buttocks. He lifted her to his erection and opened his eyes to see her acceptance of him.

Seychelle smiled, "Yes, take your time. I want to remember this."

Vance entered her easily. Her juices were flowing, and the throbbing of her muscles made it easy for him to penetrate her. They became one, dancing to a new rhythm keeping their bodies entwined. They moaned together as they changed the pace.

Vance pulled out his stiffened rod and positioned Seychelle on her stomach. She wanted to warn him that the position turned on another level of ecstasy for her, but she needed to be pleased completely. She got on her knees, and as he spread her, he began to throb. He used his fingers to fondle her while he pumped himself. He knew it would only take a touch of her outer lips on his firmness to cause an explosion. Her pulsating and his throbbing was the beginning of what he knew would be as he dreamt it. He slowed down his movements anticipating his entry to her moistened cove.

Seychelle needed him to satisfy her need. She had pleased herself with her ever-ready dildo for months. She moved closer to him knowing she would feel his stiffness. She knew he needed to be satisfied too. As Vance turned her again, he and opened her legs above his shoulders. The tease was too much for her. She wanted his next move more than the position before. Seychelle was tingling as her juices flowed meeting his tongue.

Vance toyed with her clitoris and softly kissed her. He turned her again and immediately penetrated her. Her moisture, warmth, and requests for it all caused an immediate reaction. Their lovemaking was complete. He was satisfied, and he knew she was too.

Chapter 27

Sasha invited Jon to join her for wine and conversation. The suite would be perfect for an intimate evening. Jon arrived later than she expected, but she tried not to let it bother her. The platters of sushi and salad were brought to the suite at seven. He arrived at eight-thirty offering no excuse.

Sasha opened the door and returned to the sofa and the movie she had no interest in watching. There was a small dish on the table with remnants of the food she nibbled on. Pinot Grigio sat on the floor near her and the glass needed filling a third time.

"I'm sorry I'm late. Aiden and I sat with the guys from the Whalen group. We had a few drinks before they got on their way."

Sasha had no response and wondered why he didn't think carefully about his answer before he lied. He sat next to her. He felt the tension as he slowly massaged her hand.

"I know, listen, Sasha, it was the last place either of us intended to be. Your brother thought it would be insulting if we didn't go with them. We had a couple of beers, nothing strong. I know what you're thinking, but Aiden is fine."

"No phone, no phone call? Well, I'm insulted, then I asked myself why? We are not in a relationship; we're not even lovers, hell, there's no commitment between us. It's okay. Well as you can see, I ordered food and wine for us. Eat it, drink and whatever."

Jon sat on the couch next to her as the tears dropped from her eyes. He pulled her into his chest and allowed the moment to continue without his assumptions or questions.

"I don't know why I'm acting this way. It's too much Jon really. I feel as though I'm watching myself making choices I normally wouldn't make. I can't believe these actions, my actions, what am I doing?"

"What actions my dear? Have you done something you think is wrong?"

"I don't know. I mean, if I think about this whole thing, I didn't expect to be here. I need a moment to grasp what has happened. I mean this, whatever you call it, with you, the business, my sister; it has all happened too fast. There is no commitment, no effort on my part and wham! I'm in business, in love and confused."

"In love?" Jon lifted her head from his chest. He positioned her so he could see her face. Her eyes answered his question. "In love and confused? What is the confusion?" He wiped her eyes and kissed her lips softly.

"It's too soon Jon. You are—"

"Shhh! Quiet now. You've said enough. Listen to me. I agree. Love is not something you rush. We have time. I'm not going anywhere."

Sasha sat up, repositioning herself to have the conversation she had with herself earlier.

"I'm going home, Jon. Across the waters, miles away. I'll be there for the next year, maybe longer. I can't expect this feeling to change right away, but with the distance, I know it won't last forever."

"Sasha, can we take it day by day. Allow it to grow or fade away, whichever, but let's allow what we have today to be a start. We will be in contact with each other. I'll come to visit during your break. No strings attached, we are adults."

"Jon, I don't want you to think I'm some love-crazed, village girl."

"Wow, is that what they call a woman of beauty on the islands? Why think that way? I don't think of you that way. Your beauty stuns me, your intelligence amazes me, and you being loved crazed has touched my heart village girl. I know I could and would wait for forever. A year won't make a difference for me."

"It's not just that. Everything has happened so fast. I come to spend time with my brother, travel with my sister, and all of this is like I'm dreaming."

"Well, my dear it's not a nightmare. Do you regret your vacation?"

"Jon, you and Aiden were prepared for the business. You knew what you were getting into. I'm hoping it's not too much. I don't want it to fall apart. Yes, it's a dream. I guess I just don't want to wake up."

"Well my dear, open your eyes. Look at me; I'm not confused. I love you, and yes, I'm ready for whatever you want and the business too."

Jon hoped he gave Sasha a reason to relax and enjoy the time they had left together. She was right. It seemed like a dream. One he too, didn't want to end. He hadn't sought to fall in love, and he was sure it wasn't a conscious decision for either of them. He didn't need Sérénité Resorts & Spa or the work he would have to put in to ensure it would be profitable. He was willing to be a part of it all. It wasn't about the money.

Sasha was beautiful. He hadn't been intrigued by a woman in years. Before meeting Sasha, he'd have pick up dates without seeking longevity. The chance of having a lasting romance ended when a fatal accident on I-5 took the life of the woman he loved. A reason to return to what almost took his life, alcohol. Now, ten years later, he found a reason to live and love again.

"What are you thinking about?" Sasha's question brought him back to the present. "I didn't' scare you did I?"

"No not at all. Would you ever consider living in the States? I mean on the west coast, close to your brother?"

"Close to you? I gave it a thought, but I don't know. My home is beautiful." Sasha began to laugh.

"You're laughing. I'm serious."

"I know, I was just thinking. Sérénité Resorts may have me living in Vegas for a while. Who knows a home in Cali, Vegas, here in Cancun? The money to be made can have me living anywhere. This is crazy. An overnight success and I'm sitting here bawling, unsure of what? Yes, I would consider it Mr. Mikels."

Chapter 28

A iden wasn't pleased when Jon called to say he would be with Sasha. He went on to say he didn't think he would be back to the suite that night. Now Aiden would be worried about Sasha as well as Seychelle. Sasha had relayed the information their sister had given her. She too would be spending the night out. He searched the internet for the man that turned his sister's head. Vance Chase seemed to be a well-established investor, a businessman who was praised in many of the business reports in Canada.

Aiden sat back from the computer trying to find a reason to object to his sister's choices. They were grown. After all, his stability could not compare to their progress. In less than four months Seychelle had successfully launched her business. She would remind him that he and Jon were assets. She couldn't have done it without them. That fact wouldn't matter to their father. Aiden wouldn't gain his father's respect once he knew that it was Seychelle's initiative that saved him from sinking deeper into depression.

Clayton Whelan called before he and the others boarded their plane. He expressed his gratitude for the inclusion of the Whelan Group. He described the potential for growth as astounding. He looked forward to seeing Aiden and Jon on Monday. Aiden feared he would have to admit he worked for his sister. What would she tell their father? She would have to be at the meeting on Monday.

It was now nine o'clock. He had been up since six hoping that his restless sleeping pattern was not becoming a habit. The ocean air reminded him of home. He'd speak with his father later. He'd let him know that all was well and the Tudjal women would be on a flight back to the island soon.

Aiden went out on the balcony avoiding the temptation of the complimentary bar. He and Jon agreed not to move the alcoholic products from the refrigerator. He would have to pass tests. Last night was just the beginning. The three beers teased his addiction, but he told Jon he was able to handle it. He didn't want to give rise to suspicion by any of the men at the table. The question would be asked at a later time, he was sure of it. Jon reminded him there would be more meetings or outings that would include eating and drinking. Aiden would have to stand tall and make a choice. His addiction needed to be second to the business at hand.

Aiden cried upon returning to the suite. Now standing on the balcony, he wasn't sure why. He didn't understand himself. He was beginning to feel needed. He would have his own part in the business Seychelle was building. She would need him and together they would grow. It wasn't enough.

The addiction spoke loudly, with force. He needed his own. Women should not be the lead. Seychelle understood the tradition, why would she put him in this situation? The addiction questioned every reason.

He looked out over the ocean as he heard his father's voice and his repeated argument. "It is dangerous for a man to allow a woman to be the lead in their home or business. This leaves a way for the man to become lazy. He will lack what it takes to be a true man. If a woman can rule, maintain herself, or take charge, there is no need for a man in her life. The man becomes her toy, and he will be a mere boy in her eyes."

Aiden's mother, Nicole, spoke of her husband's point of view as tradition. She reminded him that the women of the islands worked and cared for home. Women had established themselves in business and hadn't lost their husbands. The respect for the men in their lives never wavered. The old tradition was fading, and those who held on to it often regretted it.

The tradition and the addiction held Aiden captive. In his confusion, he would drink. He was not the man for any woman. Although, he hadn't stopped satisfying his desire to be pleased, or be loved. He often wrote to a few of the women he dated on the island. He teased a few women in California long enough to satisfy him for a few nights. The need to have a lasting relationship hadn't been on his mind. No one he would introduce to his parents or his sisters. He had one true love, Tristan. He was scared to call her when he felt weak. He didn't want to be weak in her eyes. His sisters broke another tradition. Neither Jon nor Vance had been introduced to their lifestyles. Their father would be disappointed in his children. Aiden thought again about the call. He would tell Seychelle to call home.

The phone rang interrupting the silence in the suite and the conversation in his head.

"Good morning. Yes, may I help you?"

"Mr. Whelan is it?" It was a female's voice, but Aiden couldn't identify who she was or if he knew her.

"No, may I help you?"

"I got the name from the V.I.P. listing for the auction held here in Cancun. How are you, sir? May I speak with Mr. Whelan?"

"I'm fine. I work with Mr. Whelan. He is not here at the moment. May I ask who you are? Do you have a specific question about the event?"

"No sir, my name is Cheyenne Minnows. I didn't see any name other than the Whelan Group. Are you an investor?"

"No, I was there with a few friends." Aiden didn't recognize her name. He became suspicious.

"I see. So you don't invest or buy property? I thought the place was filled with interested parties only."

"Well, there were quite a few of us who were there with a group of investors. I'm sure not everyone was there to buy or sell as you say."

"Your accent is beautiful. Where are you from?"

"Ma'am I don't want to be rude but exactly what is it you want?"

"Well, you see, I am an investor. I'm looking to help those who are new buyers and need financial backing for properties they purchase."

"Ms. Minnows I have stated I was in attendance with friends. So I won't need your backing."

"Well if you'd be so kind to answer one more question. ... Who are the friends?"

"Have a good day Ms. Minnows." Aiden hung up the phone. He checked his incoming call list on his cell. The call was marked unknown.

Chapter 29

Seychelle listened as her brother revisited the call.

"Who does that? She's aggressive." She replied wondering what motive caused Cheyenne Minnows to call Aiden.

"A trait I wouldn't expect from a strange woman. Any woman, for that matter. I looked in the packet and found her company. She's an investor and a buyer. I don't really know what she wanted but I'm sure it was not to be a financial backer."

"I met her."

"When?"

"Vance introduced us. Aiden I think she's trying to find out who is a part of the Whelan Group. I don't understand how she got your name though."

"We were registered for the V.I.P. room. It was under the Whelan Group. She asked for Mr. Whelan. That tells me she has no idea who's handling the sale."

Seychelle drifted in thought for a moment. She wondered if Cheyenne saw her enter the room.

"Did she ask for anyone specific in the group?"

"No, she just asked for Mr. Whelan. It didn't sound like she had done business with them before. She was fishing. Who is she?"

"A problem. Vance had business with her years ago. I thought she was upset because I was with him, but he said she was a competitor playing games."

"So if she were looking for Mr. Whelan—" Seychelle cut him off.

"It's Westlake. She's interested in the property. She and Vance talked with buyers after the auction. After talking with one of the guys from the group she probably thought she'd call. Did she ask about the property?"

"No, I didn't think that was her interest. Her questions seemed to be personal. Did you tell her you were interested in the auction?"

"No, I pretended I was Vance's arm piece; that pissed her off. I don't know if I should discuss her with Vance. I don't want him to become suspicious. He mentioned she would be calling the Whelan group. That's got to be it; she's interested in the property."

"Clayton said the property would bring out the vultures. I guess you were right not to be in the spotlight."

"What does that mean?"

"Seychelle, you said you needed me to be the face of the business. After speaking with this woman it appears I need to be the voice as well. We really should consider going into this business together. The way I see it, you wouldn't have to worry about other businesses or Father."

"Father? What are you talking about Aiden? I asked what you and Jon wanted more than once. On paper, Aiden, what do you want your position to be? Your title means little to me. Are you suggesting that I become a financial backer for you? Aiden, I am sharing with you as much as I am willing to share. At this point I could just use The Whelan group and dismiss you and your sponsor."

Aiden ignored her response. She knew what his concerns were.

"What will you tell Father about this business? How long will it be before Ms. Minnows calls again? Once she finds out who bought the property, who is renovating, etc. ... Seychelle, people will be watching from all angles. You will be on sight often. Jon said...."

"Jon said? What is Aiden saying? I thought you and Jon understood what I wanted. You are a part of this process but you are not the lead. Aiden this is my idea, my business, my money. I'm giving you a chance to re-build everything you seem to have lost. Jon has his own, but I've included him as well. You both are a part of listed executives, but I am the head, the lead. If you're looking to run my company behind my back, get out now."

Aiden was ready to accept defeat. He didn't want to argue or be "fired".

"I understand Seychelle, but your father will be relentless and it seems others will seek you out as well. Ms. Minnows has taken the first stab. I'm just presenting this to you so we can be ahead of a potential problem."

"Our father knew what my intentions were before I left home. Cheyenne Minnows is not a problem. She's looking and all you have to do is keep a straight face. She doesn't realize the game isn't poker."

"Well on another note, call Father. You can't fly out until you've met with the group. It's best for the closing of the property and the start of the renovation."

Seychelle didn't want to make the call. There was much to be said and too much to interpret. She would text the flight time for Sasha's return. Seychelle would stay another week without anyone's prior knowledge. Her parents would have questions. And Vance? Well, he would have to wait for her call.

Chapter 30

It was the beginning of the week and Seychelle already decided she was no longer needed. The meeting lasted most of the morning. It was agreed that they would fly to Vegas to visit Westlake on Tuesday. There were no further meetings needed.

Aiden and Jon were handling the renovations and all papers had been finalized. The Whelan Group agreed that Clayton Whelan would handle all the financial matters, which put Seychelle at ease. Once the intricate details were sorted out they discussed projection dates for the openings of the four locations.

Clayton and Seychelle met privately to discuss future investments leaving Jon and Aiden in the conference room.

"What's that about?" Aiden asked expecting Jon would ease his bruised ego.

"Probably nothing. Seychelle is eager to rush things. Westlake will be enough for at least a year. She should wait to seek other properties. I think Clayton will explain better what we've been trying to tell her."

"I told her to let me handle the negotiations. You know, be the voice for the company. I wouldn't have wasted his time seeking other properties. Look at this, there's so much to do to get this up and running."

Jon put down his pen and sat back from the large table. "I need coffee, how about you?"

"Nothing to say? I need to know what you think."

"We didn't get into this to be the voice. We're the support."

"More like the connectors."

"Well, yes. Aiden for me that's enough."

"Jon, we could be so much more."

Jon poured his coffee and paused hoping his response wouldn't offend his friend.

"You can't steal from your sister. The thought of taking over her business went out the window once she bought Westlake. It was too big for us Aiden. The Whelan Group is monitoring the finances and us. You and I don't have the money to purchase."

"And us? What do you mean?"

"Aiden, Seychelle has agreed for them to handle the finances. If we were to make a move it would have been with the company money. No luck my friend. Our hope now is to grow with the business. At least that's my hope. I put in a few thousand as an investor. My money will grow and I'll see it. That was why it didn't matter to me if I had a salary. I invested Aiden. I suggest you do the same."

"Oh, so you're okay with a woman handling this business and your money?"

Jon laughed. He took his coffee and walked to the windows overlooking the busy streets. Jon had been in the midst of many men who thought as Aiden did. Men who felt that a woman's place was in the home or in the shadows of the successful men they knew. He wondered if men like Aiden understood that most successful men lived among women that gave them direction and encouragement. They shared their accomplishments with the women who raised them, loved them, or simply cared for them. Success was shared with those who inspired them, or struggled with them through it all. Women, who became their reason, their explanations and their foundations, were capable of handling the business if they had the opportunity.

"Aiden, Seychelle had a dream. We weren't a part of it. She had a vision she shared with us and we saw an opportunity. I thought that she had an idea without a goal, without any knowledge of executing it. I was wrong. Your sister took that dream, shared her vision, and we became a connection to what would have taken her another month, no more, to find. Without serious investors she would have stumbled, but

Aiden she still would have been successful. It's a part of her DNA. It's instilled in her, Sasha, and you. Learn the business, take the money you will make in the company and invest. Invest in yourself and release this anger or fear you have because your sisters succeeded first. Success has no time limit in life. Today you are successful. You've been clean for more than six months. You have a goal and direction and your sister forced you to accept it all."

Silence returned between the two men as Jon finished his coffee. Aiden took another dose of reality and although he should have felt better it was from Jon, he was upset.

"Jon can you answer the question. Leave out the opportunity to be a sponsor."

"I'm no longer your sponsor Aiden. You haven't called me in months to help you with your addiction. So I consider you a friend. No, I don't have a problem with a woman handling my money or making decisions for how it is used. As long as she is watching her money, she is watching mine. Again, it's not about the money or my relationship with any of you."

"Does tradition matter to you?"

"Some of it. But a lot of it has changed as the world has. Let it go Aiden. Let your sister handle your father. That is the problem right?"

"Yes, I am worried."

"Go home with Seychelle. Stay a few days and come back. There's no court order that precludes you from visiting. The visit, a talk with your father and mother, family time. It will do you some good. Sasha will be happy to see you are home. It will be good for everyone."

"The renovations?" Aiden held a few pages of the paperwork in the air and let them fall gently to the table.

"What else do we need? We'll fly to Vegas tomorrow with Seychelle and get the specs. Submit them within the next few days and that's it. You'll leave with her and return in a week or so."

Aiden could only nod in agreement. He needed to go home.

Chapter 31

"Vance I thought if we worked this together The Whelan Group would be glad to talk numbers."

"Cheyenne go for it. I'm really not that interested."

"Oh, when I said I was interested in buying you gave me a run for it. What do you mean you're not that interested? Listen, don't you want to know about the buyer? You can't possibly believe it's The Whelan Group."

"Why not? They've bought property before. They're not new buyers. Why does this matter so much?"

"Call it my intuition. Whoever bought it is new."

"Cheyenne, it doesn't matter. I offered to invest. Clayton assured me if—"

"Yes, he told me the same thing. I called them this morning and yesterday. I can't reach Clayton. I just don't see them investing in four locations when they have two others in Vegas. Six in the same area? It doesn't make sense to me."

"You're not making sense. Who says they own the other locations? They invested there as well."

"You're right Vance. The Whelan's name isn't on any of the properties they own."

"Well, there you have your answer. Give it a few days. The owner will put their name on it. It's too soon. Once they look it over and renovate you'll see who your new competition is."

"Competition, I'm not competing with anyone."

"Cheyenne it's in your system. It's not worth it if you can't fight for it. I told you before — you're a woman. Your natural instinct doesn't fit this line of business. You need to invest in sales. Buy a house and flip it, maybe commercial buildings but definitely not resorts."

"Is that meant to be a low blow? I would have had that property if it wasn't for Clayton Whelan and his cronies."

"No, I would have had it. I couldn't allow a woman to ruin what can make millions."

"And I guess it would kill you for the woman to make the millions. Vance you didn't stop The Whelan Group from buying it."

"You would have been selling it at the next auction. I'm excited to see what those boys will do with the property."

"A matter of trust?"

"No the knowledge of the business. I'll give it to you, you're hungry. How many women do you see in the audience of these auctions? You're one in a million but I wouldn't trust you to be patient enough to make the million. The Whelan Group will see a profit on this in three to five years. This business holds no place for the homemakers."

"So you don't see a woman capable of dominating this field. Vance how ignorant is that? Homemakers? Please!"

"Well, I don't see you dominating in it. You're temperamental sweetie. Mixing emotions with business is typical for females. You play games and the Whelan Group showed you they play better."

"You play too. Parading the Queen of the Nile around didn't get you much. You use women to get you a seat in the right row for the deal. Who is she representing?"

"Who, Seychelle? Is that your new problem?" Vance knew she would soon question his relationship with Seychelle.

"Vance it won't be long before she realizes you're not a man seeking a relationship."

"You weren't seeking a relationship. We could have been a force for buyers and investors. We could have defeated the investor groups and private resources. But like I said, women don't have a place in this type of business."

"So what makes her so different? Did her accent soothe the hurt and pain of your past? Did her color mesmerize you? Has she put you on a pedestal declaring you are the best she ever had?"

"Stop it Cheyenne! You said you were better than the average woman. You could handle rejection and still be a friend. I never led you on. That rollercoaster ride you wanted us to be a part of wasn't my idea. I told you to walk away because I couldn't love you. I couldn't give you what you wanted. Why do we need to talk about this every time we see each other? You can't keep it business and I can't ignore what being with you revealed."

"What Vance what?" He could tell she was yelling through her tears. Another collapse of her guarded emotions.

"Nothing, nothing that you would understand. Your vision is not how I see what happened. I have no words to soothe you or reason to comfort you. Cheyenne, you said you were strong in your spot. Stay there and don't call me again."

Cheyenne looked at her phone. The picture of Vance faded as she threw it on the couch. It was obvious she knew him better than he knew her. Westlake Resorts was a lost that she wasn't sure she would recover. She wouldn't lose Vance too.

The Test

Chapter 32

Naomi prepared the table for breakfast. Cole and Sasha took a morning stroll on the beach. Sasha begged her father to walk with her. She returned to the islands and resumed her ritual of her beach walks. A saunter in the morning air along with the rising sun started the Tudjal's day when the children were no older than toddlers.

Naomi stood on the veranda where she could see her husband waving in the distance, an acknowledgment they were on their way. Sasha promised to tell them about her time away from home. There hadn't been many phone calls and her parents were anxious to hear the truth about Aiden.

The wind chimes glistened in the sun as an ocean breeze touched them. The soft sound added to the peace of the home. Naomi left the screen door open for their entry. The table was ready, adorned with breakfast. Fish, papaya, eggs, breadfruit and vanilla tea were prepared. A bowl of assorted fruit sat as the centerpiece.

"Mother, this is so beautiful. I did miss your meals." Sasha sat waiting for her father to join them at the table.

"Did you enjoy the foods your brother cooked?" Cole questioned his daughter as he took his seat.

Sasha looked at her parents wondering if the breakfast would become an uncomfortable query. She bowed her head and said a silent prayer.

"Tell me you didn't have to pray before answering me." Her father laughed trying to ease the sudden tension in the air.

"No, Aiden was a great cook. Whenever he did cook. We were out and about a lot. Sightseeing and we traveled with Seychelle. So he didn't cook often. Seychelle cooked a few times and Jon cooked too."

"Yes, we've heard about Jon."

Sasha took a deep breath. She didn't want to seem surprised but what her parents knew about Jon worried her. She wanted to be the one to tell them about their relationship.

"Can you bless the food Father? It's getting cold."

Chapter 33

S eychelle listened to the voice message from Vance for the second time. She didn't want him to know she was in Vegas. She would be meeting with Jon and Aiden after lunch. She reviewed the pictures sent to her from The Whelan group. Most of the interior décor met her approval. The exterior would be a discussion.

The jitney stopped a few doors away for the entrance of the first of the four locations. A Westlake sign with a flamingo pointing to direct all guest would be the first to go. The same fuchsia flamingo held a top hat at the door as a greeting. Seychelle could only laugh as she counted the bird on wall placards in the front hall.

She could hear the muffled male voices as she approached another smiling Flamingo who pointed to an opened glass door. Upon her entrance the men, Aiden, Jon and Clayton stood to give hugs and greetings.

"The flamingo is the first to go." Seychelle pointed to the door as they all began to laugh. "It looks like a drunk flamingo. The green and gold vest with that top hat? A cheap image of an island bird."

"I knew you'd love it. Your favorite colors. You've always loved the vibrant colors." Aiden teased her pointing to her fluorescent Nike bag and sneakers. Her jogging outfit matched the sneakers. She stood next to the flamingo and posed.

"Take the picture, it's the last you'll see of this ugly thing."

The tour of the Westlake Resorts ended early in the afternoon. Seychelle was amazed there wasn't much more to change. Top quality materials were used for the flooring and rooms. She was pleased with the colors and décor. She walked through each area prepared to write changes. She left Aiden and Jon to argue about the sauna and gym. Minor changes were needed for the kitchen, and decks. Clayton was pleased that the sale of the property included the furnishings and supplies.

"I believe after talking with the staffing management we could be open for business within six months."

Aiden and Jon waited for Seychelle to reply. She walked away from the men into the main lobby. She wanted to have a grand opening. Six months would take them into early January. A New Year celebration would fill the resort. She could watch from the upper level and not be noticed. She'd surprise her parents and Vance.

"Yes, I agree. Clayton have we checked with the prior owners? Had they begun to hire employees?"

"I checked. The only staff that had been employed was maintenance and grounds. We can have the management begin interviews immediately."

"Clayton, I'm serious. Get rid of the flamingo. Aiden, call me when you get a chance. I am going to take it down for a couple of hours. You and Jon going out before your flight back home?"

Jon walked out the door with Clayton leaving Aiden with Seychelle.

"I love how the stairs open to this floor. I can see the stage and the floor from above. It gives it a flair of mystery."

"You see more than I do. What's so mysterious about it?"

"See that office in the corner. The large one. It will be for management only. I can watch everything from above and slip into that office without anyone noticing."

"Why not be seen Seychelle? Let the people know you're the owner, the face behind the name."

"Doesn't matter. When you travel do you know the owners? We don't need to know who owns it. When people travel Aiden they want to know they're getting what their money paid for. We'll satisfy them with a piece of our heritage. This will be the main stage. The other locations will be extraordinary, but this, my brother, will be where we host main entertainment and large parties. This location will be the drawing card. No one needs to know any other name than Sérénité Resort and Spa. Don't tell our parents. I want to surprise them too. I want them to think I'm still looking around. I hope Sasha didn't tell them I bought the property."

"When are you going back to the islands?"

Seychelles excitement had suppressed the desire to leave immediately for home. She didn't want her brother to know she wanted another night with Vance. She hadn't spoken with him since the weekend but she was sure he'd be pleased to see her.

"I'll book a flight for Thursday or Friday but I wanted to leave from here."

"Seychelle, let's fly home together. I think it's time we talk to them about all of this before it gets any bigger than it is."

"Really Aiden. What is it we need to discuss with them?"

"Your business and my part in it. I think I need to confront my fears before I run a business."

"Well before you decide to confront Father you need to understand what or who you are afraid of."

Seychelle left her brother standing in the middle of the floor. Her anger wasn't with him. She was preparing herself for an argument with tradition.

"Seychelle call me. I'll try to fly home on the same day or something. I just want everyone to understand me and what I've gone through."

"Aiden this, all of this has nothing to do with you and what you went through. Let it go. It's a part of your past and you passed brother. It's over, time to re-build. If that means you need your own so be it. Take control of whatever you need but you and I know it's more to it than that don't we? Invest and get your money back. Aiden you can buy your own after we make this one the best in Vegas."

"What will you do then? Who will fill the job when I separate from this? I'm caught in your success Sis."

"No you're growing in my success and there's no fault in that. I'm safe Aiden. You can't lose with me. I have no holds on you and thanks to you and Jon I've got what I need to be successful. The Whelan Group is stable Aiden, they'll see their money grow and we'll both grow with them. Accept it my brother. Don't worry about Father he'll get over it. Invest in Tudjal Export and he'll be just as proud."

"Congratulations Seychelle. Call me if you need to."

Clayton and Jon walked in on their conversation. Jon suggested they say their goodbyes.

"Aiden, I'll meet with you later this week or the beginning of next week. Call me and let me know what's better for you." Clayton waved not waiting for the obvious response.

"I will, thanks. Jon I'll be right there."

Seychelle didn't know what else to say. Being as proud as her brother was there was no need to think he would understand her point of view. They said their goodbyes and she promised to book the earliest available flight for their return home on Thursday.

Chapter 34

Vance didn't give a second thought to accepting Seychelle's invitation to dinner and a show at the Wynn Theater. He didn't bother to ask what else she had in mind. He hoped she missed him as much as he missed her.

The 90-degree day didn't promise the temperature would taper down enough for a pleasant evening. In Vegas the heat without humidity made it somewhat bearable. Vance wore a tan linen blend suit. The jacket would take care of the chill should Seychelle complain about the air conditioning during dinner. They agreed to meet at the entrance.

The night performers on the boulevard were beginning to captivate onlookers. Vance walked hurriedly through the crowd hoping to arrive earlier than Seychelle. He didn't want her to think he was anxious to see her, but he wanted to be the only man to greet her. He stood on the stairs, which positioned him higher than the sidewalk. This gave him the perfect view to spot her approach from either direction.

He thought about flowers but it was too late; he spotted her among the crowd. He allowed his senses to envelope his emotions. She was beautiful. Seychelle let down her braids and they fell softly below her shoulders. She wore an ivory jumpsuit that had a sheer top and long sleeves. Her gold accessories twinkled against her cocoa brown skin. As she got closer she began to smile. He no longer had a reason to question her missing him. She quickened her pace and carefully climbed the stairs. They kissed and held each other. Vance felt his heartbeat hasten. His emotions were getting the best of him. He spoke quickly avoiding embarrassment.

"It is so good to see you again. This is a surprise, I thought you were across the waters."

"Ahhh, business kept me in California. You look nice. I'm loving your jacket."

Vance stepped back and turned slowly showing off his ensemble. He took her hand and spun her around.

"I had to be sure I would complement you in some way. You always look fabulous. I didn't want to embarrass you."

"You never would. I've learned that much about you. It's not your style."

"So business you say? Is Tudjal Exports coming to the United States?"

"No, business with my brother. He's traveling home with me on Thursday."

They began to walk into the venue. The show would begin in an hour giving the audience time to eat and drink. Once seated, they continued the conversation while waiting to be served.

"Is everything okay?"

"Yes, he hasn't been home in years. It's time. You know how family is. It's something that needs to be resolved so we all can move on. I guess he's ready to handle it. We spent some time together when Sasha and I were here but he asked me to stay longer. I did and now he wants to talk to our parents."

"Sounds serious. I wish I would have known you were still here."

Seychelle hated lying but the need to keep the business a secret was a priority.

"If you can believe it, my big brother needed my support. So I stayed, he stayed with Sasha and I until she went back home."

"And her friend?"

"Her friend?" Seychelle was thrown off guard. "She traveled alone. Who are you talking about?"

"The gentleman she left with the night I met you."

She was stunned he remembered Jon and Sasha on their first meeting. He was right, she told him Jon was her sister's friend.

123

"No Jon is someone she met in our travels." She needed a dose of the truth. She didn't want to forget anything she said. It was apparent he paid close attention to what was and wasn't said. Seychelle was glad he hadn't seen Jon to remember who he was. She hoped he wouldn't ask to meet Aiden. They would be at the auctions and he'd make the connection for sure. She wasn't ready to tell him about her business.

"So tell me how you got away from your brother tonight."

"He flew back to California. He'll meet me here to fly home on Thursday. I met him here yesterday. We tied up the loose ends he had here and now I can relax."

"Relax, I'm sensing your brother or his business left you tense."

"Tease me Mr. Chase. What if I told you I knew you would take care of me and ease my tension?"

"I'd tell you that being your masseur is a pleasure."

The dinner and show was entertaining and Seychelle was pleased the subject of Aiden and their reason for returning home was no longer a part of their discussion.

"I want to take you to my home." Vance waited for her excuse to stay on the strip. He didn't ask where she was staying. "Check out. Stay with me until you leave on Thursday."

"You don't have any appointments? Here I could lounge around until you're done with your day. Vance I don't expect you to drop everything because I'm here." She leaned in to him and winked slowly as she waited for his response.

"Now who's teasing who, Ms. Tudjal? Understood, there I go again. I don't want to move too fast. I realize, we don't officially have a relationship or do we?"

"Not officially, but I do think that we both know our limitations. If there were none, would we?"

"Yes, I believe if you let go we can work around the limitations. I won't push you though. You tell me when. There's a jazz set at a club off the boulevard. I'd love for us to go there. The entertainment there is above the expectations of most vacationers."

Seychelle didn't mention checking out of the hotel. She'd heed her mother's warnings about having her own. *"Never settle because you are unprepared."* If she became uncomfortable she had an option.

Chapter 35

The music was inviting. The Trumpet's Jazz Club was filled with a vibrant audience. Laughter and music filled the air. The atmosphere held no confines for the couples that wanted to mingle, dance or enjoy the band. The stage could be seen from the entrance. The six musicians and the vocalist were heard as the guests were greeted and escorted to vacant tables.

"Good Evening Mr. Chase. Follow me, sir, will you be dining with us?"

Vance allowed Seychelle to walk ahead of him as they proceeded through the crowd following the host. "Just the usual setting. How have you been my friend?"

The man, small in stature looked back at Vance smiling as he nodded his head. He waited until the couple was seated to speak. His attention to detail was often rewarded with large tips. Vance asked for Jared each time he frequented the club. They met years ago when Vance and the new owner finalized an investment.

"I've been well. It's good to see you. I have a wine I think you and the young lady will enjoy. Shall I bring it to you?"

"Yes, of course. Thank you."

Seychelle listened as the two exchanged pleasantries. She scanned the audience wondering how many were natives of Vegas compared to those vacationing. Jared left the table promising to return momentarily.

"Do they have many clubs like this in Vegas? I don't remember seeing them along the strip."

"They have a few. You have to go to "Old Vegas" to see club performances. Not many are devoted to just jazz, but they have live entertainment."

"Vance, I'm assuming, you've invested in more than just vacation properties?"

"Only a few. I've been successful, no blessed. This club actually belongs to a man who has become more than a business associate."

Seychelle listened as the rhythm slowed to a sultry beat matching the voice of the lead singer. The dimmed lights and couples moving closely to embrace each other caused her to relax and close her eyes. Vance took the opportunity to touch her hand softly. He stood hoping she wouldn't refuse to dance.

They swayed onto small dance floor and allowed the music to define the moment and their movement. Seychelle felt at ease as she laid her head on Vance's chest. She could feel the warmth of his body. As she inhaled the scent of his cologne, she wanted him to be with her longer than the night. She drew in a long breath allowing her emotions to tease her senses.

Vance kissed her gently on her forehead as he held her close. The music allowed them to glide as though they were lifted in the air. Their bodies and the movement blended with the others on the dance floor. The warmth of her body tempted his desires to please her.

The music faded as the band announced there would be a brief intermission. Couples continued to dance to the music played by the club's D.J. as Vance and Seychelle returned to their table.

"What's next Ms. Tudjal?"

Seychelle was still in a trance. Vance was different, in a pleasant way. Prior relationships taught her that every man wasn't ready for a woman that had goals and the potential to accomplish them. Her ex-boyfriends wanted to rescue her in one way or another. There were those who knew nothing about Seychelles Island. They assumed it was bush country. They would ask what tribe her family belonged to or they would ask her about living in communes with the lack of ample water or food supplies. Seychelle labeled them assholes and didn't bother to see them again or answer their calls. Dating or seeking to be married was not a goal. She often wondered where, if ever, it would fit on her bucket list.

Her mother and Sasha stopped asking about prospects or if she ever thought about marriage. Looking into Vance's eyes, she felt her walls of emotional protection melting away. What was next? She could tell him about her dreams for her business, but personal goals didn't exist.

She whispered, "I don't know Mr. Chase."

"Leaving me, I don't know if I can stand it."

Seychelle laughed. Vance asked again. "What's next?"

"Vance, I won't lie to you. I enjoy your company, and yes, I don't want to leave, but I must go home."

"I don't want to be redundant but…"

"Okay, where do you see this relationship going?" Seychelle had fought with her thoughts and lost to her emotions. She didn't have time for a relationship, but she loved his company. "I live in another country. Relationships are difficult enough without that distance between them. After hearing what you do, are you ever settled in one place?"

"Yes, more than I want to be."

Seychelle thought he was teasing. She waited for an explanation, and when he offered none, she assumed he had said all he wanted to say. The band returned to the stage as Vance waived to the waiter for the check.

"Sir." The waiter smiled as he handed Vance the check and a leather folder.

"I'll come in on Friday to go over this. Let Eli know that I glanced at it. I won't take it with me tonight."

The waiter nodded taking the folder and the check. "Have a good evening Sir, Miss."

The crowd was vibrant again. The voices that were whispering were now talking loudly over the music. Vance leaned toward Seychelle as he spoke.

"Come, my dear, I want you to see something." His smile eased Seychelle's fears. She thought the evening would end with her last question.

The couple walked to the parking lot. Confused and curious Seychelle held his hand tighter.

"It's okay my car is parked here."

They approached the black Audi 600, and Vance opened the passenger door. The buttercream soft leather seat was more than comfortable. Seychelle turned in her seat to view the car's interior. It was beautiful. She fastened her seat belt when Vance started the car.

"I love this vehicle. It's beautiful."

"Thank you. Believe it or not, I bought it for a friend."

"A friend?"

"Well, it was a business associate. I'm no longer invested in their business, and they returned the car."

Seychelle wondered was it a woman who no longer held his interest. She didn't want to think of the possibilities, women she didn't know, but Cheyenne was at the top of any list.

"It's nice." She kept the answer short. She didn't want him to have to explain a lie later. "What type of car do you have?"

Vance hesitated before answering. "I have an Audi and a BMW. If I could have predicted the future; I wouldn't have this Audi. I didn't want to take it back to the dealer, so I kept it. Listen, let me show you a few things about Vegas that you won't get on a tour."

He drove on the road that led them away from the center of Las Vegas entertainment. He pointed out landmarks as he told stories of the meetings and business mistakes he made.

"I wanted to buy houses, sell them after some major changes, and get rich. I didn't make what I expected, so I decided to invest in the resorts. It worked well in Cancun, so I thought it could work here. I fell in love this area."

He drove up what seemed like a never-ending winding road. Signs were pointing to an overlook area. It was eleven thirty, and the lights throughout the tourist area made an awesome view.

Vance parked the car. "Let me show you another highlight here in Vegas."

They walked up an incline on a path that Seychelle was glad ended less than five hundred feet ahead of the parking area. The path was lined with trees and bushes that seemed to have been trimmed and treated. She felt a welcomed breeze as they stepped into the preserved opening.

"This site is second to the Grand Canyon. You can see Vegas in its entirety if you stand here. I've been to many places, but this is home for me. The land there, where there are no lights, is the future. It's like many of the islands; they have so much land waiting to be discovered or developed."

"It is quite different from this point of view. I've heard about the Grand Canyon. I guess its beauty is why it's never been developed. Nature has a way of expressing simple beauty. We have overlooked such as this on the island." She paused to laugh. "You would have to be a nature lover to get to them."

"And you, Ms. Tudjal, not one for that walk through nature?" Vance laughed and wrapped his arms around her. She leaned back, responding to his embrace, allowing her back to rest on him. He kissed the side of her face and turned her to face him.

"You're right. I'm not the one to walk between bush and trees. Bugs, snakes, and whatever is out there waiting for the fool to walk between them. But it is as beautiful as you said it would be."

They walked along the railing that provided maps and information depicting the sites that surrounded them. The larger casinos were marked with stars other places had different icons.

"So much open land. I believe we saw that area when we were arriving on the plane."

"Yes, the airport is just beyond the lights over there." Vance pointed to the opposite side of the overlook. The view on that side had a vast amount of undeveloped land. "I live just beyond those lights. The area is called 'The Ridges,' I've had my home there for almost ten years."

"Do you have a home in Canada as well?" The thought of having a place to live in America crossed her mind after her purchase of Westlake. She decided against it; she'd always have a place to stay at the resort.

"My family lives there, so I visit or stay there when I need to."

"Hmmm." It was only response Seychelle was willing to give.

Vance looked at her and with his brows raised, "And?"

"No, no and I was just thinking about what you said."

"Does it shock you that I stay with my family, or that I have a home here?"

"No, I just imagined you as being a settled businessman. It seems like you travel more than I thought an investor would."

Seychelle hadn't thought about the time she would spend with her family or business. The question of travel, being on the road would damper what her family honored. Family time was another value that her father instilled. Over the years, neither she nor Sasha challenged the values that had become a habit. Now with Aiden away from home, she and Sasha would have to discuss how their father would respond. She dismissed the thought hoping she didn't appear distant to Vance.

"Let me continue with my mini-tour. Promise to keep an open mind until I finish, okay?"

"Okay, I will."

The couple returned to his car, heading toward The Ridges.

Chapter 36

Aiden called a nine o'clock meeting with Clayton and Jon at The Whelan Group Corporate offices. He sat in the office they provided waiting for the men to arrive. He shuffled through the agreement they signed before the purchase of Westlake Village. He was sure there was a clause that no shares were to be sold without Seychelle's signature. This would leave room to question the men about Cheyenne. After internet searching he found Ms. Minnows, her properties, her investments and her associations. He would later call Seychelle about her acquaintance with Vance Chase.

He heard the morning greetings as the men were approaching the office. Quickly he put the papers back in the folder and stood to shake their hands.

"Good morning gentleman. If I had known to join you for breakfast, I would have. You left me to the office coffee."

"Then you, my friend, did better than either of us," Clayton replied.

"I had a long night as well," Jon stated as he poured himself a cup of the freshly brewed coffee.

"Well, I won't take up too much of your time." Aiden handed them folders with his findings.

"I'm uneasy about Ms. Cheyenne Minnows. I don't quite know why, but my instincts tell me she may be trouble in the future. I wanted to make sure that our agreement stands firm that there will be no other investors signing on with your company. The Whelan Group is our investment team, and any investors that you sign on for Serenity Resorts and Spa must be approved and signed by Seychelle. This woman is looking for something, and I'm sure she'll reach out to you or Jon soon."

Clayton and Jon didn't respond as they looked through the search results.

"I'm not—"

Clayton cut Aiden off, finishing his thought. "You're not saying that she is not worth including, but you're right. She called and left messages for me. I haven't returned her call, but in light of what we discussed earlier it's worth the value of the project to see what she wants or is up to."

"Well, may I ask what the discussion was earlier?"

Jon gave Aiden a side eye. Aiden hadn't shared his prior conversation with Clayton, and he didn't understand why.

"I told Clayton what I told Seychelle. I couldn't reach you. This woman called, she thought I was an investor. She wanted to know about Westlake, that's my assumption. When I spoke with Seychelle, she said they met at the auction. It seems she's an acquaintance of Vance Chase. If Seychelle wants to remain in the background at the auctions, she may be exposed by Ms. Minnows."

"I don't understand her reason for hiding. Can either of you shed some light on that for me?" Clayton sat back in the high back executive seat preparing for the in-depth response.

The men continued their meeting for more than two hours. The discussion concluded with their cravings for lunch. They agreed Wexler's Deli, one of the best downtown, would satisfy their tastes buds.

"So Aiden, your family has strong traditions that you all stand by. I admire that." Clayton started the conversation and ended it, before they left the office.

"I wish I could say we stand by them. My parents have no understanding of American traditions. I don't think they've even vacationed on this side of the water. More importantly, we try not to disappoint them. They wouldn't understand Seychelle's position or why I have not succeeded with my own company."

"How would they take the partnership between you and Seychelle?"

"Jon, I don't know. I'm hoping my return home will answer this and more."

"Seychelle has good business sense, and her foresight will take the company far. Setting the foundation is key."

"So you understand her point of view?"

"Aiden, it's a new era, my friend. Women make beautiful wives, mothers, and business owners. To be truthful, that saying behind every good man, well it applies to businesses too. The secretary in the office is often the one holding it together for that CEO. I'm proud of the woman who takes on the challenge to compete and win. It's not about their gender; it's about their ability to be one of the best in what they do."

Clayton's words hung in the air for a moment. Aiden was still reluctant to agree, but he had to admit to himself, Seychelle was ready to compete. Her first competitor would be Cheyenne Minnows.

Chapter 37

Cheyenne tossed the papers on her desk, frustrated she hadn't found any updated information on the Westlake purchase. The calls to The Whelan Group hadn't been returned.

"Diane, get me the number to Clayton Whelan, please. Oh, not the office, I want his personal number. It should be on correspondence we sent to him last month."

The secretary disconnected the intercom without a response. Cheyenne didn't need a response, Diane had been working with her for more than ten years; they had an understanding. She stepped away from the desk and into her private bathroom.

The full-length mirror, Diane's idea, gave its compliments as she turned looking at the side view of her attire. The woman in the boutique asked did she want the next size. Cheyenne didn't answer understanding the woman simply sold clothes with no sense of fashion. The suit fit perfectly, yes it was tight, but that's what left memories in the minds of those who watched Cheyenne enter and exit a room. Salmon in color, the perfect match to her stiletto shoes; the color gave her gold-toned skin a soft glow. She checked her makeup, applied more lipstick and stood back to give the mirrored image her approval.

Cheyenne was the only girl and the middle child of the Minnows. Her father, Jeffrey Minnows, was well known as the next possible candidate for Mayor. He had been in politics since her freshmen year in high school, and no one remembered the Minnows children without mentioning his name.

Her mother Sophia Minnows taught in the elementary school. She had been a teacher promising to retire for more than thirty years. Just like her husband, her position was cause for conversation leaving no room for their children to make a significant mark of their own.

Cheyenne was different. She hid behind no one and set out to make her appearance known whenever and wherever. Her mother tried to explain to her daughter she didn't need to be the center of attention to be prominent in life.

Cheyenne graduated a year early after enrolling in an excel program and accepted entry into Spellman College. Her family expected her to take an interest in business, but they had no idea it wouldn't be on the east coast. Cheyenne left the east coast and their Maryland home to reside in Las Vegas.

She checked herself again before returning to her desk. Her business, Minnows Investors was one of the largest investment firms in Las Vegas. She was known to invest, buy and sell property that brought large returns. She found no difficulty persuading others to include her as the money grew and changed hands.

The Whelan Group was a thorn in her side. Larger than she could imagine, she wanted what they had. Minnows Investors had a staff of twenty, including her. Her father's words ate at her each day. *"Take it slow; you're young you have years to develop."* Taking it slow in her business was costly. The Whelan Group was a multimillion-dollar operation. The group started in the business more than twenty years prior. Their base was in Las Vegas, but it was obvious with the new offices in Mexico and Florida they were expanding.

Cheyenne wanted to be sure they weren't the shadow standing behind a smaller company that would plummet into success with the Westlake property. She couldn't afford to lose the ground gained to a new competitor.

"Mr. Whelan on line one." The intercom sang out. Cheyenne rushed to the desk but paused to compose herself before answering.

"Mr. Whelan." Cheyenne softened her tone.

"Hold on; he will be with you in a moment." The voice of his secretary annoyed her. She spoke with her more than she cared to remember trying to make the connection with any of the brothers.

"Diane!! I thought I told you to get his cell phone number. I didn't need to be connected—"

A baritone voice interrupted her scolding. "Clayton Whelan, how may I help you?"

"Clayton, you've been a hard man to catch up with these past few days. I was sure after our conversation in Cancun I wasn't barred by the red tape."

"Cheyenne, I'm sorry but as you know new properties are new business, and new business requires attention."

"That's what you have staff for is it not?"

"Once things are in order. I like the personal touch that we give new clients."

"Well, it is that new business that I'd like to discuss."

"What new business?"

"The Westlake property." She paused waiting for his reply.

Seychelle's conversation with Clayton included the possibility of a call from Minnows Investors. He assured Seychelle that Cheyenne Minnows would not be provided with any information regarding the property.

"Great property, we really lucked up with that one. It will be a signature spot for Vegas within the next five years."

"Clayton, c'mon, who is the buyer. Let me get in on the shares at ground level."

"We can't sell the shares. The owner has requested to sign off on all investments and selling of shares. To be honest with you I don't blame them. Four properties, within Las Vegas, that's prime real estate. The return should be enough to raise an eyebrow."

"What's your stake in the property? Investor?"

"Cheyenne, you've never been this invasive. Be as you are, direct. Exactly what do you want?"

"Give me a chance to talk to your client. I'm sure with your backing and mine we can all make money."

"I can't give you that, and you know it. Confidential, my dear. I can keep you in mind when any of our properties are offering shares. With the right money, you can profit from any of our clients. Business that slow?"

"No Clayton!!" She slammed the phone. She'd have to find another way. Vance was right. The registration for the newly named property would convey the name of the owners.

Clayton smiled as he dialed Aiden's number. It was a pleasure to assist him and his family in formulating a foundation for their business. They would take Serenity Resorts & Spa under The Whelan Group as a pilot program. He agreed with Seychelle; her business wouldn't fail with their support.

Chapter 38

Seychelle turned over in the king sized bed smiling at the sight of the morning sun. The smell of breakfast and coffee teased her taste buds. The sound of the sizzling bacon and the thought of Vance cooking gave her an at home feeling. Her father would cook for the family whenever they stayed up late talking and reminiscing. Her mother would purposely pretend to be too tired to rise. Seychelle and Sasha would leave their rooms to share their parent's bed. They'd snuggle next to their mother awaiting their father's loving surprise.

She pulled the sheets around her and closed eyes. Her naked body tingled as she remembered the night's end. Vance's home in The Ridges was large but moderate. He was a lover of art and sculptures. As he showed her each room of the home, he explained his reason for the décor. He enjoyed music as well, and the Boise sound system played softly as they continued the tour.

The home had five bedrooms, enough for family visits, a media room complete with a full screen for films, and a recreation room. Vance explained his sister had children and they utilized that room more than he had. His study and office, though attached, had its entrance from the outside of the home. This was for client appointments.

The landscape complimented the home with an in ground pool, deck and hot tub.

Seychelle permitted herself to let go. It was a moment of relaxation that she wouldn't find on the Vegas strip. Vance teased her with his version of a tantalizing massage, a prelude to sexual pleasure. She could see herself visiting his home during her returns. He'd become her reason for her frequent travels.

"Good morning, I thought you'd be a bit hungry."

Seychelle opened her eyes slowly. Her smile told him she was pleased. "Thank you."

"It's early, but I didn't ask your schedule for the day."

"There is none. Let's eat."

They decided to eat on the deck. The morning sun didn't discourage them, as its warmth hadn't reached its peak. Wearing one of Vance's football jerseys and a pair of his socks Seychelle laughed at herself as the reflection in the window gave her a glance at her morning appearance.

"You're still beautiful."

"Thank you for sharing this beautiful outfit."

"It's one of a kind. A Vance Chase line that only you could make worth millions."

"I don't know that you would get that much."

Their laughter was genuine, a comfort they appreciated. It was the first time since leaving home that Seychelle didn't compare her experience. She had none like it to compare. Her moments with Vance were her first as a business owner, her first as a woman who would be traveling abroad, her first that she would consider bordered on true love.

They spent most of the day lounging. Vance excused himself a few times to take calls. It was close to three in the afternoon when Seychelle decided she needed to get back to her hotel.

"No, I won't allow you to leave me like this." Vance declared sarcastically.

"Funny. I have a plane to board in the morning. I've got a few things to do before I leave."

"May I ask?"

"No, you may not. It's nothing. I told you my brother was meeting me at the airport in the morning. It's family stuff, a continuous mess."

She checked her bag for her phone. She ignored it the entire time she was at his home. There were a few missed calls, two from Sasha and one from Clayton. She'd need to return his call.

"Yes, you did say your brother was meeting you. Let me not hold you hostage."

The ride to the strip was shorter than Seychelle remembered it from the night before.

"You don't live that far from all of the action."

"Twenty minutes to be exact. I was seeking to buy property further out, but I fell in love with The Ridges."

"I see why. It is beautiful. So when your clients come to your office, have they questioned your living?"

"No why would they?"

"On the island, there are those who question my father, our family. As though we live better only because of what they pay for our goods or their labor on the docks."

"I see. Well those who can afford to be in business with me have their own."

"Do you find it to be more men than women?"

"Women? What do you mean?"

"That are in business with you. Have you dealt with individual business owners?"

"A few. The owners are usually men. I would guess they have women within their companies. Most women sit home and reap the benefits; raise the family, take the vacations and spend the money. The men make the negotiations and business deals. I simply keep them in business."

"Women in business are complex on the islands. They do it all, and it shows. Men have always reaped the benefits of having a good woman in their lives and their business."

"Do they sit in on the meetings, make the contracts and negotiations? I can't believe that women are in the business at that level. Why would they be?"

"You are right; they don't make it to the boardroom. Times have not changed that much. But Vance, tell me, you don't think as my father and brother do you?"

"And how do they think?" He parked his car and turned off the ignition. He looked at Seychelle as she prepared her answer.

"It's difficult to say. They encourage women to achieve but once

140

they do they stifle their growth. My sister teaches, yet my father was against her teaching at the University or abroad. My education is in business, yet he wants me to stay buried in the family business instead of acquiring my own. What do you think Vance?"

The answer would seal their future, and he knew it. His thoughts needed to be what she wanted to hear. Over the past few months since the auction, he mentioned women in his field and their absence. He dared not ask where her question would lead.

"Women have evolved. Many of the career choices they may have ignored in the past now interest them. I applaud their persistence on the path to advance. Seychelle, I hope I don't offend you when I say, some careers just aren't for women. There are some business ventures that they will never dominate or be the best. Investments, I believe is one. Maybe your father has his reasons beyond the island tradition."

"So you believe that women should be teachers, shop owners, secretaries, mothers and the base of the family?"

"No, I'm not saying that. It's been proven that women can be so much more but any job where travel is a must, I believe women should reconsider. I mean that is if they want a family."

"Have you given up on the thought of having a wife and family?"

"No, I haven't thought about it, but I haven't given it up either."

"And what about your travel would you give that up once you marry?"

"No, but it would be less. A lot less. I would want to be with my family."

"But your wife would have to be home?"

"Once we have children, yes. I'd expect her to be home."

"Interesting. Well, you're not married and for today that's a good thing." It became obvious that the conversation was ending.

"Yes," Vance replied unsure if he should say more. "I'll call you later, or you can call me once you've handled matters."

"Thank you for showing me a wonderful time," Seychelle spoke quickly trying to hide her disappointment. She hoped Vance would understand her passion to be in business.

"I don't know. I feel the need to expose who I am. Please don't misunderstand me Seychelle. I've never met a woman like you. You make it so easy to love you and I want to give you the world if you'd allow me."

"Time plays a part in all romance. Let's allow time to work its magic."

"Fair enough. I'll wait for your call."

They shared a kiss goodbye. Seychelle understood she'd have to teach him how to love the woman she was determined to become.

Convinced or Convicted

Chapter 39

"Clayton, Aiden is not appointed an overseer of the business or any of the money allocated to the business. That's why your group is paid. Any investors should contact you. I will sign any and all necessary documents if we choose to include stockholders or investors. Why would he question our conversation? What else did he ask?"

"There's no need to delve into the details. It's obvious that he's worried who is included in the business. I called to tell you that we are willing to give your company office space with us. Aiden can work from there and be a part of the process. Seychelle, as I said before, Serenity Resorts & Spa is a springboard for what is to come. We have plans to help you expand your business. Aiden only wants to be a part of that expansion, and I understand it."

"Clayton, Aiden's fear is my father. He wants to prove that he is the head of Serenity Resorts & Spa. He is not; I am. If having the office will quell his fears—"

"Seychelle, our group will benefit from your progress. I'm not in business to quell fears. Being scared is not good for any business. Aiden can't continue to question what my group does for your business or what you and I discuss. I'm the broker you've chosen, and we have to have a trusting relationship. I know it is your company, you don't have to convince me."

"Thank you. I thought we had a misunderstanding. I don't need the spotlight. I want to be in the background, but I didn't step aside to give Aiden control. I know it may sound strange to you but our traditions on the island are what he follows. The tradition is what he fears. I won't bore you with what the elders say or what is believed to come of a man without stability."

"Well I believe being here in the office around others that will be doing the same work, he'll be stable. I can show him how to handle your business, and maybe he'll take the initiative to get other clients as well. If he wants, we can bring him on with The Group. That will solve any potential problems."

Seychelle gave his words a moment's thought. Aiden needed that security, which she understood.

"What potential problems?"

"You want to remain as an anonymous owner. Cheyenne Minnows is seeking to find the new owner of Westlake. She called me several times and Aiden once. She won't stop there, Seychelle. Aiden told her he was a guest at the auction. His connection can be a dead end if he has an office and is a part of our group."

"What can she gain by knowing the owner's name?"

"I don't know what her intent may be. She's an investor. It could be she sees the possibilities we saw before the bid. She's a fighter, and she's done this before. The difference is, we didn't give her the buyer's name. I think it's her ego. Her purpose is to be one of the top buyers or investors. So she researches the owner's names, their longevity in business and any other information she can find. She's persistent. I ignore her as should Aiden and you. After your explanation for not wanting to be in the forefront, we will make sure your information is buried within our company. We can't guarantee she won't obtain it once the resorts open. Aiden can help with that. Since she has spoken to him, there shouldn't be a reason for her to contact him again."

"I wouldn't be so sure of that. Will we be ready to open by the beginning of next year?"

"Yes, by the Christmas holiday, all the sites will be fully operational. What were you thinking?"

"Just opening and on to the next."

"Your next? Let me know when. We don't have to wait."

Seychelle thought about the timeline. "I'll give it a thought, thanks, Clayton. Enjoy the rest of your day; we'll talk soon."

Chapter 40

Seychelle sighed deeply after disconnecting the call. She'd have to say an extra prayer for her brother and their relationship. The last thing she needed was a feud over the business, her business. Sasha came to mind as she tried to rid her thoughts of the conversation she and Aiden would have during the flight to the islands.

Her sister hadn't called. Although she had been home close to a week, Seychelle expected to hear about her parents questioning Sasha about their summer escapades. Sasha never felt the pressure their parents openly directed to Seychelle and Aiden. They never talked about Sasha's involvement in the family's business. Seychelle never asked why. She was sure they were proud of her accolades as an educator and didn't expect much more. As the youngest, she wasn't expected to manage her older siblings. Nevertheless, Sasha would be the first to be questioned about Aiden's apparent mishaps and Seychelle's intentions. She wondered what Sasha told them about Jon. The questions and assumptions bothered her as she packed.

She looked over the Westlake renovations and decided to write a welcome letter for the promotional material. The signature line would indicate the letter was from the management staff of Serenity Resorts and Spa. After talking with Vance, she'd reveal her name as owner once there was a buzz about the property and its success.

There were loose ends to tie before the next purchase. She spent the rest of the afternoon making a list of what was "next." It was close to six when she realized she hadn't fed the emptiness in her grumbling stomach.

The phone rang as she slipped a simple flowing sundress over her head.

"Hey, what's up? I was thinking about you earlier."

Sasha's whispered response caused her to take a seat on the bed.

"Where are you?"

"I'm at our house, but Father is here with me. The pipes for the waterline are clogged or something. He and the plumber are here. Seychelle, you know they have questions."

"I imagined they would."

"Your imagination can't possibly cover the query they gave me. You'd think we ran off to commit a crime."

"You're okay though, right?"

"Oh yes, school starts in a week. It was postponed because of this waterline thing. The whole island is affected by it. Father thought, of course, our home was on a different line. It's a mess."

"I thought something happened the way you were whispering. I'm as prepared as I will be. I just hope it doesn't break Aiden. Does anyone other than us know he's coming home to visit?"

"Some family. Tristan called asking for him."

"Tristan? Has she been in touch with him?"

"She said they've been in touch off and on. She even visited him when he left home. He tried to break off their relationship after he lost the last job. She said they've had their ups and downs. Maybe seeing her again will be just what he needs."

"What does that mean?"

"C'mon, we're adults. We all need a shot of life. You know someone to talk to, someone to love, someone…."

"Okay, I get the picture. Do you think it's been that long?"

"Only one way to find out. We'll know the difference when he and Tristan hook up."

"What about the talk in town?"

"I haven't heard anything. Father said there was nothing stating Aiden couldn't come home. After all, he's not staying here. How long will you be home?"

"Aiden will go back in a week. I'll be home while the renovations are being made. I don't want to be where I can peek in on the work."

"Yes, that's best."

"Have you heard from Jon?"

"Yes, he's good. I miss him, really I do. I didn't tell our parents about my relationship with him. I didn't answer many of their questions. I told them we all wanted to talk to them together. They finally accepted my answer. Hold on."

Seychelle put on her sandals and grabbed her wallet. She thought about where she would be eating alone. There was no need for fancy dining. Maybe a salad, not much more. She wasn't for another night of dining or entertainment.

"Father is ready to leave. I'm going with him to town. I'll see you tomorrow."

"Okay, tell Father 'Hello' for me."

Chapter 41

The sunset was beautiful. Seychelle walked through the lobby determined to sit poolside. She'd allow the chatter of the guest, the soft music in the background, and the warmth of the evening's air soothe her anxiety. She ordered a glass of wine and laid back on the poolside lounger waiting for the ambiance to take over. Her phone buzzed, giving her a startle, as it vibrated on the small table near her chair.

"Hey there," she answered. "I thought we agreed that I would call you."

"Yes, we did. I, well let me say it this way, I thought you enjoyed the auction. You seem interested in the process, so I wanted to invite you to another. It will be in two months, and it will be a reason for us to get together. The properties are in California, a new market for me."

"Hmmm, I might just take you up on that. I don't know how interested I'd be." Seychelle replied making a mental note to talk to Jon and Aiden about it.

"I think you enjoyed it more than you would admit."

"That's probably true. Okay, so two months, that's October. I'm sure you'll send me the information so I can make arrangements."

"I'd like to make those arrangements if you don't mind. I invited you, so I'll just send you the confirmed flight and hotel information."

Seychelle's silence stunned Vance.

"Did I say something wrong?"

"No, it's fine. Yes, send me the information for the auction as well. Do they give you a preview?" She questioned him knowing the answer.

"Yes, once you respond confirming a reservation. I'll send you a copy of the booklet. So how are you spending your evening?"

"I've packed, had dinner and now I'm relaxing. I've got some work to do when I get home, so I'm enjoying the moment."

Seychelle tried to remain calm. Getting the Westlake property was unexpected and the expense well below what she calculated. Obtaining another property so soon excited her spirit but she needed the purchase to be sound.

"I'll be in my bed by eleven I'm sure, and you?"

Vance smiled hoping there would be a chance to see her before her departure.

"I've had dinner, wine and a conversation with you. My night is almost complete."

"If it is not on your agenda now, your night will remain incomplete." Seychelle's soft response teased him.

"I guess you're right. What time is your flight?"

The conversation lasted longer than either of them expected. It ended when Seychelle noticed she was one of a few left on the pool deck. Giddily she explained her need to lay down as she took the last sip of her Merlot. She said good night and gathered herself before returning to her room.

Vance had never been assertive in romance; he understood when he was losing ground. He felt a need to be closer. He wanted to know if there would be or could be a relationship. Seychelle mentioned the distance between them would matter. Vance understood her concern even though he wasn't willing to accept it.

Time would move slowly over the next few months. His usual business wouldn't fill his days as his mind wouldn't stop thinking about Seychelle. His emotions were stirred the moment he saw her. Now peaked, he needed to know if she felt as he did. He stopped in the middle of his bedroom and smiled. For the moment he allowed the memory of past romances to creep into his thoughts. In comparison, Seychelle was different. His feelings for her were different. The prelude to loving her was easy. She didn't seem to need his wealth. She appreciated his life without the glitter. He had no reason to impress her.

He googled her name. He hadn't thought to search her name when he searched the island. There was nothing that connected her publicly. He typed in Tudjal Imports and Exports. There he found enough information to keep him reading for an hour. He became interested in the history of the company. He read the company's policy, their employees and Seychelle's father's biography. It was clear; her father worked hard to build a company that had become the leader in imports and exports. He read article after article that spoke of awards the company and the man received over the years.

Seychelle said she wanted to leave the family business. Vance couldn't understand her reasons. Seychelles Islands was beautiful and full of opportunity and wealth. She questioned what he felt about women who worked; women who went against tradition. Now he understood her questions. After reading the business her father had established and wanted her to remain in, he agreed with his wishes as a father. The tradition of the island spoke clearly. The families were close, and most of the businesses were built on those traditions. He'd back her dreams no matter what she decided to do. She needed to know that he'd be there for her. Vance was sure she was determined to break away from their traditional lifestyle.

He didn't think much of the traditions held in his family. They seemed to be pleased that he took the initiative to move on. After all, they had a new home and loved the gifts and money his lifestyle provided. His father worked hard and still worked part-time as a mechanic. He loved working on cars although he was the manager of his own business.

It was one of Vance's first investments. His father had been in business over twenty years when he suffered a major setback. Vance understood his father's concern. If the business fell under, he'd lose credibility and the trust of his employees. Vance negotiated with the banks and backed the business. Now ten years later Laurence Chase lived and worked without worry. The business grew, and he had two locations he managed.

It wasn't tradition; it was love and a test for Vance. He helped his father set up a model business and made money for himself and the family. He couldn't imagine his father talking to him about taking over the business. Seychelle was right. The tradition left no room for the children to fulfill their dreams.

He poured another drink; the clock read twelve thirty. Her flight would be departing early. He stood at the bay window overlooking the lights of the city. Vance had to admit it. He had fallen in love.

Chapter 42

Aiden sat in the airport waiting for the flight to Las Vegas. Seychelle would be meeting him during the two-hour layover. His thoughts on returning home held mixed emotions. He hadn't been there in more than five years. Although his mother told him not much had changed, he knew everything had changed.

Tristan had been his love then. Their love kept him from suicide many nights. She talked to him into the early morning hours through the prayers and tears. They toyed with each other through the college years and found each other again off, and on once Aiden returned home. It wasn't until he invited her to California that they understood they had a relationship that neither of them would find with another. Tristan kept his secrets. She talked him through his loss and his small triumphs. She promised him she'd be with him regardless of his past.

During their intimacy, he found his emotions were intact. He wouldn't let himself lean on her strengths. As he sat waiting, she teased his thoughts. Aiden called her the night before. She let him know she'd be with Sasha when his plane landed. He wondered if Sasha knew how close he and Tristan really were. He could no longer worry about what anyone thought. Tristan was what was missing now that he secured a job within The Whelan Group. He spoke with Clayton before leaving California.

Clayton explained it as a genuine offer. Since The Whelan Group was the primary investor for Serenity Resorts & Spa, having Aiden in the office would be an asset. Aiden called Jon who immediately congratulated him without hesitation. It was obvious that Jon and Clayton had talked. Aiden didn't want to be negative. The offer pulled him out of his self-imposed depression. He'd talk with Seychelle about both of them.

He allowed his thoughts to drift. The last time Tristan visited him was before he met Jon. They spent most of their time in Berkeley, a city east of Los Angeles. Tristan loved the shopping, the Arts District and the sites in the Visitors Bureau. He remembered her laughter and smiles as they stopped to eat while touring the section "South Africa." They dared not make a comparison with the Africa they knew and loved. The pictures showed their happiness. Aiden hoped it was the beginning of a lasting love. He would have another chance. He wouldn't waste it. It was time for him to do as his sisters had done. Find love and share his passion.

Seychelle's dream ignited his passion. She had no idea the depth of his depression. Tristan knew when he called he had been revived. She listened as he told her the details of Seychelle's business and the role he accepted. Now he could tell her how his sister's dream would be the catalyst for his passion. He hoped she would see him in a new light.

He passed the time reading and surfing the web. As the hour got closer to their check-in time, he wondered what happened to Seychelle. While dialing her number his worry was dismissed when he heard her voice.

"Don't you call me," she teased. "Father has checked on me twice, Sasha about three times, and never mind Vance and Jon."

"Come, let's check in." His response was dry dismissing the humor she wanted to share in her greeting.

"What's wrong my brother? You haven't spent your time dwelling on our father, have you?"

"No, I was worried about you. Maybe too much."

"I had a time checking out. I should have done it earlier. Are you excited about our visit?"

Seychelle was overexcited. Clayton confirmed the renovation phase was going well. They would be able to open earlier than expected.

Seychelle was sure Aiden was aware of the progress. She never understood his reactions. They seemed always to have been the opposite of hers. She'd ignore his mood until he was ready to talk.

"Did Clayton tell you I've accepted the Group's offer?"

"He did, but I'd love to hear your point of view. Will you be working with other clientele?"

The conversation was interrupted by the announcement of boarding. Aiden didn't hesitate to gather his reading material and Seychelle's carry on. He was more than prepared to dismiss the questions he would only have to answer again once they settled in at home.

Seychelle didn't bother to pick up the conversation once they were seated. She expected her brother to be uneasy, but he looked as though he had a panic attack.

"Aiden, how's Tristan? Sasha mentioned the two of you in the same sentence. Are you doing the long distance thing?"

"What does that mean? Are you doing the long distance thing?"

"I wasn't prying, and no I'm still doing the friendship thing. You should ask Sasha about the long distance thing. I wanted to know your opinion; I know what Sasha's is."

She opened her I-Pad. He gave no response. An indication the conversation was over. There was silence between them for more than two hours of the twenty-hour flight. Aiden broke the silence after dinner.

"Tristan and I have been doing the so-called distance thing. I'm going to ask her to come to California with me. I want to marry her."

"Marry her?" Seychelle hoped it didn't sound as condescending to Aiden as it did to her. "I didn't know the two of you kept that passion lit. So the distance didn't cause issues?"

Aiden took a deep breath. "I hope Mother doesn't have the same reaction. I know what Father will say."

"What will Tristan say? That's what really matters."

"We've discussed it before. She was giving me time to be a better me. At least that's what she said. Seychelle we speak often, and the feelings are the same. She's gone through this hell with me. She's been more than a friend, and I've always loved her. I want to live with her and for her."

"What about living for you? You can't live for someone else and lose yourself in that love. What happens if her feelings are different or if you lose her love? What happens to Aiden is important."

"You sound like her. She's told me that time and time again. So you see, between her, Jon, you and Clayton, I'm better than I was. I found there is a reason embedded in this downfall. I've learned about love on many levels. Family, friends and a woman who I want to be with the rest of my life."

"So you're marrying her and living in California? Does she know about your dreams? Don't bring her to California only to find she doesn't understand your dreams."

"My life is on the mend. I know what you're thinking. I've had those thoughts over the years. Tristan has been there for me. I want to spend the rest of my life loving her. Seychelle, you don't know how you've changed my thoughts about living and loving."

"You're right. I didn't understand what happened to you or how you allowed people to take advantage of you. Aiden, that's what Father will ask. I'm not prying but have you lost all of the money you were given?"

"I have a little of it. Jon refused to let me take it out of the bank. I put it in a different account, and yes, I still have it. But Seychelle, it's nowhere near what I have lost or thrown away. Right before you and Sasha came to California, Tristan and I talked about the job I had. She was upset when I told her I wanted to quit again. Then I met Jon; things changed rapidly. I didn't realize God was preparing me. I thought He had forgotten me."

"Aiden?"

Aiden told it all to her. He told her that over the years Tristan had been his salvation. He prayed for better days. He met Jon and was able to kick habits that filled empty time and covered errors. It seemed as though his life had changed. He explained his depression and his fears. Jon and Tristan helped him through it all. He was rebuilding himself when she and Sasha visited. He had just stopped drinking and popping pills for his anxiety attacks. It wasn't until they landed the Westlake bid that he realized he was a part of something bigger.

"But I was reminded that the "something bigger" was your dream. I feared that I lost my chance at dreaming."

"Aiden."

Aiden put his index finger in the air and waited for his sister to take a deep sigh.

"Wait, let me finish. Depression had been my out for years. I stopped thinking I was living out my dreams. I was living, and some days I didn't want to finish the twenty-four hours God gave me. Tristan was my go to, she listened and dissected each hour I thought I suffered through. Jon filled in my void. He bought my groceries, helped me keep a place to live and a car. When you called and said you were coming, I had to step out of it. The problem was I didn't know what "it" was. I was rebounding from drinking myself until I fell out most days. I had given up on me. Suddenly I needed to be Aiden, the Aiden that you and Sasha expected. The brother and son that Mother and Father prayed I still was."

"I had no idea. I'm sorry you went through this alone. I didn't know. Father nor Mother said you didn't sound yourself or...."

"Or what? You did what I needed. Your offer to be a part of your dream sparked my vision. Then Clayton's offer let me know I was still able to dream. Seychelle, I was wrong to think that you couldn't handle the position you needed to fill. I was willing to step in for you. I hadn't stepped in for me."

"Aiden I didn't want you to step in for me. I didn't expect you to. You put that pressure on yourself."

"I understand that now. But at that moment, those few weeks, I thought I was about to drown. Clayton threw the life preserver that was tied to your rope. I didn't hear you when you said you didn't need me to handle the business. I didn't think you understood what you bought into. I'm ready Seychelle. God prepared me, and I'm ready. I've got so many aspirations to be fulfilled, with me being a part of The Whelan Group. Serenity Resorts & Spa will be my first client. The papers will be drawn up that way. Clayton will be as you wish, the liaison. That way there will be no conflicts between us. Also, anyone seeking vengeance won't be able to come through me."

"I don't know, that Minnows chick seems to be sniffing around for something."

"We'll deal with it when we return. I'm looking forward to this mini-vacation. Family, friends and my rebirth; it all matters."

"I'm happy for you Aiden. You're right it all matters, but of it all, you matter. Well, I might as well tell you now. Vance invited me to come to California in October. There's an auction for property, resorts I expect. Clayton said we'd be in a good position if we want to buy the next property."

"Really? This soon? Okay, well if Ms. Minnows peeps her head into this sale, we'll be ready."

"Between now and then I hope we can find out what she's trying to find."

During the balance of the flight as the hum of the engines became a soothing sound most passengers found a way to pass the hours reading and watching movies. Seychelle allowed herself to visit her past. The years after her brother left their home was problematic for her and Sasha. Questions from friends and insults from neighbors were brushed off. It was as though Aiden hadn't been raised by the same parents. There were those who would ask if Aiden had found peace. She couldn't believe she had missed the effect of her brother's turmoil. She had thought his leaving home was the great escape. He didn't have to deal with their mother's tears or the hardened response their father prepared when asked about his only son. They all went through a period in their lives when they weren't sure who would survive. She didn't know why she hadn't called more often. She didn't know why she thought he would be okay.

She had questions for her parents and her sister. The first was why they hadn't discussed the gap his move left. An obvious question that should have filled the emptiness they all felt after Aiden's move.

Aiden had found comfort in his seat, and his snoring confirmed if only for a moment, he was at ease. Seychelle smiled as sleep had become contagious. There were still a few hours before they would be landing on the island.

Chapter 43

Tristan couldn't contain her joy as she hurried herself through her morning rituals. Her mother watched as she packed her overnight bag with what appeared to be clothing for more than a week.

"You are leaving for the week, eh?"

"No Mama, I am to return on Monday. I have to be at work on Monday. I wish I could take time off."

"You will miss your pay if you take off the time. You need to be mindful. There are many who have not had a second chance at a job they once lost."

Tristan's mother spoke from her bedroom. Marietta reminded her of the two weeks she spent in California visiting Aiden without enough time to cover her pay. The missed days were documented as "no call, no show" a cause for termination. Tristan never told anyone other than her boss her reason for not returning. Mr. Funaye not only gave her the job back but knowing the Tudjals and the problems Aiden left the island with, he commended her. Aiden recommended her for the position of health aide and Mr. Funaye the director of the clinic appreciated her knowledge and compassion. After successfully passing her studies as a Medical Assistant. She chose to take the challenge to develop a program that would provide aftercare to new mothers and their children. It fit her perfectly. Since having the job for more than five years, she was promoted twice.

Marietta concluded mumbling, "You know you shouldn't take your job for granted."

"Mama that was years ago, not last week. I don't have that position any longer, nor do I work for the same boss. I keep telling you I am my own boss and I manage my own counselors and health aides. Do you remember me telling you that?"

Tristan peeked into her mother's bedroom, as she expected her mother was still mumbling to herself.

"You know I didn't forget. I think you forgot. You've had a time getting where you are. Are you so willing to risk it all for someone who may not understand what you've sacrificed?"

"What makes you think he wouldn't understand?"

"Tristan, let's sit a minute. I know you have to go, but give me a minute."

The two women walked to the kitchen and sat where they often enjoyed the morning sun. Tristan took the time before her packing to prepare breakfast and tea so they could eat together.

"You must be leaving for more than a weekend. This is a signal here." Her mother teased smiling at her plate. "Maybe I ought to get sick more often."

"Mama, please. You weren't sick. If you were, you'd still be in your bed. You left your job and came home early thinking I was leaving yesterday."

"Okay, but I did want to tell you something. It's been an afterthought for me since your father passed. The men here are driven by the traditions we followed raising you. Your father, had he lived would have wanted you to wait for a man who followed those traditions. This new way of living your generation has will cost you and your family. When you lose the traditions, you were raised by you lose family value. We instilled our way of life in you because your father and I wanted to see it be passed on to our grandchildren."

"What traditions Mama? I've lived here with you all my life. We've got through the past ten years without any man, without my father, without mentioning this tradition. You work, I work we support each other. If you're scared of me leaving you, I never would. I want you to feel good with me and for me. Aiden and I have loved each other since childhood. Father knew that. We talked about love and its splendor. We talked about love and its storms. We talked about love and its confusion. Mama we never talked about love being distant or denied. Funny we didn't talk about love being a part of a tradition."

"I'm not talking about our love or our relationship," Marietta replied sternly.

"Nor am I. It was not my intention to mention the love I saw between the two of you. Mama, I don't know when the two of you began the business of love, but Papa didn't speak of possibilities. He spoke of what he knew was true love. I remember when I knew you and he had what I wanted. Aiden and I started our love with that tradition. His parents and my parents, we knew loved each other, and we wanted that. Mama, Papa, lost his willingness to live when tradition told him he wasn't the man he had been. The tradition stole his life, his love, and his happiness. I love Aiden, through it all. I want him to know it. I don't want to have to pray about it or whisper it at night before I go to bed. I want him to hear me say it. I don't want to pray for forgiveness when he's gone."

Marietta listened as the tears fell from her eyes. She and Joslee married young. They grew up together as they continued to live on the islands. Joslee Paigon was Marietta's first love, and it was two years after their marriage that her older husband revealed he had been unfaithful. Marietta tried to erase the truth, trust their love, stand by what she thought was her forgiveness and accept his attentiveness over the years, but it wasn't the same. The island traditions kept the couple together. Neither denied the other, and the birth of their only child seemed to bring them joy. Tristan was a daddy's girl; she always had been until the day he died.

Joslee developed a respiratory infection. The doctor's treated him but pneumonia set in. He passed away in his sleep after battling with his sickness for months. Marietta and Tristan remained in the home. Marietta couldn't let go. She hadn't let go in all the years of their marriage, and she needed him to know it, she needed God to know it. Maybe she needed to be given permission, but she wouldn't let go. Hearing her daughter speak reminded her that she loved Joslee through it all. What had tradition done for her?

Marietta rose from the table without a word. She nibbled on her food not tasting anything other than the salt from the tears that still fell from her now swollen eyes. Tristan left without saying goodbye.

Marietta stepped out on the wooden porch. The water was calm, and a walk along the shore would settle her spirit. She prayed for peace to be with her daughter during her travel although she would only be an island away. She prayed Tristan wouldn't regret loving Aiden Tudjal.

Chapter 44

Tristan met Sasha at the airport. She decided to drive her car after the emotional outburst with her mother. The need to leave her home became urgent and with an hour to spare she hoped the drive would bring her comfort. She prayed her facial expressions wouldn't prompt questions. She hadn't been close to Sasha after her last visit with Aiden. Tristan wanted to avoid any questions and the temptation to expose Aiden's secrets.

Most families on the islands extended their condolences after the death of her father but distanced themselves weeks later. Sasha invited Tristan on day trips, shopping sprees, and mini vacations. The ladies enjoyed their time together, but Tristan's loyalty was to Aiden. Sasha teased Tristan often saying she was under a love spell.

The parking at the airport was more than frustrating. She drove her car following the parking signs. She found a space on the fourth level of the garage. *"Who parks this high up for an arriving flight?"* She closed her door and laughed to herself as she saw her friend walking her way. Sasha threw her hands in the air, a sign of her struggle with parking as well. Sasha's smile erased Tristan's frustration and nervousness. She immediately returned a loving grin. The two hugged as though they hadn't seen each other in more than a year.

"Let me look at you. You've changed your hair." Sasha turned Tristan around admiring her auburn colored locs. "How did you get your soft hair to loc? It's beautiful, Tristan!"

Tristan always complained that her hair texture, neither straight, curly nor kinked, could not be managed. She had cut it, added weave and color often without satisfaction.

"Other than the color, it's the same old mess. Thanks, I twisted it up and tried something else. Well, this is it. Thanks for noticing. How are you, my friend?"

The island sun was sitting high, and both ladies responded by putting on their sunglasses. They shared the news and gossip as they walked through the crowded airport.

"Wow, so Seychelle is finally launching her business. I remember her saying she wanted to travel and visit resorts. Did you think she'd own one?"

"No, but Tristan it's an exciting job to go from place to place and enjoy the amenities. We'd take it all in and then write a review packet. Seychelle handled all the business contacts. I handled myself as a guest. You know, watching the staff, what the décor was in each area sparked my interest. Girl, I noticed things I would never pay attention to. Tristan, I made comparisons to the excursions offered and the sites that surrounded each place, all while having a great time. Before I could take it all in, we'd be flying off to the next resort. I love teaching, but I love traveling more. It's a new lifestyle for me."

"So you're giving up teaching?" Tristan couldn't imagine living a permanent vacation. "What about your home? Where would that be?"

"I don't know. I don't think we'll have to travel like we did now that she's purchased her own resort."

"Really! She bought her own? How exciting! Where?"

Sasha looked around as though others waiting for the plane's arrival were overhearing their conversation. She moved closer to speak softer.

"In Las Vegas. It has four locations. Serenity Resorts & Spa." Sasha couldn't contain herself. She hadn't told anyone how happy she was. "It's being renovated to the specs we submitted. Each location has the same theme. They have suites, salons, gyms and an area for special occasions. I thought of that area. You know anniversaries, retirements and weddings; things of that nature, a room for live music and a DJ."

"I'm so happy for her. She'll be home for how long?"

"She'll be here for a few months. We'll go back together for the grand opening. Aiden will go back sooner."

"Yes, that's the other reason I drove my car. I've made reservations for the two of us at the bed and breakfast on the east side."

"Tristan, you could have stayed with us."

Tristan gave her friend a side-eyed smirk. They both laughed causing the lady sitting across from them to look up from her book.

"Girl, I didn't even tell him I booked the room. I hope he doesn't get upset, but it's been a while since we, well you know. Sasha, I missed him so much. Anyway, it's a necessary booking.

I only have the weekends so we'll have a private spot, away from your parents."

"Tristan, he'll be here longer than the weekend."

"It's me girl. I've got to work. Can't take off a day. An arrangement I can't mess up if I want my job. So the weekend is ours. The other days I'm not sure how we'll meet up. I don't want this to be a problem for us or my job. I want him to enjoy his time at home with family too."

"Yes, I'm hoping this is not a time bomb for disaster. My parents don't know about the business or what Aiden's part in it all is."

"Aiden? They bought the resort together?"

"No, no Aiden is working with Seychelle just like me. For now, there are no financial shares. He's managing the investors, and I guess he'll be managing the operations of the business behind closed doors."

"He didn't tell me." Tristan could only wonder why he hadn't mentioned he had finally spoken to his sisters. She felt relieved. Now that they knew he was suffering from depression and alcoholism, there would be no need for secrecy.

Chapter 45

"Cole, do you think we have enough fish?" Naomi paused to count the expected guests again mentally. "Well, if not we'll just have to make more chicken curry. I have the Coconut Curries and the Cassava Pudding here. Cole, please tell me you remembered the rice platters."

"Yes, my dear, they are there on the table. There will be more than enough I'm sure." Her husband yelled from the veranda. As he dressed the tables with lanterns, he could only smile at the thought of the surprise they planned for Aiden. The decision to have a small gathering of a few family members and friends seemed to have changed to an island celebration. There would be a steel drum band and dancers, a DJ and plenty of food. Friends of Aiden's volunteered to help Cole with setting up a stage. A dance floor and chairs had been provided and set an atmosphere for entertainment.

Naomi had been cooking for two days preparing salads, and fruit platters. The fish would be grilled, and chicken would be barbequed with creole spices. The Mahé Island was known for its nightlife, but nothing would compare to the celebration planned for Cole Tudjal's son. There would be plenty of Seybrew and Takamaka Rum, Aiden's favorites.

166

Once the news of his visit spread, Naomi had been counting guests. Each was told the party was just a small gathering but Aiden's parents were prepared for more than fifty guests to celebrate his arrival. Tudjal Import and Exports closed early on Friday an extension of Cole's gratitude for the help he and Naomi received to prepare for the occasion.

Sasha was told to take Aiden and Seychelle to their parent's home and wait there until she received a call from them. She would simply explain their parents wouldn't be home until late but asked them to wait until they returned. Sasha thought their plan was simple enough. The party would be at Sasha and Seychelle's home awaiting their arrival. A second call would be the signal; all was ready.

"Naomi, we have to move all of the food to the veranda. I'll help you clean the kitchen. It will be obvious something is wrong if we leave a mess."

"Sasha's kitchen is a mess. That would be normal." Naomi laughed as she entered the kitchen and a sigh quickly followed. She glanced at the clock mounted on the wall. There was time; it was early. Their flight would be landing in three hours. Sasha would detain them she hoped for another hour. She would stop to pick up Tristan, and that would delay them for sure. A few of the women from the village would join her to help serve. As she stood to put things in order mentally she had to admit, Cole was right. Neither Sasha nor Seychelle would leave their kitchen in such a condition.

Pots and pans were on the counters joined by mixing bowls and utensils. Naomi couldn't remember her daughter's counters ever being full. The island, centered in the middle of the floor, held the desserts. The refrigerator held those that needed to be chilled. There were completed dishes in serving trays waiting to be placed on the veranda. She decided to start in the dining area where the mess seemed to be the less.

"Knock, Knock, hello?" The melodic voice brought Naomi into the living room. The small frame, cinnamon brown toned woman entered the home smiling. Her friendly glow brought another level of warmth to the room. Her resemblance to her brother was notable but nothing compared to her spirit.

"Who is that woman entering?" Naomi teased.

The response caused the women to chuckle as they hugged. Lorian Tudjal, Cole's sister, was always the first to arrive and the last to leave at all family events. Naomi was sure the other women would be arriving shortly.

Cole waited until the last truck was unloaded and the chairs were in place before he approached the man who stood at the edge of the beach. The hypnotic water held an onlooker locked in thought. Cole was sure that was why the man stood watching the waves without turning to recognize Cole's presence.

Years passed between them: time they would never regain, time they would never forget. The two were raised together on Seychelles Islands. As boys they were inseparable. They were in business together, attended their wedding ceremonies, and were present at the births of their children. However, Aiden's mishap affected Marlon Harvier. His nephew was paralyzed, and his best friend's son caused the injury.

Marlon's family didn't understand why he would defend the Tudjals. Peace between the families was needed. He kept his distance hoping Cole would understand his reasons. He learned of Aiden's visit and prayed each day his family would understand his reasons, his need to attend.

He missed his companion. Marlon refused to take sides. He decided Aiden's visit marked a time for all to rekindle. Their business, long before Cole started one of the largest import and exports business, was fishing. Marlon had problems, but Cole saw him through. He couldn't keep the business. He settled, now working on the docks as a fisherman. He had women and drugs, and Cole stayed true to their friendship. He lost it all after the fight between Ibn and Aiden.

The transition was a process. Marlon returned to the docks, returned to what he loved. He bought a fish market and was doing well. His wife was still a part of his life and he no longer used drugs or sought after other women.

"Good evening sir," Cole spoke as he placed his arm around Marlon's shoulder. Marlon turned with tears in his eyes. They embraced in silence. "Where have you been my friend?" Cole whispered his question in Marlon's ear.

"Lost, my friend. Today, I decided to find my way. How have you been?" Marlon turned to the water while waiting for the answer.

"Empty but, I prayed. God answered, and you are here. I thank you for coming. Please say you will stay for the festivities this evening."

"Thank you, yes I will." Silence fell between them again.

"Marlon, why didn't you come when I called?"

"Cole, it wasn't you. You and I have had our battles and moved on. Ibn is my sister's child. I didn't have the strength to battle with my family. Our friendship would have been forever lost. It's better this way."

"And after tonight? What would you say to them? They will find out you are here.

"Ibn has moved on. He and my sister have been gone for more than a year. I battled with the past and what you would say. I know how I felt and could only imagine your feelings. I bring my apology, and I would understand if it wasn't accepted."

A hush fell between them. Voices could be heard coming from the house. The guests were entering. Their greetings and laughter broke the silence between the men. Without another word, the two turned toward the house. Cole put his arm around the shoulder of his friend. Marlon, though nervous, understood his friend's acceptance. There was peace between them.

Chapter 46

People were filing onto the veranda. Naomi was greeting each of them with the directions to be followed just before Aiden's entrance. Hugs, handshakes and nods were exchanged between the groups as the guests increased in number. Cole nodded to his wife whose reply was a smile. Now he understood why Naomi questioned the amount of food. He took his place at the grill knowing the extra fish would soon be gone. The chicken's aroma had begun to permeate the air.

"Do you need help my friend?" Arie, the dock manager offered his assistance. The two men worked in unison placing the chicken on platters and replacing it with the next meat to be grilled. The women helped Lorian and Naomi bring out the prepared salads. Lorian closed the veranda doors and faced the guest.

"Naomi is calling Sasha. She asked that we be reminded this is a surprise so keep the talking to a whisper. She and Cole are really excited about giving Aiden a warm welcome home."

Cole handed his apron to Arie, who shook his head no causing a few men to laugh. Marlon took the apron from Cole and shook Arie's hand. The laughter turned into whispers.

"It is all good my friends and family. There is no ill will here and I pray this is what has been needed over the years, forgiveness. Please enjoy yourselves, this night is dedicated to uniting our families and rekindling friendships."

Cole's comment was followed by soft claps and hushed laughter as Naomi waved her hand at the veranda doors. A signal that Sasha, Aiden, Seychelle and Tristan had arrived.

Cole and Naomi stood waiting at the front door. A greeting with kisses and hugs was the prelude to Lorian screaming.

"Oh, holy God the Father. Look at you my Aiden. You look great my boy. I am so glad you are home. Seychelle, how was your visit to the big city?'

"Auntie, how are you?" Aiden picked up his five-foot tall aunt. Lifting her off her feet caused her to laugh. Her laughter was infectious, everyone joined her.

"Here take the bags Cole. We are sorry we didn't make it back to the house. We decided to cook a little here for all of us. Seychelle, I hope you don't mind."

"Uh, no. I can't wait to eat whatever it is I am smelling. Father, put those bags down. We can move them later. What have you cooked? It smells delicious."

Sasha grabbed Tristan and Seychelle allowing Aiden to be the first to open the veranda doors.

"It's a surprise for Aiden."

The ladies stood with Naomi, Cole and Lorian. As the doors parted, the guests anxiously waiting outside yelled, "Surprise"

The band played an upbeat island melody. The party started as Aiden walked through the crowd getting reacquainted with family and friends he hadn't seen for years. Seychelle, Sasha and Tristan followed his steps. Greeting the well-wishers was easy until Aiden stopped suddenly causing everyone around him to notice the apprehension between the two men.

"Aiden, welcome home. You've been missed. I missed you." Marlon's smile eased Aiden's approach. Aiden appreciated the man he grew up calling uncle.

"Oncle, avez-vous été?" Aiden asked in their native tongue

The two stepped into each other's arms. It was a sight that brought tears to Cole's eyes. His son, his best friend together as it should have been years before.

"Alright, let's begin to feast." Arie shouted from the grill. The steel drums brought many to the dance floor. Cole and Naomi stood by overjoyed that their dream of Aiden's return had come true. The food, the guest and the weather was perfect.

Aiden continued to greet the guest. The questions, comments and simple greetings was all he needed to shake the nervous feeling he had. He couldn't imagine his parents pulling together such a gathering without Seychelle or Sasha's help.

Tristan met him standing near the veranda entrance. He seemed as though he was separating himself from the others.

"Did you play a part in this grandiose welcome?"

"No, I only spoke with Sasha last night. I think they had been planning it since finding out you were coming home."

"So you knew and kept it a secret?"

"Aiden, does it really matter who planned this? I think it's nice. They now know you are well and it's a celebration welcoming you where you should have never left."

"Oh, I don't know. I may have left eventually, over time. I've seen and learned so much since leaving. Things I needed to know to be a man. I've been challenged and today I feel it was all worth it. I thought I didn't deserve the failures or the triumphs, but today I know I needed it to continue on with my life. I resented being born here on this secluded island. Living in America, I learned to appreciate what we have here. I've learned to be balanced in my life. The stability is what sustains quality living. I don't have to be rich in my pockets to fulfill my dreams."

The conversation was cut short when Sasha grabbed her brother's hand, leading him to the dance floor.

"No, no Sissy." Aiden tried to resist. The crowd stood surrounding the floor. "Oh no, Sasha please." Her brother begged. Sasha pulled until Aiden reluctantly gave in allowing her to maneuver him to the center of the dance floor.

The DJ handed the mic to Cole. He stood silent for a moment waiting for everyone's attention.

"As you all know we did this for Aiden. I want to thank you for helping us pull this small gathering together."

Laughter and whispers filled the air as each guest knew the gathering was larger than any of them expected.

"Now, now I know it was Naomi's fault." He waited again for the laughter and comments to cease. "We are grateful to have family and friends who can drop their plans and replace them with our plans. Most of you who are my children's ages would be at the Riverbank. Some of you I haven't seen in years. I just want you to know this night is special for my family and me."

The Tudjals stood together with Cole as he spoke. He invited Marlon and Lorian to stand with them. There were tears of joy as he expressed his love for his sister and the man that would remain his brother. It was obvious Cole couldn't continue to speak without his emotions taking over. Naomi stepped in for her husband.

"I know everyone is wondering where Aiden has been and what he has accomplished that would keep him away so long."

Aiden began to cringe. Just as he thought, his parents wanted him to tell of his accomplishments. He felt like he was at his first AA meeting. He could feel pressure surrounding him. From Seychelle's questionable grin to his father's proud stance, Aiden didn't get the nudge of confidence. Sasha squeezed his hand as he reached to receive the microphone from his mother.

"Uh, I don't know what one says when their parents put them on the spot. Thank you all for this. I left before saying farewell to most of you. Yet I return to see you weren't too mad to welcome me home."

He paused hoping that was all he was expected to say. His parents were looking into the audience, smiling and waiting just as the guest were, for him to continue.

"It is different in America, especially when you are the stranger. I went there with high expectations and dreams. Although I was not prepared for many of the encounters, I was blessed. I am blessed to be here. There were days and nights that I wanted to come home. I'll be here for a week or two and then I must return."

Aiden attempted to pass the microphone to his father. Cole ignored the gesture with a hearty response.

"My son has taken on a great business opportunity in America. It has to be. After all he could have come home and worked with me." Cole ignited laughter from his workers who stood gazing at the Tudjal family. Aiden wanted everyone to understand.

"The business is not solely mine. It is a great opportunity and the prospects will bring me financial stability. I work with The Whelan Group in California. We invest and buy property all over the world.

173

Some of the property we buy is for our clients, while other property is developed and sold. We also invest in properties such as the property my sister has acquired to start her business, Serenity Resorts and Spa."

There was an uncomfortable hush that surrounded the dance floor. Aiden refrained from continuing what he thought everyone wanted to hear. His family, as shocked as some of the guest, were stunned. They all had questions with the exception of Seychelle. She understood clearly. When one is pushed into a corner they bite back. Aiden had taken his bite. He bit anyone who put him on the spot in the middle of the dance floor. The problem was he bit Seychelle. She snatched the microphone causing the whispers to elevate to audible shouts of "no".

"I hope you all understand what my brother is saying. You look shocked. We, the Tudjal children, have used what our father has instilled in us and made a few decisions of our own. My brother has landed a remarkable position with The Whelan Group, while I have purchased a resort in Las Vegas. What The Whelan Group does for others it didn't have to do for me or us. Father gave us each a dowry upon our graduation seeing that we would not have a pre-arranged marriage. It was my choice to save money years after my graduation and I purchased the resort without any investors. Aiden is my liaison and confidant. He is with The Whelan Group to grow as an investor so Serenity Resorts will put its mark on resort from America to right here on Seychelles Islands."

There was applause from the audience. Seychelle looked to her parents hoping their response would be more than the smirks they held.

"Aiden, Sasha and I have made a remarkable step into the resort business and we have decided that this will benefit our family and the island."

Seychelle paused again while the guests applauded their success. When she noticed her words had not brought a visual sign of joy from her parents, she handed her father the microphone. Aiden signaled the band and the music gave them a reason to exit the middle of the floor.

Chapter 47

“And this should have been discussed before we were embarrassed in front of guests, don't you think?”

Cole was pacing back and forth in the house away from the rest of the family. Aiden sat listening, for more than thirty minutes, to his father's rant. He stopped trying to explain he was the one that was embarrassed.

“Father what are you so upset about? I have a job, a secure job and I'm a part of Seychelle's business. Something you would have suggested if I had called to talk to you about it. I have a chance to recoup the money I lost over the years and build a business we can pass on to our children.”

Cole wanted to explode. “What do you think Tudjal Imports is? The business I've lived my life building; the business that is to be the family business to pass on. Son, this was the plan since your birth.”

“Father that business can still be a family business. Just not with us working there. We can hire people to manage and work that dock.” Aiden knew within the sudden silence his father would find the words to belittle him and his achievements.

“Aiden, can I trust your business judgment. How much of your money and yourself have you lost in America? So much that your sisters leave here to bail you out? How much of their money will it take my son? You, Mr. Businessman? How will you repay them, no, no will you repay them? Aiden you were not shown this way of living. You are the man and they own a business with you handling it. I do not understand what you have agreed to do for your sister. How will you give her anything once it is all lost? Has Seychelle lost her mind to the American way as well?"

"Enough of this talk. Cole, allow him to visit with these guests. No answers will be heard this evening. Aiden take another tray of rice from the counter out. It is warm enough for serving. Also the Tiki Lights must be lit." Naomi had heard enough. Naomi held Cole's hand stopping him from following his son into the kitchen.

"Cole, now is not the time. Let us enjoy our guests and family."

"Why do they think I've worked so hard? Seychelle did this Naomi. This is her effort to spite me. Why would she lead her brother on? She can't have a business that will bring more profit than imports."

"Let us wait to talk with them. Not tonight my dear, please. We will talk about it over the next few days. Not now."

Naomi leaned in and kissed her husband on his cheek. She wiped the lipstick stain from his face and smiled. He rolled his eyes as he reluctantly gave in. The couple paused at the kitchen counter watching the guest from the window.

"Naomi, is it me? As a father have I failed to provide for them? Why would they feel the need to build their own when I have built this foundation for them?"

"You have given them a foundation. It is that foundation that has kept them stable, but a foundation is meant to be built on. They are building their own."

His wife made a point but he would never admit it. He walked onto the veranda hoping he hadn't caused anyone discomfort. The music kept the atmosphere lively. No one seemed disturbed that Cole and Aiden were missing for close to an hour. Aiden, following his mother's instructions was lighting the Tiki Lights.

Sasha noticed the discord her father was trying to disguise. He stood on the veranda gazing at the guests. She wondered what had caused his mood to change. As she walked through the seated guest searching for Aiden or Seychelle she found them together in what seemed to be hushed conversation with Tristan.

"What's going on?" Cutting their conversation short Sasha knew there was a problem. "Is everyone ok?"

"Father is not okay. He asked about our reason for wanting another business. I just sat there not knowing what to say. Anything I could tell him wouldn't satisfy him. I was just telling them what happened."

Sasha looked back at the veranda where Cole was standing. He hadn't moved. "Well now he knows. He's been asking, what you were doing, were you stable, who is Jon and what is he to you? So many questions that I didn't want to answer without you and Seychelle being here. Good, he knows."

"Well I guess he'll be overjoyed when he finds out you're dating Jon." Seychelle's comment eased the tension.

"He'll definitely blame me for that." They couldn't help but laugh with Aiden as he added mockingly. "You set the two of them up without thinking about family tradition. I wonder what tradition that violates."

"I heard Father was saving Sasha for a rich candidate." Seychelle laughed harder. "The problem is he hasn't been born yet."

"Funny, funny. You'll be married off first. So you wait on the rich kid's birth. Tell Vance he's number two." Sasha waited for her sister's comeback.

Seychelle's cell phone rang. She stepped away from the group and the stage area so she could hear.

"Hey, just called to set up a time to talk tomorrow." Clayton waited for her response.

"After lunch. Has something come up?"

"Just paperwork. The construction is almost done. All repairs will be completed by the end of the month. Everything should be done by mid-November."

"Okay well let's talk about two tomorrow. I should be up by then." Seychelle hung up the phone after the time was confirmed. The sun was setting and the orange glow set a beautiful hue on the calm water. Seychelle found Sasha who was clearing tables and humming to the music played by the DJ.

"Aiden and Tristan slipping off?"

"No as strange as that seems. If I were Aiden that would be my next move. They went to walk the beach. I think this party was a bit much for him."

"I think it was being put on the spot."

"Father insisted. I wonder if Aiden would have told him. I mean maybe tomorrow, certainly before he went back to California. I was thinking he would have left that up to us knowing that Father wanted him to speak up."

"Father wanted him to be proud and brag a little. He didn't expect to hear what Aiden so boldly announced. His reaction was to pull Aiden inside and scold him. Sasha we're next."

Sasha knew they would be questioned. Again she was praying for an understanding. She was glad Seychelle was home.

Chapter 48

It took less time to clean than it had to plan and arrange the gathering. The women worked together making sure the extra food wouldn't be wasted. It was wrapped on plates and given to the remaining guests as they said their goodbyes. After putting what was left into the refrigerator, they worked to clean the dishes and the kitchen. The men remained outdoors clearing the veranda and beach area. It served its purpose, all would agree as they dismantled the stage and the dance floor. Leaving the equipment to be loaded they sat drinking one the last beer. The truck would be arriving shortly. The scheduled time to pick up the equipment was midnight. The Tiki lights remained lit as they waited to be of assistance.

There was no more talk about Aiden's work or questions about his stay on the island. Aiden sat with his father and Marlon. Marlon passed a beer to Cole and Aiden declined the offer.

"How long have you lived in California?" Marlon's question broke the silence among them.

"I've been there since I left the island. My forethought was to live closer to the Mexican border. After seeing the bay area in Santa Monica I thought about living there but I settled for the South Bay area in Los Angeles. There's really no difference."

Aiden hadn't expressed his regret for not moving when he had the finances. He hoped his father didn't remember their conversations and his complaints regarding his frequent address changes.

"So will you move now that you have this position and business with your sisters?"

The question stung. Aiden took a deep breath before giving an answer.

"Father, my choice not to live on the bay..." He was stumped when Cole finished his sentence.

"I'm sure it had nothing to do with the money you lost taking risks or gambling, or drinking yourself to sleep most nights. Tell us the truth Aiden. Please, I can't get past you losing your all and thinking you won't make the same mistakes with your sister's money."

"I won't be handling her money. Mother was right, we need to have this discussion later. Goodnight Mr. Harvier I hope to see you again before I leave next week. Thank you Father for this gathering, it will be a lasting memory. Everything was almost perfect."

Aiden shook Marlon's hand and turned to shake his father's hand. Cole stood hesitating before he rendered his hand. Aiden shook his father's hand and then hugged him. Cole was taken aback as he hugged his son. It was a gesture that hadn't been done since Aiden's sophomore year in college. He tried to fight back the tears as his son walked away.

Aiden found his sisters, mother and Tristan sitting at the kitchen table. The change from the tense atmosphere to the gaiety that circled the room eased Aiden's entrance. He didn't know what he was going to say when he entered the room. There was no need to speak so he simply smiled.

"Sit a moment son. Your sisters were telling Tristan and me about California. You never told me about these places they visited. I should leave with you. It sounds so beautiful."

"Mother I would love for you to visit but believe me the beauty is on the islands."

"Well I would love to stay and chat with you guys, but I need to get some of that breeze that's coming across the waters. Tristan would you join me. We'll be back shortly."

Naomi waited until the couple became a silhouette walking along the shoreline. The darkened sky became the backdrop of a romantic scene. The sparkling stars shined like diamonds. Naomi hoped her prayers were answered. Aiden needed a strong woman that would love him as much as he loved her. Aiden often spoke of marriage and Tristan. As the tears dropped from her eyes she whispered "thank you" before turning to face her daughters.

"So my dears we will talk with your father tomorrow. We will leave you to settling for the night. Tell your brother I look to see him at my breakfast table with the two of you"

Sasha nor Seychelle objected. The discussion over breakfast would give them a chance to explain Serenity Resorts and Spa.

Tristan took off her sandals so they wouldn't get wet. She was quiet, waiting for Aiden to let go of his annoyed spirit. There was a gentle breeze that could be felt as they walked close to the dampened sand. He held her hand and she wondered if he understood that he also held her heart. She wanted to step in for him, defend his point of view, and speak the words that would silence the anger.

She learned over the years not to push until he was ready to talk. There was so much to say, and so many questions she wanted to ask. Aiden slowed the pace of their walk and then he suddenly stopped. He turned to face her.

Tristan had always been beautiful to him. When asked to describe her he would simply say "beautiful". She was not one to wear a lot of make-up and her complexion was lighter than most of the women on the island. Her eyes were light brown. At first sight one would think she had contacts. Standing there, speechless he allowed the calm that surrounded them to speak for him. She smiled sensing his feelings.

"I love you too." She closed her eyes waiting for his lips to touch hers. The kiss was gentle, but filled with passion. He took her face into her hands and kissed her letting go of the barrier he held since his arrival.

"I missed you," he whispered. "I want us to be together Tristan. I can't leave without you."

Tristan heard him as he repeated the words she had longed to hear. She tried to speak but the desire to leaving Seychelles Island was no longer just packing and catching a flight.

"Aiden, I love you, I do. But…"

"No Tristan. I want you to marry me."

She couldn't stop the tears. She didn't know if she was happy or scared. Tristan wasn't the risky one in their relationship. She had a budding program she developed. She couldn't possibly leave what she had built while Aiden was living across the waters. Every time she thought she could speak aloud what her racing thoughts were, she cried more.

"I didn't say this to upset you."

She moved away from him needing space and air. "Aiden, we can't do this now. I can't. We need to talk this through."

"Do you want to marry me? Is there someone else?"

"No, and yes, marrying you is what I want but I can't leave what I have built here."

Aiden smiled confusing her more. He took her in his arms and kissed her forehead repeatedly. "We are not in a hurry. Take the time you need. I just needed to know you were willing to love me as you have for a lifetime."

"I have so much to tell you, then you will understand. I want to know about this business you have with your sisters. We have to plan around these things. Oh, I am so happy Aiden, but let's not tell anyone tonight. I made arrangements for us to stay on the eastside at the bed and breakfast."

"Is it still there? I thought they wanted to turn it into, what was it, a time-share location or resort."

"I believe the Sauters still own it. Maybe they did convert it."

The Sauters Bed and Breakfast on the east side was a popular spot for travelers and those who visited the island and didn't want to be where the tourists were. It was an attraction that brought many to town expecting to mingle with the people who lived on the island for years.

Tristan took Aiden's hand. "I remember that being our first romantic spot."

Aiden laughed. "I was just thinking of how scared you were that someone would tell your mother you checked in with me."

"I didn't tell her this time either. She thinks I'll be with your sisters."

"I think that's what you told her then. Well let's hope Sasha doesn't call you in the morning as she did then. What did your mother say when Sasha asked for you?"

"She told my mother I left with Seychelle that morning and she didn't know if I was coming back later that day. She can keep a secret. Aiden, I'm glad you told them about your gambling and drinking. Did you tell them everything?"

"I told them nothing."

Not wanting to spoil their time together, Tristan didn't ask any questions. Aiden wouldn't be pushed into telling them. It wasn't an argument she was willing to start again. They sat reminiscing with Sasha and Seychelle for an hour more. Aiden grabbed his bags and put them in Tristan's car.

"Aiden you are coming back here right?" Sasha teased him pointing to the items in the car.

"No, I'm going to convince your girl here to spend the two weeks with me. Either the bed and breakfast or at the Savoy."

"Nice, so you are taking off Tristan?"

"No. Same plans but Mr. Tudjal said a weekend just wasn't enough."

The women laughed as she and Aiden got in the car. They waved their goodbyes.

"So that's new for him. What do you think?"

Seychelle threw up her hands. "After Father's behavior I guess he does need a place where he can relax and not be questioned about his actions. Father was a bit much. Did you notice Mother wouldn't say a word? She should have shut him up long before she did. He'll be in a great mood for morning breakfast. Trust me sister, he'll have a time trying to break me down, watch Sasha, he'll go for Aiden. I wish I would have warned Aiden, we both need to be prepared."

Chapter 49

“Tell me you never made it to your room last night?”
Sasha stood over her sister's shoulder at the kitchen table. “What's this?” She picked up one of the pages Seychelle had spread over across the table.

“It's the invoices for the items that were changed and this is what they were replaced with. These pictures are fabulous but so are the prices!”

Sasha took a seat and began looking through the pictures and the invoices. There were printed emails in a small pile. Seychelle pushed them toward Sasha. She sat back closed her eyes and waited for Sasha's response.

“I need to match the before and after pictures with the invoices. Seychelle you can't possibly understand what was asked to be done, what was done, and the before and after if you don't put them together. How long have you been up trying to sort through this mess?”

“I couldn't sleep.” Seychelle didn't move as her sister took over. I waited for the emails thinking it would be easier to put everything together. These are the quotes over here. I want to start a file for each contractor. I've never been good with filing. I started an e-file but…”

"You're frustrated. Let me do my job. Go lay down, it's just three o'clock. Remember breakfast is at..."

"Whatever time we get there. Aiden will come here first."

"That's good, I was going to suggest we talk first before we get drilled by Father."

"Sasha, he was wrong. Aiden didn't deserve that impromptu attack. Mother should have done something sooner. She knew he was going to go at Aiden."

"I think we should make sure we all know what has transpired since I left to come home. I didn't know Aiden would be working with The Whelan Group."

"Clayton gave him a position. This will give him a piece of his own."

"You didn't have a hand in his being hired did you?"

"Clayton asked me what I thought. It was after he offered Aiden the job. It doesn't matter. He's employed, he can still work our deals from the inside and no one be the wiser."

"Who's checking Ms. Minnow? I'm sure she'll remember your name. If she's so determined to find the owner of what was Westlake, she'll match your name to his."

"I'll have to find a way to get Vance to tell me more about her, including her intentions."

"Well I'll take care of this. Since this is my assigned job."

Sasha blew a kiss to Seychelle as she exited the room mouthing "thank you".

Chapter 50

"This is why it was so hard for me to tell them that I was moving again, or my reasons for my failed jobs. You should have seen, no heard his reaction. He didn't give a thought to trying to understand. We are not living in the same times or with the same traditions. He won't even consider visiting America."

Aiden told Jon while Tristan was in the shower. He hadn't slept well thinking about another arranged setting...the breakfast. Seychelle's quick thinking kept him from ignoring the mandatory invitation. Jon and Seychelle said the same thing. Their father could be displeased with their decisions but after breakfast they still would be in business together. Aiden would still be working at The Whelan Group and returning to California in two weeks. Tristan told him to think about getting settled. A new job, a new business and a marriage were a lot to take on.

"Well my friend, seems that everything is in your favor. This breakfast shouldn't spoil your visit home. Just sit there and listen, your father may have a valid point for his intentions. Remember, he thought you couldn't manage things so he was there for you with his solution. Things are different now and when he sees the business is solid and will be profitable, he'll calm down. He's your father. Parents worry."

"I guess. Well e-mail me those papers you wanted me to see and I'll print them at Sasha and Seychelle's place."

"No problem, but I think Sasha has them. Clayton probably sent them to Seychelle."

Aiden thought about what Jon said. *"If he was to be the liaison between the Group and Serenity, why didn't he have the papers?"*

"Hey you still there?" Jon questioned after a pause of silence.

"Just wondering why I wasn't included in the e-mail."

"Your name is included in the copies. Maybe it went to your spam folder. It wasn't marked like the other e-mails."

"Yeah, well I'll check. I will address Seychelle about it. We all need to be on the same page."

Jon heard Sasha's words. *We've got to find out about Ms. Minnows. I think she's interested in the property because of Vance. If she finds out who owns it, I'm sure she'll tell him. Seychelle said Clayton is going to accept her calls, a diversion, so she won't speak to Aiden.*

"Aiden, did that lady Ms. Minnows ask for your name?"

"No, I don't think so. She was looking for Clayton. I told her I was a friend. I was listed as a friend on the invite."

"Seems she may have some other motives regarding the owner of the property. It may have to do with Vance, so if she calls again don't mention the property or your name. Seychelle wants to bid again in October. If this woman is upset about Vance not being available because of the relationship with Seychelle, she may tell Vance that Serenity is owned by Seychelle."

"So what?"

"Well how do you think your sister knew about Westlake Village?"

"Vance? He doesn't know he gave her the inside tip?"

"He has no clue. I guess she'll tell him in time. But if he's as big as they say he is then we can rise as he does."

"Clayton know about this?"

"I'm sure he does. Remember he was at the table when we told them we got information about Westlake. Like I said Clayton knows and he'll leave your name out of any paperwork."

"But how does Ms. Minnows get to see any in-house business?"

"She's got clients attached to the Group. That may be a burp in future buys, but for now we need to be a few steps ahead of her."

"And the race is on. I'll find out more, I guess, this morning. Okay so everything else is cool?"

"Yeah. Hey enjoy yourself. Stay sober man."

"You too."

Aiden pulled out his laptop. He typed in Cheyenne Minnows and began to browse the information. She seemed to be a legitimate businesswoman. Why she wouldn't back off the Westlake property became the question. He typed in a few of the properties she owned, nothing appeared to be unusual. He typed in Westlake Village. He had to alter a few of his words to get the property they acquired. He found what could be of interest to any investor. He wrote notes and decided he wouldn't show Seychelle until he verified what could be a problem. Tristan came out of the shower combing through her dampened hair.

"What time is the breakfast with your parents?"

"I should be leaving now. Do you need something?"

"After last night? Hmm ... I think I'll be okay until dinner tonight?" She grinned leaning over his shoulder.

"Okay, so are you going to your house later?"

"I thought I'd go there after work on Monday."

"When you do, I want to speak with your mother. I haven't seen her in years. It can be any time before I leave."

"No it is best to see her as soon as you can. She'll have a new name for you if we wait for any time."

They both laughed as Aiden stood to leave. He watched Tristan pin up her hair in the full-length mirror before he walked to the door. She followed him to the door anxious for their parting kiss.

"Okay, let's make it later today or tonight. I'll call you when breakfast is over. I'm sure it won't be long."

They kissed goodbye. Aiden was sure Tristan would be bored in the suite but she insisted he take the car. He explained the business to her as he would explain it to his parents. She was proud of him. He was proud of himself. She could finally believe that he had no desire to ruin it with alcohol. Tristan prayed that he could see the difference, embrace it and continue to grow.

Chapter 51

Breakfast was filling. Naomi said the blessing of the food and within her prayer she included that peace prevail as they ate. It was that statement that her children and husband respected. There was no discussion or question about their business while they ate.

The temperature promised to be ninety degrees at noon. The morning breeze from the ocean through the windows wasn't enough to circulate through the home. The French doors that led outdoors were opened to bring comfort to the sitting room. The family helped clear the dishes. They talked through breakfast sharing with Aiden and Seychelle the news of the island. Sasha spoke of her new year expectations at the school. Cole went into the sitting room and waited.

"He knows I wanted to speak to you before this so-called meeting. I want all of you to remember. Stop, turn now and listen."

Just as they had been obedient children, Seychelle, Aiden and Sasha stopped to hear their mother's whispered words.

"Your father had a dream too. We both did. We didn't know what the future would hold. We watched you grow into fine adults, independent adults. Over the years we didn't stop preparing for failures that can be devastating in life. Aiden, you hit a rough time, moving on

189

too soon. Yes, we know it wasn't your choice or your fault but all the same the decision was for you to move on. Your father wouldn't have agreed to that arrangement if he knew the challenges you would face. It lies heavy on our hearts and now that you are here, we want to ... I don't know what we want to do but we feel we wronged you."

She stopped as though one of them would comment. They stood silent. Sasha returned to the sink, Seychelle continue putting up the silverware and Aiden returned to the dining room to wipe down the table. Naomi prayed they would carry her words and its sincerity she truly wanted them to understand.

The kitchen and dining room were cleaned thoroughly. Naomi waved them on. As Aiden went to pass her, she pulled him close enough to kiss his cheek and give him an encouraging smile.

Seychelle sat her tablet and a stack of paperwork on the table. Aiden reached on the side of the love seat and got his satchel. Cole watched closely as they prepared the table with the information on Serenity Resorts and Spa.

"What is this?" Their father asked. He was certain his mood would be teased and tested. He too was prepared. "Naomi, give me those papers there on the desk please. Oh, and the others on the counter under that folder.

They talked through the paperwork. Seychelle didn't have much to say. She told their parents that it was as it had been when she explained her vision. She carried it out and now was the owner of a resort with four locations. She explained the process, the auction, the bids, the sale and her plans to expand.

Cole flipped through the pages and he had to admit he was impressed. Every question he asked was explained in detail. Naomi sat by his side praying this would end his thoughts of betrayal. They all waited for Cole's next question or concluding statement. Sasha gave a brief description of the renovations, as he stacked the packets and reached for the pictures.

"Father, what exactly are you looking for?" Aiden's patience was fading. "Everything is in order. Lawyers have gone over the contracts and The Whelan Group, one of the largest investment groups in America is our backer. It is the same group I now work for. Please, whatever your disappointment is, it is with me not with the dream Seychelle has made possible."

"Exactly, you ruined your dreams and now you attach yourself to your sister's? How is that fair to her?"

"So it has been told to me over and over again. I'm regaining what I lost and Seychelle has graciously looked beyond my faults. Why can't you?"

"You should have looked to come back home. This is where your foundation is and it is solid. I struggled to see it through all these years to be a foundation for the family. I had dreams of you being where I am. Your struggle would be over."

"Father, why is it that we are to blame when you never told us of this foundation until Aiden failed and I've succeeded. We are a family and as one, I included Aiden and Sasha. I told them they didn't have to stop what they were doing. Sasha could still teach and Aiden could seek a career anywhere he chose. Aiden and I talked before I left here. It was his advice that made it easy for me to establish the beginnings of my business. What is wrong with that? Is it that we did it without you? Father, should we have asked permission? I don't understand this. You make it seem as though we are no longer a family if one of us doesn't take over your business."

"What would you understand? What would you know, any of you? Do as you wish and leave your mother and me to work until we die. Then what, where does my years of duty as the father, the husband, the provider go, huh? To the highest bidder, you will sell it off. Just like that."

"Father please, no one has said that." Sasha felt his pain. She sat next to him to show her support. "It's okay Father, we understand, but we have dreams too."

"This life you've worked hard for is your life Father, not mine."

"Seychelle!" Naomi snapped knowing what Seychelle would say next. Seychelle always felt her father would be content in marrying the girls off.

"You worked for Aiden to succeed. Sasha and I would be under Aiden's watch if something happened to you. That's tradition Father, the world is nothing without the supervision of a man!"

Aiden needed a drink. Feeling overwhelmed he stood to leave. He began packing his satchel without saying a word. The room fell silent.

"Father please..." Sasha stopped mid-sentence as she turned to see Seychelle was beginning to pack her paperwork as well.

"Stop! This is not the way to work through this!" Naomi stood in the doorway blocking both Aiden and Seychelle.

"Mother, Father has his mind made up. He can't shatter my dreams as he has Aiden's — I won't let him. We're doing as any parent would want their children to do. We're standing on our own and making our own way. Well Father if you think it is disrespectful, a slap in your face, or a scar to all that you have done… then it won't bother you if we move from your presence."

"Let them go Naomi. I have heard enough of the America way. They are no different than the others who have left the islands. Living here is no longer a desire for them. Working and raising a family here is no desire for them. Let them go. When we're dead and gone their desires will change."

"Mother, I will be talking to you later. Sasha I'll see you at our home later."

Aiden and Seychelle walked out in silence.

Chapter 52

Monday morning came quickly. Tristan couldn't find an excuse that wouldn't cause a problem with her mother or her employment. It was early but it was time for her to prepare for work. The time spent with Aiden was well worth it. Rekindling their love for each other gave the two lovers a reassurance of their future.

"What will you tell your parents?" Tristan had one more question nagging at her.

"There's nothing to tell them. I can't step into my father's chaos again. Tristan, did you know it was my father's idea that I leave the islands? It was his idea to send me a monthly allowance to keep me away from home. He knew of my problems each time I wrote or called. Not once did he mention the possibility of my taking over Tudjal Imports. He just kept my head afloat. When I would tell him of the problems, jobs, alcohol, women, and yes even when I thoughts of killing myself, I talked to my father. He would say don't burden your mother or sisters with this. He told me that they wouldn't understand. Manhood was different. It's bothered me over the years. Now, I come home and he plans this big party; invites people that care about him more and know nothing about me; and then embarrasses me by criticizing the choices I've made to survive. There's no need to tell him about anything else in my life. Trying to please him, I lost me. I can't be the man he wants me to be. I am repairing the damage. I can't allow him to destroy the repairs."

Tristan understood. She continued to dress looking in the mirror at the reflection of herself and the man she loved. Their eyes met in the mirrored image. "I love you Aiden Tudjal. Remember that today and always. Whatever you decide to do is fine with me — I'm with you. I just don't want this misunderstanding to cause a wall between you and your father. My father is gone and I miss him so much. I even miss our spats. Don't leave the island with a wall between the two of you."

Adam listened and decided not to argue. Tristan was being rational something his parents wouldn't understand. He promised Sasha, he would visit them on his way to the airport. He hadn't answered any of the calls from their phone. He assured Sasha he wasn't sick and no longer could their father offend him. Seychelle was right, they had a business to manage.

"Your parents are worried, that's all." Tristan moved closer to the mirror applying her makeup. "Aiden, I know what you do with Seychelle, but what is your job with The Whelan Group?"

"It's the same job. Seek out new property for clients, and those who need investors, or have interest in investing I refer to the Group. I am glad my father told me to major in business. Can we meet for lunch?"

"Ooo Baby I would love that. The only problem is I don't have a set lunch hour. If someone comes in or placement takes longer I may have to change my hour."

"I'm flexible. We'll do lunch. I'll take you to work, we'll do lunch and I'll pick you up. Is there anyone that needs to know I'm in town?"

"What? What are you talking about?"

"You know, I've been gone for quite some time. There's someone peeping you out."

"Peeping me out? Is that West Coast slang?"

"You know what it means that's all that matters. You know what was going on with me. What about you? A love interest that you've been ignoring? Someone who's been waiting for you to weaken?"

"C'mon if you're taking me. I don't want to be late."

Aiden's day was planned. He would drop off Tristan and go meet Seychelle. They were checking the resorts on the island. They had visited a few over the years but without the intention of being a competitor in the business. As he drove along the shoreline he could see the difference that Sasha pointed out every time they rode around the bay. There was no comparison to "God's Country", the name Seychelle declared fit for only the islands. The breathtaking views of the mountains as the framework and the beauty of nature took its place on each island. The splendor of the islands was more than the simple traditions his father continuously sermonized about. It carried an ambiance of pride. The colors of nature blended with the dress of the women who wore prints so often seen on the Pacific shoreline. Sold by vendors hoping to encourage the tourist to get a bit of the islands in America. The clear waters that rushed to the shore brought a sense of peace as it reseeded returning to the Indian Ocean. Aiden remembered his childhood, what he missed when he left the islands, what he yearned for over the years.

The morning ride helped his mood. He was sure Seychelle wouldn't try to convince him to apologize. Sasha would be at the school so there would be no one to oppose his decision. He thought of the pictures his sister's sent him when they moved from their parent's home. They did well for themselves. No one would have thought Seychelle would leave the security she had to venture into a new business, in a new world.

"Well you look better in this morning's sunlight my dear brother."

"I could say the same for you. I can only say it has been years since I slept as well as I did the last time I saw you. Being with Tristan stabilizes me when I think all has become chaotic."

"Do you plan on taking her with you when you leave? Has she agreed?"

"I didn't ask. We talked about it and of course I told her how I felt, but I didn't ask for her hand properly. I will before I leave. Even if she can't come to California right away, I'll ask."

"Will you ask her mother to bless your union? Will you tell our parents?

"Yes and I don't know. I don't know that either of them care including her mother. She isn't that fond of me."

"Aiden, she isn't fond with who you were. Father is stuck in the past too. Who you were, is not who you are today. What you are able to do today, you hadn't imagined before. Your dreams can still be, you just can't return to who you were."

"And was I so bad Seychelle? So bad that I don't look back and see what I wanted in life, what I studied in school to be, what I loved about Tristan, my home and my family? Am I to forget that I stopped someone from disrespecting an elder? I followed the stupid tradition taught by father and then what? I was deemed to be an outcast? Maybe later Seychlle, right now I'm ready to leave."

"Well I may have to leave with you. Something came up with the renovations. I too felt the control Father was crying over. Aiden, can't you see? He has lost control and of course, I am a woman. Women can't have dreams, desires or anything that belongs totally to them without the mind of a man. I love him, truly I do, but I would be less of a person if I allowed him to control my life."

Aiden thought again he would be blamed if Seychelle decided to leave and live with him.

"Are you going to wait the two weeks to leave with me?"

"Yes, I'll probably go to Vegas shortly after arriving. I need to see the problem. Clayton said it could wait until then. They'll work around the problem until then."

"Why didn't he call me?"

"You are to seek properties, set up the particulars so we can acquire it. Get yourself set with new clients. Renovations have to be approved by me no matter how I get the message. Aiden, you will be set and on your own. I will lose you to others but you will be able to rise without owing anyone, including me."

Aiden had no response. It was what he prayed for, having control of his own business. Jon was right they would win after all.

Profits

Chapter 53

C layton looked over the documents again. It was clear. The property Seychelle purchased was part of a franchise. The previous owners of Westlake Village proposed a fair price for their remaining properties. The owners were willing to discount the price for the other properties. Their offer was not made public, as they wanted to offer the purchase to the new owner of Westlake Village.

Clayton was surprised Seychelle fell into a remarkable deal without any negotiations. He sent her an email regarding the progress of the renovations but decided not to reveal the new proposal. He was certain she would take the deal. If she refused the offer the properties would go up for bid. No one would be the wiser. She would become the owner without the fanfare. Currently there was no obvious connection to the Westlake property. Each location had its own name, management, and brand.

He spent most of the morning running the numbers. Seychelle never mentioned the need for an advance. Timing would be the issue. Clayton would give her the pros and cons. The auction in October would never bring her the return she would get from the new locations; two properties in Cancun, one in San Juan, and one in Nassau. Serenity Resorts and Spa would create buzz.

The Whelan Investment Group would support her decision and finances if needed. After speaking with his partners, they agreed it was a deal that couldn't be ignored. If Seychelle declined the offer, the Group would negotiate to make the purchase. They couldn't afford to let the property go to the highest bidder at any auction.

"Cheyenne Minnows on line one Mr. Whelan." He realized the calls from Ms. Minnows would increase. Serenity Resorts and Spa would soon be the group's top client.

"Ms. Minnows, what can I do for you?"

Cheyenne pushed the button for the call to be placed on speaker. "Listen Clayton, I know there's more information on this Westlake property than in this auction brochure. I was wondering if you had information that the others at the auction should have known."

"What's the problem Cheyenne? The information was given to everyone. The seller released what they wanted to be known. You can't believe that the bid placed was because someone knew more."

"Clayton, you and your partners always know more."

"Okay guilty. We research all the time Ms. Minnows. Now if doing our job brings great results, well…"

"Clayton! Who is the owner? Why is that such a big secret?"

"The owner wishes to be anonymous for their own reasons. The purchase was legit. Everyone was given the same information and opportunity. Put the money up or shut up. Again, Ms. Minnows the field was even. You just play from a different playbook. Anything else I can help you with?"

"Let me find out you're fronting with a company that can't stay afloat."

"What? What could be the harm in that? What do you want from the property or the sale? What's got you itching?"

"That bid was mine. I know it was. The Serenity Resorts and Spa owner or spokesperson wasn't there. It was The Whelan Group who picked up the paperwork and signed for it. I'm good if you tell me your group is the owner."

"No ma'am we do not own the property. That's all I'm at liberty to say. Off the subject you looked lovely that night."

Her response was the phone's dial tone.

Cheyenne wondered if she would get better answer from one of the associates. She'd wait a few hours before calling the Group again. She would see if Vance found anything strange about the transaction. In three weeks they'd be bidding once again. She flipped through the pages of the Bidding Wars. The success in bidding section had the articles about the progress of the properties that were bought during the last auctions. There was nothing reported for Westlake Village other than it being bought by Serenity Resorts and Spa.

Cheyenne dialed the next number on the list. She was determined to find out who else knew about the franchise. Cheyenne was told if she bought the property she'd be in line for the properties that were connected. She wouldn't have to buy another property to be recognized. Someone stole her glory, she needed to know who. There was a slim chance that the new owner wouldn't be offered the other properties and they would be a part of the next bidding.

The receptionist put her on hold. "Mr. Gaines will be right with you unless you'd like to have him return your call."

"I'll hold, thank you." Cheyenne waited and after a few minutes became anxious. Just as she was about to hang up, Kevin Gaines picked up the blinking line on his phone.

"Good morning, Ms. Minnows?"

"Yes, it's Cheyenne Kev.

"What's going on? How can I help you?"

"There was a deal on the table for the buyer of the Westlake Property. Clayton claims the owner is anonymous and wants to remain that way. I just want to know if the deal will still go to this so-called buyer. Kevin I know your firm knows who the buyer is. You don't have to tell me but you know I was in line to get that property. Clayton and I have had our spats but this is business. I just want to know about the rest of the property. Can you help me out?"

Clayton, Kevin and Claude had discussed the possibilities of the deal well before the offer was drawn up for Serenity Resorts. Seychelle would be in their office next week and one way or the other The Whelan Group would be a part of the sale.

"Cheyenne there's nothing I can say regarding the ownership. Once the paperwork is done the owner's name will be on it. Public information, so you will know then. Before then I can't help you. Now as far as the offer after the sale, that's not our business. I don't know of any offers."

"Bullshit!"

Cheyenne slammed the receiver onto the base disconnecting the call. Vance would know what to do.

Chapter 54

Seychelle hadn't been to town since her return to the island. She promised Sasha she would meet her at the marketplace once she finalized the monthly report. It seemed as though she was spending more of the finances allotted than she was quoted. Sasha and Aiden reviewed the reports and explained it was all written in the quotes given. She looked at the bank account summary again and shook her head. The money was dwindling fast. She was proud of herself when she departed to begin her dream. The expenses, or researching, cost more than she expected, she wanted to account for every penny. Clayton agreed with her sister and brother, it would all pay off in the end.

She held the deed in her hand and said a silent prayer of thanks. She was still in awe. She certainly purchased more than she expected. Seychelle wanted her father to see that her first purchase would bring more than enough profit to replenish her seed money. Her father didn't question any of the paperwork, nor had he looked at the deed. She was still upset with him.

Seychelle and Aiden would be on the island for another week. Her mother called daily with a reminder that her independence and instant separation from the island was new to them as parents. It was hard when Aiden left but her departure was different because she was their oldest daughter. Seychelle was direct and stubborn, a trait she inherited in her genes. She didn't need to explain her reasons; there were discussions over dinner, lunch, family visits, all of which she took the opportunity to speak about her dreams. Before leaving the island to begin her journey, she gave her father notice that she wouldn't be working with him at the docks. She wouldn't leave her work undone and she was willing to stay on until there was someone to replace her. She stayed in touch with those who worked in the front office. Although her father had no idea she was talking with the staff members, her mother was well aware of her input. Seychelle did everything she could to make the transition easier for her parents.

Sasha stepped in after the third day of her mother's pleas with hopes she could curtail the calls. The calls didn't stop and now, Tuesday morning, Seychelle ignored the constant ringing of the phone.

The temperature was approaching its highest of the season. Seychelle raised her head saying a silent prayer of praise. She loved the sun and basked in it often. The clean smell of nature gave her a nudge to exercise. It was still early. School would be in session until three. She planned to walk the beach and spend some quiet time listening to jazz. Aiden was right, the islands were a piece of heaven.

Vance called earlier than he promised. The conversation allowed her to relax. After talking with him she longed to be on the plane and landing in Vegas. She wanted to tell him she would be there at the end of the week, but business came first. They promised to face-time later that day.

She grabbed her pre-packed straw bag. She checked it making sure she had everything needed. She had to readjust to carry the lounger. She wanted to be sure it wouldn't cost her the balance needed to make it to the beach.

Owning a beachfront home had its benefits. She put the chair in her favorite spot. The leaning palm tree provided a shaded area and after a morning swim she'd relax until it was time to meet Sasha.

The water was warm. She'd miss the calm of the waters and the welcomed breeze that met her as she walked along the shore. She wiped the sand from her feet and left the towel at the foot of the lounge chair.

"Good Morning." Her mother startled her causing them both to smile.

"Hey, I don't know when I was scared like that."

"Your mind must have been miles away."

"I didn't expect anyone to be here. Did you come through the house?"

"No I walked around. I saw you coming out of the water."

"Do you want to sit with me here? I'll bring a chair from the veranda." Seychelle waited for her mother to answer. She looked up to her mother. She seemed to be in a trance looking toward the water. "Mother, do you want to…"

"I need to talk with you Seychelle. Can we sit on the veranda?"

Seychelle felt unnerved. Her mother's demeanor always set the tone. Usually Naomi's talks held a warning. It seemed this talk would have a permanent effect. They walked slowly to the house. Seychelle carried her lounger and her beach bag. Her mother insisted she should help with something. They laughed as Seychelle awkwardly arranged the possessions to carry them back to their original place.

"I carry all of this stuff to keep from going back and forth to the house."

"You'll miss this once you start your business, or will you?"

"I haven't decided yet. I was thinking about it last night. I know I don't really want to live in Vegas."

"You don't want to live so far from your business do you?"

"Aiden is in California. It's not that far away, but I don't want to live there either. The business is about creating a place of enjoyment, entertainment and relaxation for tourist. Have you been to any resorts?"

"No, your father sees it as a waste of money. We live right here with the ability to enjoy the weather, the beach and the things we've seen in the brochures."

"Well there are thousands, maybe even millions that want to escape their everyday lifestyles. They seek to visit other places that offer what we enjoy here. They are located all over the world. I guess that's why I haven't decided if I would move to any of the properties. I can go there at any time and stay as long as I like. I would still have this home. Enough of my mixed thoughts. What's on your mind? I have fresh fruit cut, would you care for some?"

"Yes, please. I'm not going to hold you here am I?"

"You may." Seychelle laughed as she brought out the tray of assorted fruits. The remains of what she cut for her lunch wouldn't be an appetizer for dinner. "I'm meeting Sasha at the marketplace when she's done today. Would you join us?"

"No I've been out all morning. I'm going to meet your Aunt Lorian this evening. I wanted to know your plans before you left. Seychelle, you know your father means no harm don't you? I think Aiden has taken this all the wrong way."

"Mother I can't speak for Aiden. He'll think about what was said and done as will Father. They need a little distance right now and frankly Mother, so do I. Has Father said anything about the business. Good or bad he hasn't said a thing to us. We can't put our lives on hold until he decides he can accept we have our own lives to live."

"What about marriage for you? A family and marriage for him. Will we be included when you live so far away?"

"Mother did Father have those thoughts when he sent Aiden away? Did he think about our future when I left to research my dreams? Mother, Father is upset and he has played on your emotions to upset you. Aiden needs time."

"And what do you need?"

"I need him to recognize, as a woman I can do anything I set my mind to. I am not just a woman who will prepare to marry and be a mother. I want so much more. If I am to marry, my husband will understand I am more than capable of owning a business, being a wife and having children."

"So will you leave here with this confusion stirring?"

"What confusion? Who's confused?"

"Seychelle, your Father and I don't understand. Sometimes our dreams are bigger than our reality. We agreed your vision often shows the surface of what is wanted. But my child beyond the surface lies the reality. It is that reality that we must ready ourselves for. Can you say today that you are ready? Your father is worried for you and your brother. If neither of you will stay in touch, visit or come home, we will worry with reason."

"Mother, you have worried for no reason. Sasha and I own property here. I live here. I will be in touch and come home from time to time. I don't like the winter months in America. I may visit there for business and continue to travel for other business. I never gave thought to not coming home or staying in touch. I just refuse to talk business with Father. His business is Tudjal Imports. I am proud to say my father built his business. I'm sorry he can't be proud enough to say that about my business and me."

"What about your brother?"

"What about your son?"

Before Naomi could answer, Seychelle's phone rang.

"Mother I have to meet Sasha. I promise, I will visit you before I leave. Do you want to lock up or?"

"Or you're putting me out."

Chapter 55

The marketplace was less crowded during the week. Islanders shopped during the week avoiding the tourist. The sound of Seggae music could be heard in the distance. The melodic sound caused a few people to dance as they proceeded to walk along the street. Seychelle told her sister they would meet at their favorite restaurant. She parked her car and spotted Tristan waving frantically across the street.

"Hey lady, how are you?" Tristan swayed to the music.

"I'm good, look at you?" Tristan twirled and the two giggled embracing one another.

"I don't know the last time I saw you in our custom wrap."

Tristan wore one of her favorite traditional two-piece outfits. Most women on the island kept their traditional dress for holidays and festive occasions. Tristan loved the vibrant colors and the heads that turned looking at her matching head wrap.

"This material is comfortable and so light with this weather, you know." She spun slowly again seeing that Seychelle truly loved her ensemble.

"Seeing you makes my effort to have the island theme throughout the resort a definite. Our culture is so beautiful I want to share it with others.

"You are right Seychelle. So much has changed, the women here have become so independent. They wait for festivals and such to remember the island traditions. They own businesses, homes, and have you seen how the political stance has changed?"

"Changed for some. My father and a few others will never change."

"Well, I enjoy the traditional ways. I hope your brother does as well. A woman should be able to balance herself but be that woman for her husband and her children. That is where our future lies. Holding on to tradition so our children will appreciate their heritage."

Seychelle didn't answer thinking about her future. She gave little thought to having a family with her business. If she married it would have to be someone that understood what she wanted in life. Her independence was important to her. Once again it was easy for her brother to marry and still be able to carry on a business. She and Sasha would have to take a back seat to their careers if they expected to marry someone from the islands.

"Are you ready to leave all of this and come to America?"

Tristan shook her head slowly. "I don't know Seychelle. Today I do but tomorrow I will want to think about it again. Today I love the idea but I fear the unknown, the uncertainty of the security I have here. I have to sacrifice what I have to move on with someone I love. It doesn't seem fair. I often wonder would there be a sacrifice if Aiden hadn't been rushed from his home. No one thought of his love for home or his love for me. Yes we were young, but your family doesn't know how Aiden made it through those times. It wasn't just his AA meetings. It was the hours we spent on the phone, the letters, the tears we shed and the prayers we sent to heaven."

"You do what you need to do for you. Don't move on temporary decisions expecting permanent results."

"You're absolutely right. I have so much to consider and most of it is temporary. I love Aiden and he loves me, I know this to be true. I guess I thought his life was spiraling and I just accepted it as such. But for prayers my sister, but for prayers."

"Well, I will continue to pray. He needs a woman like you, he needs you."

"What about you Seychelle? Have you honed in on one of those American men?"

"I may have. I'm just like you. I'm at that 'not yet' mode."

The two laughed. Sasha was approaching them as they were saying their goodbye.

"Hey don't be leaving when I show up. You know I'm insecure."

"There's no room for insecurity between us ladies." Seychelle grabbed their hands lifting them in the air. "In spite of tradition we will rise, be lovers, housewives and in business."

Tristan blew kisses as she left the sisters standing at the car. She told them she and Aiden would be talking with her mother later. "Wish us luck."

"I hope you're hungry my sister. I didn't cook at home so we'll need something to hold us over."

"There's a new place near the courthouse. Let's try it instead."

Chapter 56

Tristan couldn't express the embarrassment she felt during Aiden's visit to her home. They had an open invitation from her mother for dinner. She picked up a few things that were needed to complete the prepared meal. Tristan stopped to get Aiden and they arrived a little before six.

The table was set for two. Tristan went into the kitchen. The food was still in the pots her mother used to cook the meal in. The pots were hot. Not understanding what was going on, she yelled out.

"Mama, we're here." There was no answer. Aiden remained standing near the door. Tristan went through the small home checking for her mother.

"Tristan, there's a note here on the table."

She quickly returned to find a note on the dining room table. She picked it up and read it twice. It was her mother's writing. She sat in the chair slowly.

"Aiden, when do we leave for California?"

"Huh? What's wrong? What does the note say?"

"She couldn't stay for dinner, something came up." She hoped he wouldn't ask to see the writing. She had to control her anger, her hurt, and her disappointment.

"Well we can still talk to her before Sunday. I thought you couldn't just leave, what changed your mind?"

"It's time I move on. My dream is to be with you. When do we leave?"

"Our plans were to leave on Sunday. I have to get our tickets tomorrow. If you're sure, I'll get yours too."

"I'm sure. Aiden, can you take the car and come back for me. I want to pack things to be shipped. I won't be coming back."

"Tristan, what's wrong. What does it say?"

"It really doesn't matter. She's set in her ways and I can't accept her treating me this way any longer. I promise, once I find peace in this I'll share it with you. Not right now. Please just come back and get me."

Aiden hesitated before opening the door to leave. Tristan whispered "It's okay" and blew him a kiss as she went to her room. After hearing the door close she walked to her mother's closed bedroom door.

She tried the doorknob. It was locked. Tears began to flow. Her mixed emotions were taking over. Between the anger and the hurt was the reality. She was glad her mother hadn't taken the opportunity to express her feelings during dinner.

She pulled her suitcases down from the shelf in her closet. She didn't want the process of packing to be prolonged. She would need boxes. She stood amid her belongings. She longed to talk to her father. It was times like these that she missed him the most. Her mother's plan to force her to stay pushed her away. There was no need to speak to her mother. The note she left said enough.

Marietta sat in her room with the door locked. She didn't want Tristan to persuade her to join them. She could hear what she thought was her daughter moving furniture. She opened her door slowly, peeking out, looking for movement.

"Mama, if you can hear me or care to hear me, I'm done. I can't pretend that I'm comfortable with living my life this way. I tried to include you. I've emptied my dresser, my closet and my armoire. Don't put a thing back. Don't touch it. I'll be back for it." Tristan shouted from her room. She didn't wait for her mother's reaction.

"I read your note and this is the solution." She shouted emphatically.

Marietta remained hidden behind her door. She didn't expect Tristan's response to be so dramatic. She knew it would prompt an angered temperament but nothing as drastic as packing and possibly leaving.

Tristan grabbed her phone. She pulled up the app for her bank account. She was saving as much of her pay as she could. After giving her mother money and buying food she didn't have much to save. Her balance wouldn't be enough to get a plane ticket and ship her belongings to California. She would need to work another month or two.

Tristan's stomach was beginning to speak to her. It led her to the kitchen. She took out a few storage bowls. She didn't turn when she heard her mother's slippers sliding across the hardwood floors.

"Do you want me to put the food up or will you be waiting until we leave?"

"Are you really going to act like we don't have something to discuss?"

"Your message was clear. If I chose Aiden to be in my life I would risk losing you. Why would there be anything else to discuss?"

"Child you picked one sentence in the message and that's it! There is so much more. Did you understand when I said I was concerned about your future with him? He's not ready Tristan and neither are you."

"So as mother you embarrass me by skipping dinner? You could have asked questions about what we see as our steps. You could have tried to see our love is not new to either of us. Instead you laid a dare in my path, my life, my journey. Have you asked me why I love him? What do I see in him? A man who was broken and yes it took a few years to put the pieces back together. Unlike you mother, I love him because of it, in spite of it all. He's a better man today, but you hid behind a door because you thought of you. He wants to marry me. He wants us to be together. We want to have a family."

"And as soon as he returns you're ready to go? I don't understand you leaving here, your home, your job—"

Tristan stopped to face her mother. "Go ahead say it. You don't understand me leaving you. That's what this is about, you!"

"If you would only listen. You're entangled in possibilities and unsettled emotions. I was the same way with your father. If I had only set my visions first. Look what I have today. This house, we're still paying the mortgage. My job is part-time when you count the hours. I have nothing to call my own because I followed his vision and dreams."

211

"You don't know any of that to be true for me."

"Don't I? You went to college for fashion and design, a talent that would pay well here. What will it pay there? Will you be able to afford your own place? Can he afford to take care of you? Leaving without a thought, maybe you are blinded by love. It is so far Tristan. Will you be able to get here if I need you? What about me visiting you? How will I get there if you need me?"

It wasn't the first time that Marietta played the desperate victim. Tristan dealt with her tearful pleas. They all were based on the same topic, Tristan leaving home.

"Mama I can't fight with you anymore. I would never leave you completely. Even living in America, my heart, my thoughts and my love will be a phone call away, a plane ticket away. I won't ask you to pick up here and live in America but Mama I have to go. It's time Mama. It's time. Even if I didn't go with Aiden, it's time I had my own."

"How long have you been planning this?"

Tristan placed the last container of food into the refrigerator. She couldn't answer her mother's question. She and Aiden talked about being together before he had to leave the island. How could she answer her question?

"It doesn't matter. There's nothing else to be said. You wrote what you wanted me to know. Now that I know it, now that I know how you feel about my love for Aiden, I can only accept it. You said make a choice. I choose Aiden. It's important to me to be able to make my own decisions and they don't have to meet your expectations. I've seen love or what I thought was love and it's that love that I'm yearning to have."

Her mother followed her into her room. "Tristan, I was upset when I wrote that. I kept thinking that Aiden was coming here to propose to you, or ask for my blessing. I can't bless what I don't believe will be the best for you."

Tristan's phone began to buzz. "That's Aiden, we'll be out of your home in a few minutes. Please don't touch any of my things. I'll be back to pack them up. It will be fine and so will you and I. You don't have to bless our marriage or our lives together. I can accept it. After all Dad is looking down smiling. He'll send a blessing from heaven."

What is Love?

Chapter 57

The plane landed early Monday morning. Neither Seychelle nor Aiden planned on working in the office. They scheduled a late lunch with Clayton. Jon met them at the airport prepared to start work once they settled in. After a quick introduction, Jon and Tristan exchanged pleasantries as the four of them headed to the baggage claim area.

Jon didn't fit the description Tristan would have given him. He was taller than she thought and he was a lot younger. They often talked after Aiden had moments of depression. Understanding Aiden's journey they became more than his support system. They became his lifeline. Tristan gave Seychelle the side eye when he asked about Sasha. It was obvious Jon and Sasha held a secret — one that neither was ready to reveal to her parents. Sasha told Tristan she was in love. Now, meeting him face to face, Tristan understood why. He was a good man and very handsome. His mixed heritage was a dominant factor. His accent wasn't as noticeable on the phone but listening to him now, Tristan recognized it.

"I understand you and Sasha were quite a pair in school. She speaks fondly of you." Jon said as he grabbed the suitcase she pointed to on the carousel. Her response was only a smile.

"I parked on the upper level you ladies can wait here if you'd like."

Seychelle found a seat. "Well alright. C'mon Aiden walk with me." Aiden followed Jon while the ladies sat and waited.

"How long do you think you'll be visiting with Aiden?"

Tristan was prepared for the questions to begin. She told Aiden they would all want to know their intentions.

"Seychelle it's really one day at a time. I told my co-workers I would be leaving in three months. That would give me time to save money for my travels. Unfortunately, I don't have a job that will carry across the waters."

"Sure you do. The program you have developed is perfect for children here, even if they are going to college. Learning how to adapt socially, off the internet, is important. You've developed a great program for them to be able to transition into adulthood."

"We'll see. Maybe they have a need for it here in America. I'm taking my time." Seychelle responded with a smirk. "Really I am. I want to make sure the program still runs. The staff is capable and there is always someone seeking to fill my job."

"So you moved out of your home? What are your plans?"

"There's an apartment connected to the center. It's one bedroom and there is no payment. I've stayed there before. I will move my things there when I go home. Aiden says he understands my actions, but Seychelle, I can't tell him what my mother said in that note. I'll stay here for the week and then I'll begin the move."

The women spotted Aiden coming through the doors. They stood and rolled their luggage to meet him. The ride to Aiden's home was filled with music and laughter. Jon and Aiden insisted on serenading the ladies. Tristan was taking in the sites and asking questions. Seychelle answered her questions with the history she was told when she arrived in California.

"It is lovely. There are so many people. I don't know if I would have enjoyed going to school in a distant place such as this. I mean not knowing anyone? It had to be a while before you became accustom to the hustle and bustle of the crowds." Tristan continued to look out of the window.

"It's the hustle and bustle that the Americans thrive on. Back home there is no rush, no urgency, but here it's never-ending. Tristan, that's what my business will capitalize on. Serenity Resorts & Spa is an outlet for those who rush all year long. It's the vacations they look forward to. My resort will give them the escape they need."

"I see that for sure. How expensive will it be?"

"Compatible with most resorts but the experience Sasha and I want to make available will bring many to our doors. I'll show you the layout. I have pictures of how it will be. Once you move here we'll go to Vegas and you can experience it for yourself."

Tristan and Aiden spent the balance of morning making room for her clothes. Jon and Seychelle looked over a few of the documents she would present to Clayton. She still had questions regarding the billing and the ongoing projects.

"How was the trip home?" Jon asked as he closed the last folder.

"Interesting. I think a lot was said that needed to be said. Aiden may not keep in touch with our parents as often as he had. My mother got caught in a mess. She's trying to support my father yet understand us. It just doesn't work, you know?"

"Yes, I do. Aiden's got a lot to work through. I think he's ready to re-start his life."

"Seems like it. Jon did he ever send in a resignation to his previous employer? He's talk about starting with the Whelan Group next week."

"He's keeping the job. He switched to the night shift a while ago. He was able to manage his travel with you and days off better on the night shift. Like I said I think he'll be fine. Tristan is the best thing for him and she truly loves him."

"Jon, what about you and Sasha? I mean the long distance thing, is it working?"

"Of course it's always better when the one you love is near, but it's as good as it gets. It's the first long-distance romance I've been in. To be honest it will be the last. I miss her Seychelle, I really do."

Seychelle thought about the last conversation she had with Vance. She never thought about being in love with him. Her thoughts stopped short once she thought of business. He was open with his knowledge, but would it be the same if he knew of her business? She was the competitor. She knew she wouldn't give up her business for love. Their phone calls, face times, quick rendezvous over the last few months were enough to call it a relationship. Seychelle wouldn't call it love. She hadn't thought about it. Now, talking to Jon, she wanted to know what Vance thought about their relationship. *Did he love her? What kind of future could they have?*

"How's Vance? The two of you have the same type of relationship right?"

"I don't know if we're as close as you and my sister. Love is a strong word. It describes so much. I don't think we've reached that point yet."

"Seychelle you're right it takes time and love is a strong word. Your sister and I have been on this roller coaster, fast-paced, exciting, anxiously we fell in love. Does it happen this way? It did. There is no rule on how you fall in love. I wasn't looking to fall in love but I did. She's so much more than I could imagine and the distance puts us to a test. Did she tell you I will be visiting your home soon?"

"Really? When? Oh, that is so special Jon."

"During the Thanksgiving week. I'm taking a few days to visit her and possibly take her to visit my family during the Christmas holiday. We want to introduce each other to our families before our relationship possibly gets deeper."

"Well meeting the family is deep, especially when you're traveling across the world to meet them. I'm happy for both of you."

"So what's next? What's on the horizon? I understand we're in the renovation phase. Have you looked beyond? Any thoughts for the Grand Opening?"

"I thought about it over and over again. I think right after the new year. I'm just wondering if I want to reveal my name then or not."

"This may be ... eh, stepping out of my place. May I ask a personal question?"

"Sure, Jon." Seychelle shocked herself. His question could cross the line but she felt comfortable enough to answer. She trusted him more than she thought.

"Why the secret? Is it something personal? I haven't asked anyone else and I guess they understand the reason."

"Jon, tradition has been the foundation in many cultures. One that has been common in most cultures is that the man runs businesses. It's a man's world, or is it? In my culture even though many women hold the title boss or entrepreneur, it is not their place. My father and others still believe that tradition should prevail. Americans speak of the women who are independent but really expect the boardroom to be predominantly seated by men."

"So you stay hidden?"

"For now. I want to build a reputation. One that most will applaud thinking a male or men have hit another mark. Another success story without a face could only be driven by a man. Right? Well once we open and the operation drives the numbers and the publicity, then and only then I will step into the light."

"I see. So you're keeping the secret as you use Vance to succeed."

"No, that was a coincidence. But how do men get their information. From their peers, other companies, researching, all that we have done. We landed this deal because I was in the right place at the right time. Is there any difference when men go to meetings, workshops or seminars? They steal ideas, thoughts, clients, and business deals daily. It seems like business as usual. It's expected. What's not expected is a woman dealing the same way."

"Hmmm and this is why you're hesitant to fall in love?"

The line was crossed. She couldn't answer. No she *wouldn't* answer. The question hit deep. *Could I be in love with my competition?*

"I don't know Jon. Maybe, maybe I am so wrapped up in the business that I don't have time for love."

Chapter 58

It was two o'clock before Clayton was able to meet with Jon, Aiden and Seychelle. They agreed to meet at a small café near Aiden's apartment. Seychelle was nervous for no reason at all. She gave the folders to her brother and mentally prepared herself for what she thought would be bad news. They ordered what could have been an early dinner and talked about their trip home. It was after the table was cleared and the waitress brought out dessert and coffee that the conversation changed to the new business matters.

"Seychelle, I want to congratulate you and your partners for moving along so well in the renovation process. There are many new businesses that get caught up in small details and become complacent. Their progress is delayed and then they're upset when the buzz for the place is slow to catch on. I've got some exceptional reviews and of course those that have complained simply because they saw the vision a bit too late. It gets so much better."

Clayton opened a folder with a list of the properties that were to be presented with the closing of the Westlake Village properties. He allowed them to look over the listings, photos and pricing. He watched intently as they tried to remain calm.

"Is this an offer to us?" Seychelle asked as her nerves caused heat to rise around her neck. She hesitated before asking her next question. All eyes were on Clayton.

"This was an offer that was to be disclosed to whoever purchased the Westlake properties. Now before you start mentally running numbers look over the properties and think of the return on the investment. I don't want you to think I'm persuading you one way or another. Seychelle this is a fantastic deal but once you turn it down, it will go to bid for a lot more money. It's a sale that most would die for. Let me explain the particulars."

Clayton began with the money invested in Westlake and the predictions based on the revenue prior to the sale. When the property was in full operation the numbers were great. The presentation ended with the understanding that Serenity Resorts could climb the charts with eight properties. They wouldn't need to expand again until their revenue grew. Seychelles understood her investment would turn into free clear money within five to ten years. There was one problem. To be fully operational with staff and equipment, she would be in debt before she started.

"Clayton, you've seen my numbers. How will I support myself and the properties? How will I pay the staff at eight sites?"

"If you take this deal, I will or The Whelan Group will back your finances. We'll keep the interest low and work with you accordingly."

Seychelle looked to Aiden and Jon who were still glancing at the pricing sheets.

"Clayton this is no way to do business. I'm sure you weren't looking to finance my business."

Clayton smiled. He understood her concern but her business was his business in every sense of the word. Having her as a client was an asset. Serenity Resorts & Spa would draw in female businesses from all parts of the country. After meeting her, he had visions and dreams regarding the growth of his business. He hired Aiden for that reason. He would head his own department with clientele that would feel comfortable working with Aiden while adopting Seychelle's business model.

He watched her as she interacted with her brother and Jon. There was another reason. Her independence and determination lit a spark. She was a challenge. Over the weeks, they talked, met for lunch or dinner, and each time she captured more than his attention. Together they would be a power couple in more ways than one. He asked Aiden about her being single. Aiden laughed as he stated she wasn't about to mix business with pleasure. Clayton would wait. He was sure if Vance Chase could capture her attention, she would give him a chance.

Clayton explained if she wasn't interested, The Whelan Group would purchase the properties and sell them separately to clients within the group. There would be no offers made to anyone other than their clients and it would not go up for bid at any auctions.

"This offer, my dear, would give you time to learn more about the business as you make each of them your own. You can keep them alive and vibrant without changing any of them. One by one whenever you're ready we will shut them down for renovations and reopen them as you like. The important thing is to have your signature on the deed. Once we close the deal we can move to your rhythm. We are here to help you. I don't want to overwhelm you."

Clayton touched her hand gently and looked into her eyes. She felt a chill run down her back. Clayton was handsome. His touch could be felt through her each of her senses. Once before while having dinner in Vegas with Vance she made a mental comparison of the two men. Clayton seemed excited that she was the owner of her business. He encouraged her thoughts and ideas explaining when and where she made have to detour or pause before taking the next step. They laughed at the bad ideas and she felt he saw her vision. She knew she could trust him. He never set perimeters or a boundary. He told her whatever she needed he would provide it.

Comparing Vance to Clayton was never her intention, but his touch and her reaction caused her to gaze into his caramel colored eyes. His features were different than Vance's Canadian mixture. They both were attractive men but Clayton's character won her over. Vance spoke of the "at home" woman while Clayton understood the "business" woman. She excused herself from the table. She needed air.

Seychelle sat on the chaise lounge chair in the woman's bathroom. She hoped no one entered asking questions about her wellness. The feelings that came over her were not intentional but she knew Clayton elevated her libido. She thought about it for a moment. This was not the first time she had an appetite for him. It was the touch. It spoke to her emotions. She thought about Vance and their last night together.

"Come closer so I can see you in the light." Vance was stretched across the bed waiting for her to come out of the bathroom.

Seychelle stood near the mirror. Where she stood gave him a perfect view of her body in the lace teddy. He could view her front and back simultaneously. It wasn't their first encounter but it would be their last for months. Seychelle planned to give him what he would miss. She hoped satisfaction would sustain their relationship. The uncertainties and questions were constantly on her mind but they mixed well.

She let the overlaying jacket fall to the floor. She still had on her heels giving her stature a models posture. She walked slowly with purpose one step then the next, crossing her legs ever so slightly. His face met her navel. Vance knew this was his starting point. He touched her thighs softly. Her spine tingled responding to the touch of what she thought would be his next move. Lifting her left leg on the bed, he kissed her ankles as he unstrapped her sandal. With her foot planted on the bed and the other on the floor, Vance kissed her inner thigh as he placed her foot on the floor lifting the other to the bed.

Seychelle giggled as she maintained her balance. The thrill of his tongue exploring each leg and pausing at her in between sent another chill. She was tempted to push him over and sit prepared for him to explore her thoroughly. She stood at the base of the bed and slipped off the teddy exposing all of what Vance dreamed of throughout the day. He loved their foreplay. She taunted him walking around the bed as if she was a lioness teasing her king. From her crown to her feet she was perfectly sculpted. Her beauty was captivating. He allowed her to crawl on him. His erection spoke to her as he prepared himself for one of his best nights ever.

Seychelle was startled when the bathroom stall slammed. She opened her eyes trying to compose herself. The woman apparently thought she was sleeping. She glanced at Seychelle from the sink.

"Are you okay dear?" The woman was about the age of her mother.

"Yes ma'am thank you. I think the wine got to me a little but I'm okay." Seychelle lied quickly.

The woman nodded her head as a sign she understood leaving her alone once again. Seychelle laughed and closed her eyes hoping to continue the thoughts.

She didn't expect Vance to please her as he did. She had sex with two other American men and the interpretation of their movements was simply to perform until they exploded. Once they dumped the condom she dumped them. She was praying that Vance was mature enough to understand there was so much more than the pleasure of one. Vance loved to kiss her body in its entirety. Her nipples hardened as he moved closer to her center. He parted her legs as she began to moan gently. Just the touch of his lips sent her to another place. She remembered looking down at him as his tongue found the sweetness he was searching. She touched him as he set a pace that would prepare her climax. As he rose to insert himself she looked into his eyes and saw Clayton.

Seychelle was shocked into the current moment. She asked herself, *"Where did that thought come from?"* She didn't even know how long she had been in the bathroom. She stood at the sink and took a deep breath. She couldn't help but smile. She felt as though she had been completely satisfied. Checking her makeup she adjusted her blouse, winked and concluded, *"Nothing better than a wet dream in the middle of the afternoon."*

Chapter 59

Vance left a third message for Seychelle. It was strange that she hadn't returned his calls at some point during the day. He wondered what was wrong but put the thought of mishaps or any serious problems out of his mind. He wanted to tell her he mailed the auction booklet with a few articles about investors. He was featured in one of the articles and he wanted to share his celebrity status. There were a few articles over the years that mentioned his investments, advice to new investors, and prediction of sales. Sharing his excitement about any of the articles wasn't bragging, he hoped she would agree.

The Premiere Auctions booklet contained information on upcoming auctions, bidding advice, and auction results. It also spoke about new investor's, owners and their grand openings or sales. Vance flipped through the pages and noticed there was an article about the Westlake Property.

The property listed Serenity Resorts & Spa as the new owners. The owners were backed by The Whelan Group. There was a real possibility that the owner was a new buyer or investor. Figures were listed showing the prospects for growth at each of the four locations and the comments noted the buyer as a smart investor. There were many who would have loved to know the profit margins before the auction. It could have caused a bidding war.

Vance's only interest in the property was to block Cheyenne. Her "rise", as she claimed would have been intolerable for many. There were a few buyers who watched her flaunt and tease to get properties, money and under the table deals over the past decade.

When he realized that her late-night calls, dinner invitations and fantasy trips were all a game, he had lost a hefty amount of money. Money lost in investments would never be regained. Money lost in love always taught a lesson. She explained with her sweetest tone, *"Baby you can't count on every investment to bring you money. You need to drop a few thousand in a purchase."* After he found out she was on the other end of the failed transactions, he dropped her.

Keeping your enemies close, a rule Vance believed was key in his business, he remained cordial with the vampirette. She sucked blood money from many that avoided being in the same room with her. All others were on her next victim list.

Vance smiled as he saw the pictures of the renovations being done at Westlake. There was no notice of the grand opening but he was sure Cheyenne would be there. He would too, but to congratulate the new owner. The purchase put a smile on many of investor's faces, all but Cheyenne's.

Vance thought about dining out, something he hadn't done in a few weeks. He wasn't in the mood to cook, which left him no choice but to choose an eatery. The phone rang just as he reached his front door. He hurried to answer hoping it was Seychelle.

"Hello."

"Before you get sarcastic let me ask my question." Cheyenne's voice caused his stomach to churn.

"Hmm, go ahead. You know it wouldn't be any harm in saying hello first."

"Vance, you and I have an understanding like no other. You would have dismissed me before I could ask anything."

"Point taken, but it's not that bad. What's your question?"

"Is anyone other than me curious about who the new owner of Westlake is?"

"Did you get you Premiere Auction booklet? I thought you'd be buried in the pages they dedicated to the Westlake property. The owner is Serenity Resorts & Spa."

"No dear, that's the new name. No owner is listed. The Whelan Group is managing the property and won't name the buyer."

"Cheyenne, why? Why is it important to know who they or it is?"

"Vance, there's a bigger picture here. A new buyer? The competition is already enough, don't you think? If this owner or investor, whatever category they fit in, has the funding to sweep until they're satisfied…"

"If my dear, if. There's nothing to stop anyone from purchasing. I don't pay attention to the competition. I know what I can handle. If you're worried about what you can't handle, avoid the drama totally."

"That's all? You're suggesting drop out of the bidding process? No Vance that's not it. We need to be in the loop."

"Alright, so how many knew of the sweet package you convinced them to give you after you bought it?"

"What?"

"Cheyenne your interest was what you planned on receiving. What was the offer? You sound like you lost more when you didn't win the bid. What was it?"

"More property at a fair price, no at a steal. I need to know if they received the same offer. I didn't convince them to give it to me. We talked about the offer going to the highest bidder. Vance whoever bought Westlake has the opportunity to being at the top. I'll admit I wanted it, but somehow my gut feeling is telling me that I was swindled."

"Well check you out. Karma is a bitch. You swindle others and then you get swindled. Too bad you didn't lose money on the deal, then I might have agreed it wasn't fair."

"Well it's a loss to many of us, not just me. I'm sure others are wondering the same thing."

"No Cheyenne. You learned about the back end deal because you were so good at convincing whoever that you were going to get it. Another one of your back door deals that closed the door on you."

"Funny!" Cheyenne's reply echoed her disgust. "The Whelan Group knows who the owner is but won't tell. That's another question, what's the big secret?"

"Cheyenne, the real question is why do you care? You didn't win move on to the next. October baby. Have you locked in on the properties they're presenting? They've got a few in California and Philadelphia. I'm going to check into a few."

"So you're not the least bit concerned, not curious? Let's see, who was new at that event?"

"Cheyenne stop. You'll worry yourself to death. There were at least five hundred seats filled. Then count those in the V.I.P. rooms and others who sent bids in. You can't possibly be that interested. You're acting weird now."

"Alright Mr. Chase. I find it strange because I know what the deal was and if the owner takes that deal, they just took over top seat. I think gloating over your little article won't mean much when there's the next feature. Serenity Resorts & Spa hits it big or some shit like that. Vance you've got to want to move up a bit. It's got to be hard on your ego."

"Baby my rating will always stand out and the last I checked I ranked in the top five. I'm good with that."

"Unless you're number five and Serenity's owner becomes number one. Then you become just like the rest of us, trying to reach them."

"You gotta love what you do. I don't mind moving down a notch. That only means everyone moves down with me. The competition keeps me sharp, without the under the desk, I mean under the table..." Vance began to laugh uncontrollably.

"Yeah right Vance!" Cheyenne slammed the receiver into its cradle.

Chapter 60

C layton was staggered when Seychelle accepted his invitation to spend a day in the Wharf district of San Francisco. He thought that the history and tourist district would be an interest to her. The day wouldn't be filled with the discussion of business. It would be an attempt to get to know her on a more personal level.

They finished the meeting with Jon and Aiden early enough for Tristan to join them for dinner. The three teased Seychelle about her acceptance to meet Clayton in the morning. She laughed with them hoping she would be able to sleep soundly without having another dream.

It was a warm evening for a late September night. Usually the temperature would fall low enough for one to notice the change of the season. The summer elements were still hanging on and autumn wasn't a part of the forecast. Aiden and Tristan walked ahead of Jon and Seychelle. Their pace left enough space between them for the conversation between the couples not to be heard.

"Jon, what do you think about the offer for the other properties? Are you thinking like me? I think it's a bit much. I don't know if getting four other properties before we learn to manage what we have is a wise decision. I'm so overwhelmed with this pace that Americans have in everything." Seychelle took a slow deep breath. "I'm sorry Jon. I know, I sounded like I was on the verge of hysteria, right?"

Jon grinned. "I'm trained in being a listener. It's an AA requirement."

The laughter between them seemed to release some of her tension.

"You have the right to be concerned, yes. It is a little fast paced, yes. Should you know a little about the management of the other locations first? Yes, but—"

"Yes but what?" She held his wrist preparing for him to say don't take the deal.

"Clayton and the rest of The Whelan Group are wise investors. You'll get this property and each will be in the renovation stages at different times. You don't have to do the renovations as you did Westlake. You knowing and working on them together as one project was a big task to take on. You don't have to take on all four properties at once. You will own them and renovate as needed. You can take your time because you have completed the first phase of Serenity Resorts. I believe these will need more work. I'm not saying that to scare you. The Vegas properties had one theme and the changes were the same. I believe these will have more changes to make them have that Serenity feel. Each of them can have their own twist, that island spill."

"So it's not too soon to purchase?"

"Seychelle, the opportunity will not wait for you. You have to either say yes or pass it on to a competitor. Right now you can jump to the top of the list as a buyer and your profits will climb. You will be in a position that others would die for. Top gun competitor." Jon was excited for her.

She thought about what he was saying and still felt pressured. She thought about talking it over with Sasha. Her sister was the rational one. Seychelle kept asking herself, *What would Sasha do?*

For the first time, she wanted to talk to someone in business, someone who knew more about purchases and sales, someone like Vance. She wished Aiden or Jon had missed the meeting. She knew they both were very interested in acquiring the other properties. She couldn't explain her fears to them. The men agreed to let Seychelle think about it for a day or so. She nodded in agreement. She needed a little time to let it sink in.

The hours passed quickly. Seychelle's nerves wouldn't allow her to skip dinner. They all agreed on Italian food and the cuisine at De

Leoni's didn't disappoint them. Tristan loved the atmosphere and the soft music that was playing in the background.

"Are all Italian restaurants similar to this?" Tristan buttered another piece of the rolls placed before them.

"Most are. I eat here often for the same reasons. I love the food and the entertainment. After nine they have a band that comes through playing music and dancing. It's great entertainment." Jon smiled knowing Tristan was in awe. "Anyone for a glass of wine?"

Tristan paused, staring at Jon as though he cursed.

"I'll have a glass. What about you Tristan?" Seychelle passed her glass to Jon. He began to fill the glass with Merlot.

"I didn't know you drank Jon." Tristan answered without addressing Seychelle's question.

"I don't and I know you know Aiden doesn't. But that doesn't stop you ladies from enjoying the finest wine this restaurant offers. It is a great blend and one of my favorites, when I did partake."

Tristan felt the verbal slap on the hand. She told herself she had to trust Jon just as she believed in Aiden.

"I'm sorry, I didn't want to be rude. I just didn't know."

"It's okay. I'm good. No I'm better with it. I get reminded at times like this. Go ahead, you and Seychelle enjoy the wine. It helps the palate adjust to the food. Good food, good company, good wine." Aiden summoned the waiter to bring another bottle.

"Yes, I believe a good toast is necessary to seal this day." Jon tapped his glass for the waiter to refill it with non-alcoholic beer. Aiden nodded he would have the same.

"So let's toast Aiden and Tristan first. May you be blessed with the happiness you share today, forever." They all brought their glasses to the middle of the table and tapped them gently.

"Jon, allow me to make the next toast." Aiden stood. "I'd like to toast the three of you. Without you I wouldn't understand the true meaning of love. You have to put it to the test — the test of time, understanding, patience and faith. You've all given me back what I lost. You've been there for me in so many ways; I want to say that you were all right. I will never forget what you've done for me and sacrificed to make sure I became who I was again."

"Okay don't ruin my little buzz from this wine." Seychelle stated as she raised her glass. They laughed as their glasses met again over the table.

"I guess it's my turn. I won't stand. I want to thank you and Aiden for being a part of Serenity Resorts. I don't know if Aiden told you Jon, I wanted to do this without any help. Other than his of course, but what I have today can't match the love you guys have shown me. Here, here let's make Serenity Resorts & Spa a business every owner would be envious of."

Jon replied, "Here, here."

Seychelle watched Tristan and Aiden as they finished their meals and the wine continued to be poured. Tristan was beginning to relax. She moved closer to him in the booth making it obvious Jon and Seychelle were about to be ignored.

"Hey Seychelle and I are going to get going. You two, enjoy the rest of the evening. Good with you Seychelle?"

"Uh yes. You guys have a good night or whatever. I'll see you when you get in."

Chapter 61

Jon said his goodbye to Seychelle assuring her he would look over the numbers again. She told him she was sure Clayton would ask her if she gave the offer for property any thought. Jon thought the deal spoke for itself. He'd wait for Aiden's input before he would add his thoughts.

It was close to eight before his phone rang. It was the anticipation of Sasha's call that caused him to answer without looking and the number flashing on the caller ID.

"Hey babe, I missed you today."

"Well, Mr. Mikels I can state that we had no meeting scheduled for today."

"I am so sorry, good evening. May I help you?"

"Maybe you can. I am Cheyenne Minnows. I saw your name in the Premiere Auctions booklet. I don't believe we've ever met. I am an investor and buyer."

The name rang loudly although her voice was soft, almost like a whisper.

"How may I help you?"

"I read that you were an investor who was listed under the purchase of Westlake Village. I thought you were with The Whelan Group, but I see you're independent."

"Yes, I am."

"Well I was wondering if you were the sole owner of Serenity Resorts & Spa or were you a shared investor."

"A shared investor as is The Whelan Group. What is your interest, Ms. Minnows, did you say?

"Yes, that's right Ms. Minnows. I've been trying to reach the owner of Serenity Resorts & Spa. It seems to be a hushed topic. I don't understand why."

"It's my understanding that the owner rather remain anonymous. For whatever the reason they've requested to be noted as Serenity Resorts & Spa on all the transactions."

"I see. Well how does that work for you?"

"What do you mean?"

"I mean, are you a part of that, what are they? They don't have any history and no submitted biography. Who are they?"

"Ms. Minnows what is your interest?"

"There are things that are done behind closed doors that others are not a part of. I know that. In this case these people or persons have stepped on what was discussed before the auction. I want to know if they were given the offer as well."

Jon immediately realized that the offer made to Seychelle had been discussed prior to the bidding. Seychelle caused a ripple at the bargaining table. Now it was clear why The Whelan Group would back her or buy the property. It was a high commodity.

"Ms. Minnows, I don't want to assume but if I may suggest you should get in touch with those who were behind those doors with you. They would be able to tell you if the offer was made and/or accepted. I won't be able to give you any information on the owner."

"I was hoping I could talk with someone who knew what was going on without them lying about the sale."

"Maybe I don't completely understand you Ms. Minnows. Any offers made regarding the sale would have to be discussed with the prior owner. The new owner has no obligation to tell you the circumstances of the sale or any offers thereafter."

Cheyenne listened intently. She kept meeting obstacles. She was annoyed but she would make another call.

"Well you're right Mr. Mikels you don't have to understand me. I guess you haven't been an investor long enough to know the goings-on behind the closed doors. Some of it goes well beyond the auction."

"Ms. Minnows I am sorry I can't be of any help. My years in investments don't matter at this point. I make all my offers, deals and goings on, as you say on paper. Verbal agreements mean nothing when you're negotiating with monetary transactions. I've learned to take the bitter and the sweet. Each bid, buy or sale is to be evaluated as such. If you look through the Premiere Auctions booklets over the years, my name appears more than once. So I am not new at all.'

Cheyenne detected his annoyance. He wasn't going to give her any information or direction.

"I wish you the best Ms. Minnows. Have a good day."

Jon didn't wait for her response. He shook his head at Cheyenne's efforts. He spent a few hours looking over the offer. He understood why Cheyenne was interested. It was as Clayton explained Serenity Resorts would be one of the top five on the sales and investments groups.

The eleven hours difference in time between California and Seychelles Island caused Jon to wait another hour before calling Sasha. The mornings for Sasha were hectic after eight. Driving on the Mahé Island in the morning traffic was her biggest complaint. She left early in the morning to get ahead of the rush. She arrived at the school each morning before eight. Jon would call during that time. She would call him during her evening hours after preparing for class the next day.

Jon poured his coffee and sat down as his call was connected. He sat the calendar on the table, a new ritual he had since calling Sasha regularly. He'd mark the calendar with a heart. Sasha was a part of his day. He wanted to be able to see how much time he committed to in their relationship. It amazed him that he put more into the calls and letters he sent then he had put in time with past relationships.

"Hello? Hello." Sasha repeated her response to the call. "The line is filled with static. Hold on."

Jon waited to hear her voice again.

"Hello? Jon I know it's you can you hear me."

"Of course I can. Are you on the veranda?"

"Yes the only place I can get across the water reception. How was your day?"

"Have you spoken to your sister yet?"

"No, should she have called? Is there something wrong?"

"Nothing she won't handle."

"Well she didn't call yet. So is it good news or what?"

"A mixture of good news and more. That woman Cheyenne Minnows called me. She sounded desperate. She wants to know who owns Serenity Resorts. I wouldn't tell her and from what she said neither will Clayton. Oh, and when Seychelle calls ask her about Clayton."

"Clayton? Is there a problem with him?"

"Quite the opposite. I'll let Seychelle fill you in."

"I was hoping she'd call this morning. It will have to wait until afternoon. Well, how is everything else going?"

"Great, will you be able to visit during the grand opening? That will be next big thing on the agenda. I was wondering if coming here would interfere with your schools schedule. You and Seychelle are working on the details, right?"

Sasha glanced at the calendar hanging on the wall near her clock. It was time for her to start her morning journey. For the first time since they had been doing the long-distance talking she was ready for the conversation to end.

"Yes, I didn't realize the renovations would be completed so soon. She said she wanted to open each one starting with a lavish affair on New Year's Eve. I didn't think of the date. School reopens that week. I really have to look at that. Thanksgiving is right around the corner, then traveling with you on Christmas. I just don't know if all of that can be done. I'll talk with Seychelle about it."

"I know she wants you there and maybe even your parents." Jon stated it as though it had been discussed. His statement made Sasha feel a bit uneasy.

"I don't know Jon. You and my brother were right. It changes things. I'm not certain my parents are prepared for the change. I don't think I am. I mean, well let me get my thought together. I'm running a little late. Let's talk later or I'll call you once I've spoken to my sister."

Reluctantly Jon didn't try to keep her on the line. It seemed as though once the school year began her attention to their relationship was lost. There were no further conversations about the future, his or hers. She seemed to be engrossed in her students, paperwork and her parents. He was surprised she wasn't overly excited about the grand openings. He wondered if she lost interest or wasn't as interested as she claimed. Jon sat back in his chair without any consolation. He knew he was losing the woman he had learned to love.

Chapter 62

“It's not the same Seychelle. I don't want to string him along just because I can. He has a different outlook on life. He's a free spirit and I don't want to keep him from being who he is.”

“Sasha, what are you talking about? You left here saying you wanted to be that free spirit. Have you changed your mind? No, what has changed you mind?”

The silence spoke to Seychelle. She knew her sister well.

“Is it Mother, has she talked with you? What did you tell her Sasha?”

“I told her nothing that you haven't said. I told her about the business from my point of view. That is all. When I mentioned travel and the beautiful resorts, I told her how excited the four of us were. Well then she questioned what four? I told her Jon was there, supporting Aiden and our efforts.”

“So you told her that you and Jon dated while we were traveling?”

“She said that she and Father thought it was odd for a man to be following another man around like that. I had to clear their minds Seychelle. They thought Jon was, you know, gay or something. I told them no and of course they asked how could I be sure.”

"Oh my God Sasha. So you told them you slept with this man."

"No but you know Father. It's all wrong Seychelle. I have a career here in the school system. It is what I went to college for. I love it I do and they reminded me that I'm good at it. The school system here is my calling and I can't ask Jon to live his life as I would mine."

"So you've decided to continue with being a teacher there. That's great."

"You're not angry?"

"Sasha everyone has a life to live, their life. I would love to have both you and Aiden be a part of this business venture. But how much better are my wants than the wants of Father or Mother? He wants us to be a part of what his dream was. I'm not mad at all. A little shocked but I understand. Now what I don't understand is why Jon is out of the picture too. I thought you and he were headed to the altar."

"Well let's just say I understood what Mother meant those years she said, '*Allowing the butterfly to fly after you have captured it is beautiful, especially when it returns to be caught again.*' I never understood it but she explained it to mean, if you capture one you say you love how do you know their love for you is true? Let them go, give them room and if it is true love they will return. Seychelle I thought about that over a few nights. I did everything I could to get Jon's attention and yes I bedded him. What did he do to show me any of that was truly love? What man wouldn't want that attention, the seduction, and the bedroom romance?"

"You're right and Mother has a point too. It may be an attraction, physical and mental for the moment. So what do you tell him about this new awareness you have for love. I know you're not going to tell him it's just a fling?"

"No, no, a fling?" Sasha laughed at the thought. "That was no fling my sister. I wish he lived here."

"Well you know the island is not the only place where teachers are needed. If you and Jon were to get together you could live in the states."

Again, the silence spoke between them.

"Sasha, Mother and Father will be fine."

"You and Aiden have left them. I don't want to leave them as well. It's hard for them to understand the American ways and traditions. Everything is so fast. You getting the property and a new business. Aiden and Tristan and you my sister what about Vance?"

"You didn't tell them about Vance too now did you?"

Sasha laughed heartedly. "No don't you worry your secret romance is still a secret."

"Good, because I don't know if I want a distance romance either."

"So have you told Vance?"

"No, I just let the butterfly go."

Chapter 63

Time didn't allow the sisters to talk much longer. Seychelle felt guilty that she didn't mention her acceptance of Clayton's offer to spend a day with him. She really thought it was his way of getting her alone to talk about the offer that was on the table. Another part of her longed to hear him say he wanted to get to know her better. She didn't understand her feelings, but Clayton Whelan peaked her interest. Vance was a good man but she couldn't be the woman he wanted her to be. She needed to have her own and make her own. She would have to change her desire of being an owner and businesswoman. Their worlds clashed because of his views.

The weather was still warm enough for a simple fall outfit. When she questioned Clayton about how she should dress he smiled and replied nothing special.

After going through her luggage and garment bag, she decided to wear a pair of jeans with a matching jacket and a cowl neck sweater. She dressed the outfit with gold jewelry and low-heeled booties. She was sure she wouldn't want to walk in her heels through the streets of the city.

Clayton arrived as promised promptly at ten. Seychelle was pleased to open the door and find him dressed in jeans as well.

"Good Morning, do you think I'll need anything other than my bag?"

Clayton wasn't sure what she meant but he told her she was fine just as she was. Her hair was perfectly pinned in an up do which accented her African features. Clayton admired her features and her natural beauty. She could have been a model for any fashion magazine. He patiently waited as she went into the kitchen and returned shaking the keys.

"Has everyone left you alone this morning?"

"Well yes, and no. Tristan is getting a tour of the area with Aiden. He will be returning to work tonight and he wants her to have access to the car so she can get around. Of course she hasn't been here so getting around would mean exploring. She's not willing to explore by herself. I guess Aiden and I will be sort of tour guides for her until she feels a bit more comfortable. When does his position with you begin?"

"Next Monday, I told him to think about it, I mean the other job. We'll be paying enough, and keeping him busy. I guess he'll let us know what he decides. I really want him to open the division that will handle the auctions and bidding process. We don't have that, although many outsiders may think we do."

"How long has the group been together?" Seychelle asked as she locked the front door.

"The group has been together for years, believe it or not. We started back in college. It's more than what it was intended to be but that's growth. We had some capital between us, put it together, bought a few great properties and decided to become investors for other companies. It wasn't long before we were interested again to buy and build. The Whelan Group as it is known now has been in business, full functioning for ten years."

"That's a success story, any downfalls?"

"None large enough to sink us. Every business has its ups and downs. It's knowing when to back up, get out, or be still. Knowing that will allow you to get up and get in again. You can't be scared of losing."

He looked at her and could only nod his head yes, answering the question she never asked.

"That's got to be the foundation for all businesses. Any other mindset would lead to defeat before any challenge."

"Exactly. Have you guys been to the Wharf?" He asked deliberately changing the subject.

"Yes, Sasha and I wanted to eat there every night. Aiden told us no. But the eateries are fabulous."

"Some of my favorites too. We're going to walk around and explore a bit. Unless you have somewhere you'd like to visit. I am sure San Francisco can't possibly top the alluring sights on Seychelles Island."

"When you live there you don't always think of the beauty that is there. Just as you will down play the Wharf, I would be the same way at home. So I am ready to see the sights. As I said we saw the eateries and shopped a little."

The afternoon went as planned. After eating lunch they walked the area. Clayton pointed out a few of the older buildings. He told her about the construction and the difference in the modern buildings and blueprints. Seychelle loved the trolley and the cobblestone streets. The Fisherman's Wharf was an attraction many enjoyed and Clayton gave her the history of each area as the trolley approached the dock. They decided to take the ferry that toured the bay.

Seychelle watched as Clayton assisted each of the women off the trolley. Instinctively she responded to him reaching for her hand as they walk quickly across the busy street. She felt like a schoolgirl on her first date as they walked to the pier holding hands.

"Are you hungry, want something to drink before we board the ferry?" Clayton asked and paused at one of the sidewalk vendors.

"Yes, how about one of those fruity drinks they advertise so often."

"Not sure what drink you're referring to but let's see if he knows more than me."

The vendor offered a list of refreshments, candy and popcorn; he also had a few souvenirs that decorated his stand. Seychelle didn't recognize the names but the different fruit smoothies seemed to meet the definition. Clayton ordered two and picked a key chain with a picture of the Wharf on it. He handed Seychelle the key chain.

"A small reminder for the day." He waited for her to put it in her leather bag. He took her hand and they continued their walk.

"How long have you been here in California?"

"My parents moved here when I was about twelve. I left and went to college and immediately returned."

"Why, didn't you finish?" Seychelle was puzzled she was sure he had a degree hanging on the wall in his office.

"I didn't finish there. I went to college in New York. My thought was I'd learn from the busiest. There's a big difference. I couldn't keep up with the pace. So my father brought me home, sat me down, and reminded me that it was my dream to have a business. I had to go to school and earn that degree. So I went to Berkeley University, here in California."

"So you don't travel much?" Seychelle began to think of him as a home boy."

"No I travel quite a bit. I do business in 25 of the states and 10 islands. We're looking to expand, maybe have an office on the east coast."

"So do you enjoy the travel or is it only because of business?"

"I enjoy both. I make time for business and pleasure. I try not to cross the two. But I must confess Ms. Tudjal you make it hard."

"Me? What have I done?"

"You've captured my attention. I honestly don't know what it is exactly but it started about thirty minutes after meeting you. I wanted to understand what you wanted to do with your business first and then I wanted to know you. Usually, one of my associates would handle new clients. Especially those with little or no business to speak of. Jon pitched for you and your brother is a valuable asset."

Seychelle stopped and looked at him with raised eyebrows.

"You knew that. His knowledge is what any business would want. It is the reason I offered the position to him. He said it was worth looking into, that your business plan had potential. After the first auction, I agreed. You allowed us to steer you lead you through the process of your purchase. A smart business woman or man understands what is necessary to building a business with a solid foundation. You had faith in my business taking care of your business. Now outside of that, I want to know about you. I want to be sure that you are okay, how can I take care of you? Seychelle I want to know more about you."

They proceeded slowly in the line waiting to board the ferry. Seychelle had another feeling of guilt as she compared Clayton to Vance. She felt comfortable being with him. He had many attributes including being sexy. His voice could lead her anywhere he wanted her to go. It was as though she was dreaming again.

She was serious about not wanting a distant relationship. She dreamed about being in love but her business came first. She looked into Clayton eyes as he spoke. He took care and would take care of her business needs. His wish to please her gave her chills, warm chills. He teased her curiosity.

Clayton was taller than Vance. His dark skin was well kept. Seychelle wondered did he consider himself a pretty boy. She wouldn't be able to deal with a man that had to have a mirror and a bunch of selfies. Although he hadn't mentioned taking any pictures, he was looking out over the water as she gave him another visual once over. He wore his clothes well. She tried to remember him in a suit, not that it mattered. She noticed he wore a black onyx stone set in platinum ring, with a matching bracelet. She wondered if she was the only one he would be caring for.

"Please step this way folks, watch your step. Go all the way to the rear as you board." The man shouted as he removed the heavy rope that held the crowd back from the docked ferry.

The ferry was larger than Seychelle thought it would be. There was plenty of room once they got pass the bow. The crowd followed the command walking toward the stern. A welcome announcement could be heard over the intercom. The voice continued to say they would be riding from Pier forty one, passing Alcatraz Island the location of the infamous prison. There would be a stop at Sausalito & Tiburon, villages off the bay, and Angel Island Park then on to Oakland. Passengers could get off at any stop or like Seychelle and Clayton stay on and enjoy the sights.

They both sat looking over the ocean as the 'voice' became the audio guide giving history and details about the points of interest.

"Your first ferry ride?" Clayton asked breaking into Seychelle's thoughts.

"No, well yes here in America. We have a ferry on the island. Most use it as transportation to and from work. There is also one that travels through the tourist areas. Like this giving a history of the area. Aiden didn't offer this excursion to Sasha and I. Sasha would have loved to hear this area's history."

Clayton listened as she talked. His prayers were answered. Her beauty wasn't a false presence meant to disguise a flawed character. She was the type of woman he could see himself dating. Getting to know what made her smile, what she loved to eat for breakfast, her favorite book or movie, what caused her pain, what caused her pleasure was all he needed to know. The relationship could grow. Seychelle being in business would provide the understanding that was missing in his past relationships. There would be no need to explain money, travel or association with clients. He knew they could grow to be a power couple.

When he decided to ask her out, he knew she would be more than the women he dated or what he imagined she would be. Clayton was never in what he would consider a serious relationship. He promised himself he would be committed when he found the right woman. Seychelle was a woman that would appreciate his status and they could share in the other's success. He couldn't deny he was in love with who she was and he wanted to be in her life.

"Aww Clayton look." The ferry was passing a group dancing on the pier entertaining a crowd. "Those colors are the same as we have at home during our island festivals. The ribbons are beautiful. Is it a special occasion or is this a part of the attractions?"

"I'm sure it is a part of the attraction. There are a few performances on the docks, especially at night. They are amazing dancers and light performers. Maybe we will be able to see a performance before you go back to the islands."

"That would be nice. Yes, I would enjoy that. Have you been across the waters?"

"Not the water that borders your island? Please say you are inviting me." He teased hoping she would extend an invitation.

"You are teasing me, I'm sure. I can see you now walking on our white sand with a wide brim hat."

"Yes, and I do have one. I see the two of us walking on your white sand. Hand in hand enjoying the weather and the water barely touching our bare feet. We would be headed to your favorite spot as you show me familiar places along the shore."

"Stop, you have a special knack for peeping into my dreams."

"Peeping? Oh, I have to change that. I want to be your dream."

Seychelle smiled. She couldn't believe how the day was going. From the weather to her present company she was at peace. There was no reason to want anything more. She looked at Clayton and he leaned in and kissed her on her cheek.

"Have you been to the northern part of California? Or anywhere where there is snow or colder weather?"

Seychelle laughed. "No, I guess I never thought about it. My sister asked about resorts with ski slopes or snow. I told her I didn't think I wanted that. California and snow? It seems like an impossibility."

"Okay, seeing is believing. Have you heard that saying before?"

Seychelle gave him a playful push on his arm. "So you have. Put that on the day trip calendar Ms. Tudjal. You may find it to be pleasurable. Remember your property is for those who find comfort and relaxation there. You can't leave out the people who love to ski or sit by a fire with a blanket wrapped around them."

"I'll mark the calendar Mr. Whelan. Don't wait until the weather is below the norm to invite me to see those places either."

"No ma'am. I promise I won't."

"Clayton, this all has been an emotional rush for me. I don't know if anyone understands me saying that."

Seychelle shocked herself she told him about feelings she hadn't shared with her siblings and wouldn't share with her parents or Vance. She wanted to dance because her dream had come true. After years of visioning the grand opening, the people applauding her success and a man at her side, it was all coming true.

"I couldn't be happy for myself without upsetting someone. Today, I feel as though I can share my happiness with you and not feel guilty. Is that strange?"

"No it's not strange. You may have to get used to being in your happiness alone if you're waiting for others to embrace it. It's nothing wrong with lifting yourself up and acknowledging your success. You're in another arena. It will be different and you'll have to find others who are in the same arena. Family, well they are happy for you. They may not say it when you want them to but there is no parent that wants their child to fail. Your siblings will be there for you and as you rise there will be questions about what you want and what they want for you. Don't beat yourself about it."

"Hmmm, you're so right, I don't have many friends because I always had different dreams. I wanted to leave the island and get started. Returning would be periodic visits, maybe holidays, or an escape from constant working. I do that sometimes."

"I can understand that. I do that as well. I'm low key. After being in a business and about business there are days that I want to escape. Can't stay away long though." Clayton laughed.

"Yes, I feel like that and I just got started. I want to shout 'I did it', but who would I be shouting to?"

"Go ahead shout. Maybe not on the ferry." They both laughed.

They talked about their childhood, and the differences in their rearing. They included traditions and Seychelle asked him about men and their female children.

"Well to answer you fairly, I don't know. I don't know about that feeling although you're saying it's tradition. I just think that the support of parents helps one grow into themselves. You can't separate that and the traditions they grew up with or planned to raise you with. Seychelle, you have so much going on and you just started. They know you as that little girl, not the business woman."

"If I stayed in my father's business would they know me better? No. I don't think so. But I'm coping with it. It's all evolving so quickly."

"Yes and I'm going to ask you this and we're going to tuck our business matters until we're at the office. Are you okay with taking on the offer you've been given?"

"Have you run the numbers? I don't want to be a broke owner. I was thinking about costs and renovations being done. I have questions about the properties. Can we look at them first? I mean this isn't a blind offer is it?"

"Of course we can and should. You can go with Aiden and Jon or whatever you like. I just want to know are you leaning toward accepting the offer or it's a definite no."

"I'm leaning toward accepting. I need to see numbers and of course the condition of the property."

"We've got your back. Whatever way you want to handle it. It brings me back to my question. What about you? Can I be a part of your support team? Can I be there to help you relax and escape?"

Seychelle smiled coyly. There was nothing left to convince her. Clayton's simplicity and warm approach did relax her. She could escape with him and there would be no fanfare. There was no need to impress her. That was the difference between the two men, Vance and Clayton. After the auction in October, she would have to make a choice.

Sweetness Is Forever

Chapter 64

The papers were signed. Aiden reviewed them again before submitting them to Kevin. He had been working full time with The Whelan Group for a month. The first auction of interest was the one being held in California. Aiden read over the invitations for V.I.P. reservations. He was sure it was the auction Seychelle would be attending with Vance. He jotted down the location and time on his calendar. He dialed Jon's number hoping he would be free to attend that day.

Clayton was right. The business of opening a new division occupied Aiden's days while his nights were filled with wedding planning. Tristan didn't want to rush the ceremony but she wouldn't hear of waiting another year. Once they got the theme, colors, and location she promised he wouldn't have to be devoted to her searching through magazines and internet sites. She would accept his simple nod of approval.

Aiden worked two jobs for a month and found himself dozing during the day. He blamed it on trying to satisfy both jobs, a sister and his soon to be bride. He quit the night manager's job and didn't miss the workload at all. He was finally doing what held his passion.

The new division of The Whelan Group would be for new investors or buyers seeking to purchase properties with the intentions of making a profit. Aiden would be responsible for overseeing their needs and handling all connections. The auction was first on his agenda.

Just as he was about to disconnect the unanswered call, Jon answered.

"Good morning. What's up?" He sounded as though he was rushed.

"Hey is this a good time? I wanted to talk to you about this auction coming up."

"Yea, Yea, it's being held where?"

"The Continental, in two weeks. Are you in town that weekend?"

"Sure, I'll mark the calendar. How's things going? Adjusting to your new workload?"

"I'm good man. Adjusting to that and having Tristan here with me. It's a little different you know? It may be what I needed. A chance to pursue a dream and live it with someone I love."

"Aiden, at some point it's got to be about you. Without the fantastic job and without Tristan there is you. Things can be disrupted or changed by the minute but you have to believe in you. You're doing great my man, don't let a bump in the road set you back."

"No bumps, I did want to keep the other job. You know a little security money. The Whelan Group salary is more than enough. I can hustle to make a little more. Listen, have you ever thought about buying property?"

"Years ago I did. Flipped a few properties and sold them. I can't see managing the property after the sale. I invest make the money over time and move on."

"So what does Vance do that has him sitting high on the list. I was reading the Premiere Auction booklet. He's hit a few milestones."

"Yeah he's been in the business for years. So has that woman that tags along Cheyenne Minnows. They were together on a few deals. I guess she cheated him too. I decided to ask around about her and found out about him. Is Seychelle serious about him?"

"I doubt it. I really don't know, she hasn't talked about him. It may be just a business connection. Listen, what would you say about you and me purchasing something like a BNB spot? We could get staff to run it. I was looking at a few this morning. They've got a few going up this round. What do you think?"

"Two weeks? Let me think about it. Are they selling the franchise outright or just the building?"

"I know what you mean. I'll check it out. It may be just the thing for Tristan to run."

"Two weeks, you better check with her too. Can't go with the maybe when you're spending money like that."

"You got it. Let me know."

Aiden planned on telling Tristan about the property but needed to talk with Seychelle first. He would need her to back him if Tristan questioned his finances. He was waiting for her call but thought it better to talk to her at home. The bid would start low enough for him to get in. He hadn't lost it all but he would need Jon and maybe his sister if it got too steep.

Seychelle stayed at the apartment even though she was invited to go window-shopping with Tristan. She was tempted but there were a few details she had to discuss with the contractors. She made arrangements to visit the additional properties before the holidays. Clayton didn't ask to tag along. She wished he had. She didn't want to sound desperate, but she hoped he would keep her company.

Tristan was her back up plan since Sasha couldn't take a leave from school. She was thrilled about the invitation and a chance to travel with Seychelle.

"I guess once all this business stuff settles Aiden and I can set a date." Tristan spoke louder than necessary as she entered the kitchen.

Seychelle had paperwork stacked and spread across the table.

"I'm sorry do you have enough room?" Seychelle questioned as Tristan moved a few of the papers so she could sit with her cup of tea.

"I'm fine. I'm going to that one boutique where we saw that jumpsuit I pointed out to you."

"Are you thinking about getting it?"

"No, I want to see what else they have in there. I'm thinking they may have a cute selection of dresses. If they do maybe I'll find dresses for you and Sasha, you know for the wedding."

"Oh, okay. I thought you'd be more traditional."

"Why? I just want the dresses to coordinate with the color scheme really. Traditional? Aiden doesn't want to have the wedding on the island. My mother probably won't come, and well let's just say I'm trying to keep my fragmented piece of mind. So nothing to nag at us during that day. Probably more of the people here. Aiden agreed to send invitations home. I know the invitations are just a way of saying we're getting married, don't really expect you to come."

"Okay, listen we'll be leaving next week for our first stop. Will you be ready?"

"Yes, I told Aiden I'd go job hunting after we return. He didn't seem pleased."

"Please tell me he didn't question why you wanted to work."

"I don't know if he wants me to or not. I need to work to keep my sanity. Plus, love him or not I want to be able to have my own."

"Understood."

Seychelle's phone rang and when she saw the number she hesitated. She pointed to the phone and mouthed "Vance".

Tristan sipped her tea with her brow raised. They talked earlier about her dilemma. She wanted Vance to be more like Clayton. As an afterthought she wanted Clayton to be more like Vance. Through her confusion she knew Clayton would be her choice. If she lived on the "edge" as her Aunt Lorian would say, she'd keep them both, separate of course.

"Hello Sir." Tristan wanted to laugh as Seychelle sank into a lazy sigh.

"I was wondering if you were avoiding my calls."

"Why would I do that? I've been busy helping my brother get settled. He's found the courage to propose to his girlfriend. She returned with us. Of course he knew we both were coming but didn't prepare for our stay."

"So are you helping to plan the upcoming ceremony?"

"No, that is not my forte. I might need her to plan my wedding one day. She's great with all of that stuff."

"Plans in the making or just a woman's dream?"

"Oh, no not even a dream. I'm not ready for that yet. I've got a lot to do before marriage."

"Well I hope it doesn't include the distance between us."

"Depends on when I'm on this side of the water. There is always that distance. I don't see myself being a bride anytime soon."

"You never know. Love takes over and then before you know it, you're waiting to deliver your first born."

"Oh my, that's too fast for me. My career will be booming before that happens."

"Well since we're speaking on it. What are your plans about your career?"

"I don't know. First I'd have to find a way to tell my father I won't be working with him any longer. Lately I've been thinking about starting a business branding a marketing program that I could teach." The lie rolled off her lips as though she had told it many times before.

Tristan began to laugh softly. Seychelle quickly wrote on a pad and passed it to Tristan. "He doesn't know about my properties."

Tristan nodded her head as she continued to listen.

"So you said that was your major in school right? Business, I guess you can dabble in it a bit. Maybe even beef up my business."

"Maybe so. What have you accomplished today?"

"Nothing. I've actually put aside my work. I've been trying to reach you most of the day."

"Now don't blame me for your lack of work. That's not what I do as a woman who understands how enterprises are built."

"Oh, do you now? Where did you get that trait? An inherited skill or through education?"

"Inherited skill. My father insisted we all learn how to build a business from scratch. It took my brother and me some time to catch on but I believe he's got it. That leaves hope for me."

Tristan began to cough repeatedly. She ran out of the room laughing. Seychelle waited to see if Vance would respond to the noises he heard.

"So my dear will I see you before the auction."

"Are you coming in for a few days? I have to do some traveling next week. Tristan, my brother's fiancé, is looking for the perfect resort for their honeymoon. She's picked out a few and my gift to them will be to treat her to at least one. Just a two-day stay but she hasn't traveled much without Aiden. My sister and I will pay for the one she chooses as a wedding gift."

"That's nice. What does your sister do again?"

"She's a teacher on the island back home. She teaches what Americans call grammar school. At home we just call it school."

"So will they have a traditional wedding?"

"I'm not sure if they've decided that or not. Are you coming to California early or staying after the auction?" She decided the conversation about weddings was getting too deep.

"Yes, that Thursday and I'll leave when you send me away."

"Hmmm. You may want to leave before I send you away."

Vance was caught off guard by her answer. "Is there something wrong?"

"No, not at all. California is no Vegas. There are a few sights and the strip but I got bored quickly here."

"Spending time with you is more than enough for me."

"Hold on." Seychelle checked to see if Tristan had left the apartment. "Tristan, I'm on my way. Vance, I am so sorry, can I call you back say about seven."

"Of course. Talk to you then."

Tristan waited a moment before she asked, "Seychelle, what's wrong with you and Vance?"

"Tristan, he's just not the one."

Chapter 65

"I think you and I made the same discovery. It was a fling of sorts. Jon fell for me and I enjoyed the attention. It was a fling."

"Are you trying to convince you or me?" Seychelle was sorting through papers Clayton sent for the new properties. Tristan chose San Juan after seeing the pictures of the others. Nassau reminded her of home and Cancun would be just another trip for Aiden.

"I don't know it just doesn't feel the same."

"Sasha it's not the same. You were seeing him every day, all day if you chose. Distance makes the heart grow fonder; or so they say."

"Well where's your heart when it comes to Vance?"

"Clayton kinda brought a few things to light."

"You and Clayton?"

"No, well I don't think so. We spent the day together a few days ago. No strings attached and no violins played. But there was some attraction."

"So what happened?"

"Nothing. We walked through the Wharf, rode the ferry, had lunch and dinner and he escorted me home. Sasha it felt good, genuine. No fancy restaurants, no need to get dressed and worry whether I was over dressed."

"Or under dressed." Sasha understood exactly what she meant.

"We talked about the scenery and history of the Wharf, but then we talked about traditions, family and anything that came to mind. There was a little talk about business. I thought that's what the day was going to be about. He didn't shut me down when I told him my expectations. He listened, heard me and understood my reasons. He didn't give me the 'women should' speech. I longed for those days with Vance."

"There's a big difference when your surroundings are the Vegas strip. Vance may have a different tune in different surroundings."

"Sasha, his opinion of women is as bad as Father's. He agrees with everything Father has said. I didn't tell him I had purchased properties, especially Westlake! He has no idea and in a way I don't want him to know."

"What difference would it make?"

"Vance is a businessman who sees no room for women. Since I won the bid and purchased the other property it makes me a competitor. I won't be bidding for any other property in the near future, but he will find out who owns Serenity Resorts and Spa. That will ruin any relationship we have."

"So tell him before he finds out."

"Even if I tell him, Sasha, his views on women and business don't sit well with me."

"I'm sure if he really cares for you his views will change."

"Did Father's view change? I'm sure he loves me and yet his views about business and women are set."

"Father's views are the same. He does believe in women being in business. It's just he wants you to be in his business."

"Sasha, I can't be with a man or fall in love with a man that wants to hold me back."

"Seychelle, what are you going to say when he finds out? It looked like you guys enjoyed each other's company and that wasn't business."

"I'm keeping it from him to keep what we have, even if it becomes just a friendship."

"So what's up with Clayton?"

"I'm leaving that up to him. I'm not rushing into anything. After all he's the top man of The Whelan Group. I don't need the headlines to have him and me on the front page. Tristan and I are going to check on the property in San Juan. She and Aiden have been to Cancun."

"She'll love the way you do your evaluations."

"No evaluation my sister, remember I've purchased these properties with the deal I was offered."

"Ah, I forgot. Yes, you are the Queen of the throne. Do you think that is why Clayton has an interest?"

"What is wrong with his interest in a woman who can handle herself and business? I have taken my dreams and made them a reality. No difference than what any businessman does. If that is his only interest I will be able to tell. I'm hoping it is merely an attraction and that he is willing to learn more about me. Vance would want me to forget my dream, have my business run by men. Clayton has an open mind for women who seek to have their own. I'm sure his interest will peak and he will want to find out more."

The sister's continued their conversation until Sasha had to leave for work. Seychelle promised to call their parents. Sasha told her they asked about her and Aiden often. Seychelle felt a jolt of guilt but couldn't bring herself to make the call.

Seychelle thought about Sasha's decision to end her relationship with Jon. Calling it a fling could only mean one thing — she was no longer interested. That was Aiden's fear. He never wanted his sister's to be involved with any of his friends. He thought he would lose a friend. There were many on the island that would become Aiden's friend just to visit and see his sisters. Aiden was able to detect their true concerns early. Seychelle wondered if he thought it would be the same with Jon. She certainly didn't expect it to be so or end when Sasha returned home. Maybe there was a suitor on the island that held her interest. A summer away could have made his heart grow fonder. Seychelle dismissed the thought. Sasha would have told her about anyone she was interested in.

It was close to seven. Tristan and Aiden would be returning soon. She decided to retreat to the bedroom and leave the rest of the apartment to the soon to be newlyweds. There were times she felt they needed to be alone. The months ahead would give them a taste of what they were stepping into. Seychelle would be returning to the island after visiting her new properties.

Chapter 66

Seychelle's sleep was interrupted early the next morning. Her brother entered the bedroom quietly and sat on the end of the bed.

"What is wrong Aiden?"

"I wanted to talk to you before the auction tomorrow. I have to go into the office and I know I'd miss you this evening. Isn't Vance coming in today? I heard you talking to Tristan about your plans tonight."

"You spy, you." Seychelle propped herself on her elbow to listen. "This must be serious. What time is it?"

"It's early. The sun is just finding its place. Remember when you were younger and you'd tell me that?"

"Oh yes and you'd run to the window to prove I didn't know anything about the sun's rotation. Then I'd find it and we'd watch the sunrise over the ocean. I loved mornings with you and Sasha. But here in California, I haven't even looked for the sunrise."

"Okay, I promise we will do a sunrise walk on the beach here. Listen I have a question. If you should get another tip from Vance this weekend can you let me know? I've been reviewing this booklet."

Aiden gave her the book and she pointed to her copy that sat on the desk across the room. He smiled realizing she was, as always, a step ahead of him.

"I want a bed and breakfast spot. They are really popular here. Something small, but quaint. I asked Jon to go in on the bid with me if the property should present itself this weekend. I know there will be other costs at closing and start up. I didn't lose all my money Seychelle I have quite a bit saved and this would be my gift to Tristan. I have nothing else to give her for our wedding."

Aiden was following an old family tradition. Both the bride and groom exchanged gifts. Usually the groom gave a home and the bride would give him her savings for them to start their life together.

"Aiden, you are starting your life new. Your life my brother the one you almost drowned in alcohol. You are just beginning to pull yourself up. Your wedding is months away. Why are you buying property now? There will be other auctions, other opportunities and you will be in a better position to purchase. Aiden I just spent money on this deal you and Clayton said was once in a lifetime. Take one of those spots and do with it as you please. There is renovations to be done, and I don't even know what else I may need."

"I need it to be from me. Not yours or Jon's. I need it to be mine. Seychelle, I'm trying to rebuild what I lost and this would be what will mold me. A wife, property that will sustain us, and a job."

"And the two of you will continue to live here in this apartment? Wouldn't you rather have a home?"

"No this is enough right now. I have two bedrooms here. It is larger than her mother's home. She likes it here. When we save again it will be for a home."

"I don't know Aiden. Jon agreed to this?"

"He told me to speak with you. I'm not talking about a resort, casino or any of that. A small BNB Seychelle. Look through the book. Please."

"Vance wouldn't be looking to invest in this?"

"Maybe he would, you never know."

Seychelle thought about the small club he took her to. It was just as Aiden described it. Comfortable and room enough for guest to enjoy themselves as the owners made money. The question wasn't would he invest. It was could she convince him to invest?

"I'll ask him what he thinks. Maybe he can give us a few tips. No promises Aiden."

Aiden stood and then leaned over to kiss his sister. "Okay, you've got time before the sun rises. It's only four thirty."

Seychelle couldn't speak. She dropped back on the bed. Sleep had found another. She was wide-awake.

Chapter 67

Vance would be arriving at LAX Airport at eleven. Seychelle decided to get up and get her day started. She went into the kitchen and began preparing breakfast. She hoped she wouldn't wake Tristan. Maybe if she ate a little she'd be tempted to return to her bed. Three hours later Tristan joined her in the kitchen.

"Wow, how long have you been up? A complete breakfast including muffins, what brought this on?"

"Your husband to be. He wanted to ask me a few questions he needed answered for the paperwork." She hoped her answer would satisfy Tristan's curiosity.

"Well I'm glad he did." She got a plate and served herself. "So what's on your agenda today? The auction is tomorrow right?"

"Yes and Vance will be landing today at eleven. I'm picking him up at the airport."

"Well, I'll meet him tomorrow. I thought I'd go to the auction with Aiden. You know, learn a bit about his business."

Seychelle kept her immediate thought to herself. She didn't think Aiden knew of Tristan's intention.

"How do they dress? I'm sure there's a decorum to be upheld right?"

"Somewhat. Business attire for most. There are a few who come dressed seeking attention and you know there are always those who have no clue. There's a lot of sitting around. Aiden and the rest of The Whelan Group have a V.I.P. room. It's usually away from the crowded lobby and the actual bidding room. In Vegas it was on another floor. The room is equipped with cameras so the special guests can watch the bidding and send their bids as well. It is an experience."

"I'll ask Aiden about me attending. I don't think he'll mind."

"I don't know how big this one will be. It's only my second one."

"So it only took one time for you to score big?"

"Bigger than most. But I told you no one knows it's me. They know its Serenity Resorts."

"I guess that's what most of them do. Buy and sell under their business names."

"I really don't know. I want to brand it that way, without my name."

"It's so exciting. Watching you and Aiden do the paperwork I understand there's some work to be done. I can't wait to see the transformation of your new properties. That's what I'd love to do."

"You may get your chance when we visit the other properties. Maybe you'd love to help me with the grand opening. Sasha probably can't be in Vegas until the weekend of the events. We've gone over some ideas. I'll leave the choices here on the table. See what you think."

"It will give me something to do during the day."

Seychelle had no response. She left Tristan eating her breakfast. She had to get ready to meet Vance. She closed the bedroom door so her call to Aiden wouldn't be heard.

Chapter 68

Seychelle didn't understand Aiden's lack of concern. If he put in a bid for any property Seychelle knew there would be an argument. Tristan would want answers since she and Aiden agreed there wouldn't be any large purchases until after the wedding.

She used the time she waited for Vance to glance at the auction booklet again. Aiden was right. The properties were quite different. Opening bid prices were less. There were fewer resort and casino properties; bed and breakfast spots were more intimate. There would be the need for a more personal touch. Seychelle wondered where Aiden's idea came from.

The voice over the intercom announced a few arrivals and departures. Seychelle listened and referred to her phone to see if she had the right flight number. Vance's plane would be delayed thirty minutes. She thought about calling Aiden again. She wouldn't see him before the auction. He'd be leaving with Jon and Tristan for an early breakfast. Seychelle passed on the breakfast invitation knowing Vance wouldn't understand. She wasn't ready for him to meet Aiden.

Clayton called to say he would be at the auction in the V.I.P. room. Seychelle was sure Aiden would tell him she would be there with Vance. He didn't seem to be moved by her being with Vance during the last auction. She wondered if it was another sign of confidence. It did cause her to blush when he told her if she could get away he'd love to see her. She wasn't the type to string men along. It wasn't good for her or business.

She wanted to "bump" into Ms. Minnows again. She promised herself not to ask Vance if she would be attending. Her name was mentioned in an ad. Seychelle wasn't impressed with her demeanor or her business. Ms. Minnows would be one who would be surprised when the spotlight revealed the owner of Serenity Resorts and Spa.

Seychelle had been working with the graphics department at The Whelan Group for a logo and the press release for the grand opening. Everything was on target for the New Year's celebration. Working with the advertising department made her realize she had a company that had full support from her investors.

Aiden told her and Tristan that The Whelan Group owned the building they occupied. He was impressed and pleased he would have his own division on his own floor. The ladies told him once he got settled in his new position they wanted a tour.

Another announcement came over the intercom. It included an announcement for a few departures, the change of scheduled landings and the arrival of Flight 745. Seychelle stood back allowing others to crowd the exit. She was tall enough to see over most of them. She waved when she saw Vance a step beyond those waiting for other travelers.

"Hey Seychelle, I am so sorry, I was annoyed when they announced we would be thirty minutes late."

He leaned in and kissed her on her cheek. She smiled and accepted his extended hand.

"Did you have to stop at baggage claim?"

"Yes I have a garment bag."

"Are you okay?" Vance didn't answer right away. "Vance what is it?"

"We can talk about it later, or maybe not. This travel arrangement didn't go well. So are you staying with your brother or are you going to talk with me all night?"

Seychelle ignored his sarcasm. She told him she loved talking to him late at night. They both had to adjust to the time difference when she was on the island.

"I didn't know what you wanted to do. I mean, since my arrangements changed. I've been here for about two weeks now. My brother and I are both the black sheep of the family. So I guess I needed a break."

"This bag is mine." He stated grabbing the garment bag from the conveyor belt. "Where are you parked?"

They walked in silence. Once again Vance gave no response to her comments. She wondered what it was that obviously upset him.

"Which hotel did you reserve?"

"The Sheraton. The auction is downtown at the convention center."

"Is the Sheraton close?"

"Yes, why?"

"I didn't know. What time is the auction?

"The first bid is at ten. Have you peeped at the booklet?"

"Yes, I see you've got a buzz going."

"Only until the next bid. There's a great article about the last bids. The owner of Serenity Resorts is still a mystery. It should be fun to find out which of those guys bought it for their wife or mistress."

"Why would you assume someone bought it for their wife or girlfriend?" Seychelle paused before opening the car door.

"C'mon Seychelle, the name. Either they bought it for a woman or a woman will be running the place."

His answer caught her off guard. She never thought of the name being an indication of the ownership.

"I never thought about it like that. I think the owner may have wanted the customers to feel coming to the resort they'd find peace among all the other amenities."

"Certainly a different angle. Your interpretation could be an advertising or marketing campaign."

"Just seems to fit." Seychelle didn't want to give any more indications that she knew anything about the business. "So if I know anything about you, you didn't leave anything for me to plan. What's the plan tonight? Don't feel you have to change because I've been here a few days."

"Well it does change a few things. I cancelled your room and the car to come and pick you up."

"C'mon Vance that's not something to get upset about. I'm still here. I can't believe that's bothering you. What is it?"

"A few calls that I got, nothing that involves you. I had some deals lined up and they fell through. I've been dealing with it all morning."

"So does this affect tomorrow's bidding?"

"I've looked at a few of the properties. I wouldn't buy any and I don't know that any of them interest me enough to invest."

"I know you don't think I understand but if you explain it you've got my ear."

"It's a long story but in short Cheyenne has always been a thorn in our side."

"Our, who?"

"Myself and other investors. The Sheraton is there on the left. Let's just say she's pulled a couple of scams, bad deals, and lost a lot of money for a lot of people."

Seychelle still didn't understand his mood. She listened to his complaint as she parked the car. Vance proceeded to check in. He got the keys and motioned for her to join him as he walked toward the elevator.

"So she's the cause of your personality change?"

"Is it that bad?"

"Well you're not the Vance I'm used to being with. Finish telling me about Ms. Minnows."

Vance opened the door to the suite. He placed the garment bag across the wing chair. He continued to check the suite without a response.

"Vance if you'd rather be alone I can call you later."

"No, no really I'm sorry. Okay here, just sit. I'll explain."

Vance began to explain his encounters with Cheyenne, including the romps he thought made a relationship.

"You can imagine how foolish I felt once I understood I was being used. Then I found out I hadn't been the only one that had problems with her. Today, a few of my colleagues questioned her telling everyone that the auction in Vegas was flawed. She felt whoever got the Westlake Village property knew about the four properties that followed. It was true. No one had picked up the property until the price on the Village properties went down. Seychelle that's normal, you know. If property doesn't sell the price usually declines. But there was more to it. No one thought of the renovations being little to none. I don't think anyone thought of it being anything but a lost. Now imagine their surprise when they read the article about the previous owner just letting it go.

263

Not because it had problems or lost revenue but simply because he was selling all his property."

Seychelle was sitting on the edge of the couch hoping Vance didn't know who the new owner was.

"Is that unusual, I mean owners don't sell all their property at once?" She hoped her question made her sound naïve.

"Usually they don't give it away. It wasn't just the auction but there was a back door deal for the buyer. A steal, literally a steal."

"But isn't that the decision for the seller to decide. They auctioned the property they wanted to and sold the other property to who they wanted to. As an owner can't they do that?"

"I guess, but it was something that Cheyenne said. She was ranting about who the new owner was because they had to have known what they would get. It seemed to her that they were persistent about outbidding her. She was the top bidder. I didn't care as long as she was beaten but when she mentioned the deal I wondered why she cared. Seychelle I thought about the deals Cheyenne swindled others out of or into. She's been ranting since the auction. Why? It's bothering me now. Women are emotional and her emotions are all over the place."

"I don't quite understand why anyone is bothered by a bid they lost. Unless like you said it was promised to them."

"Exactly. Just because it's Cheyenne I imagined she did something to secure the purchase and it didn't go her way. She wants to know who beat her to it. Probably someone who didn't have to lay on their back for it before the sale."

Seychelle was stunned. "Is that the only way she could have won the bidding?"

"Not just her. I told you this business wasn't really for women. Like Ms. Minnows, they go to unmatched measures to get what they want. It's about a level playing field and once a woman throws on a sexy dress and stilettos it's an unfair challenge."

"Vance! You can't possibly believe that this theory of yours is truth. I'm sure there are women who can capitalize business deals without laying on their back, as you call it. You have so little faith in women and business."

"No, that would be women in business. This is what really gave me a headache. You've read or glanced at the booklet right?"

"I have." Seychelle hoped he wouldn't push the issue too far.

"Okay. Did you see the ratings for buyers, investors, bankers, and such?"

"Yes I vaguely remember that listing." She lied and shook her head in spite of herself. She sighed waiting for the rest of his explanation.

"Cheyenne concluded that we needed to find out who was the owner of Serenity Resorts and Spa. Our concern, she emphasized, would be our place on the chart. A lot of an investor's clients refer to the listing to see who's approaching them. For example, I currently rank fifth. As an investor, a company that needs my services may choose one who is listed above my rank."

"That's nonsense I'm sure. What if the owner is a banker, not seeking to invest or a buyer outright? You're not fifth on every list are you? I'm sure you rank differently as a buyer right."

"Yes, as a buyer I rank fifth. That's what I was saying."

Vance walked over to the kitchen area and retrieved two glasses.

"Wine?"

"Sure. So I'm still lost. Why is this owner of importance to any of you? What if they do out rank you? Does the ranking change with each auction?

"Sometimes it does, depending on the publication. The bigger auctions update the rankings. I was surprised to see it for this one."

"Hmmm, seems like a lot of fuss over nothing. I mean it's one thing to be swindled and scammed but it doesn't seem that the buyer scammed anyone."

"Not unless the buyer is Cheyenne or someone connected to her. I can see her pulling this off as a diversion."

"Vance I think you've gone way out thinking she would buy the property and then bug everyone about who the new owner is."

"Maybe you're right." He handed the filled glass to her. He stopped pacing and took a seat.

"I can't do business with her. She watches my every move."

"Why would you be doing business with her?"

"Seychelle I know you don't understand this business and all. Cheyenne is vicious. The problem is, she has a strong financial backing. Sorry I didn't mean 'backing,' you know that lying on her back thing. Like I said, that female advantage."

"There are men that lie on their backs, I'm sure."

Vance gave her a questioning look and followed it with an uncomfortable laugh.

"Why are you laughing? My father has a lucrative business and I've seen men bend and cower for favors, information and let's just say everyone has an angle. The one with the better advantage usually wins out. Man or woman, you use what you know will work."

"Really Ms. Tudjal. Are you insinuating that business is a game of chance?"

"It is sometimes, other times, it may take skill or experience. Maybe all of those traits. I just don't believe its gender specific."

"I don't trust the skill or experience of Ms. Minnows. Any other woman in this field will be about the same antics or have a tweaked version of their own."

"Tweaked, Vance I'm glad we had this discussion. Does it matter what the business is? A woman in business intimidates you and your friends? So women just work for someone not for themselves....wow."

Seychelle put down the glass and walked to the large floor length windows. The sun wasn't as bright as it had been earlier. It looked like rain. She didn't know why her eyes were filling with water. She wanted Vance to be a friend maybe more but he'd never understand her and her need to work for herself.

"I'm going to call out for dinner if you don't mind. Anything special?"

"No whatever you'd like. I'm really not hungry."

Chapter 69

Sasha listened as Seychelle whispered her feelings. The sadness in her voice told it all. Although she wouldn't admit it, Sasha knew her sister. Seychelle had been hurt again in less than two months. Their father still hadn't mentioned the business or asked how the renovations were coming along. Seychelle sent pictures that Clayton had updated in his office. Sasha was obedient to her sister's wishes and showed them to their mother. Naomi seemed to be impressed but discouraged Sasha from showing them to Cole. Sasha couldn't bring herself to tell Seychelle what her mother said after hearing how her meeting with Vance went.

"It is better that way my sister. If you did not know what his thoughts were you may have fallen in love with him and look at the confusion that would have brought on. Are you ready to tell him you own the property?"

"No. I don't care how he finds out. What difference would it make to him or that woman? Maybe this is a lesson for him. A woman that has gained the rank and business status without lying on their back. Sasha can you imagine. Something we would regard as a blessing, something to be proud of, this man thinks there is no other way to gain it but to be used by a man. It cut me Sasha."

"How will you stay there all night without saying something about your feelings? I may have told him. I would have bragged about it."

"After this auction tomorrow, Sasha our relationship can't be what I thought it would be."

"So are you going to help Aiden?"

"I'll call him in the morning. I may have to lay on my back one more time."

"What are you saying Seychelle? Leave there if you want. Where are you calling me from?"

Seychelle laughed. "I'm in his suite. He's on the phone in the other room. I'm talking about Aiden and this property he's talking about. Maybe that's what he needs to feel secure. It's what Vance needs to know not all women lie on their backs to get ahead."

"That's true. What do you think he will say once he finds out Serenity Resorts is your business."

"You mean all eight properties?"

"My sister, I almost forgot the others. I see what you mean. It was bad enough that you had the Village properties. Vance may lay on his back."

"How are you and Jon? Have you thought about coming to the grand opening? The ideas you sent the other day are perfect. I want you to be there Sasha."

"I told Jon I couldn't do both. The holidays and then New Years with you in Vegas. He said he understood. I don't want him to get his hopes up. It's hard with the distance. Harder than I thought. Jon believes in love. I'm still thinking it must have been a fling. He says no. Seychelle, he's willing to hold on and take it one day at a time."

"I hear Vance. We had dinner without his complaining about Cheyenne. I don't know what he'll do when he finds out its not her. Better yet I can't wait until she knows it's me. It would be nice for them to have V.I.P. invites. Yes, Sasha let's send invites to the top ten in each listing. Maybe section off a place for them to sit and eat. A touch of something special before it's announced who the owner is. I'll call Aiden in the morning though."

"Okay, let me know how it goes at the auction. Jon will be sure to call me I'm sure."

"Girl don't you give up on Jon or the love he has for you."

"Sure, you are one to talk."

"Goodnight my sister."

Chapter 70

The Los Angeles Convention Center's lobby was filled with prospective bidders. Seychelle felt a surge of excitement as she and Vance walked through the crowd. There were many who nodded and smiled as she passed them. Seychelle spotted Aiden, Jon and members of The Whelan Group standing among those who were sharing greetings and coffee prepared by the caterers. Men and women admired the couple who looked as though they stepped out of Forbes rich and famous magazine.

Seychelle's ensemble, a taupe two-piece Tahari pantsuit, was tailored to fit. Vance didn't bother to wear a suit but his Hounds Tooth blazer and pants spoke style. His gold accessories coupled with her studded pearl earrings set in gold and matching necklace added a subtle hint that they were a pair. Her makeup was flawless and she knew it. As she walked with confidence sizing up the crowd, she imagined how many of them would be attending her grand opening.

"I love your suit." A woman said to her as she and Vance paused to greet people he knew. There was no introduction and Seychelle realized what her purpose was for the event.

"Thank you."

"This is such a put on for those of us who just tag along, don't you think?"

"Yes it is quite a crowd today." Seychelle and Vance moved on. She thought about the woman's wording, "tag along". It seemed to fit the opinion that Vance had about women and "the business".

"Have you ever sent your bid in from the V.I.P. rooms?" She asked as he continued to acknowledge another greeting.

"No, I really prefer to bid where I can see the others or at least those who don't hide behind closed doors."

"Is that what the V.I.P.'s do, hide?"

"Not really but I've always wondered why be secluded. I like meeting others and showing off my lady."

Vance smiled at Seychelle hoping his comment made her feel better than she had the night before. After talking with Sasha she showered and went to bed avoiding Vance's touch. When he asked was she okay, she simply said she had a headache. As an afterthought she should have told him the truth. She held a new opinion of him and his attitude regarding women. Seychelle knew she probably wouldn't see him again until the grand opening, if he attended.

"Where are the V.I.P. rooms here?"

Vance looked around the spacious lobby. He was sure the rooms or the area wasn't near where they held the reception.

"It may be on another level. They've got so many different areas in this building."

"Well for a listings that you have no interest in, there are many who do."

"Or they're here to network, see who does bid and win, there's other reasons as well."

They walked to the opening of the grand hall, which held well over two hundred seats. Once the doors closed, Seychelle knew the V.I.P's would be following the auction by closed circuit viewing.

"How much time before the start?"

"About thirty minutes. Are you alright?"

"I need to go to the restroom before we take our seats."

Seychelle left his side headed in the direction of the restroom. Cheyenne Minnows stood at the sink. She saw Seychelle enter the stall. Seychelle couldn't make a private call to Aiden. She was sure Cheyenne would be listening; so she sent him a text message:

Where are you? I can't tell where the V.I.P. rooms are.

She got an immediate response:

The rooms are where the signs are marked 'Press Only'.
You have to have a pass to enter. Let me know if there
are any tips.

Seychelle flushed the toilet and hoped Cheyenne wouldn't be still
pretending to adjust her hair and makeup. Just as she suspected,
Cheyenne was still there applying lipstick.

"Good morning. You must have some interest in properties. It
can't be just Vance Chase that keeps you coming to the auctions."

"Good morning, just Vance. I enjoy his company."

"That's about his only attribute, his business."

"Well not everyone handles business the same way. Some work to
become owners, others enjoy investing their time, and some will always
be customers. Once you know what his business is and how he handles
it, you find its growth and value. Not everyone understands his
business or how to handle his growth."

Cheyenne didn't respond immediately. She was obviously stunned.
She opened the door and then turned in Seychelle's direction.

"Bitch, I know you're about business, I'm just not sure if it's his."

"Regardless, you're neither a client nor a customer of his. So for
me you, your opinion or your concern does not matter. You're right,
I'm the new bitch."

Another woman opened the door wider so she could get pass
Cheyenne and her shocked expression. Seychelle put her hands under
the hand dryer. At the sound of the dryer Cheyenne left the restroom.
She noticed Vance across the hall waiting for Seychelle.

"You better watch who you keep as a bedmate. She needs to go
back to whatever island she came from."

"What's the problem now Cheyenne?"

"Why is she with you? There's something not right with her. She
thinks she's better than me? What the hell gives her that idea? What
have you told her about me?"

"What did she say?"

"Nothing, just keep her in her place." Cheyenne left as Seychelle
was approaching.

"What, was she telling on me?" Seychelle laughed at the thought. "I think she's upset that you've moved on."

"We haven't dealt with each other on that level for at least two or three years. Why would she be upset?"

"You're number five. I'm a sign you've moved on. Does she need another reason?"

Vance pulled Seychelle closer to whisper in her ear.

"I can think of another reason. He kissed her cheek twice."

"Alright you made your point I see smoke rising from her head." Seychelle winked at Cheyenne as they passed her holding hands.

The gavel sounded. The hosts for the auctions began their introductions. They thanked all of the dignitaries and other noted guests for their attendance. They made reference to the V.I.P's and internet viewers giving an estimated total of more than eight hundred possible bidders.

"Have you decided to be a spectator today or did you find something of interest? I thought of these listings as perfect fits for bed and breakfast spots or like the jazz spot we went to."

"Now that's a thought. A combination of both." He flipped through the pages. "I like this one. It seems promising. I don't think I want to buy though."

"So tell Cheyenne to buy."

"I just told you I didn't trust her. You've got to be joking."

"Keep your enemies close, that's what my father says. You don't have to ask anyone about their next move. They'll tell you more than you want to know."

"No, hey this one is a solid spot. How about I bid on it for you?"

"What would I do with it? Would that be permitted? Me having property and turning it into profit, spoils your theory."

"You could do the interior designs."

"SOLD to the gentleman with thirty three on his fan."

The audience clapped. Whispers began to take over the room. The auctioneer stepped away from the podium and soft music began to play.

"What is going on Vance? I don't remember this as a part of the process."

"Each auction is different. The properties are put into categories. He was the auctioneer for the properties he presented. The categories are usually selected by the property's worth or estimated value."

"I see. Well I don't think I'm the one for interior designing."

"Your loss Ms. Tudjal. Ownership adds to beauty and you indeed are beautiful."

"You are too kind sir. If I was inclined to take you up on this purchase which property would you suggest?"

"This one, perfect for a bed and breakfast. Two levels, I think it said there were let's see, yes read here."

Seychelle took the booklet from him. The price caught her eye immediately. Aiden could manage the price. The listing included three acres of land and all new appliances and furnishing.

"I don't know about a bed and breakfast. It's not really my style, maybe for my mother or someone her age. I'm not ready for the long dress and apron. Would you invest or buy?"

"Either. There is no lost with this one, with the right management I see profit."

"Buy it for Cheyenne and have her work out the details. She's better on her back."

"Unfair Seychelle, you know I wasn't talking about you."

The gavel sounded. The property Vance showed her wasn't within the next group. She needed to call Aiden. She wondered if he saw the property earlier and thought of a bed and breakfast business. Her phone began to buzz. She glanced at Vance.

"I have to take this. I'll go to the back."

She excused herself as she moved between the seats to the center row. "Hello, hold on." She whispered. She stepped into the farthest corner as not to disturb anyone.

"Aiden? Did you see the property?" She flipped through a few of the pages. On page 32. It's perfect Aiden. Yes, now if the price goes higher for some unforeseen reason it's still in a range you can handle. New renovations are complete with new appliances. Go for it."

Seychelle returned to her seat only to find Vance pouting. She didn't say a word. She noticed Cheyenne staring at them. Her phone buzzed again. *"Clayton said yes, definitely. Thank you my sister."*

She smiled and gave Vance a side eye. He was still pouting.

"Are you uncomfortable with me?"

"No but who is calling you like that if you don't mind me asking?"

"My brother. Small problem. Wrong time to discuss it. I gave him a solution, I hope he takes my advice."

"I thought he was the oldest."

"But I am a female. So is his fiancé. So he *needed* a woman's opinion. Small problem. Wrong time to discuss it. He's nervous I know and he doesn't want to argue or debate with her. Which bid are they on?"

Vance seemed to relax again. If Clayton began to act this way she'd leave the thought of a relationship to God's intervention.

Chapter 71

Bidding from the V.I.P. room made it easy for Aiden. He could sign the papers and make all the transactions without anyone knowing who he was. He signed the papers using The Whelan group's purchase code. The auctioneer left the room after informing Aiden the final documents would be sent within ten business days. If he decided not to take the property he would have to contact them before the final documents were sent.

Aiden and Jon left Clayton and the others in the V.I.P. room. Jon saw Cheyenne first. As she quickened her steps to approach them Jon pushed Aiden back in the room. He closed the door and motioned to Clayton.

"It's Ms. Minnows. We don't want her talking to Aiden do we?"

"She can't do us any harm. Besides we don't want her to become suspicious." Clayton opened the door to find her waiting for someone to exit.

"Clayton, how are you? I see you and your bandits purchased a bed and breakfast spot? Are we lowering our standards now?"

Clayton closed the door behind him. "Ms. Minnows, tell me you're not watching our purchases. May I ask why?"

"You know why. I'm on the verge of proving you've been getting tips on sales. An advantage no one else here is getting."

"My, you are paranoid. Listen our purchases are legit. I'm not going to explain what goes on behind our closed doors."

"Clayton for the last few sales you've purchased the property that will get the most return. What is one to think?"

"The Whelan Group is number one on all the rankings. We couldn't have made it to the top without purchasing and selling. While we are the top of the line, I can't help to think that your little accusation is to sabotage our company purposely. Be careful you don't overstep a boundary you know nothing about."

"Is that supposed to be some sort of threat?

"No not at all. I know you don't know where you're stepping or on who. But you don't care about that, so it's just a warning to be careful."

"I refuse to believe you don't have some sort of connection on the inside of the sales."

"Cheyenne, we bought more than one property today. Why are you questioning just one?"

"Does it matter? Dirty deals are dirty deals. What client bought this one? Serenity again? Clayton if you just tell me who the real owner is I'll let it go."

"Well there will be a grand opening, if you're interested, be there."

Clayton left Cheyenne standing at the door as he re-entered the room.

"Give it a few minutes. I'm sure she won't stand there long."

Vance and Seychelle were standing in the lobby when Cheyenne approached them. She looked disheveled.

"What's wrong, what happened to you?"

Seychelle didn't want to misunderstand his concern. She didn't step away to give them any privacy. Cheyenne paused waiting for Seychelle to object to her intrusion.

"Vance, I need to talk to you. Alone."

"What's wrong? You can tell me right here."

"Without her, please? Vance, please!"

Seychelle sighed but remained at his side.

"Cheyenne what is it?"

"They did it again. That bed and breakfast property. Didn't you pay attention? Someone told them about the property before the auction. Another one sold to The Whelan Group but the owner has not rendered their name. I think they're buying property and then making a deal with the new owners."

"Cheyenne the paperwork will be made public once the new owners take over."

"Just like the last one Vance? That Serenity bullshit! The Whelan Group is obtaining property that...."

"That you made deals on."

"Have you made any? You can't invest as long as the group has it. They hold the investment on any property they purchase. The others on the list aren't worth the time or the money."

"Okay and...."

"And they have a monopoly going. How did they know about the BNB?"

"Cheyenne, I don't know and don't care. It hasn't stopped my business or any of the purchases I'm interested in."

"Can you call them? See if they'll talk to you."

Seychelle became bored with Cheyenne's questions. She wanted to know if Aiden had signed the papers. Just as the thought crossed her mind, she spotted Aiden and Jon headed toward the exit. She smiled as her brother threw a "thumbs up" signal her way. Returning to Cheyenne's nonsense filled conversation, she leaned on Vance's arm.

"Cheyenne I'm sure you're just being paranoid. The Whelan Group has too much to lose if they were running a scam. More like your speed sweetie."

"I asked him again about that Serenity Resorts sale. I simply asked for the name of the owner. He told me to come to the grand opening. Why would he say that if he didn't think I'd be surprised? I don't know what it meant but there was a message in it somewhere."

"Well you got your answer. Go to the grand opening."

Chapter 72

V ance made dinner reservations for himself and Seychelle at a small restaurant on the San Francisco Bay. Seychelle didn't question the conversation he had with Cheyenne. She was sure he'd be convinced to go to the grand opening with her. Since it would be during the holidays, she would use the excuse of being home with her family if he asked her to join him. It would be the end of their relationship for sure.

"I thought you would love this atmosphere. Has your brother brought you here before?"

"No, this is too intimate for a sister brother dinner. I'm sure he would love to bring Tristan here. I love the ambiance."

"The eateries here are the best. I know you've told me about the Wharf but I think you'll love the eateries here as well."

"So you didn't bid today or invest? Why do you go?"

"Like I told you. Networking is key and most of the people I deal with go to the auctions."

"So I see. You've only introduced me to Cheyenne. The others you converse with are clients, I guess, not friends or close associates."

"Seychelle, I am sorry. I didn't think you would want to meet other men through me." Vance replied sarcastically but noticed Seychelle's

278

expression. "Seriously, you're right they are not friends. I don't have many friends. I guess I'm a loner. A lot of my friends don't live in Vegas and since I travel a lot I don't see them often. I go home a few times a year, visit those I choose. That's my story, sad as it may seem. I'm a rich loner."

"That is by choice, I'm sure. However, just as you thought I would be rude enough to talk to a man while I'm with you; you thought the same about introducing me to your associates. I thought you to be different. I wonder if I had not introduced you to my female friends what your reaction would be."

"I'll keep that thought to myself. We both know women don't introduce someone they're interested in to their friends or any other woman. It's not the same. I'm not the jealous type."

Seychelle heard his excuses. His actions spoke differently.

"Remember your words Mr. Chase."

"What I'm really not a jealous man. It's more to it than just the introduction. I would have to see how you would be interacting with the man first."

"Hmmm similar to the interaction with Cheyenne. Vance let's just finish the meal and save the rest of the evening if we can."

Vance cut his steak and dropped the subject. He was beginning to feel the entire trip was a waste of time. Seychelle asked him to drive her to her brother's house. Vance declined the opportunity to meet Aiden and Tristan. His decision was fine with Seychelle and she kissed him for what she knew would be the last time.

Vance needed answers. Cheyenne was right — something was amiss. The ride to the hotel cleared his mind. He wasn't worried about his relationship with Seychelle. Every relationship had its rocky moments. He couldn't peep into Seychelle's world without hesitating. She wasn't overly impressed with him, or what he had to offer. Most of the women he met were pleased with his display of richness. He could wine and dine them into the bedroom and they still would call for more.

Showing Seychelle his home was his second attempt to raise her awareness of whom she was dealing with. His rank as an investor impressed many even the media, but she didn't care that he ranked in the top ten. She couldn't have been as naïve as she pretended. His money, status and not even his past relationships shook her.

Vance realized she had bruised his ego. It was as though she didn't need him to walk through the lobby of the auctions. Seychelle seemed to be her own. Her character set demands he had to meet and he hadn't fulfilled her needs. He walked into the hotel lobby and was flagged by the concierge.

"There is a message for you sir at the desk."

Vance went to the desk and was given an envelope. As he went to the elevator he opened it and read the message.

"Vance, I really enjoy your company when you're not overwhelmed with your work. This weekend I told myself would be the proof I would need to continue dating you or just being a friend. Vance I will always consider you as a friend, but with the distance and—"

Vance tore the paper and the envelope in half and paused. He pushed the button for the elevator again. As he continued tearing the paper into small pieces he decided to finish his night at the bar.

Chapter 73

S eychelle's flight was scheduled for six in the evening. She promised Aiden she wouldn't leave on an early flight since he had a project to tackle at the office. She cancelled the week she'd be spending in Vegas to return home early. Vegas would have tempted her to see Vance again. She wanted him to pursue her; she had little doubt he would. Aiden and Jon assured her everything was going well with the renovations and a visit the first week of December would be better timing. She explained her reasons, but the men overruled her, emphasizing she wouldn't be able to get any interior designing done. In fact her presence would only delay the final touches.

During the week she shopped with Tristan, ate until she ached, and watched her brother turn into a doting fiancé. She was happy for the both of them. Aiden dared not ask about Vance but he kept an eye on his lovely sister and Clayton.

He had "dropped by" three days during the week. Aiden and Jon agreed they liked Clayton being around. Neither cared if Vance was no longer Seychelle's choice.

Seychelle finished packing while complaining she had to stop shopping while traveling. She always needed to add another carry-on or bag to be checked in on the return flight.

"Tristan, I'm meeting Clayton for lunch. I'm sorry I didn't say anything earlier but he just called." She listened for Tristan's response.

"You like him a lot don't you." Tristan walked into the den where Seychelle was searching through her bags. "What are you looking for?"

"My ID pouch. I don't carry a purse, with this carry-on I don't need one but my pouch has all my credentials. I thought I put them in this bag."

The two began to search where she sat the night before.

"Ah near the television. I'm sure you were checking the flight times when you called Sasha."

Tristan left the room and returned with the burgundy pouch.

"Thank you. You've been the best sister during my stay. I'll really miss talking to you."

"And eating." The women responded in unison.

"Seychelle so what will you do now?"

"Wait for the renovations to be done. I sent your ideas along with those Sasha and I suggested. We should get the designers input and drawings soon. I wanted to go and meet with them. Aiden and Jon said December. I don't know if I'll be able to wait that long."

"We have plenty of time. It's easier than you think. I did a lot of the restaurants during the festive season at home. I did them with one maybe two people helping. You have a crew. It will be beautiful."

"Time is slipping away or so it seems. I really want to know the reaction of the patrons. I'm praying they won't be disappointed."

"You worry too much. Go home and relax in your lounger. Meditate and pray. It all will work out for you, including that love light you have for Clayton."

"Oooh, no girl! I'm trying to remain calm. He's asked me to join him for a few of the holiday festivities here. I told him it would depend on how much time I would need for the resort. Clayton has showed me a new way of looking at business. I wish I could be as calm as he is. He's so sure of himself and what is to be. I certainly don't want to rush things with him."

"Well Vance taught you that. I think Clayton is different. He wants you to have and that's important for a woman like you."

"American men, they are hard to understand."

"Any man — the island men, too. I think I fell in love with your brother, he was so different. Maybe Clayton has shown you the same difference."

"Tristan, am I being unreasonable? I want what we've seen as children. You know, happiness in the home, the job, in life; I want to know how it is to be loved and be secure."

"I think you have found it my sister. You may need a jacket today. The weather is changing." Tristan went to the window and touched it. "I have to get used to this type weather too. No jacket, maybe a sweater."

"Yes, I hear you. Do you see Clayton's car?"

"You come and see the car this man has brought here for you."

Tristan spoke as though she couldn't believe what she saw. The black limo was parked in front of the building. Aiden and Jon were standing outside talking with Clayton.

"Why didn't he ring the bell or call?"

They looked out the window and turned to each other. "Men."

Chapter 74

They all rode in the limousine together. A safe travel dinner, as Aiden called it, meant so much more to Seychelle than the gifts he sat on the table.

"Why would you get me a gift Aiden? You've done more than enough for me these past few months. I don't know how or if I can repay you or Jon."

"And here is your gift box my dear." Aiden gave Tristan a red box with a pink bow as well. "Together now, untie the bows and open the boxes."

Inside each box was a set of keys. Clayton and Jon looked between Aiden and the women. They both had a questionable stare.

"I recognize the one to the apartment but what door does this key open."

Tristan fumbled the keys between her fingers. Seychelle smiled. Her brother found a way to surprise Tristan with the bed and breakfast purchase.

"I tried to finalize everything this morning so we could see the property this afternoon."

"Property? Aiden, what property? We agreed to keep the apartment."

Clayton raised his glass followed by Jon and Seychelle.

"Congratulations are certainly in order. Aiden you've made a complete turn-around. There's so much more for you to gain."

Clayton and Seychelle were the first to tap glasses in agreement with Jon's toast. Tristan slowly raised her glass.

"Well I'm left in the dark. What is this key for?" Tristan looked at each of them. Aiden gave her an affectionate kiss on the cheek.

"Seychelle this is the work I had to tackle this morning. Tristan, you are the owner of your own property. I've purchased it for you, as my gift for you accepting my proposal to be my wife. It's a bed and breakfast property. Clayton and I went there this morning to meet with the previous owners. The place is closed due to the sale but it will re-open when you're ready for it."

Tristan's smile through her tears was all he wanted to see. They finished their lunch with enough time for them to stop by the property.

Tristan and Seychelle walked through the front door of the three level building and stood looking around the large living room.

There was a living room, dining room and sitting room on the first floor. They walked through to the large sliding door that led outside. The door was attached to the huge deck area, which had a large grill and assorted outdoor furniture. There were a few umbrella tables with matching chairs on the grassed area. There was a cemented walkway that led to the fenced in pool.

They returned to the kitchen, which had all new appliances and cookware. Tristan covered her mouth in awe of the island with pots and pans hanging overhead. The two noticed the stairway from the kitchen. It led them to the next level. There were five suites on the second floor and three on the third floor. Proceeding down the front stairway, they returned to the living room where Tristan took a seat to gather herself.

"Seychelle, it's beautiful. Oh my, I never expected this. My own bed and breakfast? You'll have to tell me where to start. So many things are running through my mind. You won't be able to help me until after your opening. What was I thinking?"

"You're happy and I am so glad you are. I told Aiden you'd be so upset with him buying property."

"Yes, that was my first thought but Aiden is a man of tradition. Even if he won't admit it, he's his father's son."

"Tristan, did you tell Aiden you wanted something like this?"

"I did, when we were in college. Years ago I thought about having one on the island. My mother talked about having one and how much fun we would have meeting travelers and such. After my father passed so did her dreams but I've kept it in my heart."

Seychelle understood her dreams. Tristan was fortunate to have someone to share them with. Seychelle's thoughts brought her to Vance. She had dreams, dreams he would never understand. Then there was Clayton. His passion became his purpose she didn't know where she stood with him. They had been out on a few dates. He was someone she could love. That love would become her new dream.

Chapter 75

Clayton made no offer to ride Seychelle to the airport. He had the driver take Jon, Aiden and Tristan back to the apartment. Everyone said their goodbyes, promising to speak once Seychelle got situated on the island. Clayton and Seychelle continued to the airport.

"Aiden told me everything should be finished the first week of December. Your firm is overseeing the project and I know you'll be a part of any future projects. I guess what I'm saying is...."

"What about us? Seychelle, I've been going out with you for a week or two. We're in the early stages of what I hope is the beginning of a relationship. I haven't discussed The Whelan Group or any business because that's not what I'm interested in. I'm interested in you. I know your business and appreciate your passion, know that I am celebrating with you for you."

Seychelle hoped her expression didn't give away the pleasure she was feeling.

"I want to know who this beautiful woman, Queen of the Nile, is since you take my breath away each time I see you. I listen to you talk on the phone and hear your voice after the call has ended. Seychelle I've fallen for you without an effort from either of us. That's unusual for me. Your confidence heightens my curiosity. You may not want this relationship and you may say there's so many obstacles why should we even try. I am willing to take it slow, rush it on, visit your island, or stay here and wait on your return. This feels right for me and I hope you feel the same way."

"Clayton, I—"

Clayton wouldn't let her finish her response. He leaned in and kissed her passionately.

"Don't go tonight, leave in the morning. I'll pay for your fare and the fare in the morning. I just want to be with you tonight, if this will be our last."

"I'm sure it won't be. I'll have to make a few calls, but yes I will stay tonight."

Clayton chose a Sheraton near the airport. The limousine pulled to the front of the hotel to unload. Clayton talked to the driver before returning to the overnight bags and Seychelle.

They checked in and upon entering the room Clayton received a call. Seychelle kicked off her shoes. She was glad she wasn't returning to the island that night. She wanted to spend the time with Clayton.

"Do you always carry extra luggage with you?"

"Yes, I travel often. I've had flights cancelled, bad weather situations, and other last minute changes. You'll understand once your properties are up and running. Some things you just can't predict so I avoid having to shop for clean underwear, toiletries and whatever else."

"I never thought about that." Seychelle felt embarrassed. Clayton didn't seem bothered by her questions. He smiled and picked up the hotel phone.

"I'm going to order a few things for the room. It's a habit. Would you like anything? Doesn't have to be here they'll go get it."

"You're a frequent customer here huh?"

"Enough, what would you like to drink? Wine, beer, alcohol?"

"Mascoto, red or white is fine."

The lights from the airport reminded Seychelle of the tour of the outskirts of Vegas with Vance. She thought of that night and how she thought it was the most romantic night she ever had. She watched Clayton as he tipped the bellman. He went to the kitchen counter where the food he ordered would be placed. He prepared a drink for himself and a glass of wine for Seychelle.

They talked about family and tradition. They compared the differences in culture and their childhood experiences. Clayton told her about his family how much he loved family gatherings. Their talk seemed soothing to Seychelle. She relaxed, and let herself go allowing Clayton's voice to lead her to her recent dreams.

Clayton kissed her after she told him about how often he interrupted her sleep. Seychelle kissed him after he told her he wouldn't dare tell her about any of his dreams. The attraction was obvious.

"I didn't want to mix business with pleasure. I wanted to acquire status for Serenity Resorts without me being the reason your firm accepted our business."

Clayton didn't say anything. He began unbuttoning his shirt.

"As a woman I thought it was the best way for someone of your caliber to take us seriously."

"Did you research my firm before approaching us with your proposal?"

"I guess my brother and Jon did. They recommended the firm. I'm glad they did. My business that I thought would be overwhelming for me has gone far beyond my expectations. It's because of your firm and my brother's input."

"This is not about business Seychelle. It's about us. Can there be us?"

"Can we stand the distance, the differences, the desires each of us have for business? Can we stand to change some of our beliefs?"

Clayton returned to the couch where Seychelle sat comfortably with her legs stretched its length. He gently picked up her legs and placed them in his lap. He began massaging her feet.

"I believe in having strong foundations — those that last and endure longer than fads and quick rendezvous. I want us and if you'll consider taking a chance to be my lady, I'll show you the best of what love can offer."

Seychelle closed her eyes allowing his words to take her away again. His baritone voice calmed her fears. He motioned for her to stand with him. He led her to the bed.

"May I?"

"Yes you may?"

She turned so he could unbutton her blouse that closed in the back. As the blouse fell to the floor he wrapped his arms around her waist and unbuttoned her slacks. They too fell to the floor leaving her in her lace bra and panties. She faced Clayton who now stood in his briefs.

Together they could have been models for underwear commercials. Seychelle with her proportional body was more alluring to Clayton than he could ever imagine. He kissed her neck causing her to sway seductively to his touch.

Their bodies entwined Clayton took the liberty of exploring her breast and the rest of her body. Seychelle felt the warmth of his body as they pleased each other in foreplay. Each taking the time to search the others desires. Clayton gently kissed her thighs before approaching her. His manners relaxed her and she gave herself entirely to his loving embrace. There was no longer a need to hesitate. She opened her legs anticipating his entrance. They moved together as though they had been meant for the moment. The pace quickened, Seychelle stilled herself. Her lack of motion caused Clayton to increase his pace and hold her tightly. He felt the rush and the release. They laid side by side completely satisfied.

His touch caused her to quiver. She hadn't had a lover who caused her to lose control. She noticed there was a difference when one makes love happen and when love happens to one.

Chapter 76

Seychelle returned to the islands and shared the news of the business with Sasha. She shared the pictures that were taken during her stay with Aiden and Tristan. She had a package waiting from the designers that Sasha was anxious to open.

"So when you return your approval they'll make the necessary changes?"

"Yes and all the renovations should be complete by early December. Sasha we can begin to plan the date for the grand opening. I believe a New Year's gala will be perfect. Each of the resorts can be opened on that date. The party will be held at Suite One."

They spent the morning looking at the designs and making their desired changes. Colors, patterns and fabrics were decided for each of the suites. Embroidered materials, tassels that were to be bought for the grand opening. White and gold would be the color scheme. The sisters worked until the evening. They decided all of the decorations were in order. They agreed they would take another time to design the invitations for the V.I.P.

"I wish you would be able to be there Sasha. I want you to see the resort from its beginnings. You are so much a part of this dream coming true. I want you to meet Clayton and of course it would give you some time with Jon. Have the two of you talked much?"

"Yes, he calls maybe twice a week. I can't get him to believe there is no possibility for us to have this fantasy he's believes in. I've been helping Father with the business. He's decided to hire two new managers. He's training them to handle the warehouse and the docks. I'm training a young woman to do your job. The others you worked with have been handling the paperwork and payments just fine."

Seychelle didn't know what to say. She was happy that her father's business would survive without her return. She hadn't been answering the emails daily. Sasha left for work leaving her sister to get re-acquainted with her daily schedule.

She decided to complete the guest list. Aiden assisted in giving her the list of ranking investors and buyers. They would be acknowledged and have special seating.

There was a knock at the door. Seychelle was sure it might be another delivery. She took her time to answer. She was shocked to find it was Tristan's mother.

"Good morning. Please, come in."

"I don't mean to intrude but I've been trying to reach Tristan. I called Sasha earlier this week looking for my daughter. The number I have to reach her has been disconnected."

Marietta looked tired as though she had been sick or wasn't feeling well.

"Would you care for a cup of tea? Please take a seat. Let me get the number for you."

"Thank you. She said she would call. I haven't heard from her now in more than a month. I just need to know she is well. I know your brother convinced her to leave here and forget me."

"I don't think Aiden would convince her of that. It was her choice to leave Ms. Marietta, she left with me."

"And you have returned without her, haven't you?"

"She made her own decision to stay, I assure you." She handed the distressed woman the paper with Tristan's number written on it. "You can call her. I'm sure she will answer."

"I don't understand why she hasn't called."

Seychelle sat through nights when Tristan would explain her choices while not being clear about her mother's dislike for Aiden.

"Seychelle, what is there in California for her? She had a good job here and the rest of her schooling to finish. Your brother gave her a peek into an American life and she's gone. He can't possibly take care of her when he's struggling taking care of himself."

"Who told you my brother was struggling?"

Marietta hesitated knowing she promised not to reveal her source.

"I spoke with your parents. They suggested if I hadn't reached Tristan by your return, then I should check with you."

It wasn't long before the woman left or felt compelled to leave.

"You call Tristan. She should be your only concern, not the business between her and my brother. Let her know I gave you the number. I don't want her to be angry with you for wanting to know her whereabouts. Especially since my brother is barely getting by."

Seychelle's sarcasm caused Marietta a bit of embarrassment. She decided to leave without making excuses for her visit or her need to call Tristan.

"I hope I didn't disturb you. You've got to understand, my knowing about your brother's downfall has me concerned about my daughter."

"Once you've made the call I believe you'll find there's a difference in the story. I don't know what is going on with you and your daughter but my brother is not the problem."

Marietta left without a word of thanks. Seychelle had no intention of visiting her parents but after hearing the story told to Tristan's mother she needed to have a word with them.

Seychelle called Sasha and told her to meet her at their parent's home after school ended for the day. She spoke with her mother and asked that she didn't tell their father that they would be visiting.

"Sasha, the only reason for this visit is to invite them to the grand opening personally. I don't want them to think that they are not a part of our success. Besides, they need to see what we've accomplished and what Aiden has done for himself. They've told Tristan's mother he is struggling."

"I'll be there shortly. Is mother there alone? Father has been leaving early the past few days. It's inventory week and only the warehouse is open. He may be there when you arrive."

Seychelle told her sister she'd wait for her to arrive before entering the home. It was the first time in her life she too nervous to just sit with her parents.

Chapter 77

Naomi spent the morning baking. The members of the Island Mothers and Daughters group would have their meeting at seven. She was well ahead of schedule. The call she received from Sasha was expected. She hoped Seychelle would come to the house before she'd have to leave for the meeting.

Sasha expressed Seychelle's feelings and she thought it would be better for them to come to the house while Cole was still at work. Naomi didn't agree but she understood and agreed they needed to talk.

Seychelle arrived before Sasha but sat outside her parent's home. She turned the car off after ten minutes of thought and prayer. Naomi opened the door as Seychelle approached. Neither mentioned or asked how long Naomi had been peering out of the bay window.

"Hello sweetie." Naomi extended her arms for Seychelle to surrender to her hug. "How are you baby? I am so glad you came here."

"Mother, I have so much to share with you. So much I want you to know about what I've been doing, what I've learned. I want to include you in my happiness. For the first time I feel I have to hide my thoughts and feelings because Father doesn't know or understand I have a life to live too."

"Come in child." They walked to the living room where Seychelle put down her bag. She took out a photo album and handed it to her mother.

"These are pictures are of my properties. I now own eight resorts. Under one title they will be Serenity Resorts and Spa. Mother I did this with the money I've saved and the dowry you and Father gave me. I've done what takes most years to achieve with the help from Aiden and Jon."

"This is truly beautiful. I thought you had just the property in Las Vegas. I love the colors you've chosen. Seychelle is this a gambling place."

"No, it's not a casino. Just a place to take a vacation and relax. The colors are changing as we speak. I wanted a fresh paint job. Now these are the pictures from the other properties. And this Mother this is Aiden's property."

"Aiden's? No you don't say! He has property as well?"

"Yes, he won a bid. He had the money to bid on it Mother, he didn't blow it all. So this property here is his."

"Seychelle your father and I thought...."

"He wouldn't allow us to explain. We are securing a future. One for Tristan and Aiden. One that I have dreamed of."

"Child, listen to me. You know we want the best for you, but all of this breeds greed as well. What about you? I understand your brother but what about you?"

"Mother what is the difference? Are you saying that it is okay for Aiden to start his own, but I must remain a part of Father's dreams? Mother is that fair? I told Aiden about acquiring property to secure a future. We listened each time Father told us we had to have our own to succeed. I don't understand why I am to do so much more to prove I can."

"Seychelle, your success depends on you. Are you satisfied? Not overwhelmed, satisfied. Your father was willing to give you what he knows is satisfying."

Seychelle was trying not to become angry. Her mother's voice of reason was becoming obscured.

"Mother, I know you don't understand us, well me. I don't mean to be defiant or stubborn as you and Father say I am. I've done everything to prove to you I am independent. Sasha and I have lived separate from you since our years in college. Aiden was forced from the only home he knew just after graduating. I watched how quickly Father was willing to rid himself of Aiden's troubles. I've often wondered did Father worry about Aiden being ready to take care of himself. There was no the thought of the damage that Aiden might have caused the 'Tudjals'. Aiden was no longer a burden to the legacy Father was determined to uphold. His plan failed again when I said I had my own plan. You ask, am I satisfied? Yes Mother I am. I am glad I didn't have to wait until I had troubles to be ousted from the Tudjal family."

Tears began to flow from their eyes. Naomi couldn't explain her husband and his love that crushed his children. He loved the only way he knew how. Seychelle couldn't accept the ripples, the moments she felt less than in the eyes of her father hurt her deeply.

"I want you to be happy Seychelle. You will someday be a wife, a mother and if you don't find happiness…I don't want you to be like me."

"Like you? What is wrong with you Mother? What don't you have? Father has provided for you and given you everything you've ever needed."

"Yes but I too had dreams. I wanted to be so much more than a mother and a wife. I wanted to be a seamstress. Sewing the costumes for the festivals and other things for the people here has been my dream. I wanted my own place. I wanted to create dresses, suits for the men, and other garments. I married your father and gave it up. I stood behind his dreams and forgot mine. I love him and anything that he has done has blossomed from that love."

"I love him too. Mother he has to love me enough to know that my dreams are there because the two of you taught me to dream. You taught me to chase those dreams. I have put my heart and soul into saving and becoming successful. I wanted you both to be proud of my accomplishments. It was forced on Aiden but I chose to be the owner of these establishments. Not one, Mother I have acquired enough not ever to have to buy again. Sasha loves to teach but should she ever need I can give her property as well."

"What shall I say to your father Seychelle? Should I tell him that you no longer appreciate his labor for you and your siblings?"

"If I were a child, Mother. He would need to provide for them and me. I am a woman, grown and standing on the strength you taught me always to have. I am able to give thanks and be grateful for if I have to stand alone as Aiden did, I don't have to struggle."

"It is well Seychelle. I don't think your father will understand your reasoning, but it is well."

"Mother, I can't stay and wait for Father to be rude to me. I will speak with you later. My love for you will not be lost. I understand you and yes, it is well."

Seychelle didn't wait for her mother to reply. She left the pictures and told her mother to share them with Sasha and her father. Sasha could bring them home with her. Naomi tried to persuade Seychelle to stay for dinner but she knew the table would be set for three.

Chapter 78

Talking to Clayton calmed her nerves. She waited three hours for a decent time to call. It was an early morning call but he told her she didn't need to apologize. She failed at making him believe it was about the properties.

"Seychelle, what's wrong?"

"Nothing, I'm just…"

"Stressing yourself. Look your brother's here, Jon's here, and I'm here. Don't you trust us?"

"Of course I do. It's just my first you know? It's a big deal to me and this grand opening is scary."

"It will be just fine. So how are the invitations going? I meant to ask you about the rest of your family."

"What about them?"

"Will your parents be attending? You said Sasha would be there but you didn't mention anyone else."

"Clayton, I don't think they'll be there."

"If it's a problem getting them there, I can help you. Don't worry yourself with their transportation. You can set them up at your resort, that's got to be exciting."

"It would be if I knew they were coming. I don't think they will. My mother won't come without my father and my father well, I explained that to you."

"You did. Listen, don't let that worry you. That night is your night and if they aren't there for whatever reason, you are not responsible for it. If you should need my help, let me know."

"Thank you. I'll ask Sasha to let me know if they'll be coming."

Clayton paused, hearing what he thought was hurt in her voice, he changed the subject.

"So tell me how I can please you?"

"No you're not asking me that again. Every time you ask that it puts me on alert."

"Just what I want. Keeping you interested, even if it's just your curiosity keeps me on your mind."

Seychelle laughed.

"Now that's better. I don't want you to feel stressed or burdened. Your satisfaction is important to me."

Seychelle heard her mother's voice echoing his words. Again she was hearing there was a need for her to be satisfied. She and Clayton talked as he prepared for his morning meeting. Shortly after saying their goodbyes Seychelle's phone rang again. The call was from Vegas.

"Hello?"

"Strangers calling you from Vegas?"

It was Vance but his voice sounded as though he was sick.

"Vance are you okay?"

"You ask? I've called you repeatedly for the past few days. I guess my number didn't say Vance this morning."

Seychelle deleted his number and blocked the calls whenever she thought it was him. She thought her message said it all. The front desk clerk at the hotel thought it unorthodox to leave the recited message at the front desk. She explained it was the best she could do. After the night with Clayton she realized it was exactly what she needed to do.

"How have you been? I thought we had at least the beginning of a friendship or something. You couldn't talk to me at least? What the hell did I do to deserve that?"

"Vance you're right and I'm sorry. Our paths are headed in different directions. I think I was a, what is it, a—"

"A damn lie that's what you call it."

Seychelle wanted to agree. She hated avoiding the truth but she couldn't tell him she felt bad using him. Even though he never would admit she was better for it. He wouldn't understand her innocence during the first auction simply because she knew what she was doing at the second auction. She owed him at least a venting session.

"You're right. I was wrong not to speak with you. Vance you've told me where women stand with you. Experience has taught me a few things too. The most important for me is to stay clear of people who try to keep you behind them. I'm a woman who seeks to succeed in business and in life. I won't be comfortable being in the background. I don't put my efforts into anything that won't advance me. Vance I'm just like you, smart, ambitious, and willing to succeed. I've listened to you go on and on about women in business. You're right we can be friends but I can't have you being critical about me wanting more than an office job."

There was silence on the other end of the phone. Seychelle hoped he had given up and disconnected the call. She called his name and there was no reply no noise at all. She clicked her phone off and didn't think about reading a text message until late that night.

"I thought you'd want to talk about this in person. I'll be at the Grand Opening in Vegas for Serenity Resorts. I was hoping we could start over where it began. The property was the one that brought on the buzz at the first auction. There are four sites but the main one is on the strip. Please be my guest and let me show you who I really am. Give me a chance to really hear you."

"Vance have you been drinking?"

"Since you left that note. You can't hold that against me. Seychelle you just can't drop what we had together."

"What did we have Vance? A few dates, pleasures included, and what no, where was that going?"

"You didn't let it really get started. We could have, I don't know. Just give me a chance."

"There's a distance Vance, between us physically and mentally there's a distance. You have your ways and I have mine. You have your values and I have mine. It's not going to work."

"Oh I see. So you just turn your feelings off like that? I know you had feelings for me."

"Vance I can't."

"You can't what?"

"I can't. I have to go. Give it some thought Vance. I'm not like the other women you've dated. Especially when it comes to being in business."

"I know you're different. Is that what you're upset about? I knew you got mad when we talked about the women being a part of the auctions and the business I'm in. I'm sorry Seychelle; it's just an observation. It's a proven point."

"Don't explain it again. Have a good day Vance."

Seychelle disconnected the call and immediately put a block on the new number he called from. She looked at the calendar and notes on her phone. She had less than a month before the Grand Opening event.

Chapter 79

C layton was at the airport when Seychelle's plane landed. She expected Aiden but was pleased to see Clayton waiting at the gate. He smiled when their eyes met. He had on a jacket with his jeans, a reminder to Seychelle to put on her jacket. They greeted each other with a kiss "hello". Seychelle waited until they got to baggage claim to retrieve her jacket from her carry on.

"It is a little breezy this morning. Did you have a good flight?"

"I'm almost comfortable with the hours. I don't know if that's good or bad."

Clayton grabbed her garment bag and suitcase. Seychelle held her carry-on and handbag. Together they went to the car that was waiting for them curbside.

"Do they let cars sit here and wait for passengers?"

"They do when they know who you are. I don't mean that to be sarcastic it's just I do a lot of traveling."

"Oh, maybe I need that. I either wait for Aiden or an Uber."

"No more of that my dear. Just let me know when and where. I'll get you where you need to go."

"So I've got a week to get ready." Seychelle couldn't contain how glad she was to see the completed renovations.

"That's not why I told you to come a week early." Seychelle gave Clayton a side glance.

"I saw that." They laughed. Clayton pulled out what appeared to be a chart from the pocket on the back of the seat.

"Here's a list of the renovations. We're going to do a walk through. Everything is as it will be on Saturday. The caterer placements and your staff will coordinate on Friday. You don't have to be there. You'll meet the staff today and they'll be glad to handle anything you need."

"Do we have enough staff for the event?"

"Yes, more than enough. All your suites, as you call them, will open at the same time on Saturday. There will be previews for the other three sites until eight that evening. All bookings will be for Suite One only. The closing will allow the staff from the three other sites to come to Suite One for the event. You have no extra overhead. It will be as though all four sites are open. The official opening of the other sites will be on Monday."

Seychelle looked over the charts. She couldn't believe all the work was done. She thought she would have to be secluded for the week tying up loose ends.

"So your firm does this work as well?"

"We invest and support where it is needed. You won't need our input soon enough. The Group will support you until you tell us to stop. They know you're a one-woman operation. One woman can't do all that is needed but you've got a hell of a crew."

"The same staff that was there before?"

"Yes, that was a plus. Not everyone came back but you don't have any jobs that are open. The work up of salaries is included in your final numbers. Now you have to get guests. Your overhead will be taken care of and you won't miss it. The business is solid, the previous owner left for the islands."

"Really, I come from the islands and they leave for the islands."

"Yes, retirement. Just him and his wife. No children, so they sold everything and if I'm correct they'll be leaving for the West Indies in a week or two."

"Okay, so what is there left for me to do?"

"You're an owner not a worker. Let your resorts work for you. When there's a problem allow us to present it to you. You'll tell us what is to be done and it will be. I want you to know that your business is our business. Again my dear, what can I do to please you?"

"Clayton I am pleased. I couldn't be more pleased."

"Okay, I'll give you that. Ride that cloud and when you come down, I'll be right here."

Seychelle understood his intention. She moved closer, they kissed and she felt it. Her thoughts were in the clouds. She didn't know if she would come down.

Winner Takes All

Chapter 80

The red carpet was in place. The spotlight's sky beam would be seen from all points on the Las Vegas strip. The R.V.S.P. guest list and the V.I.P. list were completed with everyone accepting the invitation. The numbers throughout the day at the other Serenity Resorts & Spa Suites was well over Seychelle's expectation. Aiden, Jon and Tristan frequented during the day all of the other suites while Sasha handled the final arrangements at Suite One.

The gold and white décor gave the interior a look of elegance. Seychelle had all she needed in her suite. She stayed there overnight, as did the rest of the team. The staff was small during their stay but they accommodated all of their needs. Sasha checked all the rooms and laughed after she was done. She returned to the two-bedroom suite she and Seychelle shared.

"We need to tell them that this suite twelve oh one is just for staff, our staff. Did you notice it has the best view of the strip and it oversees the rest of the property here? I thought a corner suite would be awkward but Seychelle have you looked at this view?"

"Yes, that's why I chose it. I think you're right. I'll make sure the plate on the door is changed to private."

"Already done. I changed it this morning. They said the plate will be here by tonight."

"Sasha, you didn't! Are you kidding me?"

"No, you're special. This is the twelfth floor. The top these rooms should be for special guest. Like a penthouse."

"Hmmm, I didn't think about that. We've got eight suites on this floor, right?"

"No there's six and a large room I guess for meetings or such."

"Okay have you plated that too?"

"Didn't have to. It says conference room."

"Well, thank you my sister. What do you think of it all?"

"It's beautiful. Is Clayton around? I needed to talk to him."

Seychelle moved from the couch and joined her sister at the large window.

"He said call him if I needed him. What's up?"

"I think I left one of my bags in the car that picked us up last night. I'm sure I did."

"I can call him if you want me to."

"I'll call Jon. He may still be with them. You continue to rest. Tonight will be enough on you. I'll find my bag."

Sasha left Seychelle to relax. She dialed Jon on her phone.

"Hey, listen did Clayton leave yet? Okay can you tell him room twelve oh three? Thanks."

There were four hours left before the doors would be open to the media, guest and onlookers. There was no fee for entrance and the security team would be there two hours earlier. Sasha had completed everything on her checklist. She went to the other suite to prepare it for the guests arrival, one Seychelle wasn't aware of.

Aiden and Jon checked on the lights and made arrangements for security to handle the media and reporters. No one would be allowed on any of the other floors unless they had a guest pass. A few of the V.I.P's would be accommodated with an overnight stay. After seeing that everything was in place the men went to their rooms to get dressed.

"Aiden, do you think Sasha and Seychelle will need my help?"

"Tristan, that's a woman's thing. Do I know of that?"

Tristan laughed and dialed Sasha's number. She left Aiden and went into the bedroom of their suite to get dressed. They were all a part of the introductions to be made. A part of the evening that Seychelle wanted to go smoothly. Aiden would talk to the guests and introduce Clayton. Clayton would thank the V.I.P.s and introduce Seychelle. It seemed simple enough. They all agreed there was nothing left to be done. They readied themselves for what would be a notable evening.

The music was blaring. The photographers and videographers were busy. The buffet was open with food from Seychelles Island as well as American favorites. The Cake stood between the hot and cold stations behind a gold roped area. The five-tier cake trimmed in white and gold roses was the perfect spot for pictures. People were eating, drinking and dancing. A sign that the resort would have many who would become customers.

The buzz and whispers all asked one question. *"Who were the owners? Did anyone hear about Serenity Resorts & Spas before this event?"*

Vance and Cheyenne were two of the few who were curious. They arrived separately but found each other at the bar.

"I don't believe they are new in the business." Cheyenne said after she received her apple martini.

"Who said they were new? You won't know the difference either way. This is The Whelan Group's signature. Look around. See the money that's collectively represented here? They backed this event and put it together. No newbie would know who was important enough, or who had money enough to buy their seat here."

"There was no mention of a cover charge." Cheyenne turned to face Vance.

"Cheyenne, you sipping too much too quick. Investments baby, future investments, this place will make the money hand over fist."

"So would you invest? I didn't hear you saying you would or you wanted to, so why would they?"

"It's all about standards and ranking. Power and prowess will beat those that sleep. I ain't sleeping Cheyenne but you were right something is strange about this purchase. I can't put my finger on it."

Vance watched as Clayton walked through the crowd greeting people as he made his way to the bar.

"Hey there Mr. Chase, Ms. Minnows welcome to Serenity Resorts, thanks for coming."

"Clayton, after tonight you won't be able to stand behind the lie you've been telling me."

"What lie would that be Cheyenne?"

"You not knowing the owner's name? I've been asking you since the property sold."

"You have and as I told anyone who asked, the owner didn't want their name revealed. Publicly the name of the business is all that's required until they sign the documents in record. If you were to look at the public books they have filled the legal requirements."

"I'm sure they have Clayton, with your help."

"For sure, that's what a reputable investment firm does. They take care of their client's business and any other matters that need to be handled. I'm sure Vance has explained that to you since you refuse to do things legally."

Vance gave Cheyenne a questionable look.

"What does that mean?"

"Listen, I've got to get this program started. Enjoy the evening you two."

Chapter 81

A collection of island music started with singers accompanied by only a guitar, but by the end of the song it was joined by a bass and percussion player. Soon there was the steel drummer who brought a roar of shouts an applause from the audience. The music of the island was cheerful, upbeat and pleasing to those on the dance floor.

The music faded into applause and the voice of Aiden, who caused everyone to look at the stage where he now stood. The lights were brought up just a bit so he could see those he was speaking to and about.

"Good Evening. We're going to keep these introductions short, we promise. It wouldn't be a grand opening without introducing those that made this happen. I am Aiden Tudjal, and I am a Client Account Representative for The Whelan Investment Group. We're better known as The Whelan Group or to those who really know us, The Group. Either way we have our stamp on this new resort. Serenity Resorts and Spa, tell me what do you think of this place? We've opened a few areas throughout the building for you to see what is here. If you've been to any of the other three suites that had their doors open earlier today you've seen what it has to offer. There are four sites, which have been labeled Suites one through four. We want you to get the best vacation you can without the need to purchase weeks, book a year ahead or worry if you'll lose points or any of that. Just book when you want, come, and relax. Now I promised you I wouldn't be up here long. Let me introduce one of the men I work for, Mr. Clayton Whelan."

The audience applauded and waited for Clayton and Aiden to exchange an embrace and a handshake.

"Vance, that's the man I spoke to on the phone."

"Who?" Vance turned from the bar to see Aiden as he left the stage. "What about him?"

"He's the guy that was in the V.I.P. room at the first auction. He was there in October too when The Group signed for the bed and breakfast spot. He's new to their group. I bet he has something to do with both bids."

"You're paranoid." The two walked back to their designated seats.

Clayton had introduced himself and told a little more about the history of The Whelan Group. He introduced his partners Kevin Gaines and Claude Brooks. When Jon Mikels was introduced and brought to the stage Vance told Cheyenne to hand him the program.

He recognized Jon as Sasha's friend. Seychelle told him that Jon didn't travel with them. As he read the program he saw Aiden's name listed under the Whelan Group's logo and photo.

"He's a Tudjal. I can't believe this shit. Cheyenne, either Jon or Aiden own the damn property."

"No, look it says right here be there to meet the owner. The owner wouldn't be introduced with all...."

"It is my honor to present this beautiful woman, a new business owner and an inspiration to those who want to stand and walk rather than sit back and ride, Ms. Seychelle Tudjal. Yes rise to your feet for the owner of Serenity Resorts and Spa."

Clayton helped Seychelle up the stairs. The V-neck white chiffon gown with the lace insets was chic and sexy. The sensual strappy back showed enough to give her more than just a glow. Her long hair was in a braided up-do adorned with golden accessories. She scanned the audience to find the V.I.P. table. She spotted Cheyenne and Vance. That's when her smile began although she didn't expect to get one back.

Vance couldn't stand, he felt weak. Cheyenne rose slowly to allow the jealous anger to move from her face. There was a loud roar and cheers throughout the crowd. Vance's phone began to buzz. He picked the phone up to find several messages."

"Man you pulled that off. Nice bro' now you are a power couple."

"I see why you kept her to yourself."

"Great choice."

The last message is the one that hit him hard.

"Nothing like teaching a woman how to handle the business. You guys will be at the top shortly don't forget us."

The messages were from the friends he met while with Seychelle at the auction. He couldn't bear the thought that Seychelle and Clayton may have begun a relationship. He watched as Clayton placed his hands gently around her waist as he announced the V.I.P. guest.

"Who is calling you?"

Vance handed Cheyenne the phone. She cut it off after reading a few of the messages. "So everyone is saying what I told you. She used you to beat you out of the bid."

"No Cheyenne she beat you. I didn't bid at all."

Cheyenne wanted to fight. Vance was the closest. He grabbed her arm before she could launch the remainder of her drink at him.

He leaned in close so no one else would hear his directive.

"Take your ass to the ladies room and fix yourself and your attitude. I ain't your man and I won't take your shit. If you don't want to be here don't return to this table." He released his grip. "Hey don't come back to this table the way you're leaving."

No one else at the table paid attention to her actions. Everyone took their seats and waited for their names to be called. They stood to receive their moment of acknowledgement.

"Mr. Vance Chase, a long time investor and buyer. Thank you sir for your work and all you do." Clayton didn't read his list of accolades and he did a few of the others. Vance understood as he watched Clayton's gestures standing on the stage with Seychelle.

"An interesting fact about our new client and owner, Ms. Tudjal. Her brother Aiden works with us because of her desire to start a new business. They are here with a business routed in America. Aiden has purchased a Bed and Breakfast Inn where he lives in California. But most interesting is they are from Seychelles Island. I'll let Seychelle say a few things about her experience in buying in America."

Seychelle looked at Clayton and he immediately read her mind.

"Okay so the stage is not her thing. May I tell the story Ms. Tudjal?"
She smiled, sighed and nodded her okay.

"Well you see, we knew she wouldn't want the mic. So let's just move on to her surprise.

Seychelle felt a sudden rush of fear. The introductions were over and she was to be escorted out to the front of the building for photos. She braced herself hoping Clayton wouldn't be springing too much of a surprise on her.

"For those of you who don't know where Seychelles Island is I will tell you. It is in East Africa near Madagascar. I know most of us in America only dream of these islands especially on that borders the Indian Ocean. It is an eleven hour difference and believe me it's rough on phone calls. But I want you to understand her efforts. Her brother lives in California. She began searching there. She spent her summer with her sister, c'mon up Sasha."

Vance was hurting. He never asked about her business. She told him she was working with her father. He tried to remember the times she spoke of work. Nothing stirred his memory. She listened intently to his conversation regarding the auctions, the bids and the business. He tried to recall his exact words. He did remember he told her women didn't need to be in the business him and others had dominated. Sasha and Clayton continued to talk about the step-by-step process, including the day of the bidding.

"She's a hustler people. I'm saying this loud and proud. You know why because she's The Group's client."

The audience members laughed again.

"So tonight I want everyone to lift their glass and give a toast to a new owner, a new business woman, a new friend to us at the Group … and so much more."

A few men in the audience gave a shout. "She is beautiful Clayton."

"Yes, we're booking a trip to Africa. That's where you guys will have to go."

Laughter filled the room. "Okay one more thing I think, Sasha. Then we can resume with the music."

"Yes, we have one more business owner, a V.I.P., to introduce. He and his lovely wife have come to celebrate with us, cause that's what families do. My mother and father, Mr. and Mrs. Tudjal."

Kevin and Claude escorted them to the stage. Tears began to flow from Seychelle and Sasha's eyes. They hugged their parents as Aiden returned to the stage.

"Oh I love you all so much. I don't know what to say." Cole took out his handkerchief to wipe his eyes. The family thanked the audience, and the music began to play.

Seychelle went with Kevin and Claude while Aiden and Sasha escorted their parents to their table. Cheyenne returned to the table determined not to lose Vance to his own pity.

"We don't have to stay. We can go walk the strip. The air outside won't choke us like in here."

"I'm good you go."

"Vance it's done. It's just like you said, 'the owner won the bid'. You can't bid over, this ain't cards."

"She's upset with me. I know why. I'll make it up to her."

"Hmm look at Clayton, he's making it up to her now."

Clayton stood at one of the tables talking with his arm around Seychelle's waist. She didn't move and didn't care if Vance saw them standing there.

"He was wrong Cheyenne."

"Who?"

"Clayton said she was a hustler, she's not a hustler."

"She put her touch on you. Believe it my friend she hustled you."

Chapter 82

Everything went well. The compliments were continuing to come in by e-mail and thank you cards. Sasha stayed another week with her sister. Seychelle wanted to be there for the first two weeks of operation. She worked from her suite and walked down to the registration office once the staff arrived on Monday.

Her first meeting with the staff included Aiden, Jon and Sasha. Business cards were given for the necessary calls to be made. Seychelle was satisfied and left giving the okay to open the doors to Serenity Resorts.

Clayton arrived shortly after ten. He had a meeting with the contractors and the inspectors. He was there to turn over all of the information that needed to be posted and put on file. Seychelle stood in the middle of the lobby floor saying a silent prayer.

"Good morning. Don't you look like a Queen standing in the middle of this grand lobby?"

"I want to thank you Clayton. Everything was beautiful."

"I think you did thank me, that night, yesterday, when I called... Sweetie this is your work. I just did what was supposed to be done. I'm pleased that you got to see this dream come true."

"Yes, it is that. My fantasy has become my reality."

"So you'll be here for two weeks?"

"I don't know. If all goes well this week, I'll come to California and be with Aiden and Tristan for a week."

"Okay, well if there's any issues we can help you with—"

"I know call The Group. I will."

"Can I accompany you to the other Suites?"

"Yes, please do. I was waiting for Sasha but she's still at the airport with my parents."

"Did they enjoy their stay?"

"Yes, they said it was a mini vacation. They seemed to like the properties, which surprised me. My father wanted to talk business. I wouldn't allow it. I told them to enjoy their stay. Sasha has been their escort since she invited them."

"I see." Clayton was briefed by Aiden. He understood the underlying reason for her cold shoulder. Aiden told him don't push the topic. Seychelle would open up when she felt better about it. Clayton agreed to be the ear. Aiden told him that would be best.

"So shall we head over to the other locations?"

"Clayton I don't want you to think you have to be with me, you know, through this week."

"Is that an invite that I didn't have a chance to accept or decline? I told you I have papers that need to be posted and put in each office. Inspection papers that are required. Your office manager is busy with this being the first day of operation. It gives her a chance to do what she has done for years. I make sure you, the owner, complies with Las Vegas Real Estate Laws. Now that invitation to stay doesn't sound bad. I can take off this suit, put on something a bit more comfortable and relax with you."

"Relax? I don't think I will be able to. I just want it all to be right."

"Well if you're here no one is going to step out of line. It's when you're not watching that things happen. So my dear, if you plan on moving here, you can maintain control. Otherwise allow your staff to run your properties. Besides we can begin to talk about the other properties."

"You're right. Give me a minute to grab a few things from upstairs. I'll be right back."

Seychelle went to her suite and called Sasha.

"Are they on their way? What happened to the early flight?"

"Oh yes, they are on it. Everything went well. I'm on my way back I stopped at the other suites to see if they were okay. Seychelle you have the best staff. They knew who I was and were setting up for bookings, already! Calls were coming in and information was given. I listened to a few calls. It's so exciting. How is it over there?"

"Everything here is the same. Calls and we have a few people who came in for the tour. I'm on my way to check the others as well. Clayton and I can meet you there if you want to wait."

"No, I was curious so I just wanted to stop at the other suites. Jon wants to meet for lunch. I wanted to say no, but…"

"But it's not a fling. Go to lunch girl and set yourself up for him to win you over."

"You should talk. Hey, I say Vance. Has he called you since seeing you Saturday?"

"No and that's good."

"I guess Clayton is the better choice. Don't let him get away. The things you could do with The Whelan Group behind you. That's all the conversations were Saturday."

"What conversations?"

"How you will be more than successful working with The Whelan group. I guess they are an expensive firm and only work with elite clients. Without Jon and Aiden knowing Clayton you may have had to wait a while before you had a breakthrough. I am so happy that you have been blessed."

"Did they enjoy themselves?" Seychelle waited for Sasha's answer. "Sasha did Mother and Father enjoy themselves."

"I'm sorry. Yes, mother was overjoyed. I took them for a tour of the other properties. They got a chance Sunday to see a part of the Vegas strip. I treated them to breakfast and guess what sister."

"I'm listening." Seychelle wanted to know what they thought of her accomplishments.

"They met Jon. We all went to dinner together — Tristan, Jon and I. I knew you were tried. I did call you and Aiden. Check your messages."

"I believe you. Did Aiden answer?"

"Yes, Tristan met us. Seychelle they're really sorry about not being able to share your success with you and Aiden. Tristan told them about the Bed and Breakfast. Mother even volunteered to help her with the balloon curtains. Tristan said she'd have to buy a sewing machine.

Mother loves sewing so you know she told her that would be her wedding gift to them."

"I'm glad they enjoyed their stay. Listen I'll call you when we're finished at the other sites. Clayton is trying to get me to invite him to stay with me for the rest of my time here."

"Will you?"

"He's been asking about satisfying me. I think I know how."

Clayton took a seat while he waited for Seychelle. He checked his messages and the LCD screen showed an incoming call.

"Hello."

"It's Vance man. Listen, we need to talk."

"Hey what's up man?"

"Seychelle Tudjal. I don't want to put her in the same light as Cheyenne. But man, I think she used me to get that property."

"How so?"

"Well, she claimed not to know anything about the business. You know, she acted naïve to me explaining the auction, the bids and the business. I told her there weren't many women in the business. I didn't expect her to be putting in bids while we discussed the properties. I remember telling her about Westlake and what the margins were. Man, I even told her I'd love for anyone to beat Cheyenne's bid."

"Vance, man, listen to yourself. You talked about Westlake, but you weren't bidding on it. You talked about margins, but it didn't hold your interest. You talked about the business, but you didn't ask about hers?

"She said she was leaving her job working with her father."

"Okay and you didn't want to know what her future looked like for her, why?"

"I don't know why. We just talked. Man I hung out with her while she was here. You saw us there and at the auction in October. I understand you're handling your business but…"

"But? But what? Vance it's all about business that's what you're talking about right?"

"Right. I saw how you looked at her Saturday. She's not that type of woman. I'm trying to build a relationship with her and I think you're handling more than the business. Like I said I played a part of her acquiring the properties and she got that deal on the back end. I don't mind losing stake in the property but I know you're not the type of man to mix business with pleasure. I guess I'm that way too. I don't need the business to build our relationship."

"Man, I don't know what you're trying to say but you're right about one thing. I don't mix business with pleasure."

"So what was that too close for my comfort moments you had with her Saturday night."

"Vance, understand this. Just like you didn't ask about her business, her dreams or aspirations? I made it a point to ask. I do that with all my clients — strictly business, man. But my business, my group has locked in. She has a representative like any other client. Her brother works for us so yes, she has an inside connection. After today, I will have completed everything that The Whelan Group needs to be sure her business is set in the right direction. Your worries on Saturday night will heighten."

"What are you talking about worries?"

"You were worried about me separating business from pleasure, right. Listen man it's all pleasure now. The business is set, it's secure. Now my time with her is simply to please her. Just like her dreams for the business, she has dreams for herself. You obviously didn't ask about that. You didn't listen."

"Oh, so that's what Saturday was? A prelude to pleasure?"

"No we're beyond the prelude."

Vance paused. His ego was bruised again. "You had one thing wrong man."

"What's that?"

"She ain't no hustler."

"No I am. She doesn't need to hustle. I'll hustle for her."

Chapter 83

Clayton laughed as he hung up the phone.

"I'm glad you enjoyed your wait."

"Yeah, every now and then you recognize your blessings. Often it humors me when God answers prayers. Are you ready my dear?"

"I am. So would I be too forward if I said I accept your acceptance of my invite for next week?"

"Ah, I don't have to break down on one knee. See that's God right there. Thank you ma'am."

Clayton thought about calling Vance back but he decided to be the better man. Seychelle could be the woman to fulfill his dreams. He'd be wherever she wanted him to be. He knew where he wanted her...by his side.

The days went by quickly. The couple stayed at Serenity and spent time visiting local nightclubs. Areas where most tourist might not roam. The locals were nice enough but without knowing where to go one could show signs of being lost.

Clayton asked Seychelle if she had been to a few of the spots. She could only name the one where she and Vance had dinner. He was sure they wouldn't go there.

Their time together brought them closer together. They shared childhood memories, college experiences, lessons taught and learned. At the end of the week one would think they had been a couple for years.

Clayton drove to the airport in silence. The feelings he had for Seychelle were more than he expected them to be. During their pleasure pleasing they both concluded it would be hard not to be together.

"Are you okay? You haven't said a word since we got in the car."

"I just, I'm missing you and you haven't left. It's hurting my ego, my senses, and my heart, I just...."

"Don't please? I'm hurting too. I told you a distance romance was too much to bear. I think only Sasha and Jon understand that type of relationship. We may have to have therapy sessions with them."

Her statement brought a smile and Clayton reached to hold her hand.

"It will work sweetie. We'll make it work."

Seychelle landed on the islands that night. Her father was at the airport gate. Her heart began to beat faster — anxiety was building. Sasha promised she would meet her at the gate.

"Where's Sasha, Father? Has something gone wrong?"

"No, I asked to pick you up. Was the flight okay?"

"Yes, you didn't have to do this."

They walked to baggage claim in silence. Seychelle walked slightly ahead of her father. She noticed his gait was slower than it had been in the past. She remembered the mornings when they would all go out for a run while her mother made breakfast. Cole was a fitness fanatic while she and her siblings were growing up. He played every sport and insisted they either walk or run each morning. He would run in the morning and walk with her mother in the evening. She missed their closeness but understood they both were getting older.

After picking up the bags, he led the way to where he parked.

"I tried to park close to this exit. I told your mother I didn't want to walk the entire airport just to get to the car. That's how the parking is set up here. Arrivals park on the top tier when the baggage is on the lower tier."

"I understand. It should be that way."

"I wanted you to know that what you have done with your properties is amazing. I am sorry that I was too stubborn to embrace your vision and accept your reality. You did it all alone and you should have been surrounded by family. I can only imagine the work you have done. Your efforts have given you more than I expected."

"Have you given Aiden this same speech? I don't want to talk about it. You were the first that I showed the layout, the designs, the financial reports and my business plan. Aiden, Jon and I spent hours preparing it so that you could look it over. You refused then. So I don't expect your praise now. Thank you for your efforts but I know that it's an attempt to be polite."

"No forgive me Seychelle. I want you to know I forgive you. You wanted more than I could give you. So you went outside of the family and now you have what you say is a dream come true."

"I…Father, I don't intend on arguing this point. You did give. My dowry and my savings was enough to start. I was blessed to have people that knew what I wanted. There is no need to forgive me because I've done nothing wrong. How is mother?"

Cole didn't answer. He didn't speak again until he said good-bye at Seychelle's front door. She'd wait for her mother to call and explain what her father wanted her to do.

The call from her mother didn't come through until two days later. Seychelle had been to town twice and didn't stop at her parent's home. There were a few shouts of congratulations as she passed through the town square. She stopped in the bakery and the butcher. She would complete her shopping at the marketplace. She drove past Tudjal Exports and waved at a few of the workers. During her entire passage through town, she never thought about her parents or stopping in their home.

"Hello, how are you? I would have thought by now I would have seen you. Maybe I would have spotted you in passing since there are others have pointed out your shopping stops."

"Good morning Mother. I would have called later today. I didn't want you to have to choose between me and Father's meal."

"Child where did you get such a notion?"

"It's nothing how are you?"

"I'm more interested in you and your father. You have to let go Seychelle. He is your father."

"Let go of what? My expectations, my loss of a support system within my own family, which should I let go of. Mother I have nothing to look forward to other than what I have. I can't share it with you or him because he cringes to here of my success. He would have me be a part of the Bed and Breakfast rather than the resort."

"Yes, we thought about bringing that up."

"It figures you would. Since it's not happening, maybe I should just pack up and go."

"No one is saying that Seychelle."

"No one really cares. I've been thinking it over. Sasha wants to teach here. She will let me and Aiden know if and when things are not going well. I think living in American can fulfill my next dream. You would sit us down when we were little and ask us about our dreams. Now when our dreams can be our reality, you both fade away."

"What is your dream now child?"

"To find a soul-mate. I want to be happy and live happy."

"So you see that with this man Clayton?"

"I don't know and living here I may ever find out."

"I see. Will you allow us to come over and sit with you before you leave?"

"Mother, it's like my dreams. As you would say, it may not happen today."

"Good that gives time for all of us. You have a good day."

Before Seychelle could ask her mother what she meant, the phone was disconnected.

Vance called twice than emailed her his information. He said he needed to talk but Seychelle wasn't ready to hear his complaints or demands for her to explain.

It was nearly a month before Aiden told her they needed to move on to the next property. Seychelle needed to choose where the contractors were to go. It would be the same company that did the work for her in Vegas. Clayton suggested they keep them on all the jobs. They would follow the interior and exterior designs.

Seychelle felt a rush of excitement come over her when Clayton told her he would meet her in Mexico. He would make the arrangements for their travel. Aiden and Tristan would be joining them.

Vance's number came up on the phone again.

"Yes, hello." Seychelle couldn't understand how he was calling when she blocked his calls each time.

"Wow, aren't you the busy business woman?"

"How can I help you Vance?"

"Well I could ask you to explain why? I could ask was that your plan from the start? I'm just trying to get over you and what you did to me. I told you that Cheyenne had run a game on me and you just kept playing yours. I don't understand."

"Vance men like you will never understand. It was a chance. I was there on business, seeking to invest or buy. I was scouting places before the auction. My brother knew more and told me to accept your invitation. Perhaps I would learn more being with someone who knew more. I didn't know anything about you or anyone else. When you said you were not bidding on the Westlake property I texted my brother. The Whelan Group, my brother and Jon looked into it and said yes, they would put in my bid. It was the same for the bed and breakfast. You were not a part of the equation. I asked you why you didn't want to bid on it. Do you remember that?"

"Yeah but, I mean do you know what I felt like Saturday to see you be introduced as the owner?"

"Do you know how I felt not being able to tell you? Telling you, would alert others. The Group agreed to keep it a secret until the Grand Opening."

"Why? Didn't I show you I cared?"

"Yes in every way except the way I needed you the most. Your words were negative each time you made reference to a woman in business. I am that more than anything else. I am a woman in business. It's new but it's my business. You have a different personality for women who have the dream to be in business."

"You misunderstood me Seychelle. Just like in everything there are exceptions — you are that exception. So now you're playing with Clayton. Don't you see what he's trying to do? Taking care of your business gives him free reign to the bedroom. I can't get what I saw that night out of my mind."

"What did you see? Business and the bedroom? Oh yeah that's when women do their business deals. You said that they used tactics; even lying on their back. Is that what you think? I had to lie on my back to get the support of The Whelan Group. You're living in a man's world, there's no room for me there."

"Yes there is. I wasn't referring to you. Just the women I've met have had no other skill."

"I didn't either. That's why you attracted me. I could learn a little from you. Nothing between us was planned, it was by fate. A passage to my dreams. I thank you but I can't be with you."

"So you've given up on me because of the distance? That's not a factor. I can assure you. I will come to you and prove myself. I'll stay there if you want me to."

"No, I don't want you to. There's more to it than that Vance. I don't like the way you think about women and their independence. We can remain distant friends or say good bye."

"Alright. I won't give up. You'll see."

Chapter 84

Seychelle took her morning walk. She was pleased to leave her mail and papers to look over on the kitchen table. The trip to Mexico was the next day and she would spend time packing later. Sasha promised to bring home dinner. She took a deep breath and stretched. She was up early for no reason and after weeks of work she was happy to take on less. The property in Mexico was still operational. The staff seemed to be pleasant on the phone. She hoped there would be no need to replace those who held titles with responsibilities — those who could handle the work without calling her every week. She would contact them, just as she did the property in Las Vegas.

When she returned to her home she began her ritual. She pulled the lounger to her favorite spot and retrieved the papers and other work from the kitchen. She grabbed her cup of tea and her I-Pad so she could listen to a few mellow songs as she meditated.

Seychelle dozed off an hour after she was lying on the lounger. The sun was shifting and the warmth kept her asleep for two hours. She would later realize she needed to rest. A breeze off the ocean passed over her and she sat up. Still in a fog, she remembered where she was. She put on her glasses and her straw hat. Her one-piece Bodycon running suit fit her perfectly and she loved her Nike sneakers that matched the yellow and green in her suit perfectly.

She checked her messages, hoping she didn't miss a call from Clayton. Vance hadn't called which was the first time over the past week. As she was placing the phone on the small mat next to her it buzzed. The text message read:

> I just landed. Wouldn't that be great? But you never gave me an address. C'mon Seychelle I need to talk to you face-to-face. I'm here let me come to you.

Seychelle dropped the phone. Vance couldn't be on the island. He would have called her. Then she thought about it. He had called every day. She sighed and readjusted herself and her thoughts. She really needed to rest before she collapsed. She hadn't slept well in a week. She called her mother to remind her she would be leaving in the morning. Sasha would have given their mother too much information.

The message from Vance wouldn't allow her to fall back to sleep. She picked up the papers and began sorting through them. A few people waved and called her name from the shoreline. She smiled and waved back. Just when they were almost out of sight she spotted a man walking alone.

His walk was truly worth watching. He seemed to be barefoot, with what she would say were shoes in his hand. He had on dark shades and a two-piece Bermuda shorts set. His head was topped with a Scala Palm Gambler hat. She could see the colors were light against his bronze skin.

As he got closer she thought there was something familiar about his movement. It wasn't Vance, though his call was still taunting her. She wondered if it could have been one of Aiden's friends who she knew from years past. She didn't want him to notice her stare so she put on her shades and laid back on her chair. She couldn't keep still she sat up again and pretended to flip through the pages.

She thought how stupid she was to think the man was her visitor. No one called to say they were stopping by and least of all, a man. He seemed to be engrossed with the ocean never looking her way. He stopped and walked where the water could meet his feet. Watching him stand there she thought of Clayton.

She closed her eyes so she could see his face. She loved his touch, his voice, the smell of his cologne. He kept his hair cut short but the natural curls were not tamed. The touch of his hair as he lay against her eased her. His lips were the introduction to their pleasures well beyond a tender kiss. She missed Clayton and the distance left her lonely. She wanted to be with him the moment they were separated.

Sasha told her she was in love. Something she wouldn't dare tell him. She was barely able to tell herself.

"I do love you Clayton." She muttered the whisper as though she were trying to convince herself. "I do love you Clayton."

"And I love you."

The man was no longer standing at the shoreline. He lifted her feet and sat with them across his lap.

"I guess I found out what to do to satisfy your pleasures."

"Yes, just be with me." Seychelle removed her shades that covered her tear filled eyes.

"Always." Clayton leaned to meet her with a kiss.

Other Novels by Nanette M. Buchanan

Family Secrets Lies and Alibi's

A Different Kind of Love

Bruised Love

Skeletons Beyond The Closed Door

Gossip Line

Bonded Betrayal

Scattered Pieces

The Stranger Within

The Perfect Side Piece

Purchase Your Copy Today
www.ipendesigns.net
www.amazon.com
www.barnes&noble.com
www.smashwords.com

Books are available in e-book format